The Sisterhood of Invisible Murderers

ALEXIA CASALE

PENGUIN BOOKS

PENGUIN BOOKS

UK | USA | Canada | Ireland | Australia
India | New Zealand | South Africa

Penguin Books is part of the Penguin Random House group of companies
whose addresses can be found at global.penguinrandomhouse.com

Penguin Random House UK,
One Embassy Gardens, 8 Viaduct Gardens, London SW11 7BW

penguin.co.uk

Penguin Random House UK

First published 2026

001

Set in 12/15 pt Dante MT Std
Typeset by Six Red Marbles UK, Thetford, Norfolk
Printed and bound in Great Britain by Clays Ltd, Elcograf S.p.A.

The authorized representative in the EEA is Penguin Random House Ireland,
Morrison Chambers, 32 Nassau Street, Dublin D02 YH68

A CIP catalogue record for this book is available from the British Library

ISBN: 978–1–405–97633–6

Penguin Random House is committed to a sustainable future
for our business, our readers and our planet. This book is made from
Forest Stewardship Council® certified paper.

FSC
www.fsc.org
MIX
Paper
FSC® C018179

Readers loved Alexia Casale's first book

The Best Way to Bury Your Husband:

'This is a book that will stay with me a long time'

★★★★★

'A page-turner from start to finish, with a really great ending to boot'

★★★★★

'A true testament to female solidarity'

★★★★★

'One of the best books I have read this year'

★★★★★

'Fabulous from beginning to end'

★★★★★

'A dark humour read which also tugs at your heartstrings'

★★★★★

'Funny, heartbreaking and thoughtful'

★★★★★

'Brimming with hope, passion, tenderness and courage'

★★★★★

'Breathtakingly thought-provoking'

★★★★★

'A must-read'

★★★★★

ABOUT THE AUTHOR

Alexia Casale is a senior lecturer in creative writing at Bath Spa University, as well as a script consultant and specialist human rights editor. Her young adult novel, *The Bone Dragon*, was shortlisted for the Waterstone's Children's Book Prize and her first adult novel, *The Best Way to Bury Your Husband*, set the darkly comic stage for her adult fiction. This is her second adult novel.

For Silvia

My homicidal tendencies have always been one of the things you love most about me, Mum; I'm so grateful for your unwavering belief in just how murderous I could become with time, practice and support.

This one's for you – I've finally killed enough people, in enough different ways, to truly do you proud.

The Rules

1. You must never kill without formal authorization from the Sisterhood. This includes killing in self-defence in cases where you have purposefully provoked an attack.
2. When you need to, you should always ask for help. You are not alone.
3. The more complex the kill, the more opportunities for failure and discovery. Simple is best.
4. All killings should be quiet and clean. There should be no mess.
5. Your internet search history must never, ever include information on targets, methods or similar. Don't get 'clever' about it.
6. Only the target must die, and there must be no collateral damage outside the target's own property, with due consideration given to the well-being of any co residents.
7. Only psychopaths get a thrill from killing people. The Sisterhood contains no psychopaths.
8. Don't draw attention with your appearance or behaviour or kills – strive to be invisible: ensure you are unmemorable.

9. Take no unnecessary risks. Never, ever rush.
10. Torture is strictly forbidden.
11. Luck is the alchemy that flows from careful planning and rigorously honed skills. You must only ever rely on the latter.
12. There are no loopholes. The Sisterhood's overarching duty is the safety and invisibility of members to ensure that we can continue to fulfil our purpose. Breaking the Rules instantly forfeits your membership, your one free kill, and the Sisterhood's protection. You may also forfeit your freedom and/or your life.
13. Our lives and freedom rest in each other's hands. The simultaneous gift and price of membership is shared purpose, courage and loyalty.

Verity

The day my sister disappeared was exactly like this: bright, warm and full of promise, as if designed to make us believe nothing bad could happen – how could it, in such a delicious blaze of sunshine?

I should have known that this morning's cloudless skies were a bad sign. Instead, I felt soothed as I imagined how the day would go.

Now it's been long enough for the ground to settle after my mother's burial, the gravestone has finally been placed, so I tumbled out of bed already picturing myself visiting the memorial she'd chosen. In my daydream, I stood before the stone and, as I read the loving inscription, I felt acceptance start to soothe my grief – not just for Mum, but for Reenie, too; the warmth from the sun settled across my shoulders like an embrace, telling me that life goes on, and so will I, and one day I'll even be happy again.

Now I'm here and *everything* is wrong. Sunlight tears through the branches above me, spattering my clothes and skin with darkness. The gravestone wavers before my eyes.

IN MEMORY OF MARY ANN BANNERMAN – 1973–2025

BELOVED MOTHER OF IREENE ROSE BANNERMAN

GONE BUT NOT FORGOTTEN

My skin flares hot, burns cold. I think that I might cry, then that I might laugh, then that I might howl at the sky, but I just stand there, the grave blurring in and out of focus.

Where is my name? Where does it even hint *that my mother had two daughters?*

I'm the only person left to ensure that they aren't forgotten, and yet I'm nowhere.

My chest heaves as if the air is gone.

I never looked at the paperwork for Mum's funeral package. I was just relieved *someone* knew her wishes. Now this.

She can't have meant it to read this way. She was my mother. She loved me. Me and Reenie both, just as I loved them.

But if Reenie and I loved each other, why is my last memory of her a glance over my shoulder as I stormed out of a party, leaving her with strangers? Why did my big sister watch me set out into the night to walk home alone? If we'd loved each other the way I tell myself we did, I would have turned back only to find her hurrying after me. Then everything would have been different.

There have been so many lies, sometimes I'm not sure that the sister I miss so fiercely was ever real. Did she really read me a bedtime story every night? I remember cuddling up against the headboard, giggling at funny voices and gasping at exciting bits, then hiding under the covers for scary ones. That was Reenie I was snuggled against, wasn't it? Or was it Mum? Was Reenie the one who plaited my hair every day for school, or did Mum have it right when she said the grief has warped my memories?

Reenie was only twenty months older than me, after

all: not-quite-eighteen to my just-turned-sixteen when she disappeared. I wanted to get back by curfew because I was the careful one, and she wanted to stay because she was the risk-taker. That's the truth. Unless I'm lying to myself, just like Mum always said. Only I'm *not*, because I don't pretend that I'm *still* careful and cautious.

Why would I be, now I know how stupid it is to mind the rules? After all, nothing happens to most of the people who do truly awful things for no reason other than their own pleasure: somewhere out there the man who killed my sister – and disappeared her so we will probably never know what happened – is living his life unscathed, and there's *nothing* I can do about it. Even if he got caught, he will never – *can* never – suffer the way we have.

I know everyone thinks I crash through life making one bad choice after another, just as they think that, after fourteen years, my grief is no excuse. But what else am I going to do when there's more rage and grief inside me than can fit, yet the world keeps trying to add more? There isn't *room* to bottle up any more pain and unfairness without drowning from the inside out.

Why can't you learn some self-control instead of blaming your troublemaking on what happened to your sister? whispers Mum's voice, as if her ghost is standing behind me. *Why do you tell yourself lies that only make your life harder?*

I feel a wild laugh bubble over my lips as I stare down at the grave.

It can't *get* any harder, though at least there's no one but me to suffer the consequences of my recklessness since Mum toppled over while brushing her teeth and died on the spot seven months ago. Apparently, that's a thing with about 15 per cent of brain aneurysms. Who knew? I certainly didn't, until the call from the hospital. They asked if I was alone, meaning 'Are you alone right now?' The answer was yes, of course. It will always be yes now.

The sun keeps shining as if looking down at the wreckage of my life and taunting me with the threat of worse to come.

Pru

Verity is, of course, late.

I am never late. Lateness is the product of poor self-control. And sloppiness.

I am never sloppy, either. Case in point, I have long since made friends with the man responsible for maintenance of the graveyard, so it was a simple thing to say I knew Verity's mother and could he let me know as soon as her headstone went up? Nice man that he is, he messaged yesterday not only to say he was watching the stone being erected but that he had let Verity know and she was due to visit in the morning, if I fancied being there as moral support. Naturally, I arranged to arrive early, so she could encounter me innocuously engaged in weeding. But it is now twenty to nine and there is no sign of her, though she has an all-day shift at work starting on the hour.

I cannot decide if I am more infuriated with her, or with myself for thinking any part of this would be simple: I, at least, should know better.

Why am I dead set that it must be Verity? I ask myself for the hundredth time.

I straighten from gathering empty cans in a shady corner of the car park, gritting my teeth when my muscles pull in ways they shouldn't – that they *didn't* – two months ago.

Taking a sip of water, I survey the area. Much better already. If only the situation with Verity could be neatened so easily. I need to approach her today or find someone else – it is as simple as that. But in eleven months of watching her, I have learnt that nothing is ever simple with Verity. Which means I should move on, and yet . . . I don't. The frustration wriggles across my shoulders like an ant under my clothing. I would say it is another symptom, like the muscle aches, if it wasn't for the fact that Verity has niggled away at the back of my mind ever since I began considering my replacement.

I don't indulge in superstitious claptrap. There has been no pricking of my thumbs in this, the most important professional decision I will ever make. And yet something tugs inside me when I think of choosing anyone else. I would like to believe it is urgency – I simply cannot afford to change my mind now – but I have a terrible feeling that some of it is emotional.

My mind goes back to the moment I realized certainty had settled into my bones – along with mortification that my choice wasn't wholly rational. How could it be, when it happened as I watched Verity absently twisting a tiny plait into her hair, the tip of her tongue poking out of her mouth as she concentrated? She seemed oblivious to the world, though the next moment she whirled round to grab a stolen toy-truck off a teenage boy and give it back to the little girl it belonged to.

Which proved that, despite appearances, Verity was attuned to the world and able to act promptly and decisively to right a wrong, I tell myself now. *That was the perfect reason to pick her.*

But I'd chosen before that, when she was still fiddling

with the silly, wonky little plait and – despite the dirty-blonde hair and hazel eyes, the freckled skin – for a mad-wonderful-frozen moment, I was looking at Hope.

The doctors told me I might hallucinate as the cancer progresses and more and more tumours spring up here, there and everywhere. But apart from that moment there has been nothing, so it seems more likely it wasn't a hallucination, but longing. Which is probably worse, being pointless and irrational rather than merely medical.

I turn my frustrations on the mess around me, but the trouble with weeding – just as with cleaning a house or reducing the number of monsters in the world – is that the job is never done. No matter how hard I scrub the bath, it will need scrubbing again soon, and no matter how many terrible people I kill, the Sisterhood always has more targets to dispatch. There is too much to do in too little time to saddle myself with a terminally late mentee. And yet I have picked Verity, and I cannot seem to unpick her.

Maybe it's the guilt. I don't know if my actions led to Ireene's disappearance, but, if they didn't, it's a hell of a coincidence that I killed a man at the same time and place she vanished.

Realizing that I have started to grind my teeth, I turn to the most soothing thing in the vicinity.

Please mind the rules, begs the sign by the gate, followed by a list of common-sense ways visitors can avoid being appalling. It boils down to *DON'T be human garbage. DO take your rubbish with you*. Rules to live by. I read the whole thing carefully, feeling my tension ebb away.

I continue clearing my way around the car park as I daydream about solving the littering problem once and for all. It would be a terrible misuse of my skills, not to mention a thorough violation of Rule 1 – and also Rule 8, since that many people missing or dying unexpectedly in the local area would draw attention.

'If you weren't strangling the lilac, I would let you live,' I explain to a tuft of couch grass, wiggling it back and forth till it rips free. 'But you are, so I can't.' I toss the weed into my trug, then start dismembering a rope of bindweed.

The last man I killed – a leisurely ten days ago, since I took a week of annual leave afterwards – had strangled his former girlfriend to death, then got away with it by claiming that she 'liked it rough'. It would have been too ostentatious to kill him in a similar way, so I settled for arranging a fatal accident in the bathroom. It is how a lot of people go, so is a favourite among the Sisterhood. It almost never draws any attention from the police or family, even apart from the fact that, when the type of person the Sisterhood targets ends up dead, the world at large usually heaves a sigh of relief.

After twenty-five years, I am aware that most paid and pro bono jobs come to what is known officially as the Special Dispatch Service – and unofficially as the Sisterhood of Invisible Murderers – through the broader law enforcement community, though exactly how that happens rightly remains a secret. However, logic dictates that the women who make up the Sisterhood are only able to quietly remove all types of human stain because enough of those responsible for stopping us are studiously looking in the other direction, pretending they never brought it to anyone's attention in the first place. In any case, the Rules have ensured that only a handful of kills in the sixty-odd-year history of the Sisterhood have ever been identified as suspicious, and none as homicide.

I cannot be the reason that changes, which is partly why it has taken so long to finalize my decision about who to mentor as my replacement when I retire. It is also partly that I have been dithering. Before Verity, I had never dithered in my life. It is, as I suspected, profoundly unpleasant.

Now, when I have finally decided that introductions can wait no longer, Verity is late, as if determined to confirm my worst fears. Although most of the compulsively unpunctual are habitual in their lateness – the majority go for a precise eight or twelve minutes overdue, which helps a lot when planning when and where to kill them – Verity defies any pattern whatsoever. After eleven months investigating her, I can say with authority that Verity defies everything and everyone – though usually in pursuit of doing what she believes is right, which is another way I can almost defend my decision.

The crunching of gravel signals a car pulling into the graveyard, and there, at last, is Verity's battered red Volvo. It comes bumping and rocking over the rutted ground. Red masking tape, peeling at one edge, barely holds the cracked wing mirror together.

While it would seem more in character for Verity to drive like a maniac, she is consistently careful, considerate and cautious behind the wheel. That this is one of the *only* ways she is consistent has given me much food for thought. For months, I put it down to the fact that the car is falling apart and Verity has no money to get it fixed, let alone replace it. But there are layers of DIY repairs to the paintwork. Where the steering wheel has started to come apart, it has been lovingly darned with golden thread.

Now, as she cuts the engine, she pats the steering wheel and I lip-read the words 'Well done.'

The door pops open with a groan and Verity climbs out. Her shoes, like her car, have seen better days: one has a fraying strap and the sole of the other flaps loose at the front – an accident waiting to happen. A series of scratches up the side of her leg indicates a blunt razor that should have been replaced a month ago.

When Verity has disappeared into the graveyard, I stride along the drystone wall to the gate, pausing just long enough to toss my keys into the grass. My feet try to steer me towards the ancient yew on the left, where Hope is buried, but I set my sights on the centre of the graveyard, stooping now and then to stuff weeds and dead flowers into my trug.

Verity is stomping along a line of graves. When she gets to the end, she turns down the next. My mother used to refer to swearing as 'turning the air blue'. When Verity gets to the end of another line without finding what she is looking for, she has a go at turning it psychedelic.

A pair of panicked pigeons flomp out of the tree above, raining excrement across Verity's arm. The ensuing swearing practically turns the air neon.

Four months ago, I nearly gave up on Verity when, during a routine observation, I saw her handbag break, strewing the contents across the pavement. Instead of snatching up her belongings, Verity turned her face to the sky and screamed the breath from her lungs. It took a commendable amount of time – and drew a commensurate amount of attention. As I hurried away, I swore to myself that I would find a new candidate in the morning. But when the morning came and I opened her file to shred the contents, the picture clipped to the inside of the cover stopped me in my tracks – Verity and her sister grinning at the camera, arms around each other; they are standing in front of a long view of fields and rolling hills, with a tower topped by a golden ball rising above the wooded summit.

In twenty-five years with the Sisterhood, there is only one death that weighs on my conscience. This is it. But now is not the moment to get distracted.

'They say it's good luck when a bird poos on you, but I have never seen why,' I call, hurrying towards Verity as I squeeze some hand gel on to a tissue.

Verity takes it with a mumbled thanks, eyes skidding away without meeting mine.

I tilt my head with a frown. 'Don't you work at the animal shelter on Robbers Lane? I came in to volunteer a few months back and the manager asked me to help with fundraising, so I have been taking flyers round, though I can't say I'm getting far. People are so abrupt these days—'

'Sorry to cut you off, but I'm due at work and I really want to visit my mother's headstone first, so maybe we can catch up next time you're in the office?' Verity interrupts, eyes scanning the graveyard. 'I don't suppose you have any idea where I should start looking? I can't remember from the funeral, so if you've seen a brand-new stone . . .'

'I saw some work being done over there yesterday.' I point towards the west wall. 'In front of the ceanothus.'

Verity's face goes blank.

'The big blue bush,' I say, rather more tartly than intended.

'Ah.' Verity's already walking away as she calls a 'Thanks' over her shoulder, mouth twitching upwards, but not far enough for a smile, as if I am no more worthy of that than I am of eye contact.

Although useful, it sometimes rankles how well I fulfil Rule 8: *Don't draw attention with your appearance or behaviour or kills – strive to be invisible: ensure you are unmemorable.* Thankfully, Verity has the same potential: she is pretty enough without being gorgeous, medium height, medium build.

I watch as she weaves between the graves, circling a quadrant of new headstones. Then she pulls taut, her whole body locked, as if a massive electrical current is flowing through her.

Twenty-five years of experience means I know exactly what even unpredictable Verity will do next, so I turn and march back towards the car park.

I am clearing around the graves near the gate when Verity comes barrelling up the path, her face suffused with colour, her eyes glazed and distant. An unobservant watcher would say Verity is furious. I recognize agony.

She stumbles on a loose stone and the sole of her shoe rips off, sending her toppling sideways. With surprising dexterity, she throws out her hands and braces herself on the wall. For a moment her shoulders heave as if she's about to cry, then she plops down on the wall to pull off her remaining shoe. Her free hand moves to stroke the slide holding her hair back on one side. It has a plastic daisy sprouting from it. The rest of Verity's attire is practical and plain. If this were the first time I was seeing her, I would assume the slide was chosen for the occasion, but she wears it more often than not. The stroking thing is a self-soothing tactic, like petting the steering wheel of the car every time she gets in or out. Both have an indifferent record of success.

Suddenly Verity bends forward and picks something out of the grass. And there it is – the sudden switch from being lost in distress to being fully alert. *This* is the Verity I'm here to introduce myself to – someone with not just the depth of pain but the instincts needed to become a member of the Sisterhood. Now she just has to pass the test of decency.

'Um, hi? Hello?' comes Verity's voice.

I lever my trowel up, then stab it back down, excavating a burdock root.

'Excuse me?' Verity is closer now. 'Ow, ow, sharp stones, sharp stones.' Closer still. 'EXCUSE ME?'

I peer round with feigned surprise. 'Oh dear. Have you hurt your foot?'

Verity winces and minces closer, holding something out. 'Are these yours? I found them by the gate . . .'

'My keys!' Snatching them from her hand, I rub lovingly at the ornament hanging from the ring – a copper heart with an age-faded photo of a smiling, dark-haired girl.

'Is that your mum?' Verity asks.

'Daughter.' I don't have to feign the emotion I know is bleeding across my face. 'Hope. Her name was Hope.' I look up at Verity, who has already half turned to go. 'Why don't we go to the café around the corner and I'll buy us some cake as a thank you and we can set the world to rights?'

This is it: the moment I become Verity's mentor, using the same words that my mentor used with me.

For a second, Verity's eyes fill with need, loneliness, hurt. 'Thanks,' she mumbles to the ground, 'but, like I said – I've got to get to work.' She flashes an apologetic look in my general direction, then rushes off . . . for all of eight steps before she has to move on to the gravel, then she winces and minces again, using patches of grass and weeds like stepping stones.

I turn my attention back to the burdock until Verity's car has slowly bumped and bounced its way out of the car park. Brushing soil off the root, I snap it in half and put the pieces in my pocket, then I wend my way across the cemetery to the ceanothus, stopping in front of the newest gravestone.

IN MEMORY OF MARY ANN BANNERMAN – 1973–2025

BELOVED MOTHER OF IREENE ROSE BANNERMAN

GONE BUT NOT FORGOTTEN

The inscription fills the headstone, leaving no space for anything or anyone else.

It's not a wonder that Verity struggles to know what to do with her rage. Still, I can be sympathetic about the day she's having *and* frustrated by her refusal to see the opportunity I'm trying to offer her. When *my* mentor engineered an introduction and then invited me to put the world to rights over tea, I said yes, because I am a reasonable, rational person: the perfect choice of mentee. Verity is an irrational nightmare creature, but since there are only two things I want out of what's left of my life, and Verity is one of them, I will have to make it work.

'Even if it kills me' isn't much of a threat at this point. What concerns me is the fact that Verity's victims need to be the correct ones and they have to be dispatched in a manner that is quiet, clean and professional. That worries me very much indeed.

Verity

The sun shouldn't be shining in the first place, but the fact that it just goes on blazing seems like malice.

As usual, I'm on shaky ground at work, behind on my rent, and maxed out on my credit card and overdraft. Naturally, I keep making it worse by doing totally understandable (though perhaps not entirely sensible) things like donating to people's vet bills and contributing to crowd-funders for victims trying to take abusers to court. I've been worse than ever lately, even though Boudicca needs serious work if she's to pass her next MOT.

Now, because I definitely need another source of misery, there's Mum's gravestone . . . though, maybe, to a person who isn't as selfish as I am, it would seem like a gift, not a punishment. After all, my sister is dead, whereas I'm obviously not. Mum always wanted a grave for Reenie, but it's not allowed without a death certificate, so this is a clever workaround. Maybe Mum intended it as somewhere for me to go to remember them both. Which would make it a nice thing – a kind and loving thing that I'm twisting into a problem because I'm me.

You have to stop doing that, Verity, Mum's voice whispers in my ear. *As if I'd ever intend to upset you.*

It's as I'm listening to my dead mother's voice in my

head that this little old dear turns up and tries to mother me. She's clearly as lonely as I am, but I can't just *go and have a cup of tea*. I have to get to work, because even though it feels like my lungs are full of oil and I can barely breathe, if I lose my job I'll lose Boudicca, not to mention ending up homeless.

The pain of fleeing the graveyard barefoot is almost a relief, since it distracts me from the gravestone. Soon I'm gentling my way out of the car park, teeth gritted as I weave around the worst of the ruts, terrified that Boudicca will simply fall apart like a metaphor for my life.

Reenie is the one who named the Volvo, on the basis that she's red and could mow down an army. Boudicca wasn't so much second-hand as one-step-above-salvage from the start. Mum's then boyfriend, TJ, traded a mate some decorating work for the rusting wreck, and it promptly became Reenie's most prized possession. Boudicca was never a thing of beauty, but there's always been a certain charm to the fact that in a crash with anything other than a tank, she'd come out on top.

Reenie hadn't been a fan of TJ, but Boudicca changed things, especially when he took her out again and again for driving lessons, whereas Mum took her twice, then kept putting it off until Reenie gave up asking.

There you go, twisting things to make the worst out of them! Mum's voice hisses in my head. *I wanted Reenie and TJ to bond – and they did! How could that be a bad thing?*

I went with them the first few times for the novelty, then got bored. The wish to have chosen differently tears at me as if it has claws.

Time heals all, they lie.

Time heals some things. Others just fester.

Like the memory of the time I went with them, slouching sullenly in the back seat until Reenie caught my eyes in the rear-view mirror and started humming the opera song from *Grand Theft Auto*: her favourite game to play with her boyfriend. She and Gavin were still together then, since they only split a few weeks before her disappearance, so we used to hear a lot of 'La donna è mobile' around the house. But that day in the car it wasn't the Italian lyrics she belted out of the half-open window but a sweary rant at every bad driver on the road. By the time she pulled up at our house we were all red-faced and breathless with laughter. And yet when she invited me to go with them again the next day, I said no.

'When I pass my test, we'll have an adventure. Just the two of us. We can go to the beach. Stuff ourselves with ice cream,' she promised, then went off alone with TJ.

Was it him? Was it Gavin? Or was it Charles Temple, the boy she hooked up with the night she disappeared? Surely it was one of them. A face to put on the monster that stalks Reenie through my dreams most nights.

Rage coils in my stomach, sending hot tendrils through my veins, but I've got to get to work. Since turning up barefoot isn't going to help my 'don't get fired' efforts, I detour to the cheapo shoe shop off the high street and buy myself a pair of trainers that probably won't last the fortnight and so manage to represent both an extravagant waste of money and all I can afford.

Mum's voice follows me around the shop. *Why on earth would you pick those?*

I can see her expression now, lips pursed with sympathy. As if every cut is made with love.

Surely thinking a little more about your clothing choices would be a way to honour your sister's memory – she had such an eye. Sometimes I think you want to forget all about her.

As if I could. As if Mum – alive or dead – would ever let me.

Gone but not forgotten. The words on the gravestone aren't so much a comfort as a threat.

I trudge back to Boudicca with birds serenading me from canopies and roofs as I think dreamy thoughts about shooting them. With a gun. A slingshot. A crossbow.

Since none of these things are available, I pause on the corner of the high street and try smelling the flowers in the window-box of the bookshop.

The flowers are plastic. And mouldy.

I walk on, stroking Reenie's hair-slide, and it comes apart in my hand. I stare in disbelief as plastic petals weep on to the pavement.

There used to be a packet of six. Over the years I've worn each to pieces, repairing and repairing them until there's nothing left to repair. As I bend to gather the remnants of the last slide, raindrops patter down around the broken petals.

At least the weather's turned to match my mood.

It's only when my nose starts to run that I realize I'm crying. The hair-slide is beyond repair. Boudicca isn't far behind. Reenie and Mum are dead. And the scum who ruined my life is free to live his, while I pay and pay and pay.

I barely register reaching Boudicca, too focused on carefully tipping the remains of the slide into an old envelope. Then I hug myself around the steering wheel.

I have to pull myself together. Except right now I'd do

anything for a second's relief from the feeling that the grief might rip my chest open if I breathe too hard.

For goodness' sake, Verity. Compared with your sister, what do you have to complain about? Mum hisses.

I cling to the steering wheel, then release it because, if there's one thing worse than sitting here trying not to explode with misery, it's having Mum in my ear while I do.

Sudden movement draws my attention. A dog is staring at me through the rear window of the car in front. Its dark eyes lock on mine. Paws come up to scrabble at the glass. I'm about to smile when the dog slumps, tongue lolling. The whites of its eyes show as it puts its ears back and whines. I can't hear it, but the heave of its misery writes the sound across the air.

I'm out of Boudicca, circling the car in front, before my brain finishes roaring, *NO!*

The windows are shut. The dog follows me, then slumps again, breath fogging the glass. A gloopy string of yellowish saliva slithers from the side of its mouth.

I spin around. No one is hurrying towards the car, face tight with worry. I rush to the nearest shop and peer in. No customers. The cashier is tapping away at his phone and doesn't even look up.

I take my mobile out and, hands shaking, walk around the car, recording. The moment I've captured the four closed windows, the dog's desperate panting, I stride back to Boudicca and open the boot. Shoving a disposable mask over my mouth and chin, I snap on a pair of nitrile gloves and heft my shovel.

I'm being stupid as well as reckless. I need to call for help, not take care of this myself. My life is enough of a mess: I can't afford to make it worse. At the very least, I should drive around the block and park out of sight.

The dog turns its eyes to me, lips twisting to reveal pale gums and foam between its teeth.

I hurry to the window furthest from where it's slumped, raise the shovel and drive it against the glass.

It rebounds, hurting my hands, wrists, arms, shoulders, but I embrace the pain. Don't people always say, 'Better out than in?'

I bash the shovel against the glass again. And again. Hurt and relief wash through me. It's the closest I've been to happiness since the last time I did something that the world would call stupid because it involves breaking the rules, even though it's for all the right reasons.

I roll my shoulders, steeling myself for another attack, and catch sight of a man staring at me from the corner of the street. He looks from the car to the shovel to my masked face, takes a step back, then legs it away round the corner again.

Reaching into my pocket, I pull out a pen. I press the nib to the corner of the glass then smash the shovel against it, driving all the force into a single point of impact.

The glass crazes, crumbling into a transparent mosaic of uneven pieces. I scrape the shovel around the window frame. Some of it comes loose in strips and strands, dropping on to the pavement or drooping down the door. The rest I hold out of the way like a curtain as the dog lurches towards the fresh air, putting trembling paws up on the windowsill. Grabbing the dog by the scuff of the neck, I heave, and it crumples out of the car, landing with a yelp, then wavering unsteadily back to its feet.

'With me,' I say, withdrawing the shovel and hurrying towards Boudicca.

I grab my water bottle and cup some into my hand, letting the dog lap urgently, then sprinkling more over its back and head, before giving it another drink. I cast a wary look up and down the street. A few houses along, I see a woman framed in an upstairs window, holding a curtain back as she stares down at me. I give her a friendly wave.

'Time to go.' I open Boudicca's back door and the dog struggles into the footwell. I throw myself behind the wheel, tossing the shovel on to the passenger seat, then turning on the engine. Quickly, I pull out and away.

I make the first turn I come to, pushing the speed limit all the way home.

The dog is still unsteady on its feet when we climb out of the car, but it perks up when I give it another drink then pour the rest of the water over its back. It shakes itself happily, spraying me, then pads after me into the flat. The flat where I am categorically Not. Allowed. To. Have. Pets. But if I'd taken the dog straight to the shelter, everyone there – including my manager, who hates me and is just looking for an excuse to fire me – would have had questions that'd be hard to answer. Whereas if I go in early tomorrow I can pretend I found the dog tied to the gate and that's why I've no explanation for where he came from.

For now, I put one of the sofa cushions in the shadiest spot, set several bowls of water all around, then hare back to Boudicca, cursing every traffic light and slow driver between me and work.

'Verity, we've talked about this,' says Manager Janet Who Hates Me when I dash into the office.

I think about mentioning Mum's grave.

You can't spend your whole life using grief as an excuse for your lack of responsibility, Mum scolds.

I duck my head, mumbling an apology, then I grab the cleaning supplies and hurry off.

Amid the cleaning, there's plenty of purring and cuddling – several of the cats even invite a tummy-tickle without turning full demon – so I'm considering smiling . . . until I turn the corner into the car park and nearly walk into Skeevy Steve.

'Hey, Vicky,' he leers, standing in the middle of the path so I have to squeeze myself against the fence to avoid touching him as I pass.

I've introduced myself to Skeevy at least seven times. After the fifth, I realized he wasn't struggling to remember 'Verity' – he wasn't even trying. At which point, I forgot his real name on principle.

I wait till he's out of sight, then make a rude gesture in his direction. Then again. Then with both hands. Then I shake my hands around a bit.

A sound of pain makes me turn.

A man and a woman are standing beside a shiny new Range Rover. His hand is wrapped, white-knuckled, around her arm.

'Everything OK?' I call.

'We'll come up to the office when we're ready,' the man grunts. The woman gives me a hopeless little smile.

I cross my arms. 'We don't let people adopt if we're not convinced our animals are going to a safe home.' I lean to the side, trying to catch the woman's eyes. 'You should come up to the office with me now.'

The man's thin-lipped mouth twists. 'You can tell that fat-cow manager she can forget sponsorship from Moss Motors.' He beeps his car unlocked then wrenches the door open, letting the woman go.

She scurries for the passenger side, looking so afraid that I slip out my phone and snap a picture of the numberplate as the man starts the engine. The woman's barely shut her door when the man guns out of the car park, sending me stumbling backwards as gravel spits in every direction.

Breath coming in pants, I march up to the office. 'What's the police non-emergency number?'

'Police?' Janet Who Hates Me blinks in confusion. 'What's happened?'

I tap at my phone, but I'm shaking too hard to bring up the browser.

'A horrible man. In the car park. Obviously abusing his wife.'

Janet peers through the window. 'Should I get the first-aid kit?'

I give up on my phone, dropping down in front of the office computer. 'They're gone. But I got his numberplate.'

'Did he hit her?'

'Grabbed her arm. But really tight.'

'Verity,' says Janet, and the disappointment in her voice tells me all I need to know.

'No!' I growl. 'If he's going to act like that in public, imagine what he does in private! What if her face is on the news tomorrow? What if he's still in a rage when they get home, and—'

Janet pulls the keyboard away. 'I know you have a

difficult history, but lots of people have arguments without anyone ending up dead. A man holding his wife's arm is not a crime. You cannot call the police on every person you don't like the look of – like that man with the bulldog?' she adds, when I open my mouth to protest.

'It had a festering sore on its back leg – and the guy wanted to adopt another animal to mistreat?'

Janet rubs at her temples. 'The dog was barely limping, and not everyone is as observant as you, Verity. If you hadn't screamed at him about prison sentences, he might have stayed long enough to get some advice on caring for his pet, whereas I had to do the best I could while he was hurrying away from the – and I quote – "crazy girl with the rolling eyes".'

I grit my teeth. 'So, he's a misogynist and an animal abuser.'

'You were practically frothing at the mouth. I thought he was quite polite under the circumstances.' She shakes her head. 'The week before that, you said there was something bad happening between that young couple. And the week before that it was . . . I don't even remember, but you also had a "bad feeling" about that bald guy.' Janet visibly resists the urge to roll her eyes.

Why do people keep telling me I see the world through a broken lens, unless it's true? My chin trembles as my head floods with the memory of Mum shouting me down when I tried to talk to her about my guilt over leaving Reenie at the party because I wanted to make curfew. Mum scoffing that it would be the first time, since Reenie was the careful one, whereas my recklessness at coming home without my sister was no surprise. She insisted I must have got bored and left without trying to find Reenie, while my loyal big sister stayed to make sure I was OK. She wouldn't listen when I tried to tell her that she had it backwards: we were in Charles Temple's room at the university when I decided to leave, so how could I have gone without Reenie knowing? There were only five of us in there.

I can still see it. Feel the beat of the music. My brain promptly presents me with a picture of the courtyard steps strewn with drunken students, then another of the packed university corridors.

We were in Charles Temple's room at the end, I tell myself for the thousandth time. *Weren't we?*

'Verity?'

I blink. Janet is peering worriedly at me.

'We both know there are bad people in the world,' she says, voice softer now, 'but think about it logically. Is it likely that at least one of them comes here every single week?'

It isn't logical. Just like it's not logical that my mother would lie to me. She loved me.

Janet glances at her watch with a frown. 'I was expecting a sponsor ten minutes ago, so why don't you get a cup of tea while—'

I grimace. 'Not Moss Motors?'

Janet nods. 'Yes, did you see him in the car park?' She closes her eyes and her whole body slumps as realization hits. 'Consider this your second formal warning,' she tells me. 'As your contract states, if there's a third incident you'll be fired, so try not to put either of us in that position.' She turns away, fussing at a pile of files.

I slink away to the sheds. I'm halfway through cleaning

a stack of litter trays when my phone beeps. It's a message from my landlord.

> When I came round to see your neighbour earlier, I heard barking, so I looked in your window. There is a large dog in your flat. You're months overdue on rent. No more leeway. Eviction notice to follow. Your deposit is toast.

I tip my head back, open my mouth – and remember that yelling will scare the animals and almost certainly get me fired. Raising my fists above my head, I shake them at the ceiling and stamp my feet and feel *ridiculous* and small and hopeless and helpless, but what am I supposed to do when I'm not *allowed* to do anything that would actually express my rage and misery? There's too much screaming inside me, and no way to let it out.

Pru

Following Verity to the rehoming centre is likely to prove explosive instead of fruitful, so her recruitment will have to wait. In any case, I am needed elsewhere.

I get to the county show early enough for a reasonable parking spot, pay my entrance fee, then busy myself among the stalls, circling for nearly an hour before I spy my target. He is here to play a set on the main stage later, but for now is wandering around, looking for freebies. Slipping a Tupperware box out of my bag, I place the contents on a paper plate, then station myself at the end of a row of stalls. As his eyes rove about, I step forward with a smile and offer him a delicately prepared mushroom wrap.

'Last one, so it's half price!' I say, gifting him my best 'harmless older woman' smile. 'Gosh, aren't you the musician? How wonderful. Here.' I push the plate into his hand. 'With regards from the community.' Obviously, this is not my community or even my county, but the broad principle applies.

He plucks the wrap off the plate and takes a huge mouthful. 'Yum,' he mumbles, spraying saliva and crumbs.

'Foraged this very morning by my own hands,' I tell him truthfully.

'Cheers, mate,' he says, lifting the rest of the wrap in a salute, then wandering off.

And just like that another collector of images of child abuse is dispatched. It is depressing how regularly I am assigned such cases now, and all my friends in the Sisterhood have said the same. Last week, over dinner to discuss our relative progress at taking on a mentee, Graziella and I tried to work out whether it is more likely that these referrals come from police forces and social workers up and down the country, or if there is one specific expert quietly feeding the names to the Sisterhood. In the end, we agreed it didn't really matter, so long as the names keep coming and we keep quietly thinning out the ranks of these predators.

It is clear from the detail in the files we receive on our targets that, somewhere along the chain, there is an investigation before each kill is authorized, though how much of that is internal and how much relies on official channels is unclear. The important thing is the surety that our targets are legitimate – at least as far as the Sisterhood is concerned.

Although the musician won't actually die for hours or even days, I know better than to stick around in case he gets an early stomach ache and sends someone to see if they can find a woman meeting my description.

Obviously, I don't hurry suspiciously away, instead taking my time at the honey stall and returning to the car with several enticing purchases. I drive off just as the microphone crackles from the main stage and my target starts his extremely final show.

As I merge on to the motorway, my mind picks away

at the question of how targets get referred to the Sisterhood. It is safer that members currently active in killing aren't told exactly how the process works, let alone who is involved, so I have never knowingly met one of the team who decide which potential cases to accept, but they must be highly skilled investigators, doubtless with access to additional sources of information (official and otherwise). I always hoped that, when my term of service was up, there would be an opportunity to move into one of these roles, but of course I'll be lucky if I live long enough to train my replacement.

Tomorrow, I will have to run into Verity at work. With anyone else, I might focus on finding the perfect words to convince her. With Verity, there is really only one question – when do I tell her how invested in her sister's disappearance I am, and why?

I fret all the way home, a pointless waste of time and energy that propels me into an evening of productivity. First, I hang a large punching bag from the hook in the roof of the garage. Two months ago, I would simply have lifted the bag so that the strap slotted over the hook; like all the women in the Sisterhood, I am stronger and fitter than I look. Now I have to fetch a stepladder and shove the bag up tread by tread. Even then it's slow going: I have to keep stopping to catch my breath. By the time it's done, I am sweaty, my muscles trembling.

Once I have my breath back, I fetch out the box of old electrical appliances, clear the bathroom and dining-room windowsills, set up a CCTV array in the living room and finally collect a range of cleaning products and old cloths, along with a battered metal tray, then set it all on the draining board of the utility-room sink for Verity to practise setting 'accidental' fires. Everything proceeds nicely while I think of my own training, then I try to visualize Verity's learning process.

This is a mistake.

I quickly redirect my attention to administrative responsibilities. Settling at the kitchen table with a handsome glass of Grand Marnier (courtesy of Graziella) and the last of my pistachio shortbread, I skim then delete the latest issues of the many local e-newsletters I am subscribed to, then do the same with my Google alerts.

One jumps out, and I click through to a county-library website advertising an upcoming talk by Claire Jeynes, the director of a small local charity 'supporting people who have turned to drugs or alcohol in the wake of trauma'. I make a note on my wall calendar. Going along will be a risk, but only a small one: there is little chance of her recognizing me from the information appeals when Hope died. After twenty-six years of grief, including twenty-five of murder, all my softness has worn away: I look as much of a stranger to my former self as I feel. In any case, I don't have time to be overly cautious.

Continuing through my alerts, I find a news item about a young woman in a town less than an hour away who had been drugged then sexually assaulted after a university party. Reaching over to the sideboard, I tap the PIN into the cabinet lock then pull out my investigation notebook for Ireene's case and copy down the details. Then I search for other versions of the story, garnering a handful of other specifics, but nothing specific enough. There are too many of these stories. Instead of a single serial predator, there are many. Still, there is something here. I can feel it. Obviously, I don't believe in nonsense like psychic powers, but twenty-five years in the Sisterhood has honed my instincts and all of them are thrumming with the electrostatic prickling that signals an important lead.

I tuck the notebook back into the cabinet on top of the stack of police files from Ireene's case. Once Verity is recruited, she can read them herself, though I expect the ones that will be of greatest interest aren't those containing information she has never been privy to before but rather the sequences of statements she and her mother gave. At the start, they told two very different stories, but, by the time Ireene had been gone a month, Verity's story matched her mother's. I can only imagine how hard it has been to grieve her sister while fighting to remember her as she truly was. It isn't a wonder it often seems as if Verity doesn't trust her own mind.

I sit back, sipping my drink, the gentle burn of the alcohol soothing its way down my throat. Something tickles the back of my hand.

I look down to see an ant creeping across my skin. A moment later the ant is no more. I peer down at the floor, and there, over by the wall, is another ant. I take the ant powder out of the cupboard and, after squashing Ant 2, I creep towards Ants 3 and 4. Once they are dispatched, I sprinkle powder into the hinge-corner of the garden door. I am not convinced I have located the source of the problem, but it is a start.

Absently, I pick up my phone and tap the app showing the tracker I put on Verity's car when I first started observing her. She is not at work, not at home, not at the shops . . .

I zoom in closer. Why is she at a set of allotments in the next town over from where she lives?

I am grinding my teeth even before I tap the Nextdoor app and, with a single search, find a local discussion thread that confirms Verity is engaging in her favourite activity: getting herself in trouble.

Verity

Last night I dreamt about Reenie, but this time she wasn't being stalked by the usual faceless, shapeless monster. Instead, we were standing beside a chain-link fence and she was beckoning me forward as she bent to lift a loose corner. I crawled through and she followed me into an overgrown nest of brambles. When I stood up, I saw a column of sheds marching into the distance above little rectangles of greenery. Reenie lifted up a curl of grass and earth, just as she had lifted the fence. She smiled at me, then curled herself down into the ground. I flung myself forward to tear it open again, but there was no seam. Just hard-packed mud and stones and roots. I tore with my hands and—

Woke to my alarm, heart punching at my ribs as if trying to get out. As I sank back into the mattress, sweaty and shaking, certainty settled into me: it wasn't just a dream – it was a message. Not from 'beyond', but from my own brain, since the allotments are my best current lead.

The moment my shift ends, I drive to the allotments near Gavin Pieper's house by way of the nearest DIY store, where I spend almost the last of the cash in my wallet on wire-cutters to go with the metal detector I bought last month instead of paying off part of my back rent.

Parking as close as possible, I stomp round to the boot, stuffing the wire-cutters into my belt and hefting the metal detector over my shoulder. Then I head off to find my sister.

An old man spots me as I hurry along the edge of the fence. He calls out, but I stride purposefully onwards, checking the plan of the allotments on my phone.

Gavin Pieper has been posting about his allotment veg for years. I called Detective Inspector Strickland, the man in charge of Reenie's case, about it the first time Gavin put something on social media, but DI Strickland just sighed and told me it would be remarkably stupid of Gavin Pieper to draw attention to where he'd buried a body. Not to mention that, since the photos he was posting clearly showed the whole plot was cultivated, he'd be risking disturbing the remains all year, every year.

When I tried to argue, DI Strickland sighed again and explained, for the fifth time, that Gavin's brother – and his brother's girlfriend – both swore up and down that Gavin was home with them the night Reenie disappeared.

'Don't you think it's suspicious that he has a double alibi all neatly prepared?' I pressed.

The detective sighed yet again. In one of our conversations, he managed twenty-seven sighs before he excused himself from the call with the scrupulous politeness of a courteous man about to lose his shit. During the allotment conversation, he only racked up eleven sighs, so his tone was still calm and gentle when he told me, 'It's more common than you think.'

It didn't stop me going to Gavin's allotment that same night with a curtain rod, pushing it into the soil in a grid pattern to check that there was no body-sized area where it refused to go deep. So I know Reenie isn't in his allotment.

Today, I'm here for his aunt's. Two weeks ago, he posted a photo of a long-overgrown allotment. I promptly called the council, claiming I was worried he'd been in my uncle's plot, thinking it unused because my uncle was in hospital. The talkative woman at the council kindly looked up the owner of the plot in question; it turned out *not* to be my uncle's (shocker). Instead, it had recently been reassigned from an old lady to her nephew. I made a joke about how long some people have had their plots, and the woman told me the Piepers had owned that particular one for twenty-five years. More than long enough for Gavin to have buried Reenie there.

I crouch beside the plot in question, snip a hole in the fence big enough to squeeze through, then scramble across to the least-tended corner and run the metal detector around. Reenie was wearing her best underwired bra when she disappeared, so unless she was buried naked—

I can't think about that.

This corner of the plot has been given over to blackberry bushes, and soon I am scratched all over as I thrust the metal detector through at intervals. Nothing, nothing, nothing . . .

Then a ping. I nearly throw the metal detector down as I kneel, reaching my arm through the gauntlet of thorns, scrabbling in the dirt . . .

It's a two-pence coin. I pick up the metal detector again and run it over the same spot. Nothing, nothing . . .

A bigger ping. I unearth a rusted can. I've just tossed it

aside when I hear voices heading my way: one angry, one professionally calm.

I hurry to the second most untended area of the allotment and start thrashing the metal detector around.

Half an hour later, the door beside me clicks open and DI Strickland peers into the back seat of the police car where I am sitting. His eyes are tired, his mouth and shoulders drooping.

'Come on out,' he says.

I scramble on to the grass and hold out my wrists. 'Ready to read me my rights?'

'You can't keep doing these things, Verity.' He scrubs a weary hand over his stubble. 'I've been trying to persuade Mr Pieper to be understanding about your continued distress—'

'How lovely that he's so understanding about my distress that HE KILLED MY SISTER!'

DI Strickland shifts from one foot to the other, as if struggling under a heavy weight. 'Stop it now, Verity. You're making a bad situation worse, and what's the point of that?'

'The point is that I'm doing something! Because *somebody* has to do *something*! We don't all have the luxury of moving on and forgetting her.'

He doesn't even flinch, just sighs, looking even more exhausted. 'I'm sorry we still don't know what happened to her. I know you feel desperate, but there's nothing to find here, Verity, apart from trouble, and as for your poor mother—'

I feel my face contort in fury. 'My mother's dead. They just put up the headstone.'

'Ah,' he says, as if suddenly all is clear.

He thinks this is grief that Mum died without answers. But it's so much more than that. It's Mum setting a place for Reenie at my birthday last year, a week before keeling over dead. It's Mum crying when I cut my cake the birthday before that because I didn't comment on how it was another year without Reenie. It's Mum apologizing the year before *that* for not being more cheerful, only she 'couldn't find it in her' when Reenie would be forever stuck a month from her eighteenth.

DI Strickland's rasping voice wrenches me back to the present. '. . . not going to find your answers stalking Gavin Pieper.'

'This was Gavin's aunt's allotment. It's been in the family for twenty-five years—'

'*Verity*,' DI Strickland snaps, then sighs (is this number three or four?). 'We've been over this. He didn't have the opportunity. *She's not here*.' He takes a deep breath, then lowers his voice. 'I'm sure that when I explain to Mr Pieper about your mother, he will agree not to push matters. But if there's another incident, you'll be cautioned or even charged.' He heaves another sigh, leaning his shoulder against the police car. 'None of us want to see that happen, but we have a duty to the whole community – and that includes Mr Pieper, just as it includes Charles Temple and TJ Howard. You cannot keep committing crimes, Verity.'

I make a *pfft* noise.

'This *is* a crime, Verity. It's not just trespass but harassment. I know you have it in your head that you've identified the only three people who had a specific motive, but, as we've discussed many, *many* times before, you have absolutely no evidence – not to mention the fact that you're ignoring every other person who was at the party that night.'

'There were only five of us in Temple's room! We hardly interacted with anyone else at the university. Nathan was into me, not Reenie, and Christophe *died* that night. I know you think he and Reenie might have had the same bad batch of drugs, but—'

'And yet here we are at Gavin Pieper's allotment.' He draws in a breath through his nose. 'Not that I want to find you at Charles Temple's house next, because it *might not have been him either*,' he says, talking over me when I try to interrupt. 'Reenie could have run into trouble on the way home. Temple says she left, and other witnesses think they saw her moving towards the university gates.'

'But they're not sure,' I say.

'No one is sure of anything, Verity. I understand why you're grasping at straws, but that is what you're doing – and I think you know it,' he adds gently. 'Go home. I promise that if we ever have a fresh lead, we'll follow it all the way to the end of the line.' He gestures towards my car.

I spend the journey home emotionally ping-ponging between rage about being interrupted before I'd finished my search and relief that I won't be spending the evening digging up my sister's corpse, grief that the allotments were a bust and disgust with myself for hoping I'd find her in the dirt under the brambles.

I wrench my thoughts away, trying to focus on the dog waiting at the flat and my plan for tomorrow, but it just makes me think about my imminent eviction. Which makes me think about the fact that, because Reenie never came home, home stopped being home, and I stopped being the Verity who had a big sister to help her stand up to Mum, and Reenie stopped having anything at all.

I try to hold on to my memories, but it's hard when Mum always swore they were lies. Like the day Reenie taught me to make daisy chains to cheer me up the first time Mum twisted the truth right in front of me. I was only five, but I remember clear as day the moment Mum knocked her boyfriend-of-the-moment's favourite mug off the table.

We stared at the pieces on the floor, then Mum shook her head. 'Verity, what did I tell you about rushing?' she scolded.

I blinked at her. 'You did it, Mummy. I'm standing over here.'

Mum pressed her fists to her hips. 'Accidents happen, Verity, but you have to take responsibility and say sorry. If you lie—'

'I'm not lying!' I pointed my finger at her, shaking with anger. 'You did it!'

'No television,' she snapped. 'Out in the garden,' she ordered.

'Come on, V! I'm going to make a fairy crown.' Reenie's hand wrapped around mine. 'I'll show you, then we can do a spell for the fairies to visit us.'

I looked between Mum and my big sister, lip trembling. Reenie tugged, and I went silently.

'Mum does that sometimes,' Reenie said as she towed me to the apple tree by the fence. It can't have been more than five metres, but it seemed like a field back then. 'She tells things the wrong way, even when they've just happened. Just nod and remember things the right way in your head.'

I pulled my hand free, glaring at her. 'But lying's wrong.'

Reenie shrugged and, even though she was only seven to my five, told me, 'Mum doesn't think she's lying. If you try to argue, she'll just tie you up in knots, then it'll be even worse.'

She always let Mum roll off her back. I never could, but it was different when Reenie was there, making faces behind Mum's back or clapping a hand over my mouth, apologizing for me, then dragging me away to do finger-painting or smell the lily-of-the-valley that bloomed at the back of the garden behind the rotting shed.

When Reenie was there to help me keep the truth and lies straight, everything was different – including me. But whoever stole Reenie stole *that* Verity, too, leaving me grieving for not just my lost sister but the life I never got to live and the person I should have been.

Pru

Finally, there are no new posts on the neighbourhood app about the police being called to the allotments, and the tracker app shows Verity back at her flat. People are idiots, and Verity seems determined to top the list on a semi-regular basis, despite the fact she's got a perfectly good brain, when she chooses to use it. Ten months ago, at the vet clinic where she worked two jobs ago, I saw her catch a medication error then promptly come up with a way to detach a crow's wing from a large sheet of fly paper without tearing off half its feathers – and that was just in the half-hour I loitered in the waiting room, pretending to peruse their range of food and toys.

That's the Verity I want to recruit. But, of course, this is the moment she has chosen to renew her acquaintance with the police. As violations of Rule 8 go, this is a doozy.

I swap back to the tracker app and check her location again. Still home. If only I could be sure she would stay put, I would happily go to bed.

Instead, I go unhappily, sleep badly and check Verity's location the moment I wake. Even though it is barely 6 a.m. she is already at work. Has she turned over a new leaf after yesterday's debacle or is this a sign of fresh trouble?

The odds are on trouble, but turning up this early will

just add to it, so I make myself useful, hoovering the living room, plumping the cushions, dusting the ornaments. I pick up the picture of Hope from the coffee table to wipe the glass, but suddenly I am lost in my daughter's face.

After all these years, I know the pain won't stop my heart, won't still my lungs, and yet I hear myself gasping for breath as I press the frame to my chest and drift over to the bookcase, trailing my other hand over the line of pictures there. Hope as a babe-in-arms. Hope as a toddler. As a little girl. As a pre-teen. Hope turning thirteen. Turning sixteen. Turning nineteen. She was dead three weeks later.

My eyes blur as other pictures paint themselves across my mind – Hope turning twenty, Hope graduating, Hope pregnant, Hope with her own daughter . . . All the pictures that were never taken but which I imagined so often when Hope was alive.

After twenty-six years, I know I will never be free of the heart-stopping moments when my brain says, *One day Hope and I must go there, do this, share that* . . . I don't indulge in denial and yet some part of me cannot believe that Hope isn't out there somewhere, because surely it is impossible for her to be nowhere. Logic says that 'gone' has to mean 'gone to' when talking about an entire person, with their own universe inside them. But death doesn't mean 'gone'. It means 'nowhere' and 'never again'. I know that, of course I do, but though I used to scold myself for my moments of foolish disbelief, I've given that up now. Apparently, even *I* am not capable of being rational all the time.

I hurry to the kitchen, taking out the file on my next case before I let myself run upstairs to Hope's room and give into the stupid, pointless urge to open her wardrobe, pick one of her dresses, press it to my face then cry until I feel ill and the pain is just as bad as before.

Thankfully, planning a murder is a wonderful distraction, especially in the case of a serial domestic abuser who has just moved in with a new girlfriend and her two young kids. According to the file Astria dropped off a few days ago, my target broke his most recent ex's jaw and her son's arm less than a year ago. I won't give him a chance to do the same – or worse – with this new family.

Per Rule 3, simple plans are always best. In two days, it will be his turn to close up at the warehouse where he works. It will be the last thing he ever does.

A few weeks ago, I had lunch every day at the greasy spoon across the street from the warehouse, though I'd learnt everything I needed to know by Day 3; namely, that my target is widely hated by his colleagues for a series of near-misses. He corners too quickly in the forklift and, especially at the end of a shift, takes a shortcut over a rough patch of tarmac.

'As if the rest of us wouldn't do the same if it weren't a rollover waiting to happen,' opined one of his put-upon colleagues. He caught my eye across the café and smiled.

I smiled back, nodding my thanks for his unintentional gift.

Now, I note down the final steps of my plan, then tuck my files securely away in the cabinet and turn my attention to baking.

Graziella lets herself in at ten on the dot and soon we are bustling comfortably around my kitchen, Graziella making the tea while I set still-warm spiced-apple shortbread on a plate.

'I know there's an unspoken Rule about recruiting mentees under twenty-five – and for good reason – but Faith's twenty-four and otherwise the best candidate I've found. Plus, she needs this. She needs us.' Graziella takes a bite of shortbread then dusts her fingers off over her plate. 'So . . . Verity.'

I can't help but sigh. 'She called the police down on herself again yesterday.' I raise a hand. 'No charges. They didn't even take her in. I am choosing to view it as a sign that it is just as well I am about to step in with an alternative outlet for her emotions.'

'You don't sound as if you think you should do this.' Graziella's sharp grey eyes regard me over the rim of her teacup.

'I think it is natural to be worried about any pick of mentee.'

Graziella's mouth bunches up at one side, briefly throwing off the symmetry of her delicate features. Then her expression softens. 'Any news from the doctor? Will you have enough time, do you think? Otherwise, perhaps we should discuss—'

'There will be time,' I say, and hope it isn't a lie.

'When Astria dropped off my latest case, she told me she'll be stepping back from delivering files. She asked me if I might take over.'

I blink at the non-sequitur.

'We'll both be busy with our mentees, so it'll be a way to see each other regularly.'

I look across the table at my closest friend of the last twenty-five years. The prescient grief of my loss is written into the lines suddenly making her look her age, though usually people can't tell if she is in her forties or fifties and would never guess she is sixty-two.

I can't help but wonder if Astria would have asked me, if not for my illness. This must be what getting tapped to move up the ranks after retirement from dispatching targets looks like. Would there have been room for me and Graziella both? Another stage to our work together?

I push away both the sadness and the envy. 'It will be lovely to see you.' I clear my throat. 'I will need to build some extra structure for Verity for when I am gone, so it will be an easy way to introduce the two of you.'

'Only once you're sure about her.' Graziella gives me a pointed look. 'We *all* need to be careful about that one.' She sighs. 'Though if anyone can turn that sow's ear into a silk purse . . .'

She grins at me, and I grin back, then we talk about our plans for training our mentees instead of the fact that I am dying.

An hour later, Graziella hugs me, holding on for an extra moment that feels both too long and too short, then heads off to recruit her mentee, while I prepare to do the same.

I lock up, then settle Hope's lucky ladybird pendant around my neck before I climb into the car and set off to the rehoming centre. Obviously, I don't believe the necklace has magical powers – per Rule 11, *Luck is the alchemy that flows from careful planning and rigorously honed skills* – but it feels right to have a little piece of Hope with me.

I press the pendant to my chest till the metal warms and, when I close my eyes, I can hear her voice, though the sound is hazy with the years. Later, I will play one of our old home movies and listen to that laugh ringing through time, carving itself fresh and sharp into my memory once more.

But first I have business with the living.

On the way out of town, I pause beside a house that is clearly mid-renovation and, after checking that the builders are absent, the house is quiet and there is no one looking, I quickly fill a bucket with gravel and broken-up driveway tarmac, stashing it in the footwell. I snatch a big cracked tub from a pile of rubbish, then continue my journey.

The tarmac and gravel are a good colour match to that at the warehouse. A little sprinkling to make the ground extra uneven, and a tub in the middle of the path, will ensure my target takes the corner even more tightly than usual. No one will suspect a thing when Mr Near-Miss becomes Mr Had-It-Coming.

Verity

I can't believe I'm at work at six-o'-sodding-clock in the morning.

Yawning, I open the passenger door, letting the dog bound out. He rushes around, sniffing everything in sight, then peeing in a bunch of places.

'None of that in the office,' I order as I lock Boudicca and march across the car park. The dog follows me inside, nose and tail working overtime.

I toss him a toy, then settle at the desk, humming 'Smooth Criminal' as I punch in the security code for the cabinet where we store the microchip scanner and microchip needles.

Kneeling by the dog, I wave the scanner over the back of his neck and break into a grin when there's no beep. To be thorough, I run it over the right shoulder – all clear. Then the left – BEEP!

The dog peers back, wide-eyed, at the things I promptly tell the scanner. I think about checking the dog's name, but looking up the microchip number might leave a trace in the system, so it's not worth the risk.

Scrambling back to my feet, I grab a microchip needle from the stash, then reposition myself with the dog trapped between my thighs. I pinch the skin between his shoulders and inject the tiny chip where it'll be picked up much more easily than the old one. According to the research I did last night, it's tricky to cut out an existing microchip – and it's definitely not my skillset. I'll just have to hope Janet believes me when I say he wasn't already chipped, so I sorted it myself. If all goes well, no one will ever scan him again. And, if they do, hopefully they'll find the microchip I placed rather than the original.

Tossing the dog a treat, I start filling out the appropriate paperwork as if I'd found him tied to the gates this morning. That sorted, I do a basic health check, then lead him to a kennel.

'You're all set now. Handsome chap like you will have a new family faster than you can cover me with slobber. Which means almost instantly.'

I fondle his ears, then close the gate and start my morning rounds. I work steadily until nine thirty, then head to the office for a cuppa, trying to persuade myself that, if I can just keep up the positive attitude, I can dig myself out of debt and then everything will be OK.

Oh, Verity. I wish I could believe you mean it, Mum whispers, distracting me so I don't hear Skeevy Steve until I turn a corner and find him backing our youngest volunteer up against a wall.

A second later my phone is in my hand. I swipe to the camera app and hit record.

'I'm sorry if anything I did came across that way,' Amy is pleading. 'I didn't mean to seem—'

'Like a slut?' He laughs, but the sound is ugly. 'Why'd you think that's a bad thing? Just 'cos you've gone shy now—'

'Smile!' I crow, stepping into their view with my phone raised towards them. 'Say hello to my lovely livestream viewers! This is Friday morning on Great British Assaults in the Workplace! Tell us your name, Player 1?'

Before Skeevy can pretend it's not exactly what it looks like, Amy shoves him with both hands, gaining enough space to tear off past me.

Skeevy glares, folding his arms. 'You ever hear of roleplay, you voyeuristic cow? Thanks for spoiling our fun,' he sneers.

'Yeah, she looked like she was having a blast,' I sneer back.

His nostrils flare, but his eyes are on my phone. 'Employees on their last strike should focus on their work. I've got to get back to the office.'

As soon as he's gone, I hurry after Amy. I find her with our newest set of kittens, her face flushed and her eyes red.

'When Janet gets in, I'll show her the video. She'll make sure—'

'Please don't.' Amy sniffs, cuddling a squirming kitten close. 'I appreciate you getting rid of him, but you weren't really livestreaming, were you?'

I shake my head. 'Just recording.'

Her face floods with relief. '*Please* delete it.'

'Why? You didn't do anything wrong, and it's proof that Skeevy Steve really is skeevy.' It's proof that I'm not crazy just because I'm alert to problems that people like Janet are oblivious to.

Amy frowns at me. 'Steve? I thought his name was Chris.'

I wave a hand. 'The point is he shouldn't get away with that sort of behaviour.'

She tickles behind the kitten's ears, making it go limp with delight. 'He didn't really do anything. Anyway, it was probably my fault. It's not the first time it's happened. My ex used to say I'm a c— That I'm a tease. If I'm the common factor—' She cuts off as Janet appears round the corner.

'Come with me, please, Verity.' She turns and walks off before I can say a word.

Any gives me a pleading look, mouthing 'delete it' as I hurry away.

'Did you log a new arrival in this morning?' Janet asks as she strides towards the office.

'Got here early and there he was, tied to the front gate,' I say, trotting to keep up. 'He's probably about two, so I doubt it'll be difficult to find him a new family. I wrote up—'

'Did you know our new arrival has two microchips?'

I attempt a confused frown. 'I couldn't find one this morning, so I—'

'It took me ten seconds to find the second microchip. Do you know what prompted me to look? A man came in to ask if we had any advice about tracing a stolen dog. Apparently, someone broke into his car yesterday.'

'If the dog was in a car, maybe someone was worried about it overheating – it was boiling yesterday. It would have been a rescue, not a theft. That must be why they brought him here.'

Janet's face is slowly turning puce. 'Yes, I'm sure the person who liberated a dog from an overheated car left him tied to the front gate overnight.'

'It might have been just before I got in, not overnight.'

'Or *exactly* as you got in.' Janet heaves a sigh worthy of DI Strickland. 'We have CCTV, Verity.'

I'm such a moron. I thought the camera was focused on the office and the storage sheds, but obviously the angle is much wider than I realized.

'You can't give the dog back to him.' I pull out my phone. 'I took a video. You can see it was an emergency—'

Janet puts up a hand. 'I don't want to see the evidence of your crime, Verity. God's sake.'

'You have to understand—'

'I understand that every time you see a problem you react in the most extreme and uncontrolled manner possible.' She shakes her head. 'I'll tell the man I've reflected on him saying the dog was in the car, despite the hot weather, and suggest he might not want to find the dog – or the thief – in case it draws attention to evidence of the dog's suffering, as then he'll be in at least as much trouble as whoever broke into the car. It might be enough to persuade him to sign the poor thing over properly.'

'I'm sorry,' I whisper. 'I'll turn over a new leaf, I promise—'

'Verity, you are so beyond fired I don't even know where to start, which is just as well because there's nothing to discuss.' She turns and walks away.

I follow her to the office to collect my things. Leaving my keys on the counter, I stumble out to the car park.

The sun is so bright it whites out the world. Shading my eyes, I take out my phone, scroll to the video of Skeevy Steve and mail it to Janet. I can't let the same thing happen to the next young volunteer.

'Hello again!'

I blink, and there, just a few steps away, is the woman from the graveyard.

'Shall we pop into the office for that cuppa?' she asks, smiling hopefully.

Pru

'I just got fired,' says Verity, her voice stripped of emotion. 'I've got to go. Sorry.' She ducks her head and scurries round me to her big red tank of a car.

It is a worry that this is the fifth time Verity's been fired in the last eleven months, but at least it is convenient.

Her face falls when she turns to slide into the driver's seat and sees me standing by the bonnet. I try not to be irritated that she so clearly can't stand the idea of an hour in my company; after all, she has no idea what we would really be talking about.

'I'm having an awful day. Please leave me—'

I give her my most harmless smile. 'I won't hold you up. Just' – I rummage in my handbag, as if it isn't perfectly organized, plucking out a business card – 'the company I work for is hiring. I've been with them twenty-five years and I can honestly say they are the best.'

Verity snorts. 'If that's true, they won't want me.'

I proffer the card. 'Can't hurt to consider it. I will have you sorted before you know it, if you give me the chance.'

Verity's face says, *Good luck with that*, but I don't let my smile waver.

After a moment, Verity takes the card between two pinched fingers. 'What type of company is it?'

'A service agency. A very select one.'

We both look at the many, many muck splatters across her shirt and shoes.

'Then they definitely won't want me. Look, I know you mean well, but telling me about a job I'm clearly not cut out for is kinda adding insult to injury.' She holds the card back out to me.

I crease my face into a sympathetic expression. 'I didn't mean to come on strong, but I can see you're experiencing a bad patch and I want to help because I know what that's like.' I let my eyes and smile sharpen: let Verity register the change. 'Twenty-six years ago, my daughter died, and all I had was pain and anger I could do *nothing* about. Until someone gave me a card just like that one.'

'And then life was fine and dandy again, and all the birds sang, and the flowers bloomed?' Verity mocks. 'Thanks, but—'

'My work gave me a purpose. That is a whole lot more than you have right now.'

Verity lets her hand fall, the edges of the card crumpling in her grip.

'I can help you – if you choose to let me. So give me a call.' I shrug. 'Though I expect we will bump into each other again soon enough.'

I back away, letting Verity climb into her car and drive off.

In my twenty-five years with the Sisterhood, I have often been simultaneously amused and discomfited by how many tricks borrowed from the stage work equally well in the real world. It's not a Rule, but 'Leave them with questions – leave them wanting more' is the best way I have ever found to entice my quarry to come to me. It has saved a lot of faff over the years: in the case of one paedophile, I expected the job to take two weeks but managed to bump him off in two and a half days.

The tracking app on my phone shows Verity heading straight home. Relieved, I follow suit. I need to plan my next move – and decide whether or not to use the one thing that is guaranteed to make her listen: information about the night of her sister's disappearance that even the police don't have.

Verity's blown it with the police to the point where, if she tried to take my information to them, they wouldn't listen, so there's no real risk there. But what if Verity blames me? If I tell her about Christophe before she knows me – before she understands the Sisterhood and why we work the way we do – she might not be able to accept what I am offering. The last thing I need is for her to plunge into a fresh spiral of self-destructive behaviour and take me down with her.

Verity

Although I can't square it with her couldn't-be-more-ordinary appearance – tallish, thinnish, grey-haired, with pleasant but unremarkable features – I can't shake the feeling that the woman from the graveyard is following me.

Yesterday, there was sympathy – or maybe just pity – on her face. Both stung, though not for the shame but the sudden, wild urge to curl myself into her arms and pretend I'm cherished. Today, looking into the face of the woman I'd written off as pathetic – an older, wearier version of the hopeless loser who stared back at me from Boudicca's rear-view mirror this morning – there was a moment when I no longer saw gentle friendliness. Instead, there was a keenness in her eyes, drawing the lines of her face into a new pattern.

Yesterday, she reminded me of a soppy woodpigeon, cooing empty comforts. Today, she looked at me like a hawk – only not like a hawk might look at a mouse, but as one hawk might look at another, deciding how I measure up.

When I pull up outside my flat, I take the business card from my pocket. The paper is thick and textured, the embossed lettering understatedly elegant. It screams 'expensive'.

Elite Services Agency –

Special Dispatch Service

Pru Lawson – pru.sds@esa.com

I sit there, holding the card, trying to work out if I feel anything. Then I realize I'm attempting to sense the energies of a piece of paper.

I flip the card over.

Providing elite service staff for luxury households on the move.

Our Special Dispatch Service offers bespoke cleaning & disposal solutions to set the world to rights.

The weirdo stalker woman thinks I'd make a high-end maid. She's clearly insane, so it scans.

I pull out my phone and tap 'Elite Services Agency' into my browser. A sleek website pops up. They offer everything from nannies to chefs, and dog-sitters to butlers. The prices are eye-watering.

I'm ridiculous to even consider it, but what other option do I have? Janet is not going to give me a reference, but perhaps Pru Lawson can fix me an interview, though the fact I keep getting fired is probably going to see the door slammed in my face two minutes in.

I know it's hard when you're having a bad day, but you really must work on a more positive mindset, my mother whispers from the corner of my mind. *You were such a bright and cheerful child. Though perhaps that was just Reenie's effect. She always was the light of our home.*

I will the taunting whisper away and, with a pat on Boudicca's bonnet, trudge to my front door. It takes a good shove to open it enough to crunch my way over the detritus of leaflets for food I can't afford and services for the home I don't own. On top of the pile is an envelope labelled **OPEN IMMEDIATELY. DATED MATERIALS.**

I step on it, grinding my foot in, then pick it up and tear my way inside.

> **EVICTION NOTICE UNDER SECTION 8 . . . RENT ARREARS IN EXCESS OF 2 MONTHS . . . VIOLATION OF TERMS OF LEASE . . . 14 DAYS' NOTICE TO VACATE . . .**

My ears fill with the sound of my blood beating and the white noise of panic.

I've maxed out my cards and overdraft. I've just been fired. And, in fourteen days, I'll be chucked out of my shitty flat. I can't even go to Mum's place, as that was a rental, too; when she died, I only had till the end of the month to clear everything out, though at least the landlord gave me back the deposit. With what she had in the bank, it was just enough to cover the grave. With sudden fury I wish that I'd cancelled the headstone. If I'd known what it would say, I'd have used the money for Boudicca. Reenie would have approved, and as for Mum . . .

Stumbling into my bedroom, shedding filthy clothes, I catch a glimpse of myself in the mirror.

You could look so nice if you just took a little time with your appearance, my mother whispers.

I close my eyes and try to fill my head with Reenie's voice instead, but it's been too long. Every time I think I've caught the thread, it dissolves. Curling myself into bed, I try to imagine myself into a memory – tucked under the covers together after a nightmare, Reenie singing softly (and offkey) as she stroked my hair.

The sudden wash of need for her feels like it'll rip me in half.

Behind the grief comes the tidal wave of fury that the person who did this to us has never suffered a single consequence. If my sister's body were found, there would be new evidence. Something to identify which of the three most likely suspects killed her. Somewhere among their belongings there must be *something* that leads back to what happened to Reenie, whether that something lies with her ex-boyfriend, Gavin Pieper, or Charles Temple, the boy she hooked up with at the party she disappeared from, or TJ, Mum's boyfriend at the time. I know that, unlike the police, if I found that one telling thing, I'd understand its significance.

As my brain cycles from how I could catch whichever of them is responsible to ideas about where her killer hid Reenie's body, I keep drifting into sleep, only to start awake again and again from nightmares of all the ways my sister might have died. I know I should get up and do something productive, like trying to find a new job, or at least tidying up the flat, but every limb aches with misery so I just lie there and doze and wake, and doze and rage that, even after all these years, I cannot find my sister or her killer. There is no justice for the dead, but it would be something to have answers – and *everything* to know the man who killed Reenie won't ever hurt anyone else.

When the light starts to dim, I force myself to get up and eat some toast. It tastes like cardboard, sticking to the roof of my mouth and nearly choking me when I swallow. Bending over, I press my forehead to the coolness of the counter. There *has* to be something I can do.

Before despair can swallow me whole, I stand up, take out my phone, close my eyes and draw in a deep breath. The air goes electric, and goosebumps break out across my skin.

I am going to stumble across something that will lead me to answers. I can feel it. Even as I think it, I know it's rubbish, born of desperation, but maybe, just maybe, the universe will take pity, or maybe I'll be lucky. Or maybe, after all these years of searching, I'm due to find *something*.

I open my eyes, swipe into my browser, ready to search for 'common ways that killers get caught', and there, next to a piece about John Worboys, is an article entitled 'Temple walls may reveal human sacrifice'.

My heart kicks, then lurches into a sprint. *Temple walls. Charles Temple. There's something at his house.*

I stare at my phone. Logic dictates that this is not a sign. It's just a coincidence.

I wrench open the wardrobe and grab a black hoodie and black jeans. I know I'm being stupid, but part of me is buzzing with certainty. *This is it. This is it. This is finally it.*

You really are your own worst enemy, Mum sighs in my

head. *Reenie was always so well behaved, so good . . . Can't you try to be a little more like her?*

But that's not the Reenie I remember.

Just look at yourself, Mum whispers as I zip a torch and black beanie into the pockets of my biggest, baggiest coat. *Think about what you're about to do. Now tell me* I *was lying when I said you were the risk-taker, not your sister.*

She's right – but only because, after what happened to Reenie, I did everything I could to be like her, though all I managed to become was an angry, self-destructive version. Maybe all I'm doing is lurching from one act of desperation to the next, but if there is *any* possibility of finding Reenie, I have to take it.

Tonight, I am going to search Charles Temple's garage. And if I find nothing there, I'll search his shed. On TV, people shove paper clips into locks, wiggle them about, and *hey presto*, they're in. I doubt it works like that in reality, but I figure a hacksaw will do the trick on a padlock, though maybe I should take a hammer, too . . .

Only a hammer isn't just a tool. It's a weapon.

My eyes fall on the eviction notice sitting next to the envelope with the remains of Reenie's last daisy hair-slide.

I stride to the door, swinging the hammer and hacksaw, the weight sending a fizz of fear and anticipation through me.

The drive passes in a blur.

Tonight, I *will* find something. A lock of my sister's hair. A piece of her clothing. And if there's nothing in the garage or the shed, what's to stop me breaking into Temple's house and standing over him with the hammer and *making* him tell me the truth?

But what if it wasn't him? I'd end up in prison, and I still wouldn't know if it was Gavin or TJ. Because it must be one of the three of them, no matter what DI Strickland says. I mean, it's not *impossible* it was some random person at the party or on the street, but it's not likely, is it? I've listened to enough true-crime podcasts to know that, when a woman dies, it's usually someone close to her.

Charles Temple had opportunity at the party after I left. As for motive, maybe he wouldn't take no for an answer – hardly a big leap with an overprivileged guy used to getting his own way.

TJ had opportunity if he caught her as she was coming in when Mum and I were asleep that night. As for motive, they'd been getting close with all the driving lessons, then suddenly they weren't. He must have done something to upset her, but she never told me what.

Then there was Gavin. The boyfriend she'd dumped out of the blue a month before. Despite all my attempts to get her to talk, she never told me why, deciding she'd rather sulk and grump for the rest of the summer. Until that day. Our last day. Anyway, Gavin had motive, and as for opportunity, he said he was home in his room, and his brother and his brother's girlfriend apparently alibied him, but what if he crept out without them noticing? 'We were all sleeping' is hardly iron-clad.

Logic and statistics say it's the recent ex, the current love interest, or the mother's romantic partner. I refuse to believe it was random: that someone stole Reenie's life and ruined mine simply because she was in the wrong place at the wrong time.

An exit sign rears up in my headlights. I pull off the dual

carriageway and wind through residential streets, finally drawing up to the kerb. Maybe, if I'm not in prison after tonight, I should move away from the area: not just to a town thirty minutes away from where I grew up but somewhere entirely new. Somewhere far enough away that I can't just jump in the car to check out a new lead. Maybe physical distance will stop the past feeling so raw and fresh.

Maybe then things could be different. Maybe I could be different.

Charles Temple's house is six streets away, but I know it's safer to continue on foot. With my beanie on, bulky jacket masking my frame, even if I am caught on doorbell cameras it'll be as a vague figure in black. There won't be a car numberplate to connect back to me.

I turn off the car, unclip my seatbelt and lean over the central console, reaching around the footwell for the hacksaw. I plonk it on to the dashboard, then fumble for the hammer. The head is caught under the seat. I tug at it, then wriggle it, then tug some more, growling in frustration. It comes loose so suddenly that I bash the back of my hand against the glove compartment.

It hurts enough that I consider giving up. My 'plan', such as it is, is stupid. I should just go home.

Instead, I take the keys out of the ignition and pull the door handle. The automatic locks disengage with a clunk.

The passenger door pops open, and someone thumps into the seat next to me.

'For goodness' sake, Verity. Do you *have* to be such a liability before we've even started?' says the woman who has *definitely* been stalking me.

Pru

I take in Verity's outfit and the hammer, then close my eyes.

'How is it possible that you are going about every single aspect of this wrong?' I rub my brow, where a throbbing headache is building. 'Why must you be so *sloppy*? I must be going mad coming here.'

'What gave the psychosis away?' Verity asks breathlessly. 'The fact you're stalking a stranger you met in a graveyard, or the bit where you climbed into my car in the middle of the night?' The words are light, but her tone is brittle with fear.

The auto-lock re-engages with a pop. Verity slams her hand on to the unlock button. 'Who are you?' She holds up a hand. 'Actually, I don't care. Just get out of my car. Get out of my life. I see you again, I'm calling the police.' She pushes the words out with conviction, though every muscle is tense.

I glance down at the hammer. 'And how will that end for you?' I ask mildly.

'Better than indulging a psycho.' Her hand clenches around the end of the hammer. It stops her fingers trembling, but the grip is all wrong.

'I am not a psychopath. And I have not been stalking you. I have been researching,' I clarify.

'Oh, research. Well, that's fine, isn't it? Only, no, it's not!

What does that even involve, apart from . . .' She gestures around the car. 'I'd ask if you'd been tapping my phone or peeping through my curtains in the hope of a show, but I really don't want to know, because either way it ends right here, right now.' Verity raises the hammer, twisting in her seat to prod my shoulder with it. 'Out. Of. My. Car.'

I look at her, at the hammer, raise my hands in surrender – then grab the head of the hammer and pluck it out of Verity's hand. 'Lesson 1: never, ever use a hammer. Do you have any idea of the mess bludgeoning makes? No, of course you don't.' A huff of frustration escapes me. 'You have done precisely zero research for your shenanigans tonight. If I hadn't checked your location—'

The auto-lock engages again, making Verity flinch then scramble for the button, but, as she depresses it, I jab my thumb into her arm just above the elbow. She howls.

'You're not injured,' I tell her as she pants with panic rather than pain. 'Your fingers will be half numb for a while, though, so stop messing around and we can get down to business. If we are going to be working together, this sort of nonsense has to stop.'

'Just let me go. Please,' Verity whispers, cradling her arm.

'Why would you want me to do that when my presence in this car is the only thing saving you from your most self-destructive impulse to date? Don't embarrass yourself by pretending you truly think I am even half as big a danger to you as you are to yourself.'

She blinks at me, then looks down at her arm, flexing it.

'Now, let's start with you telling me about your plan for bashing Charles Temple's head in.'

Verity flinches, a whole new level of panic flooding

across her face. 'I wasn't . . . I wouldn't . . . I was just going to break into the garage.'

'And maybe, if you failed to find proof he killed your sister, you would have tried the house. Maybe taken a few whacks at him to see if he would confess. Only, if you had hit him with the hammer, he'd be too concussed to say anything.'

'How do you *know* all this?' Verity whispers. 'What do you want from me?'

I can't help but roll my eyes. 'I told you – to offer you a job, based on comprehensive planning and research. Though I can't say I'm not having second thoughts. And third ones,' I add morosely. 'But let's move on, shall we, and hope for the best?'

I pat the hammer into my hand. 'So, Lesson 2: since you don't have the skill or *will* to commit to using the hammer, chances are you would have ended up in a fight: one you would have lost. If Temple did kill your sister, all you would have achieved tonight is gifting him the perfect claim of self-defence to kill you, too. But for my intervention, that is, so I hope you are starting to appreciate what a gem of a colleague I am.'

Verity's throat bobs as she swallows.

'I have invested far too much time to allow you to get yourself arrested – or killed – to absolutely no purpose. And before you snipe at me about whether purpose makes a difference, I assure you that it does. It makes all the difference in the world.'

'You don't know me. You don't know—'

'I know you can do better than this.'

Verity's face twists with misery.

'I am going to help you,' I tell her softly. 'And before you argue – yes, I can help. You just have to listen to my offer, then say yes.'

Verity purses her lips. 'I can't work out if this is a really weird trick or legitimately the most aggressive piece of job recruitment the world has ever known,' she croaks, gaze fixed on the windscreen and the dark street beyond. 'Anyway, how's becoming a high-end maid going to help me when it comes to . . .' She gestures to the hammer then the street.

'Providing standard household services is a small part of the role I am offering you. You would be joining the select number of employees who are part of ESA's Special Dispatch Service – the Sisterhood, as it's more affectionately known. All of us have suffered terrible loss and injustice and, as a result, feel a deep need to make the world a better place by ridding it of dangerous human garbage.'

Verity turns her head to stare at me, the rest of her body frozen. 'What do you mean by "ridding it"?'

'Exactly what you think I mean.' I smile. 'We are an all-female group, partly because women are much less likely to be suspected, and partly because most women who kill don't make a mess, nor do they get a thrill from it: both things the Service is categorically averse to. Rules 4 and 7.'

'There's a rulebook for your hitman – sorry, hitwoman – squad?' Verity says faintly.

'It helps with the temptation to run amok with hammers.'

Verity's mouth falls open, her breathing speeding up. 'You're serious. You're really a—'

'*We* are highly skilled professionals,' I interrupt, 'doing important work with precision and discretion. That is why we have entirely separate clientele when it comes to ESA's standard offerings and the Special Dispatch Service. The standard work provides cover for being in the same vicinity as non-local targets, so separation is vital.'

I lean forward to catch her eyes. 'This job offer is the *only* way you are ever going to gain the skills and assistance you need to figure out who killed your sister. Not to mention that, even with the best research and planning in the world, it is highly unlikely you would get away with killing that person yourself, whereas the Sisterhood offers a very special bonus when you pass your training and become a full member – one free kill against any target who meets our requirements, to be carried out by me, as your mentor, on my retirement.' I spread my hands. 'You see, I really am the answer to all your problems.'

Hearing the words aloud, I hold up a hand. 'No, that's incorrect. Nothing I can offer will fix the past or give you back the life you would have led, as the person you would have been. But I *can* give you a path to a life worth living.'

In the year after Hope's death, I alienated every colleague in turn till I was restructured out of my job. I promptly threw myself into volunteering with a zeal that often led to shouting and unkindness rather than compassion – something I recognize in Verity. My marriage had long been centred on Hope and, without her . . . It felt like a relief when Robert left for Australia and neither of us had to try to salve a grief that can't be healed.

After he was gone I had a go at drinking. The effort lasted five days, culminating in the police interrupting me in the process of going door-to-door, telling off my neighbours for every tiny infraction I had ever witnessed. The next day a leaflet about a garden show plopped on to my doormat. Desperate for a distraction – any distraction – I set off within the hour. I had barely been there ten minutes when I bumped into an older woman, knocking her coffee to the ground. Although she brushed off my profuse apologies, she accepted my offer to buy her a fresh drink in the café. Half an hour later, Paloma offered to mentor me into a fresh career and, by the afternoon, I was part of the Sisterhood, with a new life opening up before me.

I try to put the weight of all this into my voice as I tell Verity the simple truth. 'Purpose helps. It's the only thing that does.' I have to pause as my voice wavers. Verity's emotional instability seems to have infected me. 'I have put in twenty-five years with the Sisterhood; now, before I retire, I have to find a replacement and, for various reasons – first among them insanity – I have chosen you.'

'I want more than purpose,' Verity whispers. 'I want . . .' She shakes her head. 'I want you out of my car. Find someone else to stalk or I *will* call the police, though probably the loony-bin is what's needed for the "international assassin" ' – she does that awful young-person thing of drawing speech marks in the air – 'who splits her time between weeding graveyards and stalking recently fired animal-charity employees, because that's *definitely* a thing professional killers do.'

I thought that once Verity understood what I was offering she would get on board with reckless eagerness; usually, she flings herself headlong at any opportunity to get herself into trouble.

'Given your penchant for vigilante tactics, you might

be interested to know that all of our targets have already done such terrible things that we are sure they will go on to do more but for our intervention. For instance, one of my recent targets strangled his girlfriend then claimed it was a sex-game gone wrong. My current target is a serial domestic abuser of women and kids – though only for the next day and a half.'

Verity's eyes narrow. 'How do you know if a target really *is* a serial domestic abuser?'

I smile. 'That is an excellent question. The answer is that those of us doing the dispatching can't know in every individual case. But whenever the death of one of my targets has been reported in the press, there has generally been mention of convictions or allegations that match what the Sisterhood has specified as the reason for the kill. Occasionally proof is included with the target's file. I have never encountered any discrepancies.'

Verity tilts her head to the side, and there it is: the curiosity I was waiting for. 'So, there's no indiscriminate murder just for the sake of money? There's, like, a moral compass element?'

'Yes, I thought that might appeal. Popular culture makes it seem that murder is thrilling, delicious – even *sexy*.' My lip curls in revulsion. 'But that is not how women go about killing in the real world. We don't *enjoy* it, let alone relish it. It's like cleaning the loo – someone has to do it. The satisfaction comes largely from our pro bono work.'

'Professional killers do pro bono jobs? How does *that* work?'

'We are paid a very nice salary, with regular bonuses, through ESA – we carry out a certain amount of the company's standard services to provide cover for our dispatch duties. More importantly to my mind – and I expect to yours – is the fact that, for every paid job the Sisterhood delivers, we dispatch an everyday monster who has been inflicting damage on people who can't fight back and don't have the money to pay someone to do it for them.'

'So you give back. That's . . . You know, I have no words.' Her tone is unnerved instead of mocking, but growing interest is sparking in her eyes.

'*Think* about what it would mean to stop flailing around, making yourself and everyone around you miserable, and instead *do* something to make the world a better place. Think about what it would feel like to help someone like you.'

I let her sit with it for a moment. 'Tonight, you might have got yourself killed or arrested. If I thought that this would be a wake-up call, I would leave this car and never look back. But we both know you won't stop searching for your sister's killer. So you can either throw your life away, without answers or redress, or I can take you on as a mentee.'

Verity's face twists. 'So, in this psycho fairytale, in exchange for taking your place when you retire, you teach me how to find my sister's killer, then you dispose of him, while my happily ever after involves spending the next quarter of a century killing people for money – oh, and for free. Mustn't forget about the pro bono.' She rubs at her temples. 'I'm going mad. This is a psychotic break. Things like this don't just . . . There's no way you're really . . .' She shakes her head. 'If this is real, then . . . why me?'

I force down my irritation at her tone because her face isn't jeering but tight. There's a desperate hope in her eyes.

'The Sisterhood, naturally enough, looks for people with a willingness to commit serious violence in the name of a just cause. People who can plan—'

'Yeah, I'm great at that,' Verity huffs, folding her arms.

'People with patience—'

'Again, so me,' she says airily.

'I will teach you patience.' I put enough warning in the words that she deflates without further comment. 'And how to plan properly. You are already willing to break the law in a good cause and take risks in order to protect the vulnerable. You are observant, when you choose to be. You are clever.' Her surprised almost-smile tugs at something in my chest, meaning that we both wince when I add, 'When you're not acting like an idiot.'

I sigh, gentling my tone. 'Your instincts aren't as bad as you think, and that's something I can't teach, only hone.'

It takes me back to that sunny afternoon in the garden centre over twenty-five years ago and Paloma watching me steadily across the tiny café table.

'You've done a good job of investigating,' she told me, raising a hand when I opened my mouth to point out I still had no answers about Hope's death. 'For an amateur, you've got yourself in less trouble than you might have, and excluded a lot of options. That will save us time when we start our rather more professional exploration of Hope's case. I can't promise we'll figure it out, but I'm – *we're* – your best shot. And, in the meantime, we'll give you a life that does something with your pain and fury.' She reached out, offering me her hand. 'It's worth it, Pru.'

But I shook my head. 'I've never . . . I don't think I could . . .'

Paloma raised an eyebrow. 'People like us are the ones who can do this the right way, for the right reasons. It's not about revenge – it's about protection. There are people who won't stop hurting others unless someone stops them. *You* can stop them, Pru. You just have to make that choice.'

Although I took her hand and accepted her offer, I didn't understand what it meant. No one does, until they start to kill, so there's no point trying to explain it to Verity now. All that matters tonight is securing her agreement to learn.

I twist in my seat so I can face her, making sure I have her full attention. 'Before I take your answer, there is one thing we must be crystal clear about: if you say yes, you can never use the skills I teach you for your own purposes. The Sisterhood will not allow it. When we identify your sister's killer, I will kill him for you. That is non-negotiable. Now, do you have any questions?'

'So many,' she breathes.

I wait until she throws her hands in the air.

'I don't know where to start, OK? Where *does* a sane person start with this? Like . . .' She looks around as if expecting the answers to write themselves across the roof of the car. 'Do we make a blood pact now . . . or is there an oath of allegiance? That was a yes, by the way. If I'm going to land myself in prison, I might as well go big.'

I thought this moment would feel like I had come full circle to Paloma offering me her hand all those years ago. I expected a moment of grief mingled with reverence and anticipation, even excitement. Instead, there is a terrible sinking sensation in my stomach that is quickly curdling into dread.

Verity

This is not what I expected.

Pru's home is a cosy little cottage like something out of a Disney movie, surrounded by a lush garden worthy of Studio Ghibli. The gate is freshly whitewashed, the hinges oiled, which is exactly on-brand for Pru. As is the fact that every border is neatly edged, the grass recently mown, and there is not one fallen leaf beneath the apple tree. Getting away with murder for a living surely requires an eye for detail, but Pru might well be more anal in her housekeeping than in her homicides.

When she gave me her address and told me to arrive promptly at 8.30 a.m. in 'clothing you can move easily in but which won't catch or trail', I was expecting a gated community with glass-and-concrete squares instead of houses. I was expecting walls and fences and no neighbours to observe the assassin-training process. But I've checked the address twice, so I'm not lost. I'm just visiting a crazy person.

The whole thing is ridiculous – but it's also ridiculous that my sister disappeared one day and no one has ever found her. It's part of why I fell for Pru's insane pitch last night . . . Well, that and the fact I was desperate and miserable and I needed *something* to tempt me away from taking that hammer into Charles Temple's property and seeing just how thoroughly I could ruin my life. Of *course* I am tempted by the idea that I could turn my self-destructive urge to right every injustice I stumble across into a career, with a whole Sisterhood to help me rescue not just over-heating dogs but vulnerable people.

Now I stare at the house and try to believe that a professional murderer lives there. It doesn't scan, but I won't figure it out standing here, so I might as well see if Pru is willing to pay me to go along with her delusion. If it is a delusion . . .

Slipping through the gate, I follow the path to the kitchen door, knocking then letting myself in, as instructed. The inside of the house is as ordered and pristine as the garden. I'd expected some clinical, empty space. Instead, there's an old tiled floor, scrubbed to a shine, and a vintage wooden table surrounded by lovingly polished wooden chairs – with floral cushions on the seats. The fabric design looks like Laura Ashley.

'While I am pleased you have arrived, I am not pleased that you are seventeen minutes late.' Pru strides through an arched opening letting on to a narrow hallway. 'You will be on time tomorrow.'

I beam at her. 'I won't stress about apologizing for today then, since I'm clearly turning over a new leaf as we speak. Do you work with crystal balls, or does your murder coven go in for some sort of scrying? I had no idea fortune-telling was part of the skillset, but it's a lovely surprise.' I wait for the frown/sigh/smile. 'There's no vow of chastity, right?'

Pru flicks the kettle on then takes out an actual teapot and starts filling it with actual tea leaves. She even does the warming-the-pot thing, which I thought was an olden days' superstition, though I suppose it can't be since Pru doesn't seem to have a whimsical – or funny – bone in her body. That makes sense, given the whole professional-murderess thing, except for the fact that things like this don't happen. At least not to me. And certainly not in a Laura Ashley kitchen.

Pru puts the pot on a doily. Then puts a knitted tea-cosy over the pot.

I can't help myself. A snigger escapes, then a giggle, then I'm laughing as I point at the pot. 'That's a tea-cosy!' I splutter. 'And a doily!'

'It's a crocheted trivet,' says Pru.

I howl until my eyes stream because I might as well enjoy this descent into insanity.

Pru moves about, setting out delicate porcelain cups and saucers. She pours the tea, then clouds milk into it, nudging a matching forget-me-not-patterned sugar-bowl towards me.

My laughter dissolves as I brush tears from my cheeks. 'Where do you keep all the gear?'

'You mean my work tools? The chainsaws and scalpels and machine guns?' Pru asks.

'Do you have, like, a secret basement with a biometric lock?'

Pru puts down her cup. 'Your tardiness we can work on, but I draw the line at training a person who sprinkles every sentence with "like"s. I would hate to have to restart the recruitment process, but there are compromises I just can't make.'

I search her face, but there is not a single flicker of humour in her eyes. She's serious.

Oh boy.

Why must you always antagonize those who are just trying to help you improve yourself? hisses Mum.

'Um . . .' I wince. 'Is "umming" a capital offence too?'

Pru closes her eyes. 'There are no chainsaws in this house. Or machine guns. There are no guns of any kind.'

I pull a face. 'Yeah, I guess that was kinda stupid of me. I mean, you could hardly train with weapons without the neighbours asking awkward questions.' I do my best to sit up straight. 'Is there a facility for that? Or do you use, like . . . I mean, do you go to a public gun range?'

Pru lifts her hands as if she is going to press them to her forehead, then lowers them to the table, splaying her fingers across the surface. 'There. Are. No. Guns. Not here. Not in a public gun range. Not in a facility. There is no facility, just like there is no basement. As I told you – weapons, when you have no skill in using them, are a liability.'

I stare at her. 'But that's why you're going to train me.' Is this where I find out it's all a . . . what? Joke? Stalker ploy to get me to her house? Would a woman with a doily and a tea-cosy really try to hurt me? I eye the distance to the door, then look nervously at my teacup. Has she drugged me? My mouth goes dry. 'If this is a real job, when do I get paid? I'm not killing anyone on spec.'

'You will receive a stipend for the initial stages of your training on a weekly basis to begin with, then monthly, once we are both assured of each other's good faith. When we move on to targets requiring a cover job involving ESA's standard services, you will receive the associated wage and appropriate bonuses. We will deal with the details later.'

I blink at her, think about saying, *I'll believe it when I see the money in my account*, then decide to keep quiet. I'm still curious, and it'll be obvious soon enough if she's legit.

'Before we proceed, you should rid your mind of any idea that the Sisterhood bears the slightest resemblance to an action movie. Instead, I would like you to think about last night's conversation and tell me how you think we *really* go about our work.'

'Carefully?' I glance about the kitchen. 'Neatly. I'm sure you're always very . . . organized and . . . tidy.'

Pru nods.

Which is when my big mouth opens and I add, 'I can't say I'm not relieved about the chainsaws. That was bothering me. I'm not very coordinated with a lawnmower, so it seems like asking for trouble . . .'

There you go. Doing your level best to ruin another opportunity, despairs the ghost of my mother: her primary and favourite setting when talking to me in life and, apparently, death. *I know it's not what you imagined your life would be like, but that's what growing up is: accepting what's on offer and being grateful.*

I want to snark back about her problem being my attitude rather than the whole 'assassin in training' thing, but arguing with the voices in my head is a level of insanity I'm not prepared for – though I'll check in with myself in an hour. Things might well have moved on by then.

'Sorry,' I tell Pru. 'It's a bit of a weird situation. What happens if I decide to back out, or you fire me? I get fired regularly, so it seems wise to check what that entails when dealing with a group of professional killers.'

Pru raises an eyebrow. 'Nothing happens if you walk

away now. You can try going to the police with a wild tale if you like, but how do you think that will end?'

DI Strickland would probably see it as the culmination of my long spiral of increasingly unstable behaviour and have me sectioned. 'But once I kill someone . . .'

'Then you'll be a murderer.' Pru cocks her head. 'Think it through, Verity.'

'What if I'm bad at it? Do you just off me?'

Pru raises a disdainful eyebrow. 'Provided you don't break the Rules I shall introduce you to later, you won't meet the criteria to become a target. Now,' she says, settling back in her chair and taking a sip of tea, 'pick up the notebook to your left and open it to the first page.'

I do as I'm told.

'We'll start with you telling me about the day your sister disappeared.'

My breath catches.

'I don't want to hear the story as you normally tell it. The rehearsed version is no use to me. Instead, take yourself back to that afternoon. You were in the park.'

I turn my teacup on its saucer, trying to align the forget-me-nots, but the patterns are slightly different sizes, making it a hopeless task. When Pru promised to help me find Reenie's killer, I didn't think we'd start immediately. Is it just a way to string out the pretence that the Sisterhood is real?

'Close your eyes. Focus on your senses. What does the air feel like?'

I wriggle in my seat, then close my eyes. 'It's hot. Sort of soft,' I answer, then take a deep breath and will myself into the memory. 'The sun's so bright. There're a bunch of us from school. We've been here for hours. The food's all gone, and the booze.'

The grass is parched into spongy prickles. Even the wind is dry with heat and dust. The world looks overexposed.

Reenie slaps the back of my calf. 'Right, we're off before we poach. See you losers tomorrow at the cinema.'

I groan and grumble, though secretly I'm relieved. My skin feels tight and tingly. Reenie and I jostle into each other as we stumble down to the road just as a car idles up and someone wolf-whistles.

Reenie is lifting her hand to flip the wanker off when we take in the fact that the car is a white limousine. I blink, wondering if I've got heatstroke. The sunroof is open and two boys are leaning over the edge, grinning at us. One lifts a champagne bottle.

'Don't suppose you ladies fancy a ride, then an evening partying at the university?'

'I fancy the limo. Not sure about you,' Reenie calls back.

The boys laugh. Then the door pops open and a third boy steps out. He's tall and slim, with wavy black hair, golden skin and a smile as sunny and open as the park behind us. He makes us a gallant bow, like a character out of a Jane Austen novel.

'Lovely ladies, we swear on our honour not to besmirch yours. We are gentlemen of yon posh and famous university, wherein there are many guards to ensure our good intentions. As for the journey, the good fellow who guides this elegant equipage will oversee our merriment.' He gestures to the open door. 'You are most cordially invited to an adventure.'

'With free booze!' yells the older and spottier of the boys leering through the sunroof.

'And what'll the ride and party cost us?' Reenie asks, folding her arms.

'Merely the pleasure of your beauteous company,' the handsome boy answers.

'And a snog!' slurs his spotty friend.

The handsome boy glares at him. 'Sit down and shut up, Christophe.' He turns back to us, smiling again. 'I promise he won't bother you.'

'Yeah, we'll thump him if he does,' offers the third boy winningly.

I look at Reenie. She grins back. Neither of us can resist a limo straight out of a movie, not to mention the best-looking boy we've ever seen in our lives.

I open my eyes and I'm in Pru's kitchen, not the over-bright summer park. Still, it's the kitchen that feels unreal.

'Reenie dived into the car, and I thought, *To hell with it. Live a little, Verity. You'll regret it for ever if you don't.*'

I can imagine myself there so easily, so physically, and yet there's no way back. It's gone, and so is Reenie, and nothing can ever undo our choices, or their consequences.

'We'll stop there for now,' Pru says. She tops up my tea then pushes a biscuit tin towards me.

Don't be greedy now, cautions my mother.

I grab a biscuit and shove it into my mouth, feeling salt and sugar explode on my tongue then rush directly into my bloodstream. I don't take a second, though I really, really want to. I feel stupid for indulging Pru's curiosity instead of demanding that she prove her story is real.

'If there are no guns, do I get to pick a type of knife to specialize in? Oo-oo-oo, can I try throwing stars? Or do you have, like, stiletto knives that fit into—'

'Verity.'

'How do I know this is real? About the Sisterhood and killing people?'

Pru raises her eyebrows. 'You took a long time to ask.' She reaches across the table for a laptop, taps in the PIN then types something before turning the screen to me.

There's a news story open in the browser: *Local musician found dead in his home.*

'Foraging for mushrooms can be such a dangerous pastime. Especially for beginners. Not that anyone is likely to identify that as the cause, since most people take days to become seriously ill – long after the evidence has worked through the person's system.' She smiles across at me. 'I could have put a beginner's guide to foraging on the table in his back garden, but that would have been . . . Well, "overkill" is probably an insensitive choice of word.'

I look from her to the laptop and back again. 'That doesn't prove anything.'

'Do a good day's work and this evening I'll give you his name. It's not been announced yet.' She tops up her teacup. 'Of course, that still won't prove anything – you haven't earned the right to information that's dangerous to me.'

I reach for my tea, clutching the cup between suddenly cold hands. 'What had he done to become a target?'

'He collected child sexual abuse images.'

Could I kill a man who did that? If I did, could I live with it?

I reach for a second biscuit.

I think I *could* kill a man involved in child abuse. Especially if I was sure I wouldn't be caught.

Pru

Although I am on edge as I take Verity through the Rules, expecting disrespectful jokes I may not be able to forgive her for, she simply nods at each new Rule and writes it down in her notebook, reading through them silently as I fetch the equipment for our first lesson.

She stares in mingled panic, confusion and dismay when I place the carbon monoxide alarm in front of her.

'You have got to be kidding me,' says Verity. 'This cannot be Step 1 of Assassin Training.'

'What part of professional murder seems funny to you?'

Verity shrugs. 'If ever there were a job for gallows humour . . .'

'Yes, but you've yet to say anything funny.' I shake my head. 'Did you really think I was going to teach you to shoot people? Did you want that?' Of all the ways I thought Verity might be problematic as a mentee, this wasn't one of them. 'Perhaps we should revisit Rules 4 and 7.'

Verity peers at the alarm's inner workings. 'Is one of those the "no torture" rule, because I'm already wondering if that isn't more of a guideline?'

I force myself to stop grinding my teeth. 'Rule 4 is that all killings should be quiet and clean – so definitely no guns. Rule 10 prohibits torture. We're not in the business of punishing people for what they've done: we're stopping them doing further harm. Rule 7 is that only psychopaths get a thrill from killing people. The Sisterhood contains no psychopaths.'

Verity raises her eyebrows. 'Yeah, you tell yourself that.' She pokes at the alarm and a battery pops out, rolling across the table. 'This is ridiculous. I can't believe I'm here, playing along with this.'

She slouches back in her chair, huffing and puffing like a small, tantrumming dragon furious that it can't yet produce a flame, let alone incinerate the kitchen. When I realize I am imagining my mentee as a baby dragon, I turn away and set about sorting expense receipts before she infects me further with her Verity-ness.

'Would you prefer me to send you outside to do laps of the garden?' I ask.

'I'm busy sulking. And reconsidering my life choices, including the potentially lethal futility of backing out. Then I'm back at sulking. So, if that's one of the lessons, I'm doing great.' She blows out a gusty sigh that is basically a raspberry. 'Look, at least tell me what the training stipend's worth. My car is dying and I need to get her fixed. If you could maybe pay me for this week upfront – as a gesture of good faith, like you said – that'd really help with my motivation.'

'Your car is female? I thought that was just ships.' I pin a set of personal receipts on the left of my corkboard, then a stack of work ones on the right.

'Boudicca,' Verity says defensively. 'My sister named her.'

'It's a good name.'

A smile softens her face before grief crumples it. She

picks up her pen, doodling a daisy in the margin of her notepad. 'Her MOT is coming up – if she even gets that far – so it would really help to know what I'm working with in terms of income so I can plan how to pay the bill. And the rest,' she mumbles.

I fold my arms. 'And what, precisely, is "the rest".'

Verity starts adding leaves to her daisy. They are botanically inaccurate. I grit my teeth, managing to keep the words to correct her in my mouth.

'I've maxed out my overdraft and credit card. I'm months in debt on rent. My landlord's kinda pissed. As in, trying to evict me.'

I take the laptop off the sideboard and place it on the table. 'Sort code and account number.'

Verity blinks at me. 'Huh?'

'What are your sort code and your account number?' I enunciate.

She keeps staring and blinking.

I sigh. 'Perhaps it *is* a bad idea to pay the money into the account of a chronic debtor. Later, you will give me your landlord's account details and I will settle up with him directly. Then we will call your credit card company and get you back into the black. Once *that* is sorted, we will drive to my mechanic and drop Boudicca off so she can get the attention she requires.'

Verity gapes at me.

'Close your mouth. Your teeth are not that pretty. Especially when you have something stuck between your molars.'

Verity closes her mouth with a click.

'From now on, your only expenditure will be essential expenses. Nod, Verity.'

She does.

'I will keep your rent paid. I will also write a letter to your landlord for you to sign asking that, since you have repaid your back rent and stumped up for this and next month in advance, the eviction notice is rescinded. You will start receiving money on the final day of each month *after* you have cleared 60 per cent of your debt to me. These terms are non-negotiable. Nod again.' I open a Word document and start the letter for Verity's landlord. 'I trust that this will remedy your distraction and allow you to focus on your training?'

'I'll believe it when I see it,' Verity drawls, then cuts herself off with a sharp breath. 'But just in case this is legit, then . . . thank you. That would—'

'Solve all of your most pressing problems and give you a clean slate to embrace the new life I'm offering you?' I resist the urge to sigh again, though only just.

Verity looks about the room with renewed interest. 'So, you do pretty well out of this whole Sisterhood gig, between the paid murders and the high-end maid duties. You mentioned bonuses, so are those just for killing cartel leaders, or are they a regular thing you can count on?'

I press a hand over my face. 'We do not kill cartel leaders. For one, there are plenty of other people to do that. Why else would we not take such cases?'

Verity shrugs. 'I guess it would draw a lot of attention, which is against Rule . . . 8? Plus everyone's bound to assume those deaths are homicide.' She stares at me as if waiting for a response. 'Would a "well done, good thinking" kill you?'

'I am clearing your debts and saving your beloved car,

and you want compliments too?' I finish the letter and send it to print. 'Sign that,' I tell Verity as the printer whirs to life behind her. 'As for rewarding you for putting two and two together, you will get home-made quiche for lunch, and you will be thankful for it.'

'Probably arsenic-flavoured,' she mumbles as she scrawls her name at the bottom of the letter.

'We don't poison people with poisons, Verity.'

She frowns up at me. 'You poison them with foraged mushrooms, though. You told me so.'

I focus on emailing the garage, leaving her to figure it out.

'I suppose you could also use medication as a poison if you overdose someone, but it would have to be something they've been prescribed or might have taken by accident, like if they got their meds muddled up with someone else in the household. Or . . .' She taps her pen against her cheek. 'I guess you could use food, if the person has a severe allergy. And I suppose if someone does recreational drugs you've got *loads* of options.'

A needle of guilt stabs through my ribs. It's only our first day together, but perhaps it is best to get everything about Reenie out in the open from the start. Only, if I tell her now, will she have the control to listen?

No, of course not.

'If everyone assumes the kills are accidents, then at least the families and friends aren't left wondering who did it,' Verity says quietly.

'Sisterhood targets rarely leave behind anyone who wants answers.'

Verity hunches over, poking at the innards of the carbon

monoxide alarm. 'One of the boys from the limo died from a bad batch of drugs the night Reenie went missing. The police said she might have taken some of the same stuff then wandered off and fallen in the river. Apparently, bodies don't always get found when that happens. Though they also said she might have crawled into a drain or somewhere else no one would ever think to look, but they searched – and so have I, so many times – and no one's ever found anything.

'Reenie had the odd drink, like everyone else at my school, but she didn't do drugs,' she says, but her tone is defensive rather than insistent. 'I was the reckless one. If one of us had taken pills off some random boy we'd only just met, it would have been me. Because I . . . I did stuff like that. Reenie was sensible and careful. She would never—'

'Is that really what you remember?' I ask, tone soft. 'Or is that your mother's story?'

Reaching over to the sideboard, I tap the PIN into the lock, open the cabinet and take out the file of witness statements from Reenie's case. Nudging aside the carbon monoxide alarm, I place the file in front of her. This isn't the moment to tell her about Christophe, but we will get there faster if she's no longer battling herself – and that will only happen when she comes to terms with the lies that leap out from the statements that she and her mother gave in the wake of Reenie's disappearance.

Verity

My mother's statements make mine read like a pack of lies. Or may it's the other way around.

Finally, after all these years, there it is, in black and white. My version: the one that matches my memories. Reenie refusing to leave the party, and me storming off home, expecting her to follow. The truth about how Reenie was in the weeks before she disappeared – angry and distant. Then slowly my story changed to match Mum's, because, without Reenie, I couldn't hold on to the truth.

Gradually, Reenie became a ghost even in my memories, faint and insubstantial, until I could barely make her out. Sometimes I stare into old photographs and it's like there are two versions of those moments playing. The one I think I remember, and the one Mum told me was true.

She said I made it up to cope with my guilt, and *I knew* she was lying but I couldn't *believe* it, because she was my mum and I wanted her to love me, though I'm not sure she did.

I think she loved her version of me, just as she loved her version of Reenie, but that's not the same thing because her versions were built on lies.

'All of this rage when I talk about Reenie as she really was – it's your brain's attempt to protect you from the guilt,' Mum told me, when we rowed on my eighteenth birthday. 'If Reenie was the risk-taker and you were the sensible one, then what happened wasn't your fault. I know it makes you feel better, but it's not true.'

'You weren't even there! What would—'

'She would never have let you walk home alone at that hour! So, either you couldn't find her and gave up, or it was so loud that she couldn't hear what you were saying about leaving – thought you wanted to carry on, so she stayed, too.' Mum pressed her fingers over her eyes. 'I should never have left Reenie to look after you when you were in one of your wild moods—'

'That was Reenie!' I yelled. '*Reenie* was the one who'd been a moody cow since the break-up with Gavin. That was the first day she was herself in weeks.'

Mum reached over and stroked a hand through my hair, her smile full of sadness and sympathy. 'Let's not fight about it, Verity. You tell yourself whatever you need to—'

'I am telling the *truth*!' I screamed. 'Why do you do this? How can you lie even about *Reenie*?'

I am shaking as I push the memory away, my heart thumping so loud I can hear it in my ears. My need for Reenie is like acid in my veins.

All these years, I've been letting Reenie slip away. Letting myself slip away. Now, finally, there's a way to hold on to the truth.

I splay my hand over my first statement and focus on breathing. Across the table, Pru watches me silently. Something about her matter-of-fact, nothing-fazes-me-not-even-murder gaze is an anchor amid the maelstrom of thought, memory, emotion. She knows what it means to have it there in black and white: a different view of Mum, of Reenie, of myself, to set against the picture the gravestone paints.

By giving me the file, Pru is letting me help myself. I've never been very good at that, but maybe if Mum hadn't alternately taken over or ignored my troubles entirely, I wouldn't believe I'm quite so hopeless at it.

'I can't think about this any more.' I push the pages into the file, then shove it away from me.

Pru rises from her seat. 'I would like a list of ways you might stop the alarm working without there being any suspicion it has been purposefully tampered with. You may use the instruction manual by the biscuit tin to help you.'

I bend to my work, bottom lip between my teeth to stop it trembling.

Behind me, Pru pauses. A hand comes down on my shoulder and presses, just once.

I have to fight to keep my breathing level, but slowly the pain in my chest ebbs.

'So it's real – the whole Sisterhood thing,' I say. 'You wouldn't be able to get these' – I gesture to the file with the statements – 'if you didn't have connections. Are you ex-police or a former spy or something?'

'I used to be a teacher. Home economics.'

I hear myself snort before I can stop myself, glancing at the Laura Ashley cushion covers. 'Yeah, that tracks.'

'I will take that as a compliment.' Pru puts two tall glasses of lemonade down on coasters. 'Mentors are given files on their mentees, but you should know that we can't ask for anything we want, any time we want it.'

'So, no police files on the people you kill?'

'Only when it is deemed necessary by the women who select and assign our targets.'

'And who are they? Do you have encrypted phones to communicate or—'

'Those are questions you don't need the answers to. You *do* need to identify at least three ways to tamper with the alarm without the damage looking purposeful.'

I huff but snag the manual and start to page through for clues, only my mind instantly wanders to the madness of the whole situation. If Pru is telling the truth about everything, then by this evening my debts will be clear, my rent paid, Boudicca saved. It would be like a fairytale, if the price weren't twenty-five years' service as a murderer.

Pru

After lunch, we deliver Boudicca for repairs, then proceed to a lesson on gas leaks and house fires.

'Is there any logic to carbon monoxide alarms in the morning and house fires in the afternoon?' Verity asks, tongue between her teeth as she fails to start a fire in a manner that could pass as accidental.

'Gas leaks are the main cause of carbon monoxide poisoning, but they can also cause fires.'

'So, it's a thematic training programme,' Verity says, glancing around from her place at the counter beside the garage sink.

'We're starting with the most common and easy-to-replicate methods.'

Verity's elbow knocks against the yoghurt pot of quicklime I set on the draining board earlier, sending it tumbling into the pan of water sitting in the sink. The pot pulls a towel with it, resulting in an instant conflagration.

While Verity shrieks, then runs for the hose, apparently determined to set the whole place on fire, I grab the ancient oven gloves and battered baking tray sitting on the workbench. By the time she looks round, I have donned the gloves and am holding the tray over the fire. The hose wilts uselessly out of her grip.

'Wash everything down the sink with plenty of water, then leave it running for a minute to be sure,' I order. 'Afterwards, you can practise using this' – I put a metal pipe on the workbench – 'to bash that.' I gesture at the punching bag.

'How does the pipe-wielding relate to fires or gas leaks?' she calls, having to raise her voice over the sound of the tap.

'It's related to my temptation to strangle you,' I tell her. 'In any case, we have to start your physical training somewhere, and we need to do it immediately.'

For the next ten minutes, I instruct her on posture and technique, then stand back to watch her efforts.

'I thought,' she gasps, 'you said' – pant – 'no weapons.' She sags over her knees. 'You specifically said no bludgeoning.'

'As a method of killing. What else could this task prepare you for?'

Verity blows her hair out of her face. Groaning, she unfolds, rubbing at her back. 'I guess if you daze someone first, it's easier to knock them off a cliff or drown them? But wouldn't the head injury be suspicious?'

'That is why, once you are used to bashing the punching bag full force, we will practise appropriate levels of impact for different scenarios. Then we will move on to angles and the need to match the bludgeoning object with something already present in the location where the "accidental death" occurs.'

Verity pulls a face. 'That's really grim.'

'You imagined we used chainsaws.' I don't point out that it is not out of the question with a target who enjoys DIY. However, where Verity is concerned, chainsaws definitely should be.

'You have ten minutes while I deliver a lecture on Rule 6: *Only the target must die, and there must be no collateral damage outside the target's property, with due consideration given to the well-being of any co-residents*. Later, I will test you on the Rules covered today.'

Verity turns back to the punching bag and unleashes her frustrations productively.

It is late when I drop Verity home, and early when I pick her up the next morning, but I find her full of beans, quips and 'like's, so instead of heading inside for Lesson 2 on carbon monoxide alarms and boilers, I continue her physical training.

'How long before I'm breaking bricks – and necks?' she asks as she stretches on the grass.

I make her run laps of the garden till she lacks the breath to joke, though it doesn't prevent a panting whinge about how I clearly enjoy torturing her and isn't that against Rule 10?

Not ready to deal with another uncontrolled fire, I set her to work exploring methods for engineering trips and falls. Verity promptly goes flying over the tripwire she just set up. She sprawls on the ground, then stares at me as if struggling to comprehend that tripwires work coming and going.

If I weren't already dying, the next hour would surely have taken years off my life. Instead, it takes several inches off my temper, which was short enough already.

When she is subdued with exhaustion, we sit in the shade of the apple tree with lemonade and muffins, Verity studying a guide to common food allergies while I finish planning this afternoon's murder.

At four o'clock, I leave Verity in the garage with the pipe – and strict instructions not to play with fire during my absence – while I drive the fifteen miles to the warehouse. I park by the hole in the back fence I discovered a few weeks ago while developing my plan for the job.

Slipping through with the bucket of tarmac and the smashed plastic tub is heavy going, but I arrive just in time to spread the broken tarmac over the cracked ground then place the tub where a forklift driver cutting the corner will have to swerve around it.

I am just creeping back through the fence when I hear the crash.

The next day, we start with exercise again, then move on to methods of 'accidental' drowning. I am learning that ringing the changes keeps Verity focused, though it feels horribly scattergun. The drowning goes as well as everything else, so it is a relief when the doorbell calls me away before I decide to give a practical demonstration.

Graziella is standing on the mat. She exchanges a stack of new files for my folder of reports and expense claims as I try not to wonder what these delivery and pick-up duties have taught her about the inner workings of the Sisterhood. I don't need to know, so she shouldn't tell me, but curiosity and envy gnaw at me all the same.

'If you're still on top of your paperwork, the sky hasn't fall in yet,' she says, glancing down the corridor behind me.

'Do you want to come in?'

She laughs. 'Not yet.' She eyes me up and down.

'I am fine. She is . . .' I sigh, and rub at my left temple, where a headache is building. 'It is a work in progress. As I am sure is the case for you, too.'

Graziella gives me her most cat-got-the-canary smile. 'My mentee is the very picture of commitment and dedication.'

'Paloma always said it is the quiet ones who end up making the most trouble.'

We contemplate this.

Graziella shrugs. 'So far, nothing could possibly be going better,' she tells me airily.

'I am shutting this door in your face,' I tell her, and do just that.

Another laugh sounds from the other side as I stalk back down the hall to regard my choice of mentee.

'Friendly postie, huh?' Verity says absently as she surveys the bathroom, hands on hips.

'You will meet in time,' I tell her, hoping it is true.

Naturally, Verity does her best to demonstrate that despair might have been a better choice than hope as she pretends to trip on the bathmat, then topples forward over the rim of the bath, pressing her forehead to the tiled wall, then letting herself slide sideways, only to end up with her head wedged against the rim of the bath, where the water level would never get high enough for her to drown.

Groaning, she slumps, despite the awkward angles she's twisted into. 'I can't see how a fall in here could guarantee an accidental drowning, though I do see the potential for a fatal head injury or a broken neck.'

'What else in this room could cause an accidental drowning?'

'I don't know!' She flings her arms in the air, gaze roving around. 'Aren't you meant to be teaching me this stuff?'

'I'm teaching you to work it out for yourself,' I snap, marching over to the cabinet and opening it to reveal a row of over-the-counter medications. 'Why might these be helpful?' I toss a packet of cold-relief tablets to her.

Verity turns it over, squinting down at the warning label. ' "Do not drive or operate machinery after a dose. Do not drink alcohol." Oh. It makes you sleepy. Maybe even a bit dizzy.'

'Everyday remedies in normal doses rarely raise red flags at autopsy, even when present with alcohol – if the decedent in question was a drinker, the assumption is that he didn't read the label, or chose to ignore it. You just need to be sure to lace a food or drink item that the police *won't* think to have examined – so, never the alcohol itself.' I snatch the pills back and put them away. 'A drugged target will often helpfully drown himself.'

Verity shudders, wrapping her arms around herself. 'Like the police think happened with Reenie.'

How long will it take until she's learnt enough for it to be safe to tell her about killing Christophe the night of Reenie's disappearance? The fact that the drugs were a red herring in Reenie's case will be a bitter enough pill for her to swallow, but then will come the realization about the other, darker possibilities.

Like the small but real chance that my actions are why her sister never came home.

I let another day pass without telling her, then another, then a week.

'Is this really all there is?' Verity groans on the fourteenth day as I slide my foot across the bathroom tiles, testing her latest attempt to engineer a fall.

My efforts produce a squeaking noise. A bubble drifts up from the toe of my shoe. I raise my eyebrows as I repeat the squeak, this time creating two bubbles. 'What else could you try?'

'Dying of despair?' She slumps against the wall. 'Don't I at least get to learn some self-defence?' She looks over at me and freezes. 'Oh my God, you're smiling – at least I think so. There are an awful lot of teeth involved, and I'm really, really wishing I knew some self-defence right about now.'

'Since you have *finally* thought to make a reasonable request that fits the Sisterhood's ethos, I will introduce you to some simple techniques this afternoon,' I concede. 'For now, wouldn't you like another run around the garden?'

'Yes! Yes, I bloody well would, you bloody . . .' With a mumble, grumble, mutter, she stomps off.

I watch through the window as she powers around the lawn. It will be a while before she is up to adequate fitness, but it is amazing what youth and a little effort can achieve even in a short period of time. Perhaps we should move on to the next stage of training. It is all very well to be building up her knowledge and skills, but until the weight of it is real, neither of us knows if she is truly cut out for the Sisterhood.

When Verity has circled half a dozen times and has collapsed, spread-eagled on the grass, I march over and put a glass of cold water down by her hand.

'Do it again, once you have your breath back.'

She groans, pressing her hands over her face to muffle something behind them.

'No attitude, or you won't get tomorrow off,' I lie.

She peeks out from behind her hands. 'It's only been two weeks and you're giving me a day off?'

'I am having some old friends over tomorrow, so I shall drop you home tonight then pick you up again at 8 a.m. on Sunday. I expect you can find some way to occupy yourself without me for a day, but I can give you some homework if you are worried your training will suffer.'

Verity pulls a face. 'I really want to tell you where to shove it, but it turns out I want to be good at this and I'm not yet, so yes – please give me homework.'

I gift her a beatific smile.

Verity replies by grabbing her water and guzzling noisily. 'That's for gloating,' she tells me as I retreat to the house to prepare a nice long list of things for her to work on.

Pru

The community hall is stuffy and smells of stale bread and cabbages. A cluster of people are chatting by a hot-water urn, dunking teabags in paper cups and spilling milk on to the floor as they wait for the talk to start. A flustered organizer is setting out chairs in rows facing a lopsided lectern. I set my handbag aside and help. It stops my hands twitching from the adrenalin.

'I'm so looking forward to the talk. I can't imagine what it must feel like to spend your life helping others escape the troubles you've had,' I lie as I push the last chair into alignment.

'And by founding a charity at twenty-two.' The organizer rubs absently at her lower back as she surveys the room, then waves at someone. 'I think that's our speaker.' She pats her hair.

I don't mention that a curl is sticking up like a horn at the back. Instead, I don my most harmless smile and keep my muscles loose and relaxed as I turn to greet Claire Jeynes.

I don't ask, *Did you kill my daughter?* This isn't the place to stun or frighten her into a confession, but that wouldn't have stopped me – my throat closing up does.

'Hello,' she says, gripping the strap of her handbag as

if she is worried that one of the slowly pottering audience might be planning to mug her. At least the nervous way her eyes dart around saves me from having to meet her gaze.

She is taller than I expected. Face pink with heat. Everything about her is soft and vulnerable. My heartbeat pulses in my ears and my fingertips buzz as if I have been in the cold too long. For a moment, I envisage taking her to the floor and wringing the truth from her.

'I'll see if I can open a window,' the frazzled organizer says, bustling off.

'Did you have a good journey?' I smile inanely, as if I am not considering whether it would be better to drown her or overdose her with whatever prescription medication would seem least suspicious. 'I left extra time for the roadworks, but they were fine from my direction.'

'I don't drive, so it's just a question of train delays for me, but it wasn't too bad.' She fiddles with the strap of her handbag. 'Are you here with someone specific in mind?' she asks, like a normal person, instead of a murderer, but then no one tends to bat an eye at me.

'Yes,' I answer truthfully, 'someone who has been gone from my life for many years, but I'm hoping to learn some crucial things. Perhaps it will lead to a degree of resolution.' I clear my throat. 'I read an interview you gave a while ago about choosing to be estranged from your family – your father, particularly. It made me wonder . . . Are you back in contact now? Was it the wake-up call he needed to change?'

She looks down, now fiddling with her handbag's clasp. 'Actually, *I* was the one with the prescription-drug problem.' She darts me a thin-lipped smile, but there's shame in her eyes. 'Prescription sedatives to begin with. Then stimulants, too. There was . . .' She swallows, expression going blank. 'I had a traumatic experience and, as a GP, my father . . . I know in his head he was doing what was best for me – was only expecting the pills to be short-term, but . . .'

'I've heard that sometimes people get addicted from just one dose. It's scary to think that applies even with prescription medication.'

She glances around as if hoping someone will interrupt us, but the organizer is still fighting with the window. 'It wasn't that simple for me,' she mumbles, fiddling, fiddling, fiddling with the clasp. 'After the . . . thing happened, I wanted my dad to call the police, and I thought the pills were just to calm me down so I could talk to them, but I was out cold for the rest of the day. By the time I surfaced the next morning it was too late for . . . for the evidence that would have supported my story.'

She shakes her head, eyes still roving around the hall. It is just as well. For once, I have no idea what my face is doing. *This is what that day looked like to Hope's killer*, my brain keeps saying, then, If *she is the one who killed Hope.*

'I was stuck,' Claire Jeynes tells the floor by my left foot. 'The only thing that helped was retreating into the oblivion the pills gave me. Obviously, my father wouldn't keep prescribing them, but I found someone else and . . .'

She seems so open, but why won't she look at me? She has no idea who I am or what I suspect. Surely it means she's lying about her history. The question is what she's lying about.

She cuts herself off with an embarrassed laugh. 'I'm

sorry. You're about to hear all this. I shouldn't be rehearsing on you.'

'Please do!' It is just as well I don't have to feign eagerness. 'In fact, I was wondering . . .' I lean forward, lowering my voice. 'I know you said you didn't manage to collect any evidence against the person who traumatized you, but if it's the type of trauma I'm thinking of . . . Well, predators like that don't just do it once, do they? Maybe a woman will come to your charity one day and tell a story just like yours and it'll turn out to be the same man.'

She flinches at the words, wrapping her arms around herself.

'If there was a second victim, you could go to the police together, even without physical evidence.'

Her eyes dart to the frazzled organizer. 'It wasn't . . . I didn't . . .' She looks past me, face brightening. 'I think I'm needed. It was nice meeting you.' She gives me an awkward wave, then hurries off to where the organizer is now fighting to make the lectern stand straight.

I pick up my handbag, fumble around inside, heave an audible sigh, then march towards the exit. A cough tickles my throat and I use the excuse to press my arm over my face as I pass a straggle of latecomers – it would be awkward to be recognized now.

It's only when I pull out of the car park and accelerate down the high street that I manage to lower my hunched shoulders. I force myself to keep my focus on the road. I won't disgrace my daughter's memory with inattention.

My brain promptly tells me that Hope is beside me. I catch a riff of her laugh. The rush of trees outside the window could be her hair streaming in the breeze.

You can still concentrate with the radio on, Mum, and I want some music.

It's so real, grief grips my throat. My eyes stay on the road, but my hand goes to the control panel. Music fills the car. For a second, I hear her cheer, then nothing. The moment is gone.

I wish I could believe there is an After where I will find her waiting, but that is just foolishness. When I die, I will be gone, just like she is, and that will be that. If I want peace, I am going to have to find it before I go.

In twenty-five years, I have never broken the Rules, but since I won't have long to live with the knowledge of what I've done – or the consequences – I have no misgivings about investigating Claire Jeynes myself. It is something of a grey area, after all, now Paloma is dead.

As for Jeynes herself . . . Until I find proof of her guilt, there is no point worrying what I will do with it. While Rule 9 – *Take no unnecessary risks. Never, ever rush* – has served me well, now the biggest risk of all is that time will run out before I've seen an end to the person responsible for leaving my beautiful daughter to die alone in a ditch on a frozen winter's day.

Verity

Why did I complain about training being boring? Boredom is bliss.

Boredom is BLISS?

Pru's voice is in my head now. Between her and Mum, I can't even be stupid inside my own skull without having to correct myself and be reasonable and rational. I signed up to be turned homicidal. I definitely was not expecting to be turned sensible in the process . . . and I've just heard myself, and I'm going to have to think about the implications.

YES, PRU! I WILL THINK ABOUT IT! I yell internally, which is probably more a sign of insanity than sensibility, but there we go.

I want to be back at Pru's cottage, getting my training all wrong but knowing it doesn't matter because it's just practice. Blissfully boring practice.

The reality of what I am training for is not boring at all. I thought I wanted excitement and adventure. I thought it would make my heart race and my blood thrill, but that's because I'm stupid.

I wanted to be ready for more – was so happy when Pru said she would let me go alone to steal our current target's rubbish so we could learn more about his habits as a basis for planning how to kill him. It felt like a big gold star for all my effort over the last two weeks. Instead, it turns out to be a test – one I'm about to flunk.

My stomach churns and my mouth goes sour as the sitting-room light goes out in the house I've been watching for the past hour. Through the window, I watch shadows flare in the hallway then at the turn of the staircase. Lights go on upstairs. I wait till they go out again before I wriggle out of the rhododendron in the garden across the street, where I've been waiting for the target to set out his bins.

Only he hasn't put out the bloody bins. Either he's forgotten, or he's planning to do it first thing and wake the neighbours, but neither option helps me. While I could climb over the gate into his garden, I'm not positive the bins are there, and I'd risk being spotted from the street. I could go over the back fence instead, but it would mean traipsing through three other properties first, and even I know that's a bad idea – especially since the bins might be in the garage instead. But can I risk going back to Pru's empty-handed?

Suddenly, the target's garden gate bursts open. With a roar like an approaching train, a man in jogging bottoms and a T-shirt bunched up on one side comes storming down the drive, dragging a wheelie bin.

Crouched on the tiny patch of lawn in front of the rhododendron, I tense, ready to launch myself behind the magnolia on my left . . . The target looks straight across the road at me.

We stare at each other in the orange glow of the streetlights as he comes to an abrupt halt. The bin clonks down on the kerb as he releases it.

I stand up and give him a sheepish wave. 'You've not seen a Pomeranian, have you?'

He blinks. 'Fluffy little dog, isn't it?'

'That's the one.' I heave a theatrical sigh and can *feel* Pru deducting marks. 'My boyfriend went one way, and I came down here.' Fishing my phone out of my pocket, I tap the sound-effects app Pru had me install and hit the 'new message' icon. The phone dings obligingly. 'Oh, thank God. My boyfriend's got her.' I flash a smile in the man's direction, already turning away. 'Sorry to bother you. Have a good evening!'

I hurry off, not stopping till I'm three corners away, even though I realize after the second turn that I've given not a single thought to where I'm going or what I'll do next. I now don't know how to get back to the target's house or even the car, which would at least give me a starting point for retracing my steps. Covering myself in glory, I am. Not to mention I'm bin-less and our target has seen me. Pru's going to be, like, so thrilled.

No 'like's! Pru shouts in my head, her voice a counterpoint to Mum's weary *Is there ever going to be a career opportunity you embrace instead of going straight for destruction mode?* But Mum's voice is easier to ignore now I've read the statements and finally – finally – have proof of who the liar in the family is.

Habit makes me hear her voice, but she's growing quieter. I'm getting faster at stopping myself spiralling into self-doubt about how I do everything wrong, for all the wrong reasons, and how Pru is going to dump me (possibly off a cliff). Slowly, I am learning to clamp down on the internalized criticism that drowns out any ability to think clearly and make sensible decisions. I figure that's why Pru gave me the statements on our very first day, though I guess it was also a sign of her faith in my ability to accept hard truths.

I'm about to thank her by demonstrating that she's chosen the worse mentee in the history of the Sisterhood. I can't even remember the name of the street where I parked to look it up on my phone. I consider drooping on to someone's front wall and having a good cry, or at least a thorough despair, but that's just going to draw attention I don't need.

Instead, I close my eyes and force myself to focus on finding a solution.

My brain fills with the memory of following Pru out to the driveway the day we took Boudicca for her MOT (brief and depressing) and repairs (lengthy and expensive) only for my mentor to walk past her own car and drop down by Boudicca's front bumper, reaching behind it and extracting a little black object.

'We don't want the garage asking awkward questions,' she said, as I gaped at her.

'You put a tracker on my car?'

'Well, how else did you think I went about looking into you, before selecting you as my mentee?' she asked in exasperation.

I opened my mouth to yell, then took a deep breath and said, 'I'd like to know how it works,' instead.

At the time it seemed strange when she promptly taught me to put a tracker on her car and sync it with an app on my phone, but now I realize, with mingled frustration and shame, that she knew I'd need it. At least I remembered its existence, so I can fix the mess I'm making of my first real task without having to call her for help. I may be hopeless, but I'm determined to do my part in stopping our target before he hurts anyone else.

The man whose rubbish I'm here to steal is a preferential paedophile. He likes dark-haired little boys aged six to eight. I cannot fail by returning empty-handed or, worse, alerting him that someone is investigating him.

I let the tracker app lead me back to the car, then carry on to the target's house a few streets away, pretending to take a call as I go. I scan each lighted window I see, checking no one's watching as I approach the house once more. I barely pause as I pull the bin lid up, snag a handful of bags, then close the lid quickly and quietly. I'm on my way in a matter of seconds, my pulse racing as if I've run a mile.

I may have screwed up my first attempt, but I stayed calm, went back and carried out my task. And I did it so cleanly even Pru would approve. Warmth blossoms in my chest at the thought that I've made good on her trust in me.

I take the first corner I come to, keeping my head ducked low so that the brim of my baseball cap hides my features. I beep the car open the moment I'm close enough, dropping the rubbish on to the plastic sheet lining the boot, then, with a quick squirt of handgel (as per Pru's strict orders), I open the driver's door and climb inside.

I barely breathe until I'm on the dual carriageway, lane markings flashing past as I hurtle through the darkness just under the speed limit. The car feels hollow and empty. My stomach won't stop squirming as if it wants to escape my body.

It feels like the whole world is watching me. Ten minutes

ago I felt so proud, so certain there was enough rage in me to fuel the lifetime of killing that lies ahead, but suddenly I just feel small and scared and lonely.

I screw up everything in my life. Did I really think that, magically, I wouldn't screw up murder? Pru gave me the simplest assignment in the world and it took me two goes to get it right. What happens when we go in for the kill? I'll get myself caught. I'll get Pru caught. Our target will keep hurting children.

I'm minutes from the turn-off to Pru's house. Should I just drive on? She said the Sisterhood wouldn't come after me if I walked away and kept my mouth shut. I should do that. For her sake and mine. For the sake of all the victims Pru will be able to help without me screwing everything up.

My hand flicks the indicator and the car glides on to the slip road.

I may be a screw-up, and I may be petrified, but I want to be part of the Sisterhood. Even if I don't think I'm good enough, Pru sees something in me. She chose me and, despite my struggles with pretty much every aspect of my training, she has never said anything that even hinted at giving up on me. I want to be worthy of that. More than that, I want to do something with my misery to give it value and meaning and purpose, just like Pru said. But I have to be willing to risk my freedom, my safety.

I have to be willing to kill for it.

The horse chestnut at the corner of Pru's street towers up in the beam of my headlights.

Bumping into the driveway and cutting the engine, I expect to sit in a frozen huddle. Instead, I climb out, crunch over the gravel and slip through the garden gate.

I step into the golden light of Pru's spotless kitchen, and she turns at the sound of the door closing behind me.

I watch her put down the teapot she's drying and walk around the table to me. Then she gathers me into her arms. Whether this is affection or just kindness, it's comfort enough.

Then, suddenly, it's too much.

As the adrenalin ebbs, the sadness comes flooding back, along with rage and despair, the misery of the fact that I can't remember the last time someone hugged me. Really hugged me and didn't let go. I'd forgotten how it feels to be in someone's arms.

A howl leaps up my throat and out of my mouth, then I'm sobbing, but Pru just holds on and doesn't say a word. Even though it feels like everything in me is coming apart, I know I'm safe enough to let it.

Pru

Verity's self-defence and fitness training are proceeding nicely, but when it comes to CCTV angles she has taken to training less like a duck to water and more like a brick to a mirror. Still, I can't fault her grit. Slowly, she has been improving, and tomorrow I will watch her take her first true step into the world of the Sisterhood. When she has crossed the threshold of her first kill, surely there will be enough trust between us to outweigh her inevitable feelings about the information I am now actively, rather than passively, withholding about the night her sister disappeared.

Case in point, Verity is presently taking me through what happened after they left the park. The drive to the university. Arriving tipsy and giggling, the handsome boy – Charles Temple – ordering the limo driver to wait in case the girls decided the party wasn't for them.

'Like I said, we mingled a bit in the courtyard and this big dance hall, but then we went back to Charles Temple's room with Christophe and Nathan – who turns out to be Charles's cousin. At some point Christophe left – I guess to buy the drugs he overdosed on. Reenie and Charles were snogging, and Nathan clearly had the same plans with me, but I was *so* not interested. I remember looking around and thinking, *I'd rather go to bed and not get in trouble for missing curfew*, but Reenie didn't want to hear it.'

I nod, doing my best to look attentive, though most of my focus is on when to tell her about Christophe. Giving her the statements was highly productive, but it doesn't mean she is ready for a fresh upheaval just as we are starting to settle into our mentoring relationship.

'When you left, did you go looking for the limo or simply set out on foot?' I ask, shifting uncomfortably as if the needling guilt has become a physical pain.

'I peered around when I came out of the university, but there was a bunch of drunk guys playing football with a beer can and it felt riskier to go past them than just walk home along the main road, since it's well lit the whole way. I mean, Reenie knew I'd be safe or she wouldn't have let me go alone.' She clears her throat. 'You've read the statements, so you know why I didn't call Mum.' Her tone turns the words into a question.

I nod, and see gratitude wash across her face. It makes me add, 'You did your best to persuade your sister to leave, then you got yourself home safely. At sixteen, those were your only responsibilities.'

Verity dips her head. She doesn't believe this yet, but at least she isn't balled up on her chair, as if trying to make herself small. Instead, she is simply playing with a water-drop, smearing it around the table till it vanishes into the grain of the wood.

'Did anything happen on the way home? Did you notice anything strange?'

She shakes her head. 'There weren't many cars. No one bothered me. When I got home, I lied that I didn't know where Reenie was and threw myself into bed, and by the morning . . .' She stares at her finger circling the same spot on the table.

The guilt needles and needles. 'The limo driver's statement claims he found drugs in the car a few weeks before Reenie's disappearance, right after driving Charles Temple to another party.' I take the file out and pass it across to her, watching as she flicks through to the right statement.

'There was a bunch of boys in the limo the night the driver found the stuff, including Nathan and Christophe, but the driver said he had several fast turnarounds where he had to do a very basic clean between clients, so he can't be sure which group left the drugs.' She sits back, tapping her pen against her lips. 'So, it could have been Temple. Or Christophe – we know he did drugs for sure. Or even Nathan, though he didn't seem the type. Or it could have been someone else entirely.' She shakes her head. 'How could the driver's boss tell him to chuck the drugs away instead of taking them to the police?'

'Why do you think?' I ask, helping myself to a snickerdoodle, then pushing the biscuit tin over to Verity.

'You know, this obsession with me working out every-bloody-thing for myself is super irritating, right?' She takes an aggressive bite of snickerdoodle, dropping crumbs everywhere.

I fetch a hand-brush and clean around her.

'Seriously?' she says, lifting her feet as I knock the brush against her ankle.

'You could just eat like a civilized human instead of a Neanderthal,' I tell her, placing a napkin in front of her. 'Can you manage like this, or should I fetch a drop-cloth?'

Verity sticks out her tongue but leans over the napkin as she takes another unnecessarily messy bite. 'I guess' – she chews, swallows – 'that since the driver couldn't say for sure whose drugs they were, it would cost the limo company business without leading the police anywhere.' She lifts the corner of the napkin to read on through the driver's statement. 'Apparently, the drugs were little white pills with a line through them, like a mini paracetamol.'

'Plenty of drugs are made into pills to disguise what they are, but there is a good chance it was Rohypnol.'

'Roofies.' Verity's voice drops to a whisper.

'It might not have anything to do with Reenie, but how could we investigate?'

Verity pushes back from the table, folding one foot underneath her. 'Is there any way to get the limo company's client list? No, wouldn't help,' she adds, before I can point out the problem. 'It could be another passenger who had the drugs, not necessarily the person who hired the car.' She picks up her pen again, clicking it on and off. 'Maybe we could get hold of a list of reports to the police about drink-spiking cases in the area in the months before and after?' She shakes her head. 'So many people don't report. Maybe a charity helpline? But then they wouldn't necessarily know the name of the caller. A help group?'

I point at her notepad. 'Write it all down.'

Verity throws her pen aside. 'There's probably confidentiality stuff that would mean no one at a help group could tell us anything and, if we turned up saying we were investigating a pattern, they'd want to see official ID.' She gives me a hopeful look. 'You don't happen to have a private detective licence?'

I glare at her. 'We are ordinary women. We couldn't be more normal if we tried.'

Verity snorts.

'Our anonymity is what protects us. Rule 8: *Don't draw attention with your appearance or behaviour or kills – strive to be invisible: ensure you are unmemorable.*'

Verity cocks her head, giving me a suspicious look. 'Why have we already spent so much time on Reenie's case, instead of it being a reward for when I actually complete a job or something?' She takes up her pen and begins doodling a bullseye of concentric circles. 'I know we need a target for my one free kill so you can off him as your last job before retirement, but are you worried about whether we can figure it out? How long did it take to identify your one free kill – or did you know from the start?'

She clicks her pen on, off, on, off.

I let it go. 'I am something of an outlier – we've never discovered who killed my daughter.'

The only progress I have made recently on proving it was Claire Jeynes is spotting an item in a community newsletter about her parents hosting an open-garden event in aid of her charity in a few weeks' time. It will be interesting to see if she is telling the truth about the estrangement. If not, it might be awkward to be recognized from the community centre, but I doubt any of them will put two and two together about who I really am. If they did, that, in itself, would be telling.

'But you and the Sisterhood are still investigating, and your mentor will do her part when you figure it out, right?'

Pushing up from my chair, I step down on an ant, then turn to survey the floor. 'My mentor died a few years ago.'

I squash another ant, then another, following them to the garden door. 'But the Sisterhood will honour my one free kill if I identify a target who meets the requirements.' I wait for Verity to ask how I kept going for twenty-five years without the reward I'd been promised.

'Can I help? I know I'm hardly a natural investigator, but I'm a fresh set of eyes.'

I am too wrongfooted to answer before she rabbits on, clicking the pen so that it punctuates every other word.

'Maybe they'll give it to me as a pro bono case, now your mentor can't see it through. There's got to be some advantage to the fact you're probably going to be training me five times longer than the average mentee.'

There won't be time for that. It's why I need to tell her about my involvement in her sister's case as soon as possible, though I've no intention of spilling the beans about my demise any sooner than I have to.

'You must have been looking for the person who killed Hope before you joined the Sisterhood. Did you ever get in trouble?'

'I did – though I broke no laws.' I fetch out the ant powder and sprinkle it over the crack where the first flagstone of the garden path meets the lintel beneath the kitchen door. 'I pestered a large and varied group of people, but there was no harassment or trespass – at least none that netted police attention.' I glare at the ground around the door, then put the powder away. 'I did drive the lead detective to distraction with emails and ideas and theories and questions. The Sisterhood arrived in my life at the point where I was "following up" once a day and it was wearing thin on all of us.'

'Why did you say yes when your mentor approached

you?' Verity turns in her chair to watch as I move over to the counter, setting out eggs and sugar. 'If you'd broken no laws so far, why jump straight to murder?'

Hope used to love raspberry mousse. After she died, I made it on her birthday, but trying to eat an entire batch solo only made the loneliness deeper. Now I need to cook something to match Verity's voracious appetite, so why not? I am sure Hope would approve. Even when she was a baby, I never had to tell her to share toys, sweets, or to take turns with other children. She just knew.

'I get that you wanted the Sisterhood's help to solve your daughter's case, but that never happened, so why did you carry on all these years?'

Subtle, Verity is not. She means: *Were you afraid to leave, despite what you told me?*

'I never wanted to leave. Oh, I've had the odd minute. There is always *one* point, in *every* case – the moment I move from preparing to kill and starting to do it: that fraction of a second where I could give in to fear, doubt, despair and just walk away. It's the hardest part.'

Stupid, I think. *Too revealing*. Then, *Maybe the truth is the best tool I have with Verity.*

'So, you don't get used to it.'

I turn the Look on her full beam and watch her flinch. 'What sort of person would ever get used to killing? I'm not a psychopath, Verity – Rule 7, remember? I've just had a lot of practice pushing through so that I can carry out my work cleanly and carefully and properly – Rule 4. When I am actually killing someone, I am too busy focusing on the job to think about the moral implications.' I lift the whisk down from the cupboard, clicking the beaters into place.

'And afterwards?'

She says it so uncertainly that I bite back the instinctive retort. Sighing, I turn and lean back against the counter, giving her my full attention. 'I focus on what the Sisterhood stands for – stopping repeat offenders in order to prevent more people becoming victims.'

Verity frowns, beating out a rhythm against the side of the table with her pen. 'So, the Sisterhood never goes after people for a one-off crime, no matter how bad?'

'You'll learn soon enough just how rare it is for people to commit the types of crimes we are concerned about on a one-off basis. It's why the Sisterhood is needed.' I set a pan on the hob, rinse raspberries and pour them in, sprinkling sugar over the top. 'Now, talk me through tomorrow's kill.'

Verity heaves a sigh. 'Do you really think I can muck up the world's simplest plan? No, don't answer that,' she adds, before I can tell her not to get ahead of herself.

I turn on the hob and watch the raspberries release their juice. It froths red as fresh blood against the sides of the saucepan. Verity stays silent, but I can feel her eyes on my back.

'No one is ever ready to start killing. But, as you said, there is very little that can go wrong with our plan, so this time tomorrow you should have a successful job under your belt.'

'Tomorrow I'll be a murderer.'

I turn, meeting her eyes before I nod. 'It's time you showed yourself what you are capable of.'

Verity

I am conflicted. Which is not helpful when I'm about to kill someone.

It doesn't seem real, despite all the planning and preparation. I suppose that's natural, but, instead of the hoped-for flood of adrenalin, I get a flood of dread. And clamminess.

When I glance over at Pru, I find her gazing calmly down at the book in her lap. She is not sweating at all. She looks like we're driving to a reading group, not a homicide.

I suppose I should be thankful it's hardly a 'hands on' job. The thought makes me shiver. I'm starting to appreciate the Sisterhood's mundane methods.

Am I becoming sensible? Has Pru indoctrinated me, somewhere between the lessons on carbon monoxide alarms and methods to make electrocution look natural? Maybe she hypnotized me during the endless repetitions of the four key wrist- and arm-locks during our self-defence lessons.

Aside from the fact I'm now a professional-killer-in-training, my life suddenly resembles that of a competent adult. I've even started eating my five a day. OK, that's only because Pru now feeds me, and she cooks everything fresh, but I'm also choosing to drink more water. And, of course,

I'm exercising every day. To top it off, since I started investigating Reenie's case with Pru, I've not stalked or harassed anyone at all. If it weren't for the fact that I'm about to commit murder, even my mother would have to admit I'm getting a handle on the basics of life.

It's only taken thirty years for you to listen to my simplest pieces of advice, sighs my mother. *Though really what you've done is find someone to replace me who has not yet had her patience exhausted.*

I wriggle in my seat, as if that will stop the whispering in my head.

For goodness' sake, snaps Pru's voice, and I almost laugh out loud. Just what I need – an imaginary beatdown between my dead mother and my homicidal mentor.

'Here will do,' says Pru, making me jump. She tucks a slip of paper into her book to mark the page, then props it in the central console as I guide the car to the kerb and turn off the engine.

I promptly freeze in place. My hands claw around the wheel, knuckles standing out white.

I can't do this.

My life was a miserable mess before, but it wasn't unfixable. Most of what was wrong was my own fault. If I had another chance, maybe I could choose differently. But if I do this – if I kill someone – I can never go back. Once my training is complete, for the next twenty-five years I'll have to carry out murders alone . . . until it's time to pick my own mentee.

I don't want that.

But I don't want to go back to my messy, miserable old life, either.

Less than three weeks ago, I was on a path to prison with no chance of solving Reenie's disappearance. Less than three weeks ago, there was desperation in my veins instead of blood. Everything kept getting worse and worse because I didn't know how to stand my loss. Couldn't face even one more tiny injustice. I *wanted* it all to end in disaster. It would have been a relief to have nothing left to lose.

I glance across at Pru, but she's staring through the windscreen. She must know what's happening, but she's not said a word to hurry me out of the car. She's not even looking at me.

In less than three weeks, something has changed in me. I feel . . . different. Not happier – and right now I'm as desperate as I've ever been – but I'm no longer flailing through life, letting things happen to me then reacting on emotion alone. I've started making choices. And today I've got to make the biggest one of all, even though it's so hugely, enormously, toweringly terrifying it feels as if it should dissolve me where I sit.

I don't know what to do. Someone needs to stop our target hurting children, but I don't want to kill him. I don't want that on my conscience for the rest of my life.

I think about asking Pru if she'd let me leave. And the fact that, whatever she says, it might be a lie – would a group of professional killers really let me walk away? But I can't believe Pru would hurt me. I can't believe anyone in the Sisterhood would hurt me unless I went to the police. So, maybe I *can* walk . . . but the target will die all the same. Just at Pru's hands, instead of mine.

I think about going back to my old life and learning

to hold my tongue and my temper. Learning not to react to every unfairness as if someone has taken a cheese-grater to my skin. Learning to hold on to a job. Learning to make and keep friends. Settling into a new place and making it mine. Maybe one day I could even fall in love . . . But unless someone stumbles on the body, I'd never know what happened to Reenie. Could I finally learn to let her go, accept what I've lost and embrace what I could have instead?

Pru would never give me the Look again. I'd stop flinching every time I say the word 'like'. There would be no more laps of the garden. No more cramming my brain with poisons and medications. No more trying and failing to work out CCTV angles. No more learning. No more changing.

I want to be able to offer twenty-five years of sacrifice with Pru's steely determination, but I don't know how to get from here to there.

I *do* know that Pru can teach me. If I stay. If I commit.

If I kill.

I may not *want* to commit murder, but I *do* want our target to die, so what right do I have to keep my conscience clean at Pru's expense?

I unclench my hands from the wheel, flex my fingers, working feeling back into them. As I click off my seatbelt my hand brushes against Pru's book. The slip of paper she's using as a makeshift bookmark drifts into my footwell. I bend to pick it up, frowning as I see it's a prescription for hydrocodone, which sounds like a painkiller, and the same sedative Mum was given in the wake of Reenie's disappearance.

I tuck it back into the book. 'Sorry, I lost your page.'

I think about asking whether Pru's trouble with sleeping is because of all the killing, but I don't want to know.

I look through the windscreen at the sunny street where I'm about to become a murderer.

With a glance at my watch, I turn to Pru. 'Shall we go?'

Pru

The job goes without a hitch and soon Verity is pulling the car back into the drive and cutting the engine.

'So, now we wait.' She shakes her head. 'I can't believe I've probably killed someone, but I don't know *when* it'll happen – assuming it all goes to plan. It's like Schrödinger's cat, only the murder-mystery version.'

I climb out of the car, rapping on the roof when Verity doesn't move. 'There is absolutely no point waiting here when there is a casserole in the oven.'

'I'm starving,' Verity says, then smacks a hand over her mouth. 'That feels so wrong.'

'If you want to punish yourself, you can run rings around the garden until you vomit, but it won't change anything.'

'What if it doesn't work?' Verity says, following me up the garden path and into the kitchen, where she starts setting the table without being asked – and possibly without realizing what she's doing, given the glazed look in her eyes.

'Then we will try something else, since no one will be any the wiser if our first attempt fails. All that will happen is that our target will get an extra week or so to live.'

Verity drops into a chair, scrubbing at her face. 'I already hate this. I am not made for waiting.'

I put a jug of lemonade down next to a couple of glasses. 'Make yourself useful,' I order, when she doesn't move.

By the time I return from the fridge with a pea and grilled courgette salad, she has poured us both a drink and is sipping hers dolefully. '*Do* I need to send you for a quick run?'

'No,' comes the sulky reply. Then, 'Maybe. I don't know.' She kicks her foot against the table leg. 'What happened to your daughter?'

The question knocks the air out of me. Which is ridiculous. My blood-sugar level must be low.

'Sorry. I shouldn't have sprung that on you,' says Verity, torturing her napkin.

I sigh as I sink into my chair. 'We lived in a little village about forty minutes from here. The closest town is two miles down a narrow, winding road – you know the type: no verge, no path, lots of blind corners. Lots of idiot drivers.' I have to clear my throat. It has been so long since I've told anyone about Hope. They either know already or don't need to.

'They found her in a ditch. She was alive for a number of hours after she was hit, but it took a while for us to realize she was missing and then find her. By the time we did, the cold had got her.' I reach for my glass, but my hand shakes so much I dare not lift it. 'Whoever hit her drove off. Didn't even call an ambulance. It was in all the local papers, of course, but the public appeal was as productive as the police investigation in identifying the driver.'

The salad tastes like mud, but I eat anyway because my hands are still shaking and I need them to stop. Verity and I have delicate work to do later, practising techniques for opening window catches from the outside without leaving any sign of a break-in.

'The police must've checked all the local garages for repair jobs that could fit, and scrapyards, too, in case the car was dumped.' Verity trails the tines of her fork through the puddle of vinaigrette on her plate, making a pattern like swerving tyre tracks. 'How big a radius did they investigate?'

'I went to every garage in a hundred miles. A few times, when an owner seemed cagey, I tried sneaking into their office to see if I could find any evidence.' I dab my napkin against my lips, making a mark like long-dried blood. 'I got caught once, but the owner recognized me from the news and realized why I had come. He made me a cup of tea, then phoned a few people at places he thought might not ask as many questions as they should. No one knew anything.'

'That they'd say.'

I let my eyes wander to the garden. 'There was quite a lot of water in the ditch – the police said she was lucky not to have drowned, though that would have been quicker. At least the cold would have numbed her so she just went to sleep at the end.'

I won't make myself tell the whole story: that she was aware enough to try to climb out. Over and over again. The banks around her were clawed to mud, plants ripped out at the roots, hedge branches broken off in the radius of her reaching hands. She fought until her injuries, the cold, the despair, were too much. Then she died. My beautiful girl.

'So the water would've washed off any trace evidence, like paint from the car. Did they—'

I push myself to my feet, gathering the dirty plates. 'I can't blame the police for the fact that there probably wasn't anything to find, given the location and the weather that day.' I put the washing-up in the sink, watching the smears of dressing swirl away. 'I still look in every open garage I see, as if the car will just be sitting there one day, with damage to the front that hasn't been repaired but is somehow so distinctive there might as well be a label saying "This is the car that killed Hope." '

Heat sears my cheeks as I draw the casserole out of the oven and set it on the table. The windows steam as the air grows rich with the scent of herbs and onion and meat.

'This was one of Hope's favourites,' I tell Verity, though I'm not sure why. Perhaps I feel I owe her a piece of truth in compensation for all the secrets I am keeping. About Reenie. About Hope. About how little time I have left. The guilt needles sharper than ever now Verity has carried out her first kill and there's no going back to her old life.

Before, I was worried about leaving the job of finishing her training to a colleague. I didn't expect it to matter to Verity who her mentor was. I didn't expect it to matter to me. But for some reason, as we eat, I tell her the story of Hope gobbling down three platefuls the first time I made the casserole and how we laughed and laughed, then spent the rest of the evening on the sofa, because she was too full to move. If I close my eyes, I can feel the weight of her head in my lap as I read to her. I can feel her fingers drawing flowers on my knee.

Verity

'I just killed a guy – hopefully – so, please don't make me do CCTV drills, too,' I beg as we finish clearing up from lunch.

'All right,' Pru says amiably. 'You can write out your confession instead.'

I nearly drop the mugs I'm lifting down from the cupboard. 'Please tell me you don't mean what I think you mean.'

Pru is filling an old brass watering can and doesn't even look at me as she tends to the herb pots on the windowsill. 'The Sisterhood requires each mentee to write a confession about their first kill. It goes with the package of physical evidence each mentor collects during training and sends at key stages to the Sisterhood for safekeeping.'

PANIC! PANIC! says the inside of my brain. It's always so helpful.

'You didn't expect the Sisterhood to take things on trust, did you?'

'You said the police wouldn't believe me if I went to them with a wild story about being recruited to a group of all-female assassins – by a woman in her mid-sixties, no less. You said they'd put me under a psychiatric hold. If I can't tell anyone, then why—'

'It's different once there's a body to go with any story

you might tell the police. From this point on, Rule 12 applies: *Breaking the Rules instantly forfeits your membership, your one free kill, and the Sisterhood's protection. You may also forfeit your freedom and/or your life.*' Pru picks a withered leaf off a basil plant and drops it into the food recycling. 'However, so does Rule 13: *Our lives and freedom rest in each other's hands. The simultaneous gift and price of membership is shared purpose, courage and loyalty.* So, wipe that gormless expression off your face and make a start on your confession.'

I don't move. 'If I screw up and the Sisterhood decides to dob me in to the police, how do you stay out of it?'

'*Verity.*'

Only Pru could pack so much disdain and weariness into my name. Even my mother never managed quite that level of disappointment.

'I am going into the other room before I say something you'll regret,' she tells me, then walks out as if *I'm* being unreasonable.

Is she trying to gaslight me that this is totally normal? It's like trying to line my memories up with Mum's statement. Only Pru's never told me I'm remembering something wrong or that I'm lying to myself. She doesn't say I'm not the person I think I am. She says I can make different choices and work things out for myself. Is that what this is? Something I should have worked out but didn't?

You'd think I'd be used to having the rug pulled out from under me. Mum could never give a compliment or do something kind without putting a sting in the tail, just as she could never offer help without making me feel small for needing it. As if it was wrong to want help, comfort, love, from my own mother. Whenever I tried to tell her how I felt, she'd sigh and pat my hand and say that I had to stop being so oversensitive.

It's exhausting, Verity, her memory whispers to me now. *You take everything the wrong way. It's like you're incapable of believing my intentions are good.*

My stomach tightens with rage – at her, and at Pru.

But Pru didn't tell me I was overreacting about the confession. She never lied that the Sisterhood would put my interests first, or pretend it doesn't compel mentees and members alike to deliver on their commitments. Of *course* the Sisterhood doesn't rely purely on the fact that few people want to double-cross a bunch of professional killers.

I figured getting fired from this job would have a whole new level of finality, but it's simpler than that. The Sisterhood doesn't want or need to kill people like me. It sends us to prison instead. But how would Pru stay out of it when the evidence leads back to her as much as it does to me? Even if I didn't spill the beans about the Sisterhood, the police would know she was involved . . .

. . . because the confession and evidence package are not just leverage to keep me in line – they're a promise. If I fail, Pru fails, too. If I go to prison, so does she, while everything stays neat and clean for the Sisterhood.

After twenty-five years of successful, invisible killing, Pru has chosen to risk it all to train me.

I want to say that I heard what she was telling me without *listening*, but really the problem is that I didn't *think*. Pru's not like Mum, trying to wrongfoot me, twisting what I remember, think, feel. She's teaching me to see things clearly. She gave me the statements when I had no training, but instead of cutting to the chase and giving me her analysis – making me depend on her and her version of the story – she let me figure it out. She could have used the opportunity to make me trust her, but instead she used it to help me trust myself. All while she was making me part of the most important thing in her life.

This is the price of belonging . . .

. . . And it turns out I'm OK with paying it.

I let the knowledge settle into me as I draw my notepad over. I write my name, and the time and date across the top.

> At 7.35 a.m. today, my mentor and I parked a few streets away from the home of Claude Jones-Smith then jogged around the area until we saw a Tesco delivery truck. We followed it to his house, then, when the driver took a crate to the doorstep, I pretended an item had slipped out and hurried to give it back. This was a tube of toothpaste doctored to include peanut oil, which he is deadly allergic to. A few days ago, I stole Claude's trash, so we knew he'd recently run out and what type he preferred. We also identified that he drank at least one banana-and-apple smoothie of a particular brand every day, so, while I was distracting Claude and the driver, my mentor tossed an empty banana-and-peanut-butter-smoothie bottle from the same brand down the side of the cabinet just inside his front door so that the police would assume he'd simply ordered the wrong flavour and drunk it without realizing.

Footsteps announce Pru's return.

'Do I need to explain how we knew about his allergy

and the Tesco order, or does that not matter for the confession, since it didn't involve any crimes? If I leave that out, I should be done in about five minutes, then you can go back to torturing me with CCTV obstacle courses.'

I hear Pru stride across the kitchen and flick on the kettle. 'Even apart from the insulting implication that I'd ever break the Rules, if you think what we've been doing is torture, I've clearly not been trying hard enough.'

Although I don't look up, I can feel that we're both smiling.

It's hard to believe I've probably killed someone. When Pru finally sends me home, I struggle to sleep. In the morning, it's all I can do not to google suspicious things from the moment I wake up. Pru keeps me busy all day, but when I let myself through my front door again, I nearly give in to temptation. Even though the last thing Pru told me as I headed home was 'Do. Not. Google. Anything.'

'Anything?' I asked.

She gave me the Look and closed the door in my face, leaving me muttering to myself about the various things I could google without technically breaking Rule 5: *Your internet search history must never, ever include information on targets, methods or similar. Don't get 'clever' about it.*

My phone pings. Pru's text simply reads: *Rule 5.* As if she could *sense* me even thinking about breaking the Rules.

Over the next two days, she reminds me morning and night.

Training is . . . happening. I wouldn't say it's going well, but it's definitely not going as badly as it was. It keeps me busy. And Pru and I . . . We're getting used to each other.

Sometimes I wonder if we're starting to become something more than mentor and mentee. She feeds me then barks orders at me, and I try to keep the whining to a minimum and the learning to a maximum. I've got a long way to go, but I'm now a fully-fledged mentee on the way to becoming a member of the Sisterhood. If I can just keep it together.

Then, three days after the maybe-kill, I stagger into my flat, exhausted after another day practising techniques for climbing fences and walls, and find another **DATED MATERIALS** letter on the doormat. I tear into the envelope.

> Although we note the payment of overdue rent, as per the previous eviction notification, you recently brought a dog into the flat, in contravention of the rental agreement, and kept it overnight. This is the fourth such incident (see previous correspondence). As such, we will proceed with eviction; in light of the advance payment of this and next month's rent, your final date to vacate is the last day of next month instead of the standard two weeks.

I crumple the letter into a ball and throw it at the wall. It ricochets into my face, wrenching a scream of fury out of me. I haven't been fired, haven't spent any money, haven't stalked or harassed any suspects in my sister's case, but I still can't keep my life together . . .

At least I have Boudicca back, so I've got *somewhere* to sleep while I pay off enough of my debt to Pru to start earning. Plus, soon I'll have a bed during away-jobs, working for cover-story clients: Pru says we're just waiting for a suitable placement to serve as my introduction to ESA's legitimate operations.

Although I asked how many members of ESA are in the Sisterhood, all Pru would say is, 'That is need to know, and you don't,' though at least she filled me in on why we need cover stories for away-jobs: to explain what we are doing in the vicinity of our kills, should that ever be necessary, as well as providing a paper trail for our income.

'But surely high-end clients have security, or even the police looking out for them? What if there are journalists and we get papped along with them? Isn't it risky?' I asked.

Pru tipped her head to one side, waiting for me to work it out for myself.

I groaned. 'I guess getting caught in press photos just confirms our . . . well, it's not exactly an alibi, but same difference. And obviously, any security would be focused on our clients, not us. If they do a background check on us, mine's going to look *great*, but I guess that I can improve it over time.'

'Good, but why else do we take high-end clients, despite the risks?' Pru asked.

'If they weren't high end, it would be hard to justify our fees, then the legit part of ESA wouldn't be much of a financial cover since our rates have to be expensive if the paid kills are going to cover the pro bono work, too.' I sighed. 'All this travelling is going to mean no pets, even when I'm financially stable, isn't it?'

At least the promise of housing being provided periodically saves me from despair as I pack a different bit of the flat into Boudicca's boot and back seats each night. Although I've still got most of the two months, I can't afford to leave it to the last minute given that I'll soon be tied up with away-jobs.

Over the next few days, the wait to find out if I've killed our target stops being a gruelling ordeal and becomes a low thrum of anxiety at the back of my brain. Compared with the days, weeks, months hoping Reenie would turn up at our door with some mad explanation, or be found in a hospital with a head injury, or be found dead, but at least found . . . Compared with that, the wait is stressful, but far from unbearable.

I'm starting to wonder if I should resign myself to the plan being a failure and having to come up with a new one when, one sunny afternoon, I look up from successfully popping a French-window lock to find Pru holding out her laptop for me to see a news bulletin.

Local man found dead in his home of suspected allergic reaction.

'Isn't that cheating Rule 5?' I ask.

'I'm signed up to a wide range of local newsletters and bulletins – have been for years.'

'Huh. I guess I should start setting myself up the same way.'

'And on all the neighbourhood apps. Though not till you've perfected your talents on the sash window in the lounge.' She closes the laptop. 'Good job.'

That's it. *Good job.*

But I don't feel good or competent. I feel sick and cold. The phrase 'someone walked over my grave' echoes in my mind. Then I pull myself together and head off to the lounge.

It is too late for regrets and, anyway, I'm not sorry that a paedophile is dead. I'm only sorry I have to live with killing him.

Pru

Our new target is a serial rapist: the most common of the Sisterhood's pro bono targets except for paedophiles. He lives half a mile from Winchester historic city centre, only six miles from our cover-story job.

Verity is practically vibrating with excitement as we arrive at our home for the next thirteen days: a Georgian manor house set in ten acres of parkland.

'Don't gawp.' I nudge her out of the way and press the doorbell.

The door opens almost immediately and a woman with wild eyes and even wilder hair looks out. 'Please tell me you're the help,' she pleads.

'Verity is here to look after the dogs,' I say, gesturing behind me. 'I am Prudence. The butler.'

The woman started to smile when I introduced Verity, but at the word 'butler' her face goes blank. 'There's got to be someone to cook. I don't cook. At least, no one wants me to cook.' She gulps. 'I tried to make my college roommate a birthday cake once. They had to take her to the hospital and pump her stomach. I don't know why. I followed the recipe. But that's why I shouldn't cook. I'm a rental agent, I—'

'My services include cooking,' I interrupt in my most

reassuringly no-nonsense tone. 'If you show us where to put our suitcases, I will make a start on lunch forthwith.'

For a second the rental agent looks like she might kiss me, but thankfully she restrains herself. Ushering us inside, she leads us, via several wrong turns, through a daunting maze of corridors and up two flights of stairs to a creaky landing, where she opens the doors to two tiny rooms – clearly the old servants' quarters. Then her phone goes and she hurries away.

I tuck my suitcase behind the door of my room, then march into Verity's. She is sprawled, spread-eagled, across the bed.

'We don't have time for lazing around. What should you be doing instead?'

'There are four similar rooms on this corridor, and a bathroom at the end. There's a fire hatch on to the roof by the bathroom. I don't see any fuse panels. There's WiFi, but only just. No second staircase, unless there's a hidden passageway.'

'There is also a hatch into the attic.'

Verity frowns. 'Where?' She sits up, sees my expression and scowls. 'Trick questions are the weapons of the petty tyrant.'

'That is not how you pronounce "diligent mentor".' I sniff. 'You should be grateful for my help in developing confidence in your memory, observation skills and—'

'The likelihood of a permanent headache,' Verity cuts in, still glaring at me.

'Yes, I have accepted that you are. Now, we will get lost in opposite directions on our way to find our client,' I say, stepping back into the corridor, then starting down the stairs.

Verity clomps after me. 'Why do we need to learn the lay of the land or, well, building? This is just our cover story. We're not doing any dispatching here.'

'Did you think your training would stop because we are away from home? Go left here.'

I busy myself exploring the corridors to the right, then make my way down to the ground floor, where I find Verity being lectured by a woman wearing what looks like fancy pyjamas and about a quarter of a million pounds in jewellery.

As I watch, Verity gives up the pretence of listening and turns all her attention on the four overbred dogs yipping and barking and jumping up at her. In moments, the dogs are taking it in turns to roll on to their backs for her to pet them.

'Verity, why don't you take your new charges for a walk, and I will get our instructions,' I say, before the client realizes Verity is ignoring her.

Soon, Verity and the dogs are gone and I am being lectured about every foible of the pampered pets and even more pampered humans, though at least in the process I manage to pin down permission to take Sunday morning off to 'visit the nearest city and see the sights'. We will do exactly as I've said – with one little detour so Verity can complete her first pro bono kill.

I am expecting the main challenge of our first away-job to be keeping Verity in line, but on the second day I wake up coughing. A cup of tea soothes my throat, but the following day the cough is back. This time it persists. First, I blame it on dust in my room, then a reaction to the cleaning products. But I am still having to cough into my shoulder periodically as I prepare lunch on the fourth day.

'You coming down with something?' Verity asks as she finishes cleaning up after feeding her charges their morning snack.

'Yes, a surfeit of dog.'

'You mean you came on this job without allergy pills? Really, Pru. You need to think these things through. Prepare for every eventuality,' says my little snot of a mentee.

'I am fully prepared,' I say serenely, 'to send you out to the shops with the horrid beasts.'

'You're not horrid beasts,' Verity tells the dogs as she starts snapping on their leads. 'You're pure delights.' She turns back at the door. 'Anyway, joke's on you. I fancied a wander.'

As the noise of their departure dies down, I finish preparing a tea tray for our client and take it through to the salon. When I return, a short, balding man is poking at the coffeemaker.

'May I be of assistance?'

The man whirls round, then surveys me up and down. 'What are you, then? Personal barista, is it?' He sniggers.

'I am the butler.'

'Do you folks come with the house?'

'If you are a guest, you will be more comfortable in the salon with your host.' I gesture towards the hall. 'I will bring you coffee shortly.'

'Right-o, Major Butler.' He executes a sloppy salute. 'Lead on, Macbeth.'

As we walk, I think about the various ornaments I would enjoy repurposing as a murder weapon. A brass doorstop shaped like a hedgehog offers particularly pleasing possibilities. The charming daydream accompanies me as I deliver the guest, prepare coffee, then deliver that, too, and finally return to the kitchen. But before I can make a start on dinner the cough starts up again, bringing with it a wave of fatigue that drops me into a chair.

All I want is to lie down and not move for an hour. I think I could even *nap*. But at least for now there's no one to pretend for or make excuses to, so I let myself lean over the table, head pillowed on my arms.

Verity is becoming significantly less oblivious, so, when we return home, I will need to switch from claiming the cough must be the dogs to saying it is hay-fever. Or should I say I have picked something up, but feel fine, so it is probably nothing to worry about? When the time comes to tell the truth, I can go to the GP, then pretend to be sent for tests . . . Verity never has to know the true timeline of my diagnosis since pancreatic cancer is often largely asymptomatic, and that is where the rest of it started. If she looks it up, it won't seem like a lie. It is a pity, but if Verity finds out I have been withholding two critical pieces of information, she will rightly wonder what else I am not telling her, and neither of us can afford for her to second-guess me at every turn.

If only we could advance the investigation into Reenie's disappearance with a lead that has nothing to do with Christophe's death, it would soften the blow of my secrecy *and* direct Verity's ire away from the possibility that I had something to do with what happened to her sister. We just need to identify the right suspect.

Over the years the police have written up Gavin Pieper for a few minor public order incidents and handed down one formal caution, but he has no criminal record. It isn't a foolproof indicator that he's not responsible, though twenty-five years in the Sisterhood has taught me that it is pretty reliable.

For the same reason, Charles Temple looks unlikely. However, his family's money and connections could have put paid to cautions or charges for minor offences – or even more serious ones, if there was little hard evidence. But if that were the case, I'd have expected to see a note in Reenie's file – the presence of a key suspect in a murder case at the scene of another serious crime wouldn't have gone unremarked. There is no sign of alcohol or drug issues in Temple's life, and of course he has no money troubles. His LinkedIn indicates he has worked at the same firm since graduation, gradually rising through the ranks. He married seven years ago and now has a kid. I went through his rubbish a few times and found no signs of mental health issues that could point to a guilty conscience.

Gavin Pieper, on the other hand, goes through a fair amount of alcohol every week, regularly takes sleeping pills and has had on-and-off money troubles since he left home. He has never married or, from what I can make out from girlfriends' social media, stayed in a relationship for long. He changes jobs regularly. But then the same can be said for the mother's ex-boyfriend.

TJ's first statement, taken two days after Reenie failed to come home, mentions her having been in a foul mood with him for weeks before her disappearance. His view was that, fed up with everything and everyone after her break-up with Gavin, she had gone off with someone she met at the party and would be back soon. It is clear that the officer who recorded the statement agreed.

TJ's next statement, taken five days after her disappearance, is a mix of fear and apology for not having been suitably panicked from the start.

The third statement heavily implies he would have broken up with the girls' mother if he hadn't felt too guilty to do it with Reenie still missing.

By the fourth statement, some months later, he had moved out of the family home and his words were resigned and weary. Perhaps a good front, but nothing in TJ's records chimes with him being adept at deceit. Still, after twenty-five years, I know that people don't wear their evil on their face.

All things considered, I am not convinced that Verity has identified the best suspects in her sister's case as opposed to the most obvious ones. But I understand that – and the desperation to believe you must be able to unravel the disaster that wrecked your life if you just keep looking: the need to ignore the possibility that you might never find any answers.

Barking announces Verity's imminent return, and I force myself back to my feet just before she crashes into the kitchen, setting up a frankly impressive racket as she feeds her charges again. Distracted by trying not to cough into my cooking, I don't realize what she's doing until it's too late.

When I turn to set the platter of grilled vegetables on the counter, I find a leg of ham already sitting there. A large chunk has been roughly chopped out of it. Beside the ham is a crumpled pile of packaging. *Jamón Ibérico de Bellota*.

Verity is sprawled on the floor, petting two of the dogs, then switching to the other two, then back again. They all,

Verity included, have looks of dazed bliss on their faces. I have no idea why. Four empty dog bowls are sitting along the counter.

'What have you done to the ham?' I demand.

Verity grimaces. 'Was I supposed to mix it with something? I looked, but I couldn't find any mention on the nutrition schedule, so I just chopped it up.' She shakes her head. 'Rich people, huh?'

'You fed the ham to the dogs.' I sag back against the counter, rubbing at my temples. 'Verity, that is a top-quality leg of Iberico ham. It's worth about four thousand pounds.'

Her eyes go wide. 'These people are cray-cray.'

I shudder. 'Never, ever use that detestable term in my hearing again.' I shake my head. 'There was a guest in here earlier – he must have brought the ham as a present and put it in the fridge when I was out of the room, not realizing he'd used the dog-fridge.'

Verity stares at me in horror. 'Are they going to take it out of my wages? What if they fire me? That'll screw our cover story.'

'I shall take care of it,' I say with a sigh. 'There is no way to dress the ham to hide the fact you've made both a figurative and literal dogs' dinner of it, but, if I serve some of it carved, then use part in a dish tomorrow, our client doesn't have to know.'

When Verity practically melts with gratitude, I feel a sudden and ridiculous welling of affection.

'Set out a coffee tray, then go and pick me some fresh mint from the herb patch,' I say, as I get to work rescuing the ham.

A few minutes later, something nudges my elbow. Glancing down, I see a cup of tea and a packet of allergy pills.

'Pru?'

I look round to find Verity hovering by the garden door. She smiles, then whisks herself away outside.

I turn back to the sink with a smile of my own.

Verity

I am about to carry out my second kill: my first pro bono case – and my first serial rapist. It's been five months since his last assault and, according to his target file, he's due for his next. Today, Pru and I will make sure he never gets the chance.

'Does the Sisterhood assign pro bono cases in the order they're registered, or is it about urgency?' I ask as we wander away from Winchester historic centre towards the target's house. 'Do targets get bumped up the list if they're an imminent risk? Ha! Bumped up for bumping off!'

Pru performs the world's weariest eye-roll. 'There will always be too many predators and not enough of us,' she says, ignoring my brilliant witticism.

'I guess it would be hard to keep the Sisterhood secret if it was too big, not to mention it would be pretty suspicious if all the paedophiles and serial rapists had fatal accidents in a single year . . . But what if someone's on the list and they commit another terrible crime before we get to them?'

Pru doesn't answer. I try to focus on the pretty houses lining the street we're on instead of thinking about how it would feel if I was assigned a target but my kill came just a week, a day, an hour too late for his final victim.

I shudder and force my mind back to the present as we

turn into the target's drive. It takes less than a minute for Pru to jemmy the battered old lock on the garage door, then I pull it up to waist height and together we duck inside. *Breaking and entering*, my brain supplies, though we haven't technically broken anything yet. Also, we're here to kill the owner, so . . .

'Verity,' hisses Pru, who's already over by the target's e-bike charger, swapping the power cable for our off-brand version, carefully frayed where the wire connects to the plug.

We spent hours last week ensuring that this combination of cable plus charger produced a spark within a minute of being connected to the relevant make and model of e-bike.

While Pru tackles the cable and charger, I take an ancient extension cord out of a sealed bag, fumbling clumsily in my double layer of plastic gloves as I shove the plug into the wall socket then connect every appliance in the garage to it, including the e-bike charger. When the fire investigators find this set-up, their only question is likely to be 'How on earth did he not burn the place down before?'

As Pru gathers old rags and boxes of paper, lining them up next to the extension cord, I loosen the screws on the door into the house so that, when the knob is turned, it will come off the bolt, preventing it from opening. Then we each collect a bottle of flammable liquid and loosen the top, placing the bottles where they're most likely to be knocked over by a man panicking in a garage on fire.

Leaving Pru to check my work on the door knob, I poke about until I find a pair of rusting wire hangers in a dusty corner. I brought some in a second sealed plastic bag in my backpack, just in case, but it's safer to use his. Moving over to the garage door, I start manoeuvring the hangers into place, ready to jam the door shut behind the target when he enters. I keep expecting Pru to slip past me, but, when I glance back, she's still standing in the middle of the garage, staring at the target's car . . . and staring and . . .

'I still look in every open garage I see, as if the car will just be sitting there one day, with damage to the front that hasn't been repaired but is somehow so distinctive there might as well be a label saying, "This is the car that killed Hope," ' Pru had told me when she finally opened up about her daughter.

I just didn't realize she meant it quite so literally. It tugs at something inside me. I do this – not staring-at-cars, obviously, but it's the same thing as letting myself believe a news story is the universe's way of telling me to search Charles Temple's garage. It's strange to realize Pru really *is* exactly like me in some ways. I mean, I know she told me, but now I *get* it.

'Pru?' I call, keeping my voice soft. Her vulnerability aches inside me.

She blinks, then purpose fills her eyes again. 'Well, let's not stand about all day!' She marches to the garage door and peers out, then ducks away into the drive to keep watch while I let the door crunch down on to the hangers behind me.

We stride across the drive as if we're meant to be there. Pru coughs into her elbow as she bends to slip a receipt for the off-brand charger into the recycling box at the mouth of the drive. As she straightens, I see her clock the tall dark-haired woman standing two houses down on the opposite side of the street, a mess of shopping bags at her feet. Pru leads me quickly in the opposite direction. I can't help casting a worried look back.

'Do you want to show her your face?' Pru hisses.

I snap my head around and hurry on, then realize I'm being conspicuous and drop back to stroll beside Pru. Despite our leisurely pace, Pru alternates between rubbing her shoulder and coughing into her elbow.

'How are you feeling?'

'Better, thanks to your pills.'

I eye her dubiously. 'Are you sure you shouldn't see a doctor? It's no good if you end up keeling over. We both know I can't manage by myself.'

Yes, heaven forfend you are ever inconvenienced by anyone else's troubles, Mum hisses, the words licking the inside of my brain like acid.

'You won't have to worry about that for a while,' Pru says sanguinely. 'Though I'll be damned if you're not ready when the time comes.'

We walk on in companionable silence.

'Good job,' she says, like last time. The only recognition that, once again, we've set the stage for a man to die.

We visit Winchester Cathedral and enjoy the leafy streets around the city centre for another hour, then return to our cover job. The dogs are delighted to see me, and the client is delighted to see Pru, but still my skin prickles as if a police officer is about to jump out from behind one of the antique standing-lamps to arrest me.

When we bring after-dinner coffee into the 'Green Salon', as we've learnt to call the main living room, our client is sprawled on a fancy settee that looks both impressively expensive and deeply uncomfortable. A massive flatscreen is tuned to the news. The sound is off, but the footage tells us everything we need to know. The camera zooms out from a fire-gutted garage to show the wash of soot staining the wall of the house beside it. The banner confirms that the report is live from Winchester.

I shoot Pru a meaningful look, opening my mouth to comment, but she gives a quick, angry shake of her head.

'I'd like you to check the smoke alarms before you finish tonight,' the client says, as Pru sets a cappuccino on the coffee table beside her.

Pru inclines her head, then turns smartly on her heels and marches back into the hall. I trot after her, astonished when she actually follows through.

'We said we would, so we will. In any case, there may be CCTV monitoring us.'

When Pru eventually judges us done, we head upstairs.

Soon, I'm curled up in bed, staring through the open window. Everything is bathed in moonlight. It's a cool, clear night after a warm, cloudless day and ground-mist is rising in front of the distant woods. The cathedral earlier – all towering columns and stone-lacework ceilings, dark wooden pews and light slanting through stained-glass windows – was magnificent, but this is just as beautiful.

Something stirs in the mist. A shadow, looming out of the woods.

For a moment, my chest tightens with fear. I must be dreaming a monster stalking out of the trees to punish me for the man I killed earlier.

A stag appears, antlers raised as he surveys the house

and the silent lawns and gardens. Then another head appears. A doe. Then another. And another. And, finally, a cluster of tiny fawns.

My breath catches. Suddenly there are tears on my face.

It's like the world is giving me a gift – a reward to show me that the terrible thing I did today was necessary, even if it was wrong. It was only this afternoon, but already it feels unreal – dim and distant, as if it happened a year ago.

Neither Pru nor I believe killing is 'good', but we *did* do a 'good job' today – everything exactly as per the Rules. It isn't justice, but leaving that man to commit more terrible crimes wouldn't have been justice, either. Maybe all we did was exchange one injustice for another, but better this than the alternative, so I can live with the fact I'm now a double murderer.

Thank God I've got Pru. Even though it's other members of the Sisterhood acting as judge and jury in determining our targets, I'm glad I don't have to play executioner alone. I know that, before long, she'll retire and I'll be working solo, but she'll still be part of my life. I'll turn up at her kitchen door and she'll feed me, and if I start doubting what I'm doing, she'll tell me to shape up. It's different being told that by someone who believes I can do it.

Back when she climbed into my car the night I nearly got myself arrested going after Charles Temple, I couldn't imagine ever trusting her. But I do.

Across the misty lawn, the deer disappear into the woods once more.

I curl down into this strange bed in this strange room in my strange new life and, for the first time since Reenie vanished, I sleep without a single nightmare.

Pru

I had hoped the intensity of an away-job with a cover story to maintain would wear Verity out, dampening her interest in chirping away as if I've the slightest interest in the rubbish that goes through her head on a moment-to-moment basis. And yet she is still at it a week later, even while wriggling over the windowsill of my upstairs bathroom, legs still inside, though her upper body is now hanging over the roof.

'What do you mean, there's a manual?' Verity puffs.

'Which of the words are you having trouble with?' I inject the question with my most long-suffering tone.

Verity glances down at me, then returns to walking her hands along the slope of the roof over the kitchen. 'The Sisterhood seriously has a manual on how to push people off high buildings?'

'It also covers defenestration and balconies, so I would start with that section.'

'Stay down there, OK? I am not interested in being your practice dummy.'

'It is for our next job, but don't tempt me with the idea of a demonstration.'

Verity ignores me to focus on drawing her legs out of the window and dropping her feet down without a thud.

She is not successful. With a groan, she slithers to the edge of the roof, then climbs down the trellis. She jumps the last foot, then turns to take the ring-bound manual I am holding out.

'*A Guide to Accidents in High Places*,' she reads from the cover. 'This is an actual thing that exists. Isn't it risky to have a physical copy?'

'Riskier than dozens of digital versions? It only takes one hack—'

'Or one burglary.'

I look down my nose at her. 'Burglars don't usually steal books, unless they are antique. In any case, we keep our manuals in lockboxes when not in use, with details on file with the Sisterhood about what, where, and any PINs, so they can be disposed of safely, should any of us become indisposed.'

I turn away to the patio, where I have set out lemonade for Verity, a honey-ginger tea to soothe my throat, and rum-raisin brownies for us both. I try but fail to resist the urge to cough into my elbow as I settle down with my back to my favourite flowerbed, where purple-black cranesbills have taken over now that the black tulips and hyacinths have gone over.

'Who wrote this?' Verity drops down opposite me and glugs unpleasantly from her glass as she opens the manual. 'Is there a sequel on pushing people in front of trains?'

'One of the early members of the Sisterhood was an expert accident investigator.' I cough into my elbow again, then take a sip from my mug.

'How come you're still coughing now you're back home? Is it hay-fever?'

'Probably. I shall get myself a pill in a moment while you sit and study quietly, rather than doing your level best to get right up my nose, as if attempting to excavate the last of my patience.'

Verity mumbles into the manual as she reaches for a brownie. '*Are* there any other murder manuals?' she asks, spraying crumbs.

'*Verity*. Manners.'

She makes a *meh-meh-meh* noise. 'Actually, park that question. Who are the other . . . architects of the Sisterhood? Are they, like—'

I clear my throat. It sets me coughing.

'Karma!' sing-songs Verity.

'Yes, twenty-five years of homicide earned me you.'

Verity blows a raspberry at me. 'But seriously . . . what's the origin story of the Sisterhood?' She rolls her eyes at my confusion. 'Who started the whole thing? Who's the woman behind the Rules?'

My fingers reach across the table to the spot where Hope, forgetting to put something under a drawing, incised a pattern of flowers and leaves through her page and into the wood. If I told Verity, she would probably imagine I was angry about Hope's carelessness, even if now I am glad for any mark my daughter made on the world. I doubt she would guess I have always loved this happy little accident.

'There is a lot of yapping for someone who is meant to be reading.'

'You've been teaching me to multitask,' says the wretch I've chosen to mentor.

'I hadn't realized I had succeeded.' I move to the herb

bed beside the table and start weeding around the just-budding monkshood. 'The Sisterhood was started by a small group of women from across the criminal justice world – and I do mean world. These experts, and the ones who came after them, took care to codify and pass on their knowledge in manuals like that one.' I tug a tuft of grass out of the flowerbed, then begin carefully pulling up herb-robert from between tender new fronds of water hemlock and young stems of deadly nightshade.

'But how did it begin? Did a bunch of colleagues seriously just sit down one day, and someone goes, "Let's form a secret society to murder people?" '

'Our founders were at a point of despair about all the dreadful men they could not stop by legal means. As long-term, trusted colleagues, they made a pact to trade kills so they could each close the one case they couldn't let go unresolved.'

The lily-of-the-valley have finished flowering, but the rhododendron behind is just starting, while the oleander is yet to bloom. I clear old leaves from beneath it.

'That's obviously the origin of the "one free kill", but how did the Sisterhood become a whole Thing if the plan was just to trade one kill each?'

I open my mouth to reply, but a cough erupts instead. Giving up on the weeding, I sink down at the table again, applying myself to my tea while Verity occupies herself with the manual – and casting worried glances at me.

'The first thing was to carry out each other's kills and make sure everyone got away with it,' I say, when I finally have my breath back. 'They agreed that they would all keep a piece of evidence of each other's guilt both to prove their loyalty and to show they would never turn on their friends. And they didn't. The proof became a bond of trust – and a symbol of what they could accomplish together.'

Verity lounges back in her chair. 'You could have led with this when you ordered me to write out my confession. But that would have been too easy, wouldn't it, so you decided to go with "Oh, by the by, Verity, you must write down every detail of your murderous endeavours to go with the proof I've taken of your crimes. Nothing to worry about. It's only life in prison if someone finds out." '

I give her a dour look. 'Don't ever mimic someone's voice or accent as part of a job.'

Verity throws her hands in the air. 'See? Instead of, "I don't sound like that," you go with the insult.'

'It was a fact. A statement of the obvious. And you know how I hate those.'

Verity grins. 'Are you clocking this?' She points at me, then herself, then me again. 'Top bantz. Guess we're mates now.'

'I have no idea what "top bantz" are – they sound revolting. And I have never been anyone's "mate". I am your mentor. It is a venerable role – named for the adviser to Odysseus.'

'OK, let's both stick to English, but I'll make it old school for you. We are now *friends*,' Verity enunciates slowly and carefully, 'because this – right here' – she does the detestable pointing thing again – 'is banter. We are bantering.'

I rub at the headache behind my eyes, doing my best to ignore the surge of something that might be frustrated fondness. 'I do not banter, Verity. You do sarcasm, and I do a spectrum of tones from weary irritation to thinly veiled homicidal rage.'

'Top bantz,' says my horrible mentee. 'Right here.'

'I'm going to pick some monkshood to put in your salad,' I reply, but it is half-hearted at best. Verity's comment about being friends stung, though she couldn't have known it would, because how can we be friends when there's so much I am choosing to keep from her? If nothing else, I could have opened up about my history in the Sisterhood, or about Hope.

I get back to my feet, but Verity props her foot on the edge of an azalea pot to block my path. 'The herby goodness can wait until you've finished the story about how the Sisterhood formed.'

'Monkshood is a poison,' I grit out, 'as you should know by now. The other lesson in store is that, if you do not move your leg, I will demonstrate the self-defence technique fondly known as, "No one has ever stood in my way once I've kicked their kneecap in."'

Verity's face lights up. 'Poisons and violence! Now we're cooking with gas.'

I give her my most withering glare, though there's warmth in my chest. I should tell her now about Christophe, get it out of the way, but Verity's smile is so easy and happy that I can't bring myself to spoil the moment. 'Have you had any thoughts about Charles Temple?' I ask instead, and feel my insides squirm with shame, while the guilt needles and needles in my chest.

'You mean, other than the hammer one?' Verity winces away from my attempt to put the Evil Eye on her. 'I've got a Google Alert on him, but he's . . .' She shrugs. 'There's nothing *there* to investigate. His family have a million properties, but they're all crawling with servants and tradespeople. Doesn't mean Reenie's not buried somewhere on one of them, but where would I even start? The reason I was going to try his garage was in case he took a trophy.'

I roll my eyes. 'If Charles Temple is a serial killer taking trophies, where are his other victims?'

Verity raises her hands. 'Maybe he goes after homeless people now. Or he only kills when he's abroad – he's always travelling.'

'And you think no questions would have been raised by now if bodies kept dropping wherever such a rich and prominent person went? While a lot of people can be bought, it is by no means all. If he had been killing on his travels, someone would have dug into his record, then they would have come across your sister.'

She deflates. 'So why are you asking about him?'

'Because I want you to think about why he is on your list of key suspects. Why not Nathan?'

Verity rakes her hands through her hair. 'I looked into him as well, but he's Temple's cousin, so it's the same story. Anyway, he was more interested in me than in Reenie, so why would it be him? Why not anyone else at the party rather than just the group in Charles Temple's room?'

I raise my eyebrows.

'That's too many people.' She doodles a long, winding path down the margin of her notebook. 'I guess, now I've got the list from the police file, I should start working my way through it.' She throws her pen down. 'How do you stand not knowing about Hope after all this time?'

'I want the right answer so I can do the right thing.' My

hand traces the imprint of Hope's design. 'I want to win, Verity. And one day I will.'

I *will* find a way to prove that Claire Jeynes did it. And then I will find a way to make sure she dies before I do. If that means breaking the Rules, so be it.

It *has* to mean something that her life went off the rails in the same month Hope was killed only two miles from Claire's family home. It *has* to mean something that she passed her driving test not long after her seventeenth birthday and a brand-new car was registered in her name shortly thereafter, but it never received an MOT. Instead, within a year it had been officially declared 'off road'. It can't be a coincidence.

'Finding the man who killed your sister and taking your one free kill will not give you your old life back or turn you into the person you would have been,' I say gently. 'But this version of Verity isn't so bad.' I force myself to my feet, gathering up our empty cups. 'You'll be better still if you stop pestering your weary mentor and, instead, start practising climbing the garage wall, crawling over the roof and climbing down the other side.'

Verity eyes the garage with misgiving. 'What happens when I fall and break my neck and you have to explain this to the police and the Sisterhood?'

I smile blithely. 'Accidents happen, don't they? Especially when we are around.'

'I thought you were training me to make good choices,' Verity mutters, but she heads over to the garage all the same. 'If this is as good as it gets, we're both in trouble.'

Verity

There have been a lot of surprises in my training, most of them unpleasant. The key exception is Pru's cooking, which is fantastic. Of course, she has to go and spoil half our meals with pop quizzes or, like this evening, demanding I revisit the night of Reenie's disappearance over and over again. It's an odd feeling to finally find someone almost as obsessed with solving Reenie's disappearance as I am. Despite Pru's iron determination to do her duty to the Sisterhood at all times, I know it's more than that. But is it just about me as her mentee, or does she feel some personal responsibility to Reenie, now the case is in front of her?

'Tell me about the behaviour of the people you met that night,' Pru says as she serves new potatoes in parsley and garlic butter on to my plate.

I shrug. 'I know you're fishing for fresh suspects, but we really did just hang with the three boys from the limo. Charles Temple was charming and kept his hands to himself until Reenie made the first move – but that was later. When we first got to the party, he introduced us to a few people. Got us drinks. We all danced together in the university hall, then we went to his room as a group. It was a few hours before he and Reenie got wrapped up in each other. Christophe spent most of the night glaring at them, so I'd have suspected him, if he hadn't died that night.'

I spear a potato and try to savour the flavours exploding across my tongue, but I can *see* Pru's frustration in the sudden tension across her shoulders.

'That's it. And, yes, I tried the sensory technique you taught me to put myself back "in the moment".' I draw air quotes around the words. 'But I didn't remember anything new, unless you think there's something in knowing the colour of the sofa Reenie and Charles Temple were snogging on when I left.'

I take a bite of scallop, but the conversation sours the sweetness, even though the seafood is delicate and moist and perfectly seasoned. I didn't know what that meant before, when I heard it on cooking programmes, but then I met Pru.

'Is it a bad sign we haven't turned up anything new in Reenie's case?' I ask before I can rethink whether I want to know the answer.

'It is early days.' Pru clears her throat as if she wants to cough, then tops up our water glasses and takes a series of careful sips.

'But when do I have to accept that it's just not going to happen? That I'm going to be like you – working away for the Sisterhood but never calling in my one free kill.'

Pru pats her napkin at her lips, then presses it to her mouth as she coughs again, tapping at her chest as if something has gone down the wrong way. 'It is far too soon for that. And if I have not lost faith, why should you?'

'If you've not lost faith, isn't that denial? Is that why you never talk about new lines of inquiry in Hope's case, only what you did at the start, before you joined the Sisterhood? Or is it that you don't trust me yet?'

Pru gives me a steady look, then stands and walks out of the room. I wait, but she doesn't return. I stare at the arch into the hall.

Pru is often sharp and easy to irritate, but I've never known her to lose her rag to the point of walking out on me. Then again, every time I've raised the question of how she copes with knowing the person who killed her daughter is still out there after all this time, she's changed the subject or ordered me to run laps or started rattling things around in the sink to drown me out.

I trust her, and I've been telling myself that she trusts me – and she does, but only up to a point. It's reasonable – sensible, even – for her to withhold stuff she's not ready to share while I'm still learning not to be a total disaster. On the other hand, she's always telling me to work things out for myself. Maybe she left me here to see what I'll do.

I don't yet know the PIN for the filing cabinet, and I can't imagine what else is worth nosing into. My eyes rove around . . . then settle on the roof of Pru's car, just visible above the garden wall.

The one suspicious thing that's happened since I started training is the sudden day off. Pru said she was having a quiet time at home with friends, but it never rang true. Sitting out in the drive is the way to find out.

I pad to the sideboard and pick up Pru's keys, casting a wary look towards the hall. Then I realize how stupid I'm being. If she catches me, I can say I thought I'd left something in the car.

Marching out of the garden door and along the path, I beep the car open before I can second-guess myself, then slide behind the wheel, insert the key fob and tap the start button. The engine rumbles to life as I scroll the display to the satnav function, then to history, then back to the correct date. It feels squirmy and wrong, but Pru will probably be proud of me for taking some initiative.

And there it is. She *did* take the car out that day – and not just round the corner for milk, but miles away. Almost an hour. I memorize the postcode of her destination, then turn the car off and hurry back to the kitchen.

It's still empty, so I take out my phone to look up the postcode. Footsteps in the hall make me click it off before the search loads.

Pru strides back into the kitchen and places a folder by my elbow. 'Hope's file.'

I feel my eyes go wide as I stare down at it, then up at Pru, withering inside at the fact that she's chosen to take this leap with me when I've just pried into her private life, as if I've any right to know what she did on her day off. True to form, as soon as things start going well, what do I do? Set about blowing it all up – literally at the moment our relationship starts to grow from infuriated mentor and worst-ever-mentee into something more.

'A fresh pair of eyes would be much appreciated,' Pru says as she retakes her seat, tapping at her chest again.

My heart hammers against my ribs. Pru may be the most ruthlessly pragmatic person I've ever met, but this isn't pragmatism. It's trust. I feel . . . honoured. I've heard people say that, and thought it was snobby bullshit. But I get it now. It sounds stupid even in my head, but I feel *bigger* somehow, because Pru's not just *giving* me this honour. She's telling me I've *earned* it.

I swallow down the guilt of what I've just been up to and open the file. I'm going to be worthy of the trust she's giving me. I will *not* ruin this job, this relationship, this life I'm building.

This time it's all going to be different.

Pru

For Verity's third kill, we have been sent to Prague: our first international job. Our cover story places us with a party of businessmen, me in the role of personal chef and Verity as maid. As for our target, until today, he made his living organizing the filming of child sexual abuse then loading it on to various paid-for sites – then re-uploading it under a slightly different name every time it was reported and taken down. Ten minutes ago, we ensured the next takedown is the last. As for the rest of those involved . . . I have to hope the Sisterhood is adding them to the target list and, over time, we will ensure a permanent takedown of more than videos.

Now, with our target lying dead on the cobbles behind us, we wind our way through crowds of tourists. The plan was to defenestrate him, and we did. And then some.

Prague is beautiful, I tell myself. *Look at the beautiful buildings. Let them calm you.*

'I'm sorry! How many times do I have to say it?'

I ignore the beautiful buildings and stalk ahead as Verity patters along behind me, squeaking out a steady stream of apologies.

'Anyway, it worked out, didn't it? The right person's dead. We haven't been arrested. No one's chasing us. It's hardly a disaster.'

I lengthen my stride, but Verity skitters after me even faster.

'I mean, it didn't exactly go to plan, but it was . . . in the right ballpark.'

I turn on my heel so suddenly that Verity nearly runs into me. 'Our target went over that balcony like a competitive long-jumper.'

'Exactly! It looked like he jumped, rather than being pushed.'

'It was *meant* to look like an accident. Rule 8 – *Don't draw attention* – went even further out of the window than he did!'

It would be counterproductive to mention the bigger problem: that I recognized a face in the crowd at the scene. Why did the Sisterhood have to send a second observer to report back on Verity's progress so soon after the last check-in? Surely Nora put in a positive report after Winchester – that was a textbook performance – but now . . .

My hands clench into fists as I march off down a narrow street between high-end shops, weaving between tourists and fed-up locals. It's unreasonably hot, and a dull ache has been thumping in my right shoulder since we arrived in Prague.

Until this morning, things were going smoothly – no Iberico hams have been fed to any animals, and I've generally kept our client and his merry band of business partners too well fed and drunk for trouble. One tried ogling Verity, but after he spent the next day and a half in his en suite, thanks to a moderate amount of laxatives in his water bottle, that was the end of the problem.

Today, our first half-day off duty, we were supposed to

quietly dispatch our target while touring the sights. Now we are hurrying away from the scene of a death that is, at best, weird. Questions will be asked, and we need to ensure they're not asked about us.

'I don't know why you're so cross. It's not like defenestrating someone was ever going to be entirely quiet and clean. Mess was guaranteed, and that's a violation of Rule 4. Or did you forget—'

'I never forget the Rules! And I have never broken them! But now there is YOU!' The ache in my shoulder is growing unbearable so I march over to a bench by a fountain and cast myself down.

A moment later Verity joins me.

'Even apart from the fact that Rule 8 most definitely *does* apply to the defenestration itself, it *also* applies to your performance afterwards. I haven't seen anyone ham it up like that since a friend I never quite forgave took me to the pantomime to "cheer me up" the Christmas after Hope died.'

Verity crosses her arms defensively. 'I was giving you something to work with.'

'No one benefits from working with a headache, Verity!'

A flock of pigeons explodes off the statue in the middle of the fountain, showering excrement over a staggering line of men in matching stag-do T-shirts. My mood lifts, just a little.

'It's normal to be a bit hysterical after you've just seen someone leap off a balcony. I think it sold the whole thing.'

'Quiet, dazed shock would have done it without tempting anyone to film us.'

Verity's eyes go wide. 'Someone filmed us?'

'Your situational awareness is diabolical. Worse even

than your CCTV skills.' I sigh. 'No one got our faces, though they have probably captured some of your shrieking.'

Verity groans. 'I can *feel* the adrenalin draining out of me.' She sits up. 'I need sugar. Sugar's good for shock.'

'If you were in shock, you would not still be operating at a volume that may well be doing permanent damage to my eardrums.'

'I'm getting us ice cream. What flavour do you want?'

'Whichever one is quiet.'

Verity mutters something under her breath as she strides off. I tip my head back and try to relish the sun.

Today's mess will be all over the news, not to mention social media and the wider internet. Constance will have to include that in her report. Still, the advantage of a tourist hotspot is that it is easy to get lost in a crowd. No one stopped us on the way out to insist we stay to talk to the police: there was no point, with so many eager gawpers telling anyone who would listen that they had seen our target launch himself over the balcony. As for him, there are distinct advantages to a target being instantly and thoroughly dead. The momentum of Verity's enthusiasm with snatching away the elasticated tripwire propelled him so far he inevitably arced down head first. No chance of telling a soul what preceded his brief and fatal flight. Constance will be clear on those points, too, at least.

Verity clears her throat. 'I got you pistachio and hazelnut, but you can have my coconut and strawberry if you prefer.'

I hold out my hand without opening my eyes. 'I do not prefer.'

Verity presses the cone into my hand, then drops down beside me so heavily the bench bounces. My bag tips over, spilling the contents across the cobbles. We bend to pile everything back in. I grit my teeth when I see Verity pick up the packet of painkillers that I reluctantly allowed the GP to prescribe. I have resisted taking any, but I may have to concede defeat. Verity looks down at the box as I snatch it from her hand, stuffing it into the recesses of my bag.

'Sit. Still,' I order.

We eat in silence. The mood, like the ice cream, softens then starts to thaw.

Although today was a mess, Verity is applying herself to training and, considering where she started, there is a lot to be pleased about. A mixed report from Constance isn't the end of the world when Nora's report will have been positive.

I cast a sidelong glance at Verity and find her staring up at the buildings around us, tongue darting out every now and then to catch drips of melting ice cream. I don't think I have ever seen her look so . . . it is not quite happy or relaxed. At ease, maybe. Despite everything, she feels safe. Because I am here. A flash of emotion in my chest, like a physical pulse in my blood.

I picked Verity for many reasons. Guilt, sympathy, the gravitational pull of her misery. I didn't expect to develop this foolish streak of fondness, for goodness' sake.

She glances over at me and grins, saluting me with her cone, then quickly bending to slurp revoltingly at a trickle of melted strawberry ice cream.

I look away, tugging my shirt straight. I should have

told her about Christophe by now, but perhaps this can be the moment.

I clear my throat. 'Let's talk about Gavin and his alibi,' I say, though shame is twisting in my stomach before the words are out. I want to pretend it is too much of a risk to tell her without a solid line of inquiry leading away from Christophe. After all, if I can soften the blow, I should. But the truth is that I don't want to disturb the ease between us.

Verity sighs. 'Why do you have to spring this stuff on me? We were having a moment.' She stuffs the last of her cone into her mouth. 'But I'm never going to turn down a chance to find my sister,' she mumbles as she chews, swallows. 'So, how do we tackle this alibi thing?'

I raise my eyebrows.

She huffs and slumps back. 'I guess that, unless he had a huge fight with his brother, I can't expect *him* to retract; I could check out the brother's social media and, if there are recent family pics with him and Gavin together, that's probably a no-go. But the brother's girlfriend might be a different matter.'

I make a 'go on' gesture.

'I could search for her on social media.'

I make the gesture again, but faster and with extra anger.

Verity slides out her phone. 'Jeez. She's active on Facebook, as if she's fifty.' She scrolls aggressively. 'Bollocks. She married the brother, so that's probably that.' She scrolls some more. 'Girls' night out. Movie. Cat. Cat. More cat. Even more cat. Happy Divorce Day To Me.' She looks at me, eyes wide. 'Do I just . . . message her? Or do I like some of her posts first?'

'How will that persuade her to tell you about her ex-brother-in-law?'

'Honest approach. Got it.' She takes a deep breath. 'What should I say? What if she just ignores my message?'

'There may be nothing to tell, or she may be unwilling to talk, but you won't know until you *send the message*. And just the one, Verity,' I add wearily. 'No harassing her if she doesn't get back to you in two seconds.'

'Would I— No. Don't say it.' A moment later there's the *zwoop* of a message sending. 'Why don't we ever do this with Hope's case? I know I'm not likely to have a brainwave you and your mentor missed, but if it's helpful to go over it again and again with a new person listening, then I'm game, if you want to . . . share.'

I cross my legs, adjusting my skirt over my knees. 'Which bit of the case should we discuss?'

Verity stares at me in surprise. 'Well . . . what do you think happened with the car? It must have been damaged, so if it didn't go to a garage or a scrapyard – and I know you checked out stolen and burnt-out vehicles in the next six counties – did someone hide it in their garage for a while before getting it fixed?' She pulls a face. 'You'd need to give it months. Who could afford not to use their car for that long?'

I shrug. 'Rich people. Someone who went to prison. Or into a nursing home . . . Someone who had access to another car through a grandparent with dementia who couldn't drive any more . . .'

'You would have looked into changes in car registration and cars written off by insurers . . .' She looks over at me to check.

I nod. 'The police checked the relevant records, as well

as looking at locals newly insured on cars they didn't own.' I suppress a sigh and end up coughing instead.

Verity looks at me askance. 'Why's your hay-fever just as bad in Czechia, in a city?'

I take out my water bottle and sip. 'I didn't feel ill when it started, but there is a hundred-day tickly cough going round. It's rare for me to pick things up, but I *have* been unusually stressed lately.' I give her a pointed look.

Verity swivels to put her back to me. 'Rude.'

I wait her out. This takes precisely one minute and seventeen seconds.

'How about locals with a history of accidents? Drunk drivers?'

'The S—' The cough erupts again.

Verity reaches over to thump me on the back. 'Should we stop by a chemist? Get some cough lozenges or something?'

I nod as I reach for my water bottle again. The cough isn't getting worse yet, but it will. Just as there is a heaviness in my limbs like tiredness but . . . not. How long until the next set of symptoms?

There is so much to do. Verity is right to be frustrated about her sister's case – though not for the reasons she thinks. With any other mentor, there would be plenty of time. But if we don't make a breakthrough soon, will I be able to do what's needed when the time comes?

'The Sisterhood got me a list,' I croak, when I can speak again. 'I spent four years working through it.'

Verity picks at a mark on her jeans. 'If the Sisterhood's kills are meant to be about preventing other crimes, rather than revenge, then . . . It's already been fourteen years since Reenie. What has the man who killed her done to other girls in all that time?'

I could tell her right now that it is possible he hasn't done anything because I killed him.

If his death had some bearing on Reenie's disappearance, there will be some comfort for her in knowing that at least he hasn't hurt anyone else, just as the possibility has comforted me all these years. It is the uncertainty that needles and gnaws at me, and Verity has enough of that already. If only we could poke a hole in Gavin's alibi, she would have something tangible to hold on to when I complicate her grief all over again with the knowledge that the one time I might have violated Rule 6 – *no collateral damage* – it could have cost her sister her life. I don't know if Verity is ready to bear that yet. I don't know if I am ready to bear her fury and pain.

Though surely there is enough trust between us that Verity will not go straight for destruction – of our relationship, her place with the Sisterhood, the life she is starting to build . . .

I can't let another opportunity to tell her the truth go by. I open my mouth . . .

A child comes shrieking across the square, dashes past our bench and leaps into the fountain.

A wave splashes over our legs. The child's father hurries over, apologizing profusely in between attempts to get his sodden toddler out of the water, where she is now trying to swim laps.

Verity and I hurry away, neither pointing out that the

child launched herself into the air just like our target did earlier, though with a lot less blood and brain matter as a result.

'We've got another few hours for sightseeing, so we could go to the Mucha Museum.'

'What do you want to see, Verity?' I ask wearily, already knowing the answer.

'Well, if we went over the bridge to the park, we could see the tiny wooden church . . . and get another ice cream on the way back.'

'Why do you think you deserve a second ice cream? I am not convinced you deserved the first.'

'You know, you could try encouraging me. I respond well to positive feedback,' Verity lies.

'Liking compliments is not the same thing,' I tell her tartly. 'And the last thing you need is encouragement. But it so happens that another ice cream would be most soothing to my throat.'

Verity cheers and springs to her feet, offering me her hand. I try to scowl as she pulls me up, but my mouth refuses to cooperate.

I wonder how long I have with her. The thought pops into my mind with such a wave of longing I stumble.

I want to see Verity grow into the woman I know she could be. I want to see her find her feet in the Sisterhood. I want to see . . . everything. But I won't. And she'll have to manage without me, though she's nowhere near ready.

There's so much I need to do, but I *must* make sure Verity will be all right. More than that, I need to know she will be happy.

Verity

I've been creeping along Pru's dining-room walls all morning, slithering under the table, crawling from chair to chair, and each time I've managed to get myself caught on her latest CCTV set-up. I'm starting to think there's no solution.

'Please tell me you're cooking up a different type of torture for tomorrow,' I groan as I drag myself to my feet, trying to stretch out the ache in my back.

'Tomorrow I am busy, so you have the day off,' Pru says, brushing past me as she moves over to the window.

'How serious is the cough for you to want a break?'

Pru gives me a Look, then shimmies herself on to the windowsill, swivels her legs neatly through the gap and drops down into the flowerbed. 'After all the moaning and groaning you've been doing, I thought you would welcome a day of rest.'

I plop down behind the laptop to watch the live footage of her attempt to cross from the window to the door without being caught by the camera. 'You're up to something. I can feel it.'

'I have a life, Verity. It has largely been on hold for your training, but tomorrow I have a prior commitment.' Carefully, she lifts herself back on to the windowsill, crouching in the opening, then she reaches out . . . and slides belly down on to the table.

I gape as she inches herself across at an angle, sliding out over the carpet until she can lower her hands on to the seat of a chair halfway down the room. She balls herself on to the seat, then eases on to the floor, slithering under a side table then cutting a sharp corner around the door into the hall. All while staying invisible to the CCTV.

'I hate you,' I mumble at the laptop. Then give the camera a middle finger.

'Your turn,' Pru orders, marching back in and shooing me away.

I climb out of the window, then back in, repeating Pru's route across the furniture. 'Are you killing people behind my back?' I ask as I slide across the table.

The last time Pru gave me a day off she lied about staying home to see friends. I still haven't looked up the postcode she travelled to, but I have to wonder if she's going back. And, if so, why.

I start transferring myself from the table to the chair. My leg slips.

'BEEEEEP!' Pru shouts as my left foot touches the floor.

I crumple over the chair and scream into the cushioned seat. When I finally drag myself back to my feet, Pru is watching me morosely.

'So, is it a job tomorrow?' I pout in the way that makes her look like she's considering tearing my throat out with her teeth. 'Couldn't I come and observe?'

'There is no job. I *do* have friends, you know.' She clocks my expression and snaps the laptop closed. 'Your astonishment about the concept of people enjoying my company is not endearing you to me. You should consider making yourself absent.'

I swipe sweaty hair off my forehead. 'See you Monday, I guess.'

Pru is already striding away down the hall, so I gather up my stuff and let myself out.

'Nice reassurance,' I grumble as I stomp down the garden path. 'I'm definitely going to come to my next CCTV exercise feeling ready to smash it.' I pull out my phone, ready to tap in the postcode of the place Pru went on her last 'day off' . . . then put it away again.

Two months ago, I would have looked up the postcode as petty revenge, but now it feels small and childish and stupid. *I* feel small and childish and stupid. Because I wanted Pru to say, *Never mind. You'll get it*. Or at least, *Have a great day off – you deserve some fun*. Which is a pathetic thing for a professional killer-in-training to want. It's not a wonder Pru is fed up with me. Even apart from the bit where I implied she was unlikeable and friendless.

Groaning, I let myself through the gate and crunch across the gravel.

The night air is fragrant and warm. Standing beside Boudicca, I tip my head back and look up at the stars. Reenie used to love reading our horoscopes. The year she turned thirteen, she whinged and whined until Mum gave in and bought the present she wanted. (Usually Mum chose what she wanted us to want, then pretended we'd asked for it until we half believed it, too.) Reenie's perfect present was this thing like a kaleidoscope, but instead of turning it to see different patterns, it showed how the stars moved through the sky at night.

From that year on, stars were her thing. A dress with a star pattern. A necklace of stars. The pair of tiny star earrings I got her to match.

The summer she disappeared, on a clear night like this one, I went up to bed expecting Reenie to be in our room, but it was empty. The bathroom was empty, too, and she wasn't in the living room, or the downstairs loo, or the kitchen. Finally, I poked my head out the garden door and there she was: lying on our tiny, overgrown lawn, staring up at the sky.

I padded over and stood looking down at her, but she kept her gaze on the stars. Eventually, I lay down beside her.

She raised her hand and traced a shape in the sky. And again, and again.

'Virgo,' she said.

I wriggled closer, pressing my head against hers so I could follow the line of her finger.

'You can see it all night in April and pretty much all night in May, but now it's . . .' She lowered her arm, pressing her hand to her chest as if something was hurting her.

'The virgin, right?'

Reenie made an odd noise beside me.

'Isn't it a bit stupid to name a sign star that when it's not like you can change your sign when you start having sex?'

Reenie flinched. 'It's more than that, you know.' Her voice was a hiss, making me flinch.

I rolled on to my side to look at her, but she was still staring up at the sky, her eyes glassy, as if she was on the verge of crying.

'Virgos are smart and practical and loyal.' Her voice was sharp, making me pull back. 'We like to help people.

We're perfectionists.' Her voice grew quieter and quieter. 'We hold ourselves and others to high standards.'

I curled back down, tucking my head on to her shoulder and wrapping an arm over her stomach. 'I guess Gavin was a crap Virgo to do something bad enough for you to dump him right before exams.'

Reenie stiffened, and for a minute I thought she might finally be ready to talk about him, but she just sniffed, her chin wobbling. I waited, but she didn't cry, just lay there breathing slow and shallow.

'Reenie, what—'

'It's none of your business,' she snapped.

I huffed and turned on to my back. 'Well, if you want to be a better Virgo than he is, you should stop being such a dick to everyone. Especially TJ. That isn't very "high standards" after all those driving lessons—'

She scrambled to her feet. 'He only did that to get what he wants!' she snarled. 'They're all liars, just waiting for the right moment to turn around and—' She shook her head. 'Why am I bothering? You don't understand *anything*.'

She stomped away. A moment later, the kitchen door slammed behind her. Though the air was still warm, there were goosebumps on my arms.

I blink, reeling back against Boudicca, and I'm thirty again, standing in Pru's driveway, and Reenie is gone. Long gone.

I throw myself into Boudicca and close the door, gripping the steering wheel as if I can anchor myself in the present when it feels as if the past is about to sweep me away.

I'd forgotten. How had I forgotten that? Or the fact that, in the morning, Reenie started getting rid of everything she owned with a star on it. The reason the hair-slides I've worn all these years were daisies is that all the star ones disappeared a week before she did.

'It's nonsense, isn't it? Childish,' she sneered, when I asked why she was throwing away her favourite things.

'You're going to keep my earrings at least, aren't you?' I asked in a tiny voice.

'They're mine. I'll do what I want with them,' she snapped.

But she didn't throw them away. Instead, a month after she disappeared, I came down to breakfast to find Mum wearing them.

'Can't I keep them? Since they were a present from me?' I begged.

But Mum just frowned. 'No, Verity. I gave these to your sister. For her last birthday.'

'You didn't!' I shouted.

Mum got up and started clattering things into the dishwasher. 'They'll be yours eventually, Verity. For now, I need something of your sister's to keep close to me.'

She wore them for a month, then they vanished. I ransacked her room one evening when she and TJ went out, but they were nowhere to be found. Somewhere, over the years, I'd forgotten about them . . . and Reenie's sudden aversion to stars. Compared with her disappearance, what did a moody patch and a change in style matter?

I crane my neck, looking over the garden gate towards the glow of Pru's kitchen windows. Then I shake my head, start the car and head back to the flat. I'm not ready to find the words to explain the memory – and why I didn't think twice about what my sister had said.

That night under the stars, when she walked away, I just huffed.

'Moody cow,' I muttered, then lay back down on the grass and carried on staring at the stars as if I wasn't lonely for my sister's warmth at my side, the tickle of her hair against my cheek.

I was so busy being angry that she wouldn't talk to me I failed to hear how loud her silences spoke.

Up till now, I've been focused on solving her disappearance. Now, for the first time, I imagine what my sister must have felt in the run-up to that night if TJ was hurting her for weeks, maybe months, until things went too far and . . .

I stumble towards the bins Pru put out earlier and hack up bile as I dry-heave again and again and again.

Pru

A red kite glides above me as I wind through narrow lanes hemmed in by ancient hedgerows. My phone buzzes in the hands-free stand as I sail out of the signal dead-zone.

I park on the verge at the top of the private road where a smartly painted sign reads *Jeynes Family Open Garden 4 Charity – Today ONLY, £5 entry*.

Fields rolls away on either side as I walk up the gentle slope. After a quarter of a mile, I pass a line of cottages where I would wager the people who actually work the land live. A car trundles past. I follow, rounding a bend on to an elegant avenue between plane trees. Ahead stands the house. A young man is guiding visitors to park along the drive, while an older woman sits at a table to the side, taking donations and entry fees.

'What a lovely day for it.' I pass over a ten-pound note. 'Do keep the change.' I pick up one of the leaflets for the charity.

'My daughter is the founder.' Claire Jeynes's mother beams up at me. 'We're so proud of her. She had such struggles, but then she did this, and it's made all the difference to so many lives.'

I force my face not to twist into a snarl as a voice in my head says, *I suspect your daughter killed mine. Are you still proud?* I turn to look at the line of cars down the drive. 'Good turnout.'

'My husband's a retired GP and I'm an ex-magistrate, so it's easy to get the word out, and people do like to support a good cause, don't they?'

I put the leaflet back, nod politely in her direction without meeting her eyes, then wander into the garden. Or rather, gardens. There's a walled garden, an orchard, an Italian garden, a huge Victorian greenhouse and a rolling lawn leading down to a lake with a tiny island rose garden. I amble towards a group of people clustered around a man in his late sixties who is holding court as he ushers everyone towards the walled garden.

'My grandparents rather let things go to weed, so it was quite the job, I tell you, to get it back to this.' Claire Jeynes's father gestures expansively around. 'But now we've a good stock of herbs and plants with medicinal uses. My daughter used to love putting them into candles and various lotions and potions. She's too busy these days with the charity, but maybe today's event will coax her back!'

I watch the lines around his eyes seep down to bracket his mouth as his smile fades and another emotion replaces it. Then he is all bonhomie again as he leads us over to the Italian garden, then out on to the lawn.

I know far more about the plants than he does, but keep my knowledge to myself, watching a little girl with wavy dark hair darting around after butterflies. When a dragonfly zooms past, she stares after it in disbelief, creeping closer, closer, as it settles on a leaf. I watch her mouth a 'Wow', her eyes wide and full of delight, and I think of Hope the first time she saw a damselfly in the garden of a stately home we visited for a bank-holiday picnic. I remember her dashing after bees in the tiny garden of our old house, just a few miles away. I remember her laughter, her joy, my joy.

Realizing the group has wandered down to the lake, I hurry to catch up, though I barely hear what Dr Jeynes is saying over the roar of memory overlapping memory.

'We put in the water feature ourselves, but the island was a happy accident. One day our daughter swerved around a rabbit on the driveway and drove straight into our brand-new lake.'

The words snatch me into roaring darkness, as if the lake has lifted into the air and swallowed me whole. Dr Jeynes's voice ripples through me like a current.

'We came running out of the house, but she was fine, though the car was a write-off. This was during our daughter's bad period, so she'd had the car in the garage under a dustsheet for months to make sure she wasn't tempted to drive while she was struggling. That day was her first time going out in . . . well, I can't remember how long.'

I am drowning. I must be drowning here, under the water, yet somehow I can see the tour group standing in the sunshine on the bank as if they're beside me.

'So, there we were, staring in horror, certain this was going to crush her just as she was starting to turn a corner . . . And she piped up, "What if, instead of paying someone to drag it out and scrap it, we use it as the foundation for a little island? Let's just upcycle!"'

The group chuckles, the soundwaves making the world waver and distort.

'So that's what we did, and the process became the first

step in her journey of healing . . . though it did also give her such a scare she never drove again. Thank God.'

The group laughs while I continue to drown. I need to fight my way to the surface, but my limbs might as well have been turned to stone.

'Thankfully, she liked the island far more than the car, so it all worked out. We put down sacking and liners, then a layer of soil, then planted our rose garden – though, over the years, we've been adding aquatic plants all around as a mini habitat for the local pondlife. And I don't just mean the challengers to our wonderful MP.'

More laughter. He keeps talking, talking, talking, as if telling a funny story, with a happy ending, not the tale of a cold-blooded murder.

All these years of searching, and there it is, just twelve metres away, topped with soil and blooming roses: the car that killed my daughter.

I thought I would be buoyed up by triumph. Instead, the truth cuts me open.

Before today, it was merely a recent, educated guess that Claire Jeynes killed Hope – I didn't *know*. Now I do.

And yet I still don't have proof because the evidence will have long washed or corroded away. All this time and it was right here, little more than two miles from the accident.

Over the years, I imagined the moment of finding my daughter's killer in so many different ways, but never in brilliant sunshine, surrounded by laughing strangers. It feels like madness. Like I am dreaming. I must be dreaming because this cannot be real. I just need to wake up and breathe.

Wake up and breathe!

The world turns over and I am back on the bank. Light catches off the water as the breeze inscribes patterns across the surface. It is so beautiful. How can it be beautiful?

I wrench in a shuddering breath, staggering back from the water's edge. Then I am bent over coughing as if there really is water in my lungs. When I unfold, hand still pressed to my chest as I wheeze and drag at the air, I see the group has moved off up the slope towards the refurbished Victorian greenhouse.

I came here to search the grounds, but my answer has been presented to me and stolen from me all at once. Maybe there is enough circumstantial evidence that the Sisterhood would agree to assign Claire Jeynes as a target, but it wouldn't be simple or easy, which means it wouldn't be quick. I'd be dead long before she was.

I don't want to leave this world with my daughter's killer still in it.

The thought echoes in my head as my heart thumps out a hard, angry beat. I need to leave before the unreality of the moment tempts me into some act of madness worthy of Verity. There's nothing here for me.

Only there is. Everything I've been hoping and searching for has been stolen from me. So, now I will have to steal myself a new hope: an invisible way to kill the woman no one but me knows murdered my daughter. Breaking the Rules isn't a legacy I want to leave Verity, but if no one ever knows . . .

As the tour group files into the greenhouse, I slip away around the corner of the house. A few metres along I find a side door, but it's locked. Hurrying around a further corner, I spot a small window left ajar. Reaching through, I lift the stay to pull the window wide, then brace my forearms on the inner wall and push off, wriggling myself on to the sill. Once I am securely balanced, I lower my arms, squirming forward until my hands touch down on the floor. From there it is an easy matter to walk myself into the room until I can drop my feet down behind me, just as I have demonstrated time and again for Verity.

I stay crouched on the floor, listening, but I can hear no movement, no voices inside with me. Drawing a plastic glove out of my pocket, I pull it on before I open the bathroom cabinet, unsurprised to find nothing of use there. Padding carefully across to the door, I listen again, then ease it open. I hurry down the corridor, glancing into each room until I find the kitchen. There, I check the windows first – no one in the little inner courtyard outside – then head for a door that I figure is at the northernmost corner of the house. Sure enough, behind it I find a larder, with a shelf for medication.

Slipping a ziplock bag out of my pocket, I scan the shelf, then pick one box and one little bottle. It will be easy enough to set things up so it looks like the ex-addict stole some pills from her father then overdosed: a perfect Sisterhood plan.

Dropping the medication into the bag, I check there is no air then seal it and zip it into an inner pocket before creeping back to the door.

The kitchen is empty, but now there are footsteps approaching along the corridor. Hurrying to the door into the courtyard, I ease the handle down, but it's locked. Cursing, I spin round, spying a key on a lazy Susan on the counter. Darting forward, I grab it and slide it into the lock.

'Owen?' a woman's voice calls. 'I thought you were with the tour group?'

I open the door and swing myself through, closing it behind me.

'Owen?' comes a louder call.

I bolt across the little courtyard, grabbing for the knob of the door on the other side. It refuses to open. Then I twist and push, instead of pulling, and I'm through, just as I hear the kitchen door open behind me.

It is dim in the old stable where I find myself, but I don't stop, scuffing my feet along the ground as I wait for my eyes to adjust. The space is now used as a garage. A mint-condition classic Rolls-Royce stands near the far doors. Instinctively, I look between the Rolls and the brand-new red Audi next to it, but of course neither is the car that hit Hope.

The stable door creaks open.

I drop to the ground and wriggle under the Rolls, breathing calmly through my sleeve so that the dust won't start me coughing.

The lights go on. I listen as the woman moves back and forth. She opens a small side door, peers through, then backs out again, muttering under her breath as she returns to the courtyard. The lights go off, the door closes.

I stay where I am for a full twenty minutes, then slowly slide out. The side door leads into a storage shed with no second exit, forcing me back to the courtyard door. I peek round, then slip through and over to the ivy-cloaked wall curtaining the courtyard from the gardens. Grabbing a thick handful of vines, I slide the toe of my trainer across the brickwork just above knee height until I find purchase, then ease myself up, reaching for the top of the wall.

A quick look over reveals a few figures wandering towards the walled garden, but no one looking towards the house. Taking my chance, I drag myself on to the top of the wall, keeping my body and head low as I swing one leg over, then the other. Coughing overtakes me and for a moment all I can do is cling on, riding it out.

'Who are you? What are you doing?' someone shouts from the courtyard behind me.

I drop over the wall, landing in a crouch, then immediately lurch into a smart march, muffling my coughing in my elbow.

The moment I round the corner of the house, I slow to a saunter, forcing myself to take shallow, steady breaths. Pulling off my gilet, I quickly turn it inside out, replacing scarlet with a pastel floral pattern. Sliding it back on, I draw a baseball cap from a pocket and tuck it over my hair.

Around a second corner, I find a group of kids playing croquet on a flat patch of lawn and sink down on the grass to watch. A moment later, I catch the sound of someone running along the path. I peer back when the kids look round and see Dr Jeynes, red-faced and panting.

'I think we had a break-in at the house. Anyone spot someone in a red top?' he calls.

We all shake our heads. He surveys the garden, then turns away.

I wait till the croquet match is over, then head back to the drive and start the long walk to my car. The sun paints the ground with splotches of light and splatters of darkness. Step by step my pace quickens as my heart beats harder and harder and faster and faster.

I cannot be here any more. I need to go.

It takes everything in me not to run. I came to see if I could prove Claire Jeynes killed Hope, but now I'm leaving with the means to finally take my one free kill. Only I am the one member in the Sisterhood who isn't allowed to deliver it.

Unless I break the Rules. It would be different if I weren't dying, but I am. I won't face any consequences except the pangs of my own conscience.

But Verity is another matter.

Verity

It's morning, but I feel like I haven't slept. My eyes are dry and gritty. My body aches as if I'm ill. Muddled dreams and memories chase each other around and around in my head, like a nightmare carousel.

Dragging myself out of bed, I realize I'm out of food and coffee. The only thing in the cupboard is a solitary teabag. This is not enough caffeine for a night spent tossing and turning, waking again and again with a sense of urgency, but no idea why.

Reenie shadows me as I pack more clothes, books, household items into Boudicca. The flat is nearly bare now. Luckily, Pru and I are leaving for our next cover-story job the day I become homeless, so it won't be a problem until our return.

I stare at the dust circling in a beam of sunlight. I need a plan: a new place to live when Pru and I get back. But I can't seem to find the . . . will? Energy? I know it's going to be so much harder to do anything about my situation when I'm in another country, caught up not just in playing nanny to the offspring of the obnoxiously rich but also working towards my fourth murder, so today is the day to get things sorted.

I'll need to ask Pru for money for a new deposit, which

will mean explaining why I'm not getting my current deposit back. I'm pretty sure she'll give me the money, but she won't approve—

I care about Pru's approval. I care about it a lot. When did that happen?

Why is that so bad, Verity? asks an inner voice that sounds distinctly like Pru.

Do I really like Pru that much? I mean, I admire her steely determination, her sense of justice and purpose. OK, she also kills people, but now I do, too, so I can hardly fault her there. So why am I resisting asking her for help? It's not like she's doesn't already know how hopeless I am – it won't come as any surprise whatsoever. What's stopping me from arranging some viewings today and tomorrow – Pru will let me out of training if it's a choice between that and my being homeless when we return from our away-job.

I think about getting to my feet, finding my phone, searching local listings . . . But I just stand there staring at the dust motes.

I wait to hear my mother's whisper, but it doesn't come. The flat is silent but for the bonging and clunking of the pipes, the thrum of a lawnmower somewhere nearby. I haven't heard Mum in my head for . . . days. Without that nagging whisper, it should be so much easier than it's ever been before to fix the mess I'm in, so what's stopping me?

It feels like there's something I should be doing instead. Something important that I'm missing.

I slip out my phone and tap in the postcode of the place Pru went on our last 'day off', then sit there with my finger hovering over the 'search' button. When Pru gave me Hope's file, I felt so guilty about spying on her by checking her satnav, but that's stupid. She spied on me for eleven months – and for good cause. Now, I've got good cause to spy on her. After all, I know she didn't stay at home last time. God only knows where she is now and what she's up to. What if it's some sort of test she's expecting me to work out?

I hit 'search', then frown at the location, zooming in. It's a community centre. I zoom out again, seeing it's about an hour's drive. It's not where she lived when raising Hope. It's nothing to do with any case we're working on. So why was she there when she was meant to be having a quiet day at home with friends?

I tap out of the browser and into the tracking app for the car, bringing up its current location. Pru is about thirty-two miles away – and this time she *is* near the town where she raised Hope. I zoom in and see her exact location is a large farm estate just up the road from her old house. This time she really is seeing old friends.

Groaning, I scrub a hand down my face, putting the phone aside. Pru probably wouldn't care – might even be proud – but it feels bad. Not just ungrateful, but wrong. Still, I can't shake the feeling she's hiding something.

Cursing, I pick up my phone again and type in the name of the drug from the prescription I found in her book on the day of my first kill.

Hydrocodone. Used to treat moderate to severe pain.

My stomach clenches. I know Pru's been feeling rough lately, but she's not said anything about really *bad* pain.

Also an effective cough suppressant.

Oh, OK. That makes sense.

Only she didn't have the cough back then. It came on

during our first away-job. So, maybe the prescription really was for pain – perhaps an old injury acquired on the job. She could have had it for ages and never filled it, hence using it as a bookmark. I try to zoom into my memory of that moment, but it stays fuzzy. I've no idea what the date on the prescription was.

The swirl of dust motes sparkles in the sunlight, the mess of my life turned magical.

Something picks away at the corner of my mind, demanding attention then sliding out of focus. I didn't leave Boudicca unlocked, did I?

I drag myself out to the kerb, but she's shut tight. I walk a circuit, checking the windows. Closed, closed, closed, closed. I peer in to see if any of my stuff looks worth stealing. As I straighten, I finally see it. The scratched-off remnant of the star decal TJ bought Reenie when she passed her driving test.

I'd been studying in the kitchen when Reenie burst in and started rifling through the cupboard under the sink, emerging with a rag and a bottle of white spirit, then storming outside. I went back to my notes until shouting erupted, then I hurried to the front door to see what was wrong.

'I thought you loved everything with stars!' TJ was red-faced as he watched Reenie scouring away at the sticker. 'You're going to ruin the car, too, at this rate! I thought you liked the decal. You said it was lovely when I gave it you!'

'Well, I don't! It's stupid. You should have told me to grow up and stop being such a child with the stars and bloody horoscopes. You're meant to be teaching me to be smart.'

'Four bloody hours a week in this rust-bucket so you could pass your test as fast as possible wasn't enough teaching? Seems like you figured out the horoscope thing just fine, but even if star signs are rubbish, stars aren't made up, are they, so what's your damage?'

'You're so stupid, TJ!' Reenie screamed. 'You're so stupid, and you don't listen. No one ever listens to me!'

She hurled the rag at him, then the bottle, leaving him cursing as she ran inside, slamming the front door.

TJ stomped over to the bin and tossed in the cracked bottle, along with the rag. 'Your sister's a right cow sometimes, you know that. Just like her mother,' he snarled. Then his shoulders slumped. 'I thought I was getting this right. Then out of the blue she's not speaking to me for days. Now this. You got any idea what set her off?'

I shook my head. 'I've got to study,' I whispered, then hightailed it to grab my stuff from the kitchen and take it into the garden, out of everyone's way.

Now my fingers trace the ghost of the sticker. Over the following week Reenie rowed with Mum, with TJ, with both of them, again and again, louder and angrier each time. The day with the sticker paled in comparison to the one when Reenie said she was going to find a charity job building schools in Africa, Asia, *anywhere* that would get her far away from her current life.

Of course that wasn't the story Mum told the police. According to her, Reenie was just talking about a gap year travelling. But reading the statements and seeing our stories shift over time, I understand now why the police didn't listen when I swore over and over that my sister wouldn't have taken drugs, and she would *never* have run away. I didn't want them to blame her, so I lied, and they knew it. At the time, I told myself the lies were necessary because I knew she hadn't run away, but the truth is that I couldn't face the prospect that she had gone without telling me. And yet I *know* as certainly as I know anything that she wouldn't have abandoned us permanently. Sooner rather than later, she'd at least have let *me* know where she was – unless something happened to stop her.

DI Strickland saw that desperation to believe my own lies from the start. He understood that, in my terror, everything I said was what I wanted the truth to be, not what it was.

For the first time, standing by Boudicca, with my hand on the ghost of the sticker, I ask myself the questions I've been resisting since Reenie vanished. *What if something terrible happened to her, but not the night of the party? What if it was a day, a week, a month later, in another town or city? What if we've been looking in the wrong places all along because neither Mum nor I could bear the thought that she'd left us behind?*

I don't have any answers, just further questions. *Why was Reenie so different in the weeks before she disappeared? Why did she throw out all her star stuff? Why risk damaging her beloved Boudicca just to remove TJ's sticker?*

What if she tried to tell me what was wrong, and I just didn't know how to listen?

If I had, could I have saved her?

Pru

In the hour since I returned from the open garden, I have had lemon-ginger tea, cough syrup and even a soothing hot toddy, but my cough will not ease.

Instead of worrying – or letting my mind go back to the car in the lake – I busy myself with packing for our upcoming away-job. Ticking items off a list usually leaves me smiling and relaxed, but today I am distracted and anxious.

Finally, I take myself to the kitchen and hide the ziplock bag of medication in a saucepan at the back of the cupboard. I have just pulled out the appropriate drug manual to calculate the required dosage when my phone beeps.

Glancing at the screen, I smile at the name on the notification. Perhaps, with the way my cough is going, it's time to introduce Verity to Graziella. It's not likely that I'll die suddenly, but it's not impossible, either, so the sooner I set Verity up with a second contact in the Sisterhood, the better. She's earned it, after all.

I tap in my PIN, finger moving to the WhatsApp icon to message Graziella back. Then I pause and tap the tracker app for Verity's car instead. This is only the second day off Verity has had since she started her training almost two months ago. How she is choosing to use it will be a good measure of her progress.

Verity's location loads. My smile vanishes.

Five minutes later, I'm in the car, grinding my teeth, splitting my attention between the road and my breathing.

Out two three four five. Hold two three four five. In two three STRANGLE VERITY!

I straighten in my seat and start again. *In two three four five. Hold two three four WRING HER NECK!*

I thought I was rubbing off on her. She has been making steady progress across all her skills – with the exception of CCTV angles. Her fitness is improving. Her investigative work is coming along, though her attention to detail in planning and preparing for a kill could be stronger. Nevertheless, she has delivered – and on her first attempt – with every job so far. Above all, she is learning to focus. The other day she worked for a solid forty-eight minutes. When she started, the longest I saw her manage was three minutes and seventeen seconds.

A growl escapes my lips, then I am shouting at the windscreen, then coughing, then shouting some more until the cough finally gets the better of me. By the time I have control over my lungs again, I can see Verity's car. And the police vehicle.

I park carefully and precisely, then march across the street to where a uniformed officer is talking to a man about my age and an elderly woman. Verity stands to one side, head down, arms wrapped around herself.

'Verity.'

Her eyes are dazed as she turns to me, then her face floods with panic.

'I thought we agreed you wouldn't be bothering Mr Howard?' I turn to him, holding out my hand. 'I'm Verity's mentor. Her very disappointed mentor.'

TJ Howard shakes my hand, frowning in confusion.

I cast an anxious look at the police officer. 'I can see Verity has been causing a disturbance, but I can assure you that we are working on her impulse control. I had thought—'

'She just turned up and started going at TJ,' the elderly woman pipes up, shooting a glare at Verity. 'One moment he was mowing his lawn, the next she was leaping out of her car and screaming in his face like a madwoman.'

TJ rubs his forehead. 'I'm sorry for the noise, Mrs B, but I told you, it's nothing to worry about.'

The neighbour tucks her chin in, accidentally multiplying it by six. 'I wouldn't put it past her to try to run you down with that big red car.'

'I can imagine it looked very worrying,' I interject, 'but I can assure you that, while Verity can be very loud and troublesome in her manner, she is not violent.' I turn to the police officer. 'Given that Mr Howard understands the cause of Verity's distressing behaviour – and I am here now to ensure that she does not cross any further lines – would you be willing to leave this with me? She will not be back.' I proffer a business card.

The officer takes it, looking between the four of us. 'Since Mr Howard has already told me he doesn't want to see charges laid, I will write this up as requiring no further action at this time. However, if there is any more trouble, Mr Howard or his neighbour can ask that we pursue this as a public order offence.'

I give him and TJ an authentic smile of relief. 'Thank you very much for your sensitive handling of this situation.'

The officer nods to me, then to TJ, and finally to the neighbour. 'Call us if you have any cause for concern.'

'I will and all,' says the neighbour, giving Verity a dirty look. 'You behave yourself. I've got sharp eyes and ears for all I'm eighty-four, so don't you think about coming back here.' She shuffles away.

I eye Verity up and down. 'I cannot tell you how disappointed I am.'

She hunches into herself.

'What on earth provoked you to come here like this?'

'She was yelling something about the sticker Reenie scratched off her car,' TJ says, drawing my attention back to him. 'Started accusing me of . . . Well, if you know the story, you can imagine.'

'What does a sticker have to do with Reenie's disappearance?' I don't have to feign confusion.

'That's what I'd like to know.'

TJ and I both glare at Verity.

She lifts her chin but refuses to meet our eyes. 'She used to love everything to do with stars and horoscopes, so TJ got her a star decal when she passed her driving test. Then suddenly she's chucking all her star stuff out and scratching off the sticker.' Finally, she looks at TJ. 'Why did she do that if you didn't give her reason? One minute you were going out for lessons all the time and everything was good, then she acted like she hated you.'

TJ heaves a sigh. 'She rowed with your mother plenty, too. And you. The day she scrubbed off the sticker, I asked her what was wrong, but she just exploded. You were right there – don't you remember? I have no idea what I'd done, or if it was anything to do with me at all. I still don't understand it.' His face sags with remembered hurt. 'I thought we were getting close. We had such a nice time on those lessons, then suddenly it was just . . .' He makes a 'poof, gone' gesture. 'I know you never wanted to hear this, but she was different the month before she vanished from that party.'

'It was Mum who said everything was fine,' Verity snaps.

TJ shakes his head. 'Your mother had her version of the story. Had her version of who you and Reenie were, too. But you wouldn't hear anyone say Reenie might have gone off of her own accord.'

'Because she didn't!' Verity shouts, then subsides, looking warily around. 'She wouldn't have just left.' She sounds desperate rather than certain.

TJ raises a hand as if to touch her arm, then lowers it. 'I didn't dare say it then, but the way she was . . . I always wondered if she'd done something . . .'

Verity frowns at him, then blanches. 'She would *never*! She didn't *kill* herself!'

'We don't know. We don't know anything.' His face creases with guilt. 'Maybe she did something foolish. Maybe she ran off. Maybe it was an accident. Maybe someone hurt her.' He raises his hands helplessly. 'All we know is that she wasn't herself. It wasn't because of anything I did, though I can't make you believe that. But if you want to blame me for something, you might as well pick something real, and that's the fact I knew she wasn't right and I didn't do anything about it. Just lost my temper when she scrubbed off that sticker and waited for her to come and apologize.' His face twists. 'There's nothing I can say to convince you I wouldn't ever have hurt your sister, but it's the truth. I don't have any answers, Verity. I wish I did.'

He casts a look at me. 'It's good you've got help. I hope it works and you can find some happiness.'

Verity searches his face, her own a mask of misery.

TJ gives her a sad smile, tips his head at me, then walks away around the side of his house.

'Are you safe to drive?' I ask Verity.

She swallows, shivers, nods.

'I'll see you at home. No detours. We have a lot to discuss.'

Verity's phone beeps. Then beeps again. And again.

'Well, look at it,' I snap at her.

She slides it out. 'It's Gavin Pieper's ex-sister-in-law.' She taps in her PIN then scrolls for a moment. 'She says she and her ex were in the garden all evening. When they went to bed, Gavin's door was shut and they just assumed he was in there. Her ex persuaded her that they would have noticed Gavin going out, and that muddying the waters with uncertainty over his alibi would have diverted the police from useful leads, so she kept quiet.'

Her throat works. '"Gavin swore he was in his room the whole time. And he could have been. But I don't know, and neither does my ex. I said we had to tell the truth, but my ex got so mad . . . He could be real nasty when he was angry, so I kept my mouth shut. I'm so sorry. Please forgive me." '

Her breathing hitching, Verity looks past me to TJ's house.

'The only thing you achieved here was destruction.

What a waste of all the chances you have been given. What a terrible waste.' I walk away before I can say anything more.

I expect to rant at the windscreen the whole way home. Instead, misery chokes me into silence.

I thought we had turned a corner, but I guess I was wrong.

Verity

We've been back at Pru's place for half an hour and I haven't apologized yet. I know I should, but 'I'm sorry' won't fix this. Anyway, Pru knows I'm sorry. It doesn't change the fact that the first chance I had to take new information on Reenie's case to her, I did my level best to blow up my brand-new life instead. Only my brand-new life is also Pru's life. How does 'I'm sorry' measure up to that?

Pru finishes rinsing her water bottle, then checks through her bag, throwing a wrapper in the bin, then pinning a petrol receipt to the noticeboard where she keeps info on expenses until she can write it into her accounting ledger: her financial organization is as precise as everything else in her life, whereas my current filing system is an old crisp packet.

I prop my elbows on the table and interlace my fingers around the back of my skull as I stare down at the grain of the table. A pair of knotholes glare at me. I sit back, craning my head to look at the ceiling instead. In my flat, there would be spiders, strands of cobweb. In Pru's pristine kitchen, even the light fitting shines as if freshly polished.

'I know it looked bad, but I wasn't going to be arrested. TJ doesn't hate me enough for that.'

'Imagine you are a responsible, long-serving member

of the Sisterhood and you have taken on a mentee. We will imagine that your mentee is striving to be worthy of this honour.'

'Oh, stuff you,' I snarl as shame burns into anger.

Pru tries to intensify the Look, but she's already maxed out the dials on 'Disappointment' and 'Withering Contempt'. 'Your careful, diligent mentee is going about her training and progressing through her early jobs. Then one day something goes wrong. She immediately calls her mentor, who steps in to help, and . . . everything is fine again. It sounds *terrible*, doesn't it?'

I sit back, folding my arms.

'Anyone can make a mistake. *You* made a choice you *knew* went against everything you owe to the Sisterhood, to me, to yourself. You made a promise when you committed to being my mentee and becoming a member of this extraordinary group of women. Today, you acted as if all of that is *nothing*.'

'I didn't even get cautioned,' I mumble defensively. 'Even without you, it probably wouldn't have been more than a warning.'

Pru stares me down. 'And what would have happened when the caution went into the system? I thought DI Strickland said the last time was the end of the line if you didn't want things to escalate?'

I wave the words away. 'He's not going to arrest me for having a loud row with TJ.'

'No, but what if we find out one of your suspects killed your sister? Even if we set you up with the world's best alibi, when your one free kill happens there will be a lot of attention on you. They won't find anything in *that* case, but what if it raises other questions? Our role is to be invisible – not just when we are at work, but all the time. Because if a kill ever goes wrong, that invisibility is our shield. You cannot afford to throw it away while you are still in training.'

'OK, fine. No more impulsive behaviour. That what you want to hear?' I try to meet Pru's gaze but have to look away.

'Now you have broken the Rules once, what is to stop you from doing it again?'

'So, no mentee has ever had a bit of a rocky start? I'm literally the first, am I?'

'You seem to think this is a little mistake, Verity, but I am starting to wonder if you have the type of steadfast loyalty the Sisterhood requires. I thought you understood the value of the gift we were offering you.' Wiping her hands, she picks up a sunhat and pair of secateurs.

'And I thought training was a process, not "one mistake and you're dead to me."'

'It isn't. Doesn't that make you the lucky one?' Pru tells me as she strides out of the garden door.

I follow Pru outside and across the grass. 'Does the Sisterhood know about my screw-up, or are you responsible for snitching on me? If a mentorship gets terminated, just how terminal is that really?'

Pru settles down by the vegetable bed, trimming the ivy that wreathes the garden wall.

'Maybe if you told me about the consequences of my actions—'

'It isn't about that, Verity!' Pru rips a strand of ivy away, then bends it over on itself until it breaks. *Snap, snap, snap,*

snap. 'No one gives twenty-five years to the Sisterhood out of fear.' She coughs into her sleeve, leaving a swipe of mud on her chin. 'If that is what is keeping you here, then *go*. Off you pop.' She gestures at the garden gate.

'You. Are. Free. To. Go,' she enunciates when I don't move.

'How about you?' I ask, moving closer. 'You owe the Sisterhood a mentee.'

The sun is shearing through the apple tree behind Pru, putting her face in shadow.

'You can keep destroying every chance of happiness and stability, but the universe is not going to see how unbearable your pain is and restore what has been taken from you. All you get to choose is whether to have nothing or to have *something*. But if you are looking to be forced into choosing what the Sisterhood is offering, then you really should walk out of that gate and not come back.'

I want to scream that I'm not strong enough to pledge twenty-five years of service when I haven't even been able to keep to the Rules in the first few months of my training, but Pru knows. She knows and yet she's still asking.

Can I really promise to do what I have to do, and bear what I have to bear, and never give myself the option to say, *It's too much, I can't,* and instead, say, *I can, so I will*?

If I can, maybe the truth is that I'm not afraid I'm weak. Maybe I'm terrified of finding out just how strong I could choose to be.

Pru

The cough tears at my throat and chest until my eyes are streaming so I can barely see. I would curse, but I don't have the breath. Pulling off my gloves, I wipe my eyes and turn around.

Verity is gone.

Snatching up my tools, I clomp back to the house, refusing to glance towards the drive to see if Boudicca is gone, too. Instead, I focus on what I am going to cook for dinner. At least I try to, only to end up rehearsing what I will tell the Sisterhood about Verity. Later, I shall have to make a plan for managing our upcoming away-job solo.

As I open the kitchen door, my eyes fall on Verity's empty chair. My chest pinches and I dissolve into coughing again. It takes me a full minute to recover enough to hear that the kettle is on.

'Why don't you sit down, and I'll top up your tea,' Verity says, pulling out my chair.

I drop into it. 'You cannot make another mistake like this.'

Verity sets my tea on a coaster, then sinks down opposite. 'I know I'll have to earn back your trust. Maybe I can start with explaining why I went to TJ's? Then there's something else I should probably tell you. You know, to put all my cards on the table. Move forward with a clean slate.'

I take a sip of tea. 'A bit less honey next time, but this is helpful. Thank you.'

'Are you sure you don't need to see the GP?'

I shrug. 'If it doesn't improve soon, I shall make an appointment for when we get back from the Dresden job.'

Verity fidgets in her seat, then tugs at her cuffs. 'So, about TJ. I know I should have come to you first, but leaving that aside—'

'I need to tell you something about the night your sister disappeared.'

Verity stills. 'You've found something. Do you know who—'

'No.' I cough into my sleeve, then take another sip of tea. 'I wanted to find the right time to talk about this. I thought it would help to have some trust between us first.'

Verity hunches in her chair. 'And I've broken that trust.'

I rub at my forehead. 'In this case, it is more an issue of my uncertainty about when to . . . introduce this information.'

'So, you've been making me revisit that night over and over, going through the suspects again and again, and all the time you knew something but didn't think I deserved to hear it?' Verity's mouth twists with anger. 'Suddenly I'm not feeling so bad about earlier.'

I sigh – carefully, so as not to set the cough off again. 'I was hoping to teach you a degree of self-control so that we could discuss the matter calmly, rather than running the risk of derailing your training. *My* caution about your reaction is not the same as *you* drawing police attention by harassing a suspect in your sister's case, after swearing to me that you would stop investigating by yourself.'

'You didn't want to tell me till I'd learnt to respect the Rules, but now you want to tell me on the day I smash a bunch of those Rules to pieces. Yeah, makes loads of sense,' Verity drawls.

'After today's mess, I think it will do more harm than good to wait,' I say wearily.

Verity starts tapping her foot against the leg of her chair. 'So, did you leave something out of the police file? Get someone in the Sisterhood to do some financial or digital digging?'

'The night your sister died I was at the university on a pro bono case. I took a batch of doctored drugs, then waited for Christophe to head towards the gates to meet his usual dealer and intercepted him. I told him the cops had rousted his dealer, so I had been sent instead and that I had something special to offer him at a discount. Then I gave him a free sample.'

Verity's breathing is quick and shallow, her face blotched white and red.

'Christophe tried the sample, then he headed back towards the party. He got thirty metres, then keeled over and died where he fell. Your sister wasn't with him. If she took drugs that night, they weren't part of the batch that killed him.'

Verity is slowly shaking her head. 'The police thought maybe Reenie died from the same drugs – that she wandered away off her head and hid somewhere so weird no one could find her.'

'It was a line of inquiry,' I concede, 'but only one.'

'It didn't have to be *any*!' She presses her hands over her face.

'You've seen the important parts of Reenie's police file, Verity. The police explored the full range of possible scenarios. There were no leads they failed to follow because they were looking into connections to Christophe's death – the time they spent searching the campus and river they would have spent anyway. The rest was part of the investigation into his death, not Reenie's disappearance.'

Verity lowers her hands, staring at me as if she has never seen me before. 'You picked me because of Reenie. Why would you do that if it wasn't your fault?'

'I picked you for many reasons. But you were on the list because of your sister,' I admit. 'She is the reason you met the Sisterhood's criteria. And your attempts to investigate, while often self-destructive and misguided, showed determination and, on occasion, an eye for detail. Not to mention your often explosive – but always passionate – need to right every wrong you stumble across.'

'What else?' Verity grits out. 'If you know for a fact that Reenie didn't die from the drugs you doctored, why do you feel guilty about it? It's not just because you were there, in the vicinity, when it happened. You're too rational to think you could somehow have saved Reenie when you didn't even know she was in danger, unless . . .' Her breath catches. 'Christophe had only just turned twenty-one. How come he was a target?'

'You know he was from an aristocratic family – wealthy, connected.'

Verity nods, gesturing urgently for me to go on.

'He had been drugging and sexually assaulting girls for over three years. Always ones from working-class backgrounds so he could intimidate them, if necessary, either through sending lawyers to pick apart their claims or hiring investigators to dig up something that could be twisted to discredit them. Sometimes he found his victims at parties. Other times, he cruised around in a limo – with or without his closest friends, like Charles and Nathan Temple, though there is no evidence they were involved in his crimes. He waited until the girls dropped their guard, started drinking a bit more freely, then he would slip them something and find a quiet place to . . .'

I fidget with my mug, wiping a drop of tea off the rim, unable to look at Verity. 'Afterwards, he would take them back to the limo, or call a cab, in a pretence of concern to see them safely home. Sometimes he would even go, too, so that the driver would be a witness to his chivalry.'

'The limo driver's statement said that when he talked to his boss about the drugs he'd found, he also told his boss he was worried about driving so many drunk, possibly drugged, girls around.'

I nod. 'His boss pointed out that it was better than leaving those girls to fend for themselves. I imagine the driver was careful not to shut the partition, so he could monitor what was going on in the back. From the statements, he made sure to cover his back by reporting everything to his boss, so I don't think he would have let an assault happen in front of him.'

Verity tucks her feet up on her chair, hugging her knees to her chest. 'How did Christophe's case come to the Sisterhood?'

'I suspect it was a referral from a police officer. Someone who had seen the same pattern again and again, kept hearing the same story involving Christophe, but knew how hard it would be to build a strong enough case to convict him – and how many more girls would be hurt while they tried.'

'You think Christophe did that to Reenie?' Verity picks at a catch in her nail. 'Before he went to get more drugs, I mean.' The nail tears down to the quick, a bead of blood welling up at one corner.

'If he had followed his usual pattern, he would have taken her home when he . . . finished – or called the limo driver to collect her. The police checked his phone records as part of the investigation into his death and there was no evidence of any calls or texts after you left the party – and we know Reenie was alive and well then.'

'But what if he took her somewhere and left her there, planning to go back, only you killed him before he could?' Verity whispers.

I swallow, then nod. 'That is possible.'

Verity's hands clench into fists, then uncurl as she frowns. 'But where could he have taken her that no one ever found her? It couldn't have been anywhere far, if she was drugged. And it can't have been anywhere too strange if he wanted to . . . to . . .' She takes a shuddering breath, looking away. 'You wouldn't go into a culvert or a crawl space to assault someone. You'd go somewhere comfortable. Where could that have been that no one ever found her?'

'It's not just that,' I point out. 'If he took her somewhere and left her there, then never returned because I killed him, why wouldn't she just have woken up and found her way home?'

'Unless she fought back and he . . .' Her lips tremble.

'Maybe he hid her body before going to get the drugs from you . . . but how could he do that without anyone seeing when the whole place was swarming with drunk people searching out corners to puke or snog or pass out in?' She jiggles her knees up and down, up and down. 'How did he seem when you sold him the drugs?'

'If he had just killed for the first time in an assault gone wrong, I saw no sign of it. He seemed calm, bored even.' I shake my head. 'It is more likely that – assuming he was involved at all – Reenie had a bad reaction to the roofies after he left her – some people do. But it still doesn't explain why she was never found.'

I wait for Verity to explode or cry, but she just sits hugging her knees and staring into space.

'Maybe you killed him the night he killed her. Maybe I've been searching for answers all these years, tearing my life apart over and over, and you . . .' She heaves out a quavering sigh. 'Maybe you stopped him from hurting anyone else the way he hurt Reenie.'

I wait to find out if grief or fury will win.

'You knew all this, but you still don't know what happened to her. Or even whether what you did made any difference.' She unfolds, resting her elbows on the table.

'It might have been *the* difference.' My voice cracks, but I force myself to go on. 'I might have been the reason that she was the only one of his victims not to come home.'

I press at the ache under my breastbone as if the guilt is a physical pain. 'I have been trying to work out what happened to your sister since the news of her disappearance broke and I realized it happened at the university the same night I killed Christophe. For twenty-five years, I have kept to the Rules, and they have seen me through every other job with no mistakes, no collateral damage. This was the one time I might have done harm to a victim, not just my target.'

The cough threatens again and I take a sip of tea to quell the urge. 'My career is nearly over, and you are my loose end, Verity. Whether or not I had any hand in what happened to your sister, whether or not either of us ever finds the answer, I couldn't rest knowing that I could have helped you and didn't. I picked you because a place in the Sisterhood is the greatest gift I could give anyone. It has been everything to me, and I thought it might be the same for you.'

Her eyes go glassy. 'So that wasn't a lie. It just wasn't the whole truth. Because you thought I wasn't ready for it. You thought I'd wreck this chance, too. Because that's what I do, isn't it?' Verity's right hand draws into a fist so tight I know the nails must be cutting into her palm.

I reach out and put my hand over hers, rubbing the back of her fist until it unfurls.

She presses the back of her free hand over her mouth, holding in a noise of painconfusionmiseryrage. 'I don't know what to do. I don't . . . I don't want it to be like this.'

'But it is, so we shall just have to make the most of it. That is what a life in the Sisterhood is.'

Verity

I'm so tired the bed seems to be rocking beneath me – I'm so tired I can't sleep. Fragments of thought keep drifting through my mind, sending a spike of emotion-fuelled adrenalin through my veins, then exhaustion washes over me again.

I don't even know where to start with figuring out how I feel about Pru. We spent the evening quietly eating our way through a huge bowl of raspberry mousse and re-reading the statements from Reenie's file. TJ and I had both said she was alternately distant and angry before she disappeared. At least our early statements said that before moving into line with Mum's. But by then the police had already looked into whether Reenie had ordered a passport. Whether she had bought a train ticket, bus ticket or plane ticket. They looked into the possibility she'd run away. They found no evidence.

So then they looked into whether she'd bought drugs from any local dealers. Whether she'd gone to the GP recently. They looked at her internet history. In every case, they found nothing.

What if Pru killing Christophe killed Reenie? I let the question shudder through me, feel a scream building . . .

Then it dies. If Pru's actions killed Reenie, why wasn't she found? It doesn't make sense.

Maybe Pru killing Christophe had nothing to do with Reenie's disappearance at all.

There could have been a second predator at the party that night – after all, women and girls get assaulted all the time. Maybe it was Charles Temple or Nathan or another boy entirely. Maybe it didn't even happen at the party – Reenie could have set off home and, in the dead of night, someone could have seen her. Dragged her into an alley or a car . . . Maybe she was never found because she was miles away when she died.

But what if it was simpler than that? What if Reenie ran away *and never looked back*?

My muscles lock until they tremble, my heart beating so hard and fast I think I might be sick.

'Why don't you like me any more?' I asked that final morning as Reenie stomped about the kitchen ignoring me, as she'd been doing for weeks.

She went still, then turned and, for the first time in days, there was a smile on her face. 'Just because I'm a moody cow doesn't mean I don't love you.'

I shot across the kitchen and wrapped myself around her, and she laughed and rocked me back and forth till I laughed, too. When I finally let go, she reached out and hooked my hair behind my ear the way she always did.

'Let's go to the park early this afternoon. We can walk around the lake, like old times, before everyone from school turns up.'

Everything felt perfect. Reenie was herself again. She lent me a dress I'd admired for months. She did my hair and make-up for me. We sang our way to the park, then skipped stones across the lake as the sun shone and shone.

We went on the swings and the roundabout like kids and got chased by a black swan making noises like something out of *Jurassic Park* . . .

Was that afternoon in the park a goodbye? Was she planning to leave me?

She started going distant and distracted the moment people from school turned up. By the time we arrived at the party she was sharp and brittle again, focused on anything but me. Was she planning to run away and use the party as cover?

I can't believe it. She loved me. She protected me – kept me sane around Mum's lies and tempers. She wouldn't have just gone off to make a new life for herself without ever a word. She wouldn't.

That's not denial, that's the truth. Reenie's dead. She has to be.

But what if that day was a different type of goodbye, like TJ hinted?

My heart kicks painfully at my ribs, then slows again as I finally ask myself the question.

She'd been so *wrong* for weeks. Then, like a switch, she was fine, and I didn't question it; I was too relieved the storm was over. But what if the only thing that was over was her fighting her troubles?

You're betraying her memory! part of me screams.

But another, quieter part whispers, *Why would you feel guilty for leaving your big sister at a party if you didn't think there was something wrong with her wanting to stay instead of seeing you safely home?*

A passing car sends shards of light fanning across the ceiling, blazing golden, then gone.

It all seems so clear now I recognize the same desperation that drove me to confront TJ instead of talking to Pru, drove me to break into the car to free the dog instead of calling the police, drove me to Gavin Pieper's new allotment, despite knowing I was bound to get caught. I knew it would end badly every time, and I did it anyway because there was too much hurt in me to care so long as, for a moment, I was doing *something*.

It was the same with Reenie that night: she was beyond caring about the risk of staying at the party because she was already hurting as much as it's possible to hurt.

Why, though? It seemed so obvious that the stars led to the sticker, which led to TJ, but he wasn't furtive and defensive when I confronted him earlier. He was sad and guilty and . . . weary. Maybe I'm being stupid, but I don't believe that's how he'd react if he'd hurt Reenie.

But if it wasn't TJ, then why wouldn't she have told? With TJ, she'd have tried to talk to Mum, and Mum wouldn't have listened, but if a stranger had hurt her, or someone else we knew, Mum would have been all over it, ranting about her precious innocent daughter. So who else is there?

It *has* to be Gavin. The things she said that night in the garden looking at the stars – it could have been him she was talking about, not TJ at all.

At the time I thought it was romantic that the pain of the break-up was so bad she couldn't bear to even mention Gavin, but what if she was heartbroken because he'd hurt her? Given their endless PDAs around school, she might have blamed herself. Mum would've said she was asking for it. Reenie usually managed to ignore Mum's lies, but would *that* have been water off a duck's back?

I fling myself out of bed and stumble to the sink, splashing cold water on the back of my neck.

Gavin was in the park that day. What if he was so angry to see Reenie going off in a limo that he waited somewhere like the alley by our house to confront her, only it all went horribly wrong? The statistics say her killer is more likely to be Gavin than TJ.

Yesterday, I would have hurled myself in the car and gone to interrogate him. Now, I think it through.

Even with the message from his ex-sister-in-law about his alibi to unsettle him, he wouldn't admit anything to me. And, unlike TJ, he'd be delighted for the police to charge me with harassment. I need a plan. And, for a good one, I need Pru, but . . .

I feel betrayed. And furious. Guilty. Hurt. Confused.

I'm so confused. What am I meant to be feeling? Am I betraying Reenie if I keep trusting Pru? Because I do trust her. Only it's not simple any more.

The other times I felt like she'd pulled the rug from under me – the tracker on my car, the confession – I could believe she'd done it partly for my own good, and partly because how else could the Sisterhood function? But holding back knowledge that might have helped solve Reenie's disappearance . . . From Day 1, I thought we were investigating together.

And yet knowing hasn't solved anything, just given me more questions without answers. And not just about Reenie.

All this time Pru's been teaching me to think things

through, spot what I'm missing. So, I have to consider the fact that this isn't the only thing Pru has withheld.

Tonight, when I asked if there was anything else about Reenie she was holding back, she promised there wasn't. Since keeping promises is practically an unwritten Rule to Pru, I know she's not lying. So then I asked if there was anything else she was keeping from me, and she just laughed.

'Where do I even start?' she said, which could mean anything.

She's never promised to put my well-being ahead of the Sisterhood, so it's time I stopped assuming her interests will always align with mine. After all, I've felt like she was keeping secrets since that first day off from training. Although my attempts to investigate have led nowhere, I've hardly been persistent.

Maybe it's time that changed.

Pru

For Verity's second international job, we are assigned a three-week cover story with a diplomat's family in Dresden. I am housekeeper, while Verity is nanny to twin six-year-old boys and one small canine. Our target arrived in the city a few hours ago to pursue his favourite hobby – travelling to meet and assault children he has groomed online. With half a day to while away before meeting up with his latest victim, he booked himself a series of spa treatments at his hotel. That is where we killed him just a few minutes ago.

The Dresden streets are helpfully teeming with tourists when we step out of the hotel, losing ourselves in the crowd strolling towards the city centre. The city's mix of modern and old architecture speaks to the legacy of Second World War bombing raids – and the impressive scale of post-war reconstruction. It is a lovely place to spend a few weeks and, with our kill taken care of, the rest of our off-duty hours are now ours to enjoy together.

'I smashed that!' Verity crows, punching the air like a football hooligan. 'Target dispatched cleanly, carefully and invisibly.'

'Indeed. Now, will you stop shouting about it before we draw attention?' I hiss, trying to hold on to my happy ruminations about the sights I want to show Verity and the out-of-the-way restaurant Constance recommended when I told her about the trip.

'I can't believe you didn't let me nick the robe. Given what we were up to, minor theft – of a disguise, no less – seems a little silly, don't you think?'

'First, stealing from a hotel will not make the world a better place, unlike dispatching a paedophile. Second, the whole point of the robe was that we were in a spa, where everyone is wearing the same. Leaving it in the toilets, then exiting with the hen party, dressed in normal clothes, means no one will ever know who went into the whirlpool room, then swiftly left again, as if she had found it unexpectedly occupied. *Why* is that the case?'

'Because it's illegal to put cameras in bathrooms and similar spaces, so the only footage will be from the corridor and I made sure my head was down with my hair hanging over my face,' Verity sing-songs. 'What if someone put a camera in there anyway?'

'Then they would hardly want to admit that to the police, would they?'

'I still feel bad for whoever has to find him. What if there's some residual electricity and they get hurt reaching into the tub to check his pulse?'

'The target had a pre-existing heart condition. A normal person wouldn't have died from the voltage of the . . . item you tossed into the water.'

Verity giggles. 'I love the way you keep calling it an "item".'

'I am being discreet,' I say sniffily as I guide our steps towards the patisserie where I promised to buy some cakes if Verity completed the job without complications.

'Did you manage to slip the receipt for the' – Verity flashes me a grin as she pauses theatrically – '*item* under the door of his room OK? What would have happened if the carpet was too tight a fit?'

'It wasn't. And there were no problems. I tripped over, spilling the contents of my handbag all over the corridor for the benefit of the CCTV. Unlike some people, I understand my angles perfectly, so, while most of my belongings fell in front of the next-door room, a few things rolled in front of his door. A quick crouch to grab them with one hand, and a little flick of the other wrist, *et voilà*.'

'You really think they'll be reluctant to look into the details just to avoid the publicity of a guest killing himself with a sex toy in the whirlpool?' She pulls a face. 'Yeah, I guess I wouldn't want that getting out if I was managing the hotel.'

'Exactly. The world is full of men who get up to far more sordid things than using a sex toy in a single-occupancy area of a spa, so it is unlikely to provoke questions. Indeed, most people want to ask as few as possible in these circumstances: a useful thing in our line of business.'

Verity catches the patisserie door and holds it open for me, then rushes to the counter like a child, practically pressing her nose to the glass. 'That one, please. And that one. Definitely that one. Oooooh, and that one. And . . .' She glances up at me with a revolting grin. 'Anything for you?'

I order a raspberry tartlet. Verity promptly adds one of her own. I let her cradle the box, carrying it as if it is a bubble about to burst. This time I hold the door as she manoeuvres outside, then sets off at a snail's pace.

'For goodness' sake.' I snatch the box and stride on.

Verity squeaks in protest, scuttling after me with her hands out.

'It isn't made of glass, and I am not going to drop it. Do you really think you are more likely than I am to get it back to the house safely?'

'You're so mean to me,' she whines, looking quite pleased about it.

My heart squeezes that we still have this ease, this growing fondness, between us, even after I told her about Christophe.

'Whatever did you do to deserve such cruel treatment as to be bought fancy, expensive cakes? Five of them, might I add. Hardly a balanced lunch.'

'There're carbohydrates in the pastry and the sponge. And there's cream and butter, so that's dairy *and* a bit of protein. Especially in the cheesecake. And there's egg in the meringue. And fruit. There's, like, a selection of fruit.'

I sigh at the 'like', then stumble to a stop as coughing tears its way up my throat. 'Here.' I shove the box at Verity while I get myself under control. 'Yes, yes, I know,' I say, when I can finally breathe properly again. 'I will make a doctor's appointment for when we get home.'

I take the box back and we walk on, though Verity is quiet now, frowning at me.

Eventually she shakes her head, though I haven't said anything. 'Any news from the Sisterhood about Gavin's records?'

'No evidence of harassment complaints at work. There were a few public order incidents – rows in a pub or after a football match. One caution. All involving alcohol. His medical file confirms that he is a drinker. He has been unemployed a few times – looks like drinking on the job, so that follows. Some money issues. Never married. No kids. Nothing to suggest a pattern of violence or sexual aggression against women, but there isn't always any evidence. His main relationship seems to be with his dog, which is ill, if the vet bills are anything to go by.'

Verity scrunches her face up. 'If he's spending all that money on his dog, then he's probably good to it. I thought violent men tended to be violent to animals as well as people, so isn't that an indication against it being him?'

We reach the smart townhouse that is our current base-of-operations-meets-cover-story, and I stand back while Verity puts in the code to unlock the front door.

I slip through as she holds it open. 'Make sure it closes.'

'Yeah, yeah.' She gestures me on.

'This is important, Verity.' I make my way along the corridor to the kitchen, listening out until I hear the telltale click. Placing the box on the counter, I set out plates and forks.

'The most interesting thing in the financial report was a recurring donation to a local wildlife charity for a sanctuary on Heathtop Hill.'

A flurry of noise erupts in the hall as the front door opens again and twin six-year-olds explode into the house. There is much shrieking as their fluffy nonsense of a dog scurries around their feet, yipping. I hurry down the corridor, Verity at my heels.

'Heathtop?' she asks, but I wave her off as I take our client's handbag and wrap.

'Oh, shoot!' Laurene turns to her driver-meets-security as he follows her up the front steps. 'Javier, you couldn't be a doll and get my phone from the car?'

He nods, turning away.

'Door, Verity!' I say, as I hang Laurene's wrap on the coat stand.

Verity shoves at the door, though her attention is on Vivaldi, the fluffy white gremlin our client believes is some sort of canine.

Ajax zooms upstairs, while Apollo runs out of the lounge, shouting, 'I'm coming, too, Javier!'

I catch hold of him. 'Why don't we have some reading time while Mummy does her email? Door, Verity!' I hiss over my shoulder.

She shoves at it again as the fluffy white rat bolts down the hall to the kitchen. 'Could I grab you a moment, Pru, about that Heathtop—'

A large man in a black hoodie wrenches the door open.

I am moving before anyone else has even realized what is happening. As the intruder slams the door behind him, I twist and shove Apollo behind me, hoping Verity is sharp enough to catch him.

As the intruder jams on the security bolt with one hand, reaching for a weapon with the other, I grab the gorgeous marble bowl with its delicate yellow orchid from the sideboard.

Laurene's mouth is still coming open as the intruder turns, lifting his gun.

Pebbles rain across the hall as I swing my arm up so that the bowl crunches into his chin, then catches his nose as his head snaps back. The impact jolts through my hand into my wrist, elbow, shoulder. He crashes into the corner between the door and wall, head smacking into the plaster. Momentum pulls me forward, gravity dragging my arm down as I put all my weight behind it.

As the bowl catches him in the side of the head, crunching into his skull, I let go, watching it rolling down his chest to land in his lap. My knee thuds on to the floor as his arm drops, the gun crashing out of his limp hand.

I flinch, waiting for the explosion as it fires . . .

Nothing.

Though the man hasn't yet moved and my chest is painfully tight, I push frantically off the ground, reaching for the gun.

I pick it up, keeping the barrel pointed to the floor as I assess the man properly.

He is not going to be moving again. At least not under his own steam.

'Verity, take Apollo into the kitchen and give him some ice cream,' I order, even as I turn to our client. 'Laurene, go upstairs and make sure Ajax doesn't come down.'

Thankfully, Verity's footsteps are already fading, so either she is propelling Apollo or, if she's got any sense, she has picked him up. They are a problem for later. Our client is still staring at the intruder.

I raise my voice. 'Laurene. Go upstairs to Ajax. Verity has Apollo.'

The moment her eyes snap to mine, she starts hyperventilating. Still, she pushes shakily off the wall and scrambles upstairs, even as a piercing wail echoes down to us.

I steel myself, then turn back to the intruder. He is blocking the door and will need to be moved so that I can let Javier in before he tries to break through one of the reinforced windows.

My lungs feel as if I have been breathing in splinters of glass, and tremors are starting to creep down my arms and legs, weakening my knees, but I can't stop yet.

Putting the gun on the sideboard, I shake my hands then crouch to grab the intruder's feet, but I am trembling too badly to pull him clear of the door. Muffling a groan, I go to my knees and, moving his nearest arm and leg into the correct positions, I rock him back and forth until I can tip him into the recovery position.

It takes me three attempts to rise again, levering myself up on the sideboard then sagging over it for a moment before I take up the gun again. I keep it pointed at the ground as I unlatch the security bolt.

'Javier!' I call, then have to pause to cough. 'It's Pru,' I croak as loudly as I can. 'I am opening the door. Don't push in on me. I need to check it's you.'

I press the release button then, keeping myself sheltered behind the door, open it an inch. Javier stares back at me from the front step. Opening the door wide, I beckon him in with my free hand, even as my eyes roam the street behind him.

'Laurene is upstairs with Ajax. Verity is in the kitchen with Apollo,' I report. 'Can I give you this?' I point at the gun with my free hand. 'I need to find a pot to see if I can rescue that poor orchid.'

Javier's eyes move from my face to the gun, then he looks at the man on the ground.

'I hit him with the orchid bowl, but I think we can save the orchid,' I tell him.

Then I realize that this is probably not the right thing to say. Older women who have just bludgeoned armed intruders are not meant to be worried about house plants.

I let my eyes go wide, let my mouth fall open, then I totter backwards and slide down the wall.

Javier leaps forward to tear the gun from my hand while I do my very best to mimic Laurene and hyperventilate like a normal person.

Verity

The intruder has been taken away in an ambulance. I expect this is for show. I keep hearing the sound the marble bowl made the second time it whacked into his skull—

No. No, no, no, no, nope. Not going to think about that. La la la la. Not hearing it. All gone.

Thankfully, Vivaldi is still yelping. Usually even my temper would be fraying by this point, but, for once, her piercing little shrieks are a welcome distraction. I take one of her freshly cooked gourmet meals from the fridge, then spoon it into her ergonomic name-embossed dish. The yipping is promptly replaced by the sounds of her slobbering it everywhere. For such a tiny thing, she sure makes a mess, even when she's not peeing or pooing on anything.

I'm not sure if I'm allowed to clean up the deposits she left in the hall in the wake of Pru bludgeoning the intruder. Javier snapped some pictures of the scene while we were waiting for the police and the ambulance, then they took a couple more once the man had been whisked away, medical treatment taking priority over forensic investigations. I was peeping around the kitchen door, trying to keep Apollo from doing the same, when they moved the bod— him, so I saw what was left. After which quite a lot of deep breathing was needed.

In the end, I wrapped a tea-towel around Apollo's head, making a game of guiding him down the hall then upstairs to his mother. Laurene's make-up had smudged, making her look almost melted. Her hair was a frazzled mop to rival Vivaldi's tail. The moment I whipped the tea-towel off Apollo's head, she launched up from where she was holding Ajax and wrapped herself around Apollo instead, bringing him to the floor then reaching out and dragging Ajax in, too. The boys protested and wriggled, but she just held them harder, then finally released them.

'Why don't you have some screentime?' she said.

They raced next door to their bedroom, leaving her limp and wretched on the floor.

'Do I . . . Do I have to go down now?' she asked, voice small and pleading.

'Why don't you stay with the boys? I'll head back to Pru and Javier.'

I had no idea what to expect as I descended the stairs, but Javier beckoned me on as he spoke quietly to the policeman standing in front of the door. I paused on the bottom step.

'We have shut Vivaldi in the kitchen. Please could you check on her then make some coffee?'

I nodded, eyes fixed on the closed living-room door. Quiet voices sounded behind it. 'Is Pru . . .'

'She is giving a statement. I am sure everyone would appreciate a hot drink.'

My eyes lingered on the door even as I hurried down the hall, bending to scoop Vivaldi up before she could make a break for it as I slipped into the kitchen.

She's back to pawing at the door now, her fluffy tail vibrating with anxiety.

With a groan, I pick her up again. 'You are a terrible menace for the offspring of a dust bunny and an angora sweater.'

She licks my nose.

'Time for a nap.' I take her over to her luxury crate, flick open the gate and slide her into the nest of blankets on top of her memory-foam pillow. She's tired enough from all the trouble she's caused to yip just once as she circles, curls up, then immediately falls asleep.

Heavy footfalls approach down the hall. There's a quick rap of knuckles against the door.

'Safe to come in, or will we get eaten?' Javier calls.

'She's in her crate,' I call back.

The door opens and Javier steps in. He is followed by a man in a suit who reminds me so forcibly of DI Strickland that I know instantly he's some sort of police detective.

'Are you feeling up to answering a few questions?' Javier asks.

He and the police officer draw out chairs as I sink down at the kitchen table.

The police officer takes a phone out of his pocket and puts it on the table, swiping into an app then hitting a red 'record' button. 'Please tell me what happened after you returned into the house this afternoon before the incident,' he asks in near-perfect English.

I try to keep my explanation brief, wincing at how halting and strained my voice sounds. Will they think I'm making it up? None of it is a lie, but obviously I need to be careful not to give anything away about what Pru and I were up to earlier.

'I didn't see what happened after I ran in here with Apollo. I dragged the table in front of the door as a barricade, then took out my phone to call the police, only I'd forgotten what the number is in Germany. I learnt it for the job, but I was so panicked I couldn't remember—' I shake my head, taking a steadying breath. 'That was when I heard Pru calling to Javier about opening the door and I knew everything must be OK. I pulled the table back and poked my head out, but Javier said to stay put. By the time he told me I could take Apollo upstairs to his mother, Pru was in the other room and— Is she OK?'

'She's fine,' Javier says. 'The shock caught up with her once it was over and she got a bit hysterical, but she's better now, and the coffee seemed to help.'

'Shall I make some more? Maybe something to eat?'

'In a moment,' says the officer. 'Your colleague . . . she is trained for security?'

'Maybe?' I squeak. 'I don't . . . I haven't been with the Sist— with ESA for long. I guess maybe, after a while, they want you to do a security course or, like, self-defence?' I raise my hands helplessly.

Pru's voice snaps, *Don't oversell it, Verity. You're not hamming it up for the stage. You're just a normal person telling the truth.*

Should I be weirded out that her voice has replaced Mum's? Am I imprinting on her somehow?

I meet the officer's eyes. 'Pru's a rock. She's been there for me since I started with the Sis— with ESA. She's always exactly where people need her to be, when they need her.

She seems rigid and fussy and cold, but she's not. She's just . . . she's determined to do everything excellently, you know?'

The police officer frowns, opening his mouth.

'And I get that doesn't seem relevant, but it's just . . . Pru gets stuff done. That's what she did today. She pushed me and Apollo behind her . . .' I have to pause to swallow down the sudden rush of emotion as I register that the first thing Pru did was put herself between me and an armed man. She didn't stop to think about it for even a second. It was pure instinct to protect me – and trust me to protect Apollo.

What on earth do you think I'm training you for, Verity? The whole point of the Sisterhood is protection. This is just a more . . . immediate version.

'She looked after us first, then she grabbed the nearest heavy object and swung it at him . . . Then did it again when he tried to get up. It wasn't, like, some mad ninja moves. It was just a really brave woman refusing to let me and the kids and Laurene get hurt.' I shudder, trying to keep it subtle.

'Some people are good in a crisis.' Javier exchanges a long look with the police officer.

The officer nods and taps the red 'record' button to off.

I try not to slump in relief. 'Can I see Pru now? I'd really like to thank her.'

'Yes, she deserves much thanks,' agrees the police officer. 'We will call if we have more questions later,' he tells Javier, then strides away down the hall.

'Why don't you get more coffee on and see about some sandwiches,' Javier says. 'I'll send Pru in once they're finished with her.'

Then he's gone, too, and it's just me and Vivaldi's improbably loud snores. I want to fold over the table and rest. Instead, I bustle about the kitchen with Pru's voice tutting over how sloppily I butter the bread, how unevenly I chop the cucumber.

Do it properly, she says, where Mum would have told me, *It's such a pity you never outgrew your clumsiness.*

'Did Apollo fall when I shoved him at you?'

I shriek at Pru's voice behind me, scattering the lettuce I was shredding across the counter as I spin round.

I've heard people say someone looked small after an illness, but I always thought they meant figuratively. People don't just shrink because they've had a shock. But Pru seems . . . diminished.

'Sit down. I'm making you a sandwich. It is sloppy and uneven, but you're going to love it.'

Pru huffs out a breath of laughter, then starts coughing. It's become a nasty, wet crackle, and she winces as she lowers herself into a chair like she aches all over.

I slosh milk into her coffee, add sugar, then a bit extra, and put it down beside her. Too busy coughing to speak, she reaches out and pats the back of my hand.

'You were magnificent,' I whisper.

Pru wipes away the tears the coughing has forced from her eyes. 'I drew attention.'

'You saved our lives!'

'Maybe,' Pru croaks. 'They don't know what to make of me.'

I crouch by her chair and wrap my arms around her. I expect a quick squeeze, but she sighs and leans in. Something about the fact that she lets me support her weight as she rests her head against mine makes my eyes sting. I hold her even tighter.

Finally, she pulls back. 'Hugging and compliments. Whatever next?' She eyes the messy sandwich. 'Well, at least some things are comfortingly familiar.'

Pru

After yesterday it is no surprise that Laurene and the boys are holed up in the lounge, keeping themselves occupied with their devices; I doubt they will be venturing out any time soon, leaving Verity to walk Vivaldi alone. I am just setting out ingredients for lunch when my phone goes. My adrenalin spikes when I see it is an unfamiliar local number. I take a steadying breath before answering.

'This is Polizeioberkommissar Fischer – I think you say Detective Inspector in UK? I am sorry to have bad news.' He waits a beat. 'The man who intruded into the house yesterday died in the hospital.'

What would a normal person say? I don't know, so I stay silent.

'We need you to come to the police station for a formal interview.'

I clear my throat, then end up coughing. 'Sorry,' I rasp. 'When . . . when do you need me?'

'Soon, please. While your memory is fresh.'

'I shall have to ask my client, but I will be there as soon as possible.' I muffle another cough.

'I will message the address,' DI Fischer tells me, then ends the call.

For a moment, I stare down at the phone, then I shake myself and knock on the lounge door.

'Come in!' Laurene calls. 'Oh, Pru. Could you possibly—What is it? What's happened?'

I glance at the twins, but they are lost to the world, headphones on, eyes glued to their screens.

'The intruder is deceased,' I tell Laurene, pitching my voice low just in case. 'They need me to go and give a formal statement.'

Laurene's shock melts into confusion. 'I thought you gave a statement yesterday.'

I spread my hands. 'Now there is a fatality, I suppose they need more details. They would like me to go as soon as possible.'

'Of course.' She shakes her head. 'I'm sorry, Pru.'

'Hopefully, I won't be long, but Verity will be back soon, and she can manage a basic lunch if I am delayed.'

Laurene reaches for her handbag. 'Let me find some cash for a cab.'

'It isn't far, and the walk would be welcome, but thank you.'

'Good luck!' Laurene calls after me.

I collect my handbag then let myself out, messaging Javier, then Verity, as I walk. My phone pings, but I ignore the notifications, keeping my focus on the app showing me the route to the police station.

The sun blazes down, forcing me to slow my steps to avoid arriving sweaty and overheated.

That would be bad when you need to keep your cool! Verity's voice pipes up in my head.

Fond frustration makes me smile, then I sigh, and then I cough. My phone keeps pinging. How long will it take Verity to come to the conclusion that it is more important for me to get to the police station quickly rather than delay while I deal with her panic?

Ping, ping, pingpingpingping. Verity will be expressing her feelings.

Since the last line of my message to her was *Be careful and stay mindful of your duties*, I have to trust that she won't put anything too foolish in writing.

The pinging continues unabated.

I switch the phone to silent; my focus needs to be on the interview.

I turn a corner, and there is the police station. My steps falter, but I drive myself on.

Fifteen minutes later, I am facing DI Fischer across an interview-room table. We are going over the incident while I try not to look down and to the left (a common sign of lying) or hold too much eye contact or too little (other common signs). I make sure I use contractions. I avoid reusing too many of the words and phrases from the statement I gave yesterday. I admit I have some self-defence training but insist that grabbing the bowl was an act of panicked desperation.

'Apollo was right there in the hall. When I realized the man was reaching for a weapon . . .'

Coughing overtakes me, but, since it isn't faked, I let it happen. It will muddy the waters regarding any tightness in my voice.

'Sorry,' I gasp, rubbing at my chest. 'I think it's an allergy. Had it for weeks.'

'Did you aim for a particular place on the body when you hit the intruder?'

I shake my head. 'The bowl was so heavy I let momentum take it. I wasn't thinking at all. I just knew I had to do something – knock him down, knock the gun away – before anything happened to Apollo.'

'So, then he fell. Did you think about locking yourself and the others in the living room or escaping through the back?'

'There wasn't time. He was in the corner between the wall and the door, and . . .' I let my eyes close as I visualize the scene. 'His hand was coming up with the gun and my arm was still in the air, but the bowl – like I said, it was heavy, so I let gravity do the work.'

I try not to look as if I am analysing his expression. Does he believe me?

'And next?' he asks mildly.

'The bowl came out of my hand and . . .' I frown, tilting my head. 'I think I picked up the gun next. Or maybe I told Laurene to go upstairs? I'm fairly sure that was before I moved the man out of the way so I could open the door for Javier.'

'And you moved him how?'

'I know first aid, so I put him in the recovery position.'

He suspects there is more to this story, but he has nothing to justify his instinct. After all, I am telling the truth and nothing but the truth. And yet I took down a man who was surely some sort of professional killer or kidnapper, though doubtless on paper he is a freelancer for an international security firm. Even people like Laurene can fall foul of bad luck, but he was not some random thug – he had to have been following her, or at least watching the house, waiting for his moment. Then I killed him.

Now I need to persuade DI Fischer that I am exactly what I seem: a shaken sixty-four-year-old woman who threw herself at an intruder in a fit of reckless bravery and got lucky.

'I had a daughter.' I let my hands spread open and empty. 'She was killed in a hit-and-run when she was still a teenager.'

The words still feel strange in my mouth, even after all this time. They are too small, too simple. Even though I know they are true, my brain sends up an instinctive message: *Wrong. Error. Does not compute.*

'Apollo and Ajax may be spoilt and loud and nothing like my daughter, but they are children. And I will never, ever let harm come to a child if there is the slightest chance I can stop it.' I fiddle with a loose thread on my cuff. 'I expect you think I'm cold and strange because a man is dead and I . . . I'm not crying, even though I . . . made that happen.'

Rule 9: *Take no unnecessary risks*, I tell Verity all the time. *Simple is best* – Rule 3.

I meet his gaze straight on. 'I know I should pretend to be distraught, but I'm not. Apollo and Ajax are unharmed. I don't know what that man had planned, but he burst into the house with a gun, and all I cared about then, and all I care about now, is that the children are OK. It isn't a crime to care more about children than about violent criminals. That is all I did. Now I want to go back to the house and make lunch for everyone.'

A frozen moment.

DI Fischer nods and closes his file. 'Thank you. We will call if we have more questions.'

'That is your prerogative, but I won't have any new answers,' I tell him as I follow him to the door.

When his lips quirk into a smile, I seize the moment and ask, 'Do you know who the intruder was? Why he . . . What he was planning?'

He pauses, considering. 'I cannot share information from the investigation at this time, but it is right that you know he had convictions for violent crime.'

I nod my thanks as he opens the door and gestures me towards the exit.

I keep my pace steady. Quick, but not too quick.

It is irrational to expect someone to stop me as I make for the street, but my shoulders stay rigid with tension until I am two blocks away. Then I have to sit down on a bench as coughing overwhelms me again. Since the fright of yesterday, it has been growing wet and crackling.

Now I spit into a tissue and find the phlegm flecked with rusty brown.

Verity

I rehearse many, *many* brilliant things to say to Pru as I walk Vivaldi and clean up after Vivaldi and groom Vivaldi and deal with Vivaldi trying to bite the decorator who has come to fix the dent in the hall wall and the gouges on the skirting board.

Now, holed up in the kitchen, Vivaldi yips in approval as I practise several snappy retorts about partnership. She pees on the kitchen floor when I call out the hypocrisy of Pru expecting me to keep to the Rules while she is surely breaking all rules of common decency.

I am so ready for this conversation. Beyond ready. I am going to *win*, and Pru is going to have to apologize. I'm fairly sure it won't kill her.

When the doorbell goes, I toss my hair back, check Vivaldi is sleeping in her crate, then march down the hall – remembering, at the last moment, to check who it is through the spyhole. Pru stands on the step. There's no one behind her. I open the door.

'Are you going to start here, or can we go into the kitchen before I get the lecture, the rant and the attempts at humour?'

All my carefully planned lines vanish. My brain is blank. 'You are a horrible woman,' I tell my mentor. 'And you look exhausted.' I throw my hands in the air. 'This is just typical. For once, I've got a perfect right to tell you off, and you're . . .' I gesture at her.

'Yesterday I was your guardian angel. Has it brought me no grace?' Pru fashions her face into a look of martyred resignation.

'Oh, for—' I pull the door wide. 'Get in the kitchen and sit down while I make you a cup of tea,' I snarl.

Pru sails past me . . . then trips on the mat.

I lurch forward just a second too late to stop her tumbling to her hands and knees. I dither between helping her and closing the door.

'What is it?' yells Laurene from the living room. 'JAVIER!' she screams.

'It's fine!' I shout, shoving the door to, then shoving some more when the lock doesn't engage immediately. 'Pru tripped on the mat. Everything's fine!' I hurry to Pru, who has pulled herself up on the sideboard but now is slumped against it, coughing.

Javier appears from the back, skirting around us to check the door is shut tight.

Laurene appears from the lounge. 'Is she OK?'

Pru straightens, then wavers into me. I grab her arm and hold her steady.

'Sorry,' Pru croaks. 'Just need . . .'

'I'll get her a lemon-honey tea and some hay-fever pills,' I tell Laurene. 'Are you OK while I . . .' I nod towards the kitchen.

'Of course. Let me know if we need a doctor.'

Pru leans on me all the way down the hall and into the kitchen. There's a trembling in her muscles that I know has nothing to do with the cough. Sixty-four isn't old, but I guess it's old enough, given all that's happened in the last twenty-four hours. I'd probably be shaky, too, if I'd been questioned by the police.

'I know you said no weapons, but I guess marble bowls don't count.'

'Is this a fresh attempt at comedy?' Pru asks wearily as she drops into a seat. 'I told you never to *bring* a weapon: I never said not to use one you find at hand in an emergency.' She sighs. 'It is such a pity about that lovely orchid.'

I fetch the box of cakes from yesterday and serve a couple on to plates.

'I'm not hungry,' Pru says, pushing hers away.

'Just eat to keep me company, OK?' I take a large, angry forkful then moan as bliss consumes me. 'Or don't eat it and I'll pig the lot. This is a-maz-ing.'

Pru contemplates the cake, takes a bite, then draws it closer and tucks in.

'I didn't tell you before I left because I had to focus on the interview,' Pru says. 'If you choose to think this is a violation of trust or withholding of information, then . . . We are past the time when you have to decide if you're in this, no matter what. No walking away if you're upset or hurt or angry.'

'You can't tell me that you – of all people – are in this "no matter what".'

'So long as the Rules prevail, then, yes, I am. To the bitter end.' Her lips quirk as if she's said something darkly funny, instead of just dark.

'If the Sisterhood sent you after an innocent person, you'd still be in?'

‘There has never been a mistake of that sort in our history.’

‘That you know of,’ I counter. ‘What if they changed the Rules?’

‘The Rules do not change. When necessary, they are augmented. Try a different excuse.’

‘What if someone betrayed you? What if someone you know from the Sisterhood got caught and gave you up as part of a plea deal?’

Pru rubs at her temples. ‘That is the American system, Verity. It doesn’t work like that in Britain. Anyway, no one in the Sisterhood would do such a thing.’

I slouch back, folding my arms. ‘You wouldn’t, but you can’t swear to it for everyone else. Do you even know everyone in the Sisterhood?’

‘I have met enough of us over the years.’ Pru warms her hands on her mug. ‘When Hope was born, I had no idea what I was facing. Never sleeping for more than a few hours at a time. Never being able to catch up on the missed rest. The endless feeding. The endless cleaning. The endless crying and *needing*.’

Despite the words, there’s a smile on her face. ‘Babies are made of need, and you lose yourself in it. Your whole existence comes down to meeting that need till you feel there is nothing left, and *still* you cannot stop. At times you hate the baby, then you hate yourself, then the love floods back again. The thing that gets you through is that you decided to have a child, so now you have to look after that child – and somehow, you do. It isn’t because the love fuels you though – sometimes you are too tired for any sort of emotion. There is just the dogged knowledge that you *must*, so you do.’

'Joining the Sisterhood is like raising a baby?' I bite out, then wince.

Oh, Verity, sighs my mother. *You say you want to be close to people, then the moment they open up you make some unkind and unfunny joke and wonder why everyone gives up on you.*

Pru levers herself to her feet. 'You had better take Vivaldi for her walk while I work on lunch.'

I watch as she starts taking ingredients out of the fridge. 'What about the police?'

'We shall have to wait and see.'

That is not comforting, but I am getting used to living with uncertainty.

Still, I loiter, watching Pru. She's moving stiffly, as if her whole body hurts. The last of my anger about earlier fades away as worry takes its place.

Pru

I love to travel, but I am always happy to be home again. This time, more than ever. It has been a long three weeks.

Verity parks next to Boudicca in the drive, then bounds out of the car, practically skipping round to the boot while I am still fighting my way to my feet. I pretend to be having an issue with the seatbelt as an excuse to lean against the car when dizziness makes the world spin around me. Weariness has settled into my bones, as if my marrow has been replaced with lead. By the time I've straightened, grabbed my handbag and shut the car door, Verity is already dragging our suitcases up the path.

I follow slowly, hoping Verity will assume I am simply enjoying the sight of my garden. When I let myself into the kitchen, Verity's suitcase and hand luggage are by the door. I wince as I hear a thud on the stairs as she bashes my case up to my room.

I busy myself taking soup from the freezer and putting it over a low heat on the hob. As I set out crackers and cheese, Verity clatters back downstairs.

'Thank you for taking the case up for me. I could have managed,' I say, though I am not sure it's true.

'Getting it off the carousel in the airport triggered a coughing fit.'

'My throat was dry from the air in the plane.'

Verity gives me a dubious look.

'Yes, yes, I have a doctor's appointment next week. Why don't you go and get some mint? I have some lime cordial, and that will soothe things nicely.'

'Only if I can put gin in mine.' As Verity reaches up for the tall glasses in the cabinet over the counter her sleeve catches my receipts corkboard and sends it to the floor. 'Sorry!' She bends to gather up the scattered slips of paper. 'Work. Work,' she says, pinning them back to the left-hand side of the board. 'What's this one?' she asks, frowning. 'Oh, that was the Sunday before we left – your day-off adventure. You've put it under work, though, not personal.'

'Did I? Could you move it across?' I don't turn from the hob, where I am stirring the melting soup.

'Am I hearing correctly? Pru Lawson nearly made a mistake in her expense accounting? Tut, tut. Very suss.'

'I thought you were fetching some mint?'

'Are you expecting someone?' Verity asks.

I glance round to see her peering out of the window, towards the drive. 'Must be the food delivery. It's very early, but at least we will have some milk. Can you ask them to bring it to the back?'

I hear the kitchen door open and close, then a murmur of voices. The door opens again and I turn to help Verity unload the crates, only to find her wide-eyed and tense.

'We've got a visitor.' She steps out of the way and in comes . . .

'Graziella! What a lovely surprise.' I embrace her, taking a moment too long to realize she is not smiling.

Still, she doesn't rebuff the hug or her standard double-kiss.

'Verity, go get that mint, please.'

She looks between me and Graziella, then scuttles off as I fetch out an extra bowl and plate.

'I know we talked about you meeting Verity soon, but I wasn't expecting you today, so I assume this is about Dresden.'

Graziella draws out a chair and settles her tall, slender frame elegantly. 'You killed a man who was not an authorized target. You did it in the context of your cover story.'

'And I submitted a report as soon as the police left.' I put a coaster and glass down in front of her, then move back to the stove. 'I did my best in the circumstances that presented.'

'But why did they present?'

I fetch Graziella a napkin, smoothing it carefully as I lay it beside her plate. 'Verity was about to take the client's dog for a walk, but the client and her children arrived home early, then the client had to send the security guard back to the car for her phone, and there was so much confusion the door didn't get shut properly—'.

'Nice use of the passive voice, but we both know who didn't shut the door.' Graziella's sharp grey eyes flick towards the garden. 'No one is questioning your loyalty or service, but whether it's Verity or your illness—'

I bring a finger to my lips.

Graziella throws her hands in the air. 'How could you think she's the right choice of mentee when she's not worked out how ill you are, and *you've* not trusted her enough to tell her that there's a literal deadline to finish her training?'

I purse my lips.

'Don't pretend to be offended by my bluntness. After twenty-five years, it won't wash. Not even as an attempt to *change the subject*,' Graziella adds pointedly.

I grin at her and, after a moment, she smiles back, reaching out an open hand. I slip mine into it and hold on as she reads my face silently and I read hers. She's had her hair cut recently: now her bob ends at her jawline, emphasizing the planes of her face. She looks thinner, taut in a way I haven't seen since her mentor died, nearly ten years ago. I am the cause of this incipient grief. It knots in my chest as I squeeze her hand, and it's nothing and everything, the way love is.

Graziella clears her throat and sits back with a little toss of her head: a tell that tears are threatening.

'I do trust Verity. At least, I want to.' I rub my forehead. 'The Sisterhood will be the making of her. It is just . . . taking a little time.'

Graziella's face is frighteningly full of sympathy as we both clock Verity trying, and failing, to creep close enough to the garden door to eavesdrop. We wait in silence until Verity gives up and strides back in, brandishing the mint.

'Hello again,' she says as she skirts the table to the sink. 'So, how long have you been in the Sisterhood?' she asks Graziella as she rinses the mint then tears it into the jug of lime cordial.

Graziella smiles. 'I came to it around the same time as Pru.'

'Here to plan a joint retirement party?' Verity suggests brightly.

I press my fingers to my temples and rub again at the building headache.

Graziella gives me an amused look. 'How very restrained you've been, Pru. You haven't killed her *once*, though I imagine the temptation will have been almost constant.'

I watch Verity's shoulders relax at Graziella's friendly tone.

'She's nearly withered me to death with her Look a few times,' she tells Graziella, as she pours lime and mint cordial for everyone, then leans against the counter with her glass. 'Is this a social call or should I prepare myself for some particularly gruelling training later?'

Graziella's gaze sharpens, and I watch the grin fade from Verity's face.

'We are being cautioned for our performance,' I tell her.

'We?' She slams her glass down on the counter and straightens. 'I'm the one who caused the situation that meant Pru had to . . .' She makes a gesture that I think is meant to represent bludgeoning but looks more like a demonstration of a cricket bowling technique.

'Pru is your mentor. She selected you. She is responsible for you.' Graziella props her elbows on the edge of the table, steepling her fingers. 'I'm sure Pru's told you this, but did you listen, Verity? You certainly don't strike me as having understood. All this friendly attempt at bonding – do you really think that is how you should be responding to my visit?'

Verity shrugs. 'Was I meant to put arsenic in your drink . . . or should I be watching out for when you try it with mine?'

'Would I do that here, in Pru's kitchen? Would that be clean and neat? Would it draw minimal, if any, attention? Or, given what happened on your last job – and your little run-in with the authorities right before that – would it put your mentor in the crosshairs of police attention in two countries?'

Verity's hands curl into fists. 'We didn't make a mistake on the job – the murder job, I mean. Why is it our fault someone tried to kill our cover story? Surely we got a glowing review from Laurene.'

'Naturally. Who wouldn't want a housekeeper able to make a gourmet meal, organize the family and dispatch an intruder, all in a day's work?'

'So, banter is out but sarcasm is in? I can work with that,' Verity drawls.

I close my eyes and will myself to remain calm.

'It is an option,' Graziella says. 'Or you could try explaining what you've learnt from this latest disaster and why you will never make the same mistake again. Maybe attempt to demonstrate passable observational skills—'

'I didn't need to be told you're in the Sisterhood,' Verity points out with so much smugness I want to shake her.

'Yet you are responding to my tone in kind, instead of steering the conversation the way you – and your mentor – need it to go.'

Verity blinks, going still.

'I'm not about to get violent in Pru's kitchen, but you seem to think that joking around is going to help. Why would you think that, Verity?'

'I . . .' She swallows, wrapping her arms around herself.

'You should know how to turn a situation to your

advantage. How to quickly formulate a strategy to maximize success and minimize damage. You should know how to work out what is actually happening so that, when things turn nasty, you're not caught off guard.' Graziella's voice hasn't risen, but the warmth and humour are gone. 'This is a warning, Verity. We don't think Pru's made the right choice with you.'

She takes a long drink of her cordial, then sets the glass down and gets to her feet. 'Mistakes sometimes happen, but they need to stop happening around *you*. You may have been too stupid to realize it until now, and goodness knows whether you even care, but your actions don't reflect only on you any more.'

I turn off the gas under the soup. 'I'll see you to the car.'

I grab our completed target files from the cabinet, then follow Graziella out.

'You could step down, Pru. I know you're bound and determined to finish your service the normal way, but no one's going to hold you to training your own replacement when . . .' She glances back to the house. 'You deserve some peace.'

'If I want peace, then I need to see this through.'

Graziella sighs. 'I know you've given up hope of seeing a resolution to Hope's case, but as long as you are a member in good stead, the Sisterhood won't forget your one free kill. Do you really want to risk that for Verity?' She reaches out to squeeze my arm. 'Let it go. Retire. Enjoy your garden, or travelling, or . . .' She purses her lips at my expression, then leans forward to hug me.

We exchange kisses, then she hands me a new set of target files and I give her the completed ones. I want to ask who she collects from and delivers to, but I keep my curiosity to myself. The sting of jealousy that Graziella has been chosen for an onward role in the Sisterhood when she retires from killing is soothed by the rush of pride.

Graziella beeps open her car and slings her bag inside. 'You need to tell her soon, Pru. I know you're worried it will be the last straw, but maybe that's for the best. Better than dropping dead on her.'

I wave her away down the road, then stand staring after the car. Every part of me aches, and the thought of the twelve-metre walk back to the house makes me want to sink down on the gravel and just lie there. But there is far too much I still have to accomplish if I am to die knowing any sort of peace.

The time is coming when I may have to choose what to leave undone. But I am not prepared to give up yet.

Verity

Pru has been staring after Graziella's car for about five minutes, swaying slightly. Then she starts to cough, raising her arm to cover her mouth and gradually doubling over.

I keep thinking I've got my head around the Sisterhood, and the Rules, and what my new life entails, only to find I don't understand at all.

Outside, Pru has gathered herself and is wavering back along the path. I hurry to serve the soup and set out the cheeseboard. When she lets herself in, I'm just topping up our glasses.

'Shall we eat before . . . whatever comes next?' I ask anxiously.

'This isn't the Last Supper, Verity,' snaps Pru, then sighs. 'Thank you for finishing.'

We sit down, but neither of us eats.

'They wouldn't actually . . . kill you because of me, would they? I mean, so long as neither of us tells anyone, Rule 12 doesn't apply.'

Pru picks up her spoon and hovers it over her soup. She seems to steel herself, taking a spoonful and drawing it to her mouth, then swallowing as if her throat is hurting her. I suppose, after all the coughing, that's not a surprise.

'Would it keep you on the straight and narrow to

worry about me?' she asks. 'You've certainly never been driven by your own best interests.' She sighs again. 'Have your soup.'

We eat in silence.

'Almost all members of the Sisterhood know who to claim as their one free kill from the start, but in the rare cases where an investigation is needed, provision is made for however long it takes.' Pru pauses, takes a sip of cordial. 'If a mentor is too old or has died, then the target of the one free kill is allocated to whichever mentee is closest to finishing her training. It becomes her final kill under her mentor's watch. Similarly, if a member dies without taking her one free kill, the investigation to identify the correct target continues.'

I take a slice of Brie and layer it over a poppy-seed cracker. 'So, even if something happened to me, the Sisterhood would keep looking into who killed Reenie and he'd be dealt with?'

'Provided you are in good standing.'

'What does that mean?' I demand, taking an aggressive slurp of soup.

Pru grimaces. '*Verity.*' She lowers the cracker she was about to bite into. 'To be in good standing, a mentee must pass her training and demonstrate her continuing competence throughout her term of service. Then, when her term is nearing its end, she must successfully train a suitable mentee to replace her. However, while she is training her mentee, the mentor is responsible not just for upholding the Rules herself but for her mentee's behaviour in respect of the Rules.'

I go cold. 'They'd take your one free kill. After twenty-five years, they'd just . . . cancel it like overdue loyalty points if I screw up badly enough?'

Pru slams down her glass, then folds forward, coughing. She hacks into a tissue, then gets up to throw it in the bin before rinsing her hands.

'Pru—'

She braces herself against the edge of the sink. 'I am trying not to lose my temper. You cannot joke about this, Verity. You cannot ever joke about anything to do with Hope.'

'But if they take your one free kill, what's to stop you doing it yourself if you find the answer? I mean, you've had twenty-five years learning to make murder look accidental. The Sisterhood wouldn't have to know, so they couldn't punish you.'

Pru goes very still. After a moment she says, 'You mean what's to stop *you* if you find Reenie's killer?'

She throws the towel she was drying her hands on into the corner of the counter. 'You want to know when the Sisterhood comes for one of its own? It's never happened because of betrayal because no one – not one single member – has ever given up her Sisters. But it *has* happened when a member decided to exercise her skills on a target of her own choosing in violation of Rule 1.'

She leans back against the counter, looking wearier than ever. 'It's also happened when a member or mentee has become so erratic that, even without intending betrayal, she risked the type of attention that could expose us all.'

I push my bowl away.

'Eat it anyway, Verity.' Pru drops back into her seat, slicing a piece of Gouda and pressing it on to an oatcake.

I match her, and we crunch away.

'I should probably tell you that my landlord chucked me out. I meant to find somewhere new before we left for the job, but . . . Well, I went to cause trouble with TJ instead. And then I moped.' I take a second cracker and smear it with garlic cream-cheese. 'I recognize that I am an irresponsible moron. And that most of my recent and current problems are of my own making.'

Pru dabs her napkin against her lips.

'You can chime in any time,' I say between bites of cheese and cracker.

'What do you propose to do about the apartment?'

I grimace. 'Ask you for some more money on account for a B&B, then for a deposit when I find a place. I'll also need some time off for a viewing or two. Sorry,' I mumble.

Pru gathers up my bowl and her own, putting them in the sink. 'Or you could stay here and figure it out after your training is complete.'

I blink, thinking I must have misheard her over the sound of the tap. 'I'm not sure it's safe for me here. I frustrate you enough during the day. If it's 24/7—'

'Perhaps I can exert more control over your most destructive tendencies this way, though I shan't hold my breath. It will, at least, give us more time to devote to the development of your core skills. For instance, what have you learnt just now?'

'Not to say the first thing that comes into my head since I'm going to be stuck here for the foreseeable and there are a million ways you can make my life miserable?'

Pru heaves a sigh. 'Rule 2: *When you need to, you should always ask for help. You are not alone.*' She walks over to the cabinet, taps in the PIN and takes out a ring-bound volume. She tosses it on to the table beside me. 'Enjoy your evening. I have reports to write up, expenses to file—'

'Not that personal one you put in the wrong place.' I look down at the file. *Edible foraged foods with poisonous counterparts*.

'Later, you may fetch some of your belongings from the car and set yourself up in the guest room – first on the left at the top of the stairs.'

'What was the thing about Heathtop Hill?'

Pru blinks at the non-sequitur.

'Just before the intruder burst into the house in Dresden and all *that* happened, you were saying something about Gavin Pieper making regular donations to a community project?'

'And so we return to the reason you were so distracted you let an intruder into our client's house.' She shakes her head, visibly reeling in her anger. 'Gavin Pieper has a direct debit to a local nature charity that's looking to set up a wildlife sanctuary near the viewpoint.'

'He used to take Reenie up there on dates.'

Could he have slipped out of the house when his brother and ex-sister-in-law thought he was in his room, waited for her to come back from the party, then coaxed her up there in the hopes of making up, only it all went wrong? Is that where she's been all along?

'If he'd buried her there, he wouldn't want a bunch of scientists and nature-lovers focused on the area,' Pru points out, puncturing my hopes. 'Not to mention that creating a wildlife sanctuary involves a degree of digging and clearing, building observation points and such. The donations might be born of guilt, but the nature of the project means I cannot believe that she is there. It is more likely the donations are simply about preserving a place where he and Reenie were happy.'

I've never thought before how much guilt and grief have in common. With a sigh, I drag over the ring-bound volume of poisons. 'Do I, like—'

'VERITY!'

'Do I just sit here and memorize this?'

'What else would you do with it?' Pru slaps a pile of folders down on her end of the table.

I turn to the first page and stare at a set of mushrooms. The ones on the left of the page look identical to the ones on the right, but apparently they're deadly. 'Next you'll say there's a quiz later.'

Pru's head comes up. She beams. 'What a wonderful idea, Verity. We can both look forward to that, can't we?'

Pru

'What did the doctor say?' Verity asks by way of a greeting as I climb out of the car.

'She's setting up some tests. Gave me some medication in the meantime.' I hold up the pharmacy bag.

Verity frowns. 'But what does she think is wrong?'

I let myself through the gate and stand surveying the lengths of rope I'd left Verity tying into various knots. 'Better.'

I head inside, resigning myself as Verity patters after me.

'There's some fluid in my lungs, and apparently I'm running a low-grade fever, so she's given me antibiotics.'

Verity hovers as I sit down at the table, pulling over a box of old electrical goods and starting to sort through it.

'And?' she says. 'Shouldn't you be in bed if you've got a fever?'

'She said not to exert myself, not laze about in bed.' I pull out an old alarm clock. 'Work out how to make this create a time-delayed spark – ideally, one that syncs with the alarm function.'

Verity plops down in the next chair and starts turning it over in her hands. 'Why don't you go in the living room and put your feet up, at least? I'll find you some paracetamol for the fever.'

'Will you let me work in peace if I agree?' I ask, though I am already gathering up the folders.

Verity grins. 'I can't promise peace, especially if I start setting stuff on fire, but I'll try not to burn down the *whole* house.'

Moving over to the oven, I pull out a battered baking tray and an ancient chopping board from the cupboard, placing them on the table by Verity. 'Make sure your device is on this when you plug it in to test the spark. And for heaven's sake,' I add, when she starts humming under her breath, 'don't touch the metal when you do it.'

Verity pouts up at me. 'I'm not brain-dead, you know.'

I womanfully resist the urge to comment. 'I am going into the other room. You may bring me tea in an hour, but if you try to plump my pillows, you will be very sorry indeed.'

I nearly groan as I sink down on to the sofa. It takes me several shameful minutes to gather the energy to shuck my slippers and twist so that I am lying back against the armrest, knees up so I can lean my files against them.

Not ten minutes later, Verity bustles in with a tray of mint tea, water, paracetamol, tissues and my phone.

'Do we need to cover telling the time in your training?' I ask, even as I reach for the mug.

Verity attempts to give me a put-upon look. 'Call me if you need anything.'

The day passes with her fussing in and out, insisting on making lunch (a cheese omelette that is simultaneously burnt and undercooked, and a salad that hasn't been washed properly), and generally getting underfoot every time I dare to get up. Nevertheless, we make adequate progress on our respective tasks, even though there is a loud yelp mid-afternoon, followed by Verity appearing in the doorway, one hand cradled to her chest, to ask where the fuse box is.

Thankfully the burn to her hand hasn't broken the skin, and the circuit breaker is soon reset. I leave her working cack-handedly, but with determination, on putting a new fuse into the alarm-clock plug to continue with her fire-starting efforts.

All is well until shortly after dinner, when I head back to my folders only for Verity to tug at my elbow the moment I step into the living room.

'Bed!' she orders with her version of sternness. 'I'm going to bring you herbal tea, and you're going to tuck yourself up and have an early night.'

I pull my arm out of her grip. 'Are you telling me when to go to bed in my own home?'

'I am telling my tired mentor, who has a fever and a nasty chest infection, that I am going to be on her case till she's all better again.'

I look her up and down, lip curling. 'I could kill you stone dead six ways without taking a step.'

Verity brightens, peering around. 'Really? I mean, there's the lamp, so that's potential for electrocution, and the door knob to fall and bash my head on. But what are the other four?'

'Stay here and work it out!' I snap. 'I'm going to bed because there, at least, I will be able to get a little peace!'

I growl my way upstairs and into my pyjamas. Settling into bed, propped against the headboard so I can read, is such a terrible relief I almost forgive Verity. Then I realize I have left my medications downstairs. I say something very rude, then throw back the duvet.

Verity is stamping upstairs in the way that means she is trying to be quiet. I sag into the pillows as I wait for her to crash through the door, making a mental note to work on methods for walking quietly on stairs as soon as possible.

'Oops!' she says as the door flies open then bounces off the wall.

'If you'd really like to be helpful, not destroying the house would be much appreciated.'

'Nag, nag, nag.' She puts a cup of fragrant tea on the bedside table, then pops my bag of pills next to it. 'Call me if you need anything. I don't want to see you downstairs again till morning.'

'Go away, you dreadful creature.'

'Don't let the bedbugs bite,' she sing-songs as she whisks herself out of the door.

'I will be doing the biting soon,' I grumble as I reach for my pills.

I wash down one of the strong new painkillers, then reach for my book. I am horrified when only fifteen minutes later I can barely keep my eyes open. I drag myself out of bed, brush my teeth and turn out the light.

I plunge into sleep almost the moment I close my eyes and wake to find sun pouring through a gap in the curtains. My whole body feels heavy.

I roll to the side with a groan. It is nearly nine o'clock. The only time I ever sleep so late is when I have been up till four killing someone.

I feel punch-drunk with the lingering effects of the medication as I stagger out of bed and attempt to wake myself with a shower. I am still yawning and stumbling as I shuffle into the kitchen.

Verity is setting a pot of tea and a rack of toast on the table. 'And you said you didn't want to go to bed early.' Her tone is cheerful, but there's something brittle in her expression. Her movements are quick and sharp, as if she is angry.

I watch her fluttering about the kitchen, moving the sugar from the counter to the table, then back again. She curses and puts it beside me, then starts scrubbing the sink. What on earth happened between last night and this morning? A realization about what Graziella's visit really means? A nightmare, perhaps?

'So, what's the line-up for today?' she asks the plughole. 'Please don't say CCTV exercises. I know I still suck, but I'll do anything except that, OK? I'll even go for round two of electrocution.'

My skull feels as if it has been filled with mashed potato. Then my eyes fall on the wall calendar and understanding dawns. It is the anniversary of Reenie's disappearance.

'We are going out today,' I tell Verity. 'You will want walking shoes and something warm in case the weather turns.'

'I'm not sure I'm up for a mystery adventure, Pru.' She pauses in her scrubbing to frown at me. 'Is it a good idea to go out when you're sick? Shouldn't we at least check if you've still got a fever?'

'I am feeling much more the thing,' I lie. 'But if it makes you feel better, you can drive. Leave the sink and get ready. We shall be off in half an hour.'

Verity is quiet as we lock up and get in the car. I expect her to ask to put on the radio, but she stays silent, focused on the road, as I give periodic directions. Finally, we pull off the motorway, stop-starting through High Wycombe and out the other side, wending our way between rolling hills. Verity's been shooting me progressively more frequent looks, but I let her realize where we are for herself.

Just past a picturesque village, the road curves and a new vista opens up on either side. A line of hills rises on the left and there, above the trees, a tower surmounted by a golden ball peeks out, flashing in the sun.

I hear Verity's breath catch as she recognizes the view from the family photo clipped to the inside of Reenie's file.

I direct her to the car park. The moment the handbrake is on she is off up the footpath. I follow, though I have to stop several times to cough then wait till I regain my balance as dizziness makes the sunny woods and fields whirl around me.

When I finally reach the summit, Verity is sitting cross-legged on the grass, staring up at the golden ball. I sit beside her and put my hand over hers. After a moment, she leans sideways and tucks her head on to my shoulder. Her hair tickles my cheek and the closeness is almost as sweet as the grief is bitter.

Eventually, she scrambles back to her feet and helps me up. We wander around, not talking, then Verity leads the way down. It is even more of a stop-start journey than before.

'You shouldn't have come all the way up,' Verity frets as I cough and hack. 'Just bringing me here was so much more than enough.'

'It is just . . . a cough,' I grind out. 'Bit . . . breathless. Wanted . . . the walk. See the . . .' I give up.

Verity alternately pounds and rubs my back until I give

her the nod to stop. As we carry on downhill, she keeps her arm around me and, together, we very, very slowly make our way back to the car.

Verity is almost serene, while I am practically vibrating with frustration by the time we arrive.

'Home?' she asks, and it goes straight to the pain in my chest.

I rub a fist over my breastbone. 'There was a charming little inn as we drove through West Wycombe. I am hungry and have every intention of sampling their fare.'

Verity laughs. 'I think it's a gastropub, not a medieval re-enactment inn.'

'Potato, potahto. It's an old-fashioned inn.' I shift in my seat, trying to get comfortable. 'Besides, I saw the menu board out front. It said, "Bill of Fare". So there.'

'Which of us sticks out our tongue at this point?' Verity asks.

I give a disdainful little sniff.

'Thank you. For knowing what day it is.' Verity doesn't look away from the road. 'Thank you for bringing me here – and coming all the way with me, even when you're so tired.'

'I wasn't going to lead you here then leave you part of the way to our destination, Verity. I see things through to the end.'

She flashes me a smile, then focuses on the road as we weave around a sharp bend.

Verity

It's a nice day to be standing in an alley beside the towpath along a London canal, even if we are here to kill a serial domestic abuser.

Pru is watching a peacock butterfly flit between the buddleia blooms arching over the high fence to our left. I am watching her.

Since the anniversary, things have felt different. Maybe it's that, for the first time since I left home, I no longer have the threat of homelessness hanging over my head. I'm still in danger of being fired, given Graziella's visit, but though that should be paralysing, the fact that Pru is in the (possibly literal) firing line, too, has just made me determined.

But determined in a new way. Not my usual hot, angry, rush-in-and-ignore-the-consequences way, or even the sullen, what-the-hell way I approached the Sisterhood at the beginning. Now it's like there's a stillness inside me. I think I'm starting to understand what Pru means when she says sometimes you decide to do something then you follow through because you don't let yourself believe there's any alternative: the only option is making the thing you promised to do happen.

Oh, Verity, I know you mean well, but you've never been

good at persisting with anything. Mum's voice echoes in my head, but instead of the words setting needle-sharp claws into me, I just shake my head and focus on the sound of the water in the canal and the caress of the cool summer breeze.

I'm wearing a baseball cap over a blonde wig. Pru has a flowery headscarf. Our eyes are shaded behind large sunglasses. While I gently roll a baby-stroller back and forth, Pru leans on a rusty old bike. A coil of barbed wire is bundled under a plastic bag in the fraying basket.

The stretch of towpath at the mouth of the alleyway is a CCTV blind-spot, but we still need our target to pass on his way to work at a moment when there's no one else in sight. As such, we've had to abort the plan two days in a row. This is our third attempt and, as per the saying, it seems our luck is in.

As our target approaches, I keep watch on the upstream section of the towpath, while Pru monitors downstream. I stare at the path, willing it to stay clear, stay clear, stay clear . . .

As our target reaches the mouth of the alley, I pull a length of metal pipe from the stroller. Its diameter, and glossy black paint, are a perfect match to the railings along the canal.

My blow catches him neatly on the side of the head as he passes, at the exact angle I was aiming for and with exactly the right degree of force. All that practice with the punching bag in Pru's garage has finally paid off.

He careens into the railing, drooping over it. I grab his legs and shove so that he dangles head first above the water while Pru hooks the end of the barbed wire into his trousers. Then over he goes. We quickly send the bike sailing after him. Even if he's aware enough after the blow to try to fight his way to the surface, he won't be able to see clearly enough in the murky water to unhook the wire, ensuring the weight of the bike tethers him below the surface until he runs out of air.

'Did you hear a splash?' Pru asks as I slide the pipe back under the blanket in the stroller.

'Must have been something quite big. I wonder if there are herons around here.'

We set off along the towpath at a leisurely pace, eventually turning on to a short, steep ramp to the main road. At the top, we only have to wait a few minutes before a bus pulls to the kerb. Pru helps me wrangle the stroller on, and off we go.

'Do you know that there are a frightening number of household products that, when combined, produce deadly gases?' Pru asks. 'Not to mention many things that, with a little application of heat, positively explode. We should look into that tomorrow, for safety reasons, but I think this afternoon is one for foraging in the woods.' Pru reaches past me to press the stop button. 'We can explore how your skills are coming along with identifying what we can and can't eat.'

The doors whoosh open. Pru lifts the foot of the stroller while I take the back and, a moment later, we're off down the pavement.

The car is only two streets away, and soon we're heading out of London, another job complete.

'So how are we going to approach Gavin?' Pru asks as I weave through the traffic.

'I know you don't want to just go over there and

challenge him about his alibi, but if the police appeals Mum and I did when Reenie disappeared weren't enough to make him come forward, I can't see why shoving a leaflet for a domestic violence charity through his door will do the trick.'

Pru cracks her window, turning her face to the cool breeze. 'Guilt sours over the years. His life has not gone the way he hoped. If that is because of Reenie, he might be starting to realize he cannot live with whatever it was that he did.'

'You still don't think he killed her,' I bite out.

'I don't know, Verity,' she says wearily. 'If he did, he was very clever about it. And nothing I have seen or read of him indicates that he is a great brain.'

We heave matching sighs. Of course, Pru's sets her coughing.

'Did they say when you'll hear back about the blood tests?'

'I expect . . . it will be . . . soon enough,' Pru chokes out. 'Now, what else f— for Gavin,' she croaks.

Worry tightens my stomach and stops the sharp comeback on my tongue. 'Maybe, instead of the leaflet thing, you could pretend to be collecting for a domestic violence charity. See if you can draw him into conversation about whether he knows a woman who's suffered abuse.' I slow for a light, beating out a tattoo against the steering wheel.

Pru nods, fumbling with her water bottle. She puts a pill in her mouth, then curses as the packet drops into the footwell. 'I shall make some plans . . . while you practise . . . flammable products tomorrow.'

I follow the signs to the motorway, eager to be out of the stop-start London traffic. 'It's so weird to imagine you doing all the same training with Paloma. You know, you never told me how she recruited you.'

Pru shifts uncomfortably, her face tight with discomfort. 'It wasn't half the production your recruitment was, if that's what you're asking.' She shifts again. 'She arranged for us to bump into each other at a garden centre. Made it seem like I'd spilt her coffee, so I offered to get her another in the café and she said, "Why not? We can put the world to rights together."'

I dart a glance at her, recognizing the wording she used on me that first day in the graveyard, then wincing at the realization that I didn't just reject her offer – I rejected her attempt to recruit me the same way Paloma recruited her. If Pru weren't so persistent, where would I be now? I'd rather not think about it.

'She must have had quite a speech prepared to persuade you to leave the straight and narrow path for serial homicide,' I say as we sail up the on-ramp and join the motorway.

'I did not take any persuading. *Some* mentees understand what they are being offered and embrace it with thanks and humility.'

'I'm so glad to hear you admit you picked me because you could see what a biddable, patient sort of person I was,' I say, instead of *Thank you for not giving up on me before we'd even started.*

Pru barks with laughter and promptly starts coughing again, folding over her seatbelt.

I take a hand off the wheel to pat her back as she hacks into a tissue. 'Is it green?'

'No. No green,' Pru says.

'Maybe the antibiotics are working?'

I turn on the radio, selecting the channel by the way Pru's face relaxes when I find some classical music. On the plus side, I'm not tempted to sing along as we fly down the motorway, the breeze throwing my hair about my face.

When we finally pull into the drive, Pru climbs stiffly out while I collect my phone and water bottle from the console. As I lean over, I see the pill packet Pru dropped earlier. I snatch it up and stuff it into my pocket, then hurry after Pru to help with lunch.

I only remember the pills later, when the sleeve crinkles against the counter as I wash up. Slipping it out, I set it on Pru's side of the table, then pause. Pru is lying down on the sofa in the living room, writing a report on today's job, so there's no one to see when I take out the book of prescription medications and look the pills up.

Tapentadol. Used to treat severe pain when other analgesics are ineffective or cause adverse reactions.

It has no secondary use for coughs. The issue date on the packet is last week.

I march down the hall . . . and find Pru fast asleep, folder spilt over her lap and on to the floor. Even from the doorway, I can see her forehead is creased in discomfort. There's a faint wheeze to her breathing.

I retreat to the garden and busy myself with strength training and climbing practice, but my mind keeps going back to the pills. Does the doctor suspect something bad and Pru's waiting until the tests confirm one way or another before telling me? If something happens to Pru . . .

I shake my head as if I can shake out the thought, like

a drop of water in my ear. A picture takes its place. The prescription Pru was using as a bookmark. The one for a strong painkiller that can also be used to treat coughs. Did she have the cough earlier than I realized? I'm less oblivious now, after all Pru's training, but back then . . . Could I really have missed that? It would be just like Pru to ignore how she was feeling in order to focus on me and the duty I represent to the Sisterhood. What if, in the process, she waited too long? What if now there's no good news to be had? If she knows it's going to be bad, she'd give me as much time as possible to focus on training, on becoming the person she hopes I can be. Only I'm not there – not nearly there yet – and maybe I could do it without her, but I don't want to. She has to be there to see it and be proud of me and . . .

I force myself to take a deep breath, then another, and another. Pru has been suffering, so it's good she has better pills. That's all I know right now, and if Pru's taught me anything, it's to work things out properly, instead of jumping straight to destructive emotional reactions. So, I'm going to be calm and collected and work on my training in between looking after her as much as I can.

In the evening, after Pru has gone to bed, I tap the PIN into the sideboard cabinet and take out Hope's file. I get nowhere with it, but patience is another thing Pru's taught me.

I continue the next day.

And the day after that.

Pru

Verity has been looking at Hope's file. She thinks she is being sneaky, doing it at night when I've gone to bed, but she never puts it back quite where I left it . . . though sometimes I wonder whether that is on purpose: her way of letting me know, without discussing it. She is becoming more precise, more careful; this seems sloppy in a way she has been steadily steering away from.

She is currently writing neat notes about how we might dispatch our latest target.

When I lean closer to read, she tilts the notebook in my direction, wincing when I stifle a crackling cough in my sleeve.

'When do you hear about the results of the scan?'

'It was *yesterday*, Verity. It will be at least a week or two.'

She glances over at me. 'Are you sure you should come with me tomorrow? You could wait in the car. The GP *did* tell you not to exert yourself.'

'What she doesn't know will not hurt her.'

'And you say I'm stubborn and pig-headed,' Verity mutters.

'I have never said that.'

'Not in those exact words, but I heard you loud and clear.'

I sniff. 'I suppose I should be glad that your listening skills are improving.' My stomach suddenly turns over. 'Work up a plan for a second method,' I tell Verity, then hurry to the bathroom.

I make it just in time, then spend a miserable and disgusting twenty minutes on the toilet. Two diarrhoea tablets and some anti-nausea pills later, I mince painfully into the kitchen and ease myself down at the table.

Verity has commandeered my laptop and is staring at the screen with a look I cannot decipher. 'Why were you looking up news items about girls being drugged and assaulted in a fifty-mile radius of here? And what does it have to do with this woman?' She turns the laptop around.

The browser is open to an article entitled *Local woman starts charity to support those who've turned to drugs and alcohol after trauma*. There's a picture of Claire Jeynes.

My heartbeat lurches into double time, pulsing in my ears.

'She started the charity twenty years ago,' Verity says, as if the information isn't right in front of me. 'You've got a whole bunch of searches about this woman going back months and months, maybe longer. Is this a case? Are you doing jobs without me?'

Relief floods through me. She doesn't know. Of course she doesn't.

'And if I were?' I shake my head. 'No, Verity. There are no secret solo jobs. When would I find the time? Especially since you moved in.'

She sits back, folding her arms. 'Do members of the Sisterhood ever recommend jobs?' She waves a hand. 'I know – Rule 1 – no unauthorized jobs, but what if one of us thinks she has identified a serial predator? Do we gather evidence then put it forward? Do things like that ever get authorized?'

'They do. Though the jobs never go to the woman who first identified the target,' I say, drawing out a chair and sinking down. 'Too traceable.'

She tilts her head, searching my face. 'Is that what you're doing?'

'What do you think I am up to?' I ask, popping a pill out of a sleeve and swigging it down. I don't want to lie more than I have to, but I have no qualms about letting her misinterpret my interest in Claire Jeynes.

Verity props her arms on the table. 'In interviews, Claire Jeynes talks about a traumatic *event*, not some long-term abuse, so why have you been looking up her family, too? If you think the trauma involved the father, hence the stuff about them being estranged, it's a bit weird the parents did an open-garden event just a few weeks ago to raise money for her charity. They can't be *that* estranged.'

Suddenly her eyes widen. 'They live in your old town! You were there at the open garden – it was when you gave me the day off so you could go to see old friends. *Do* you know them? Is this' – she gestures at the laptop – 'an investigation *for* them or *into* them?'

'Think it through,' I tell her, settling back in my chair as if I am quite at ease.

'You know that's wearing really thin, right?' Verity rubs at her forehead as if *I* am giving *her* a headache. 'I'm behaving myself nowadays, so you could give me a straight answer once in a while.'

'And deprive you of an excellent learning opportunity?'

'I'm putting arsenic in your dinner.'

'Not some of those lovely Destroying Angels we found in the woods the other day? What is the point of cultivating them in the garage if you are going to forget all about them? Since they are right here, in my own home, it would pass muster even with the Sisterhood, given that most accidental poisonings and overdoses are caused by things people have lying around. Of course, you could also poison me with my medication – or anything you have been legally prescribed. Things do get muddled up in a household. But no arsenic, Verity. Too suspicious.'

'You're changing the subject. Why are you so interested in Claire Jeynes and her family? *Are* they old friends?'

'No.'

'But it's not a case. At least not yet.'

'I have . . . insufficient evidence of what I suspect to take anything to the Sisterhood. And, no, I shan't be discussing my suspicions. You can work it out – or not.'

She wrinkles her nose at me, then turns to glare at the screen. 'Do you think there's something suspicious about her father medicating her with the stuff that set her on to the illegal drugs? Maybe a reason he didn't want her going to the police about the fact she'd been . . .' Her face twists. 'Surely a father wouldn't want to protect the person who'd done that to his daughter . . . Unless he cared a lot about that person, too. Were you trying to find out if she had a brother? An uncle?'

'Why else might someone not report a crime?'

'Because they think they won't be believed.' She glances at the cabinet with Reenie's case files. 'Or the person who did it is rich and powerful.' Her eyes return to me. 'Like Charles Temple and Nathan and Christophe.'

She draws the laptop back in front of her and clacks away. 'All of these searches, they're . . . well, not local, but it's all within an hour's drive.' Her eyes snap up to mine. 'You've been looking for the person who hurt Reenie. You think Claire is another victim.'

I shake my head. 'If anything, Reenie's case speaks to an inexperienced criminal making a mistake, but it is later than what happened to Claire Jeynes, so the timelines don't track.'

I cannot lead her astray about Reenie's case. She accepted why I withheld the information about Christophe, but hiding anything else would break the trust between us permanently. I can't – I *won't* – tell her that I think Claire Jeynes killed Hope, but I can and should share the fact that I have long wondered if she – or someone like her – might hold the answer to Reenie's disappearance, even if they don't know it.

'Someone like Claire Jeynes hears a lot of painful stories – among them, she might notice a pattern: telling similarities, striking details that speak to a particular predator. It might not be enough to take to the police, especially if the victims don't want to come forward, but I bet people like Jeynes have questions, perhaps even theories. The difficulty is how to persuade them to share their information, given both confidentiality and the fact that charities don't always know the names of the people who call their helplines or turn up to self-help groups.'

Verity shakes her head. 'You really have been looking into Reenie's case all this time. Investigating every possibility. Searching for the one bit of information that might give you a lead.'

'I came across Jeynes in a different regard,' I admit, voice tight, 'but it did make me wonder if there might be something in this general line of inquiry that could help with Reenie's case.' I sigh, rubbing my eyes.

Verity sighs, too, sinking back in her chair. 'You should rest before tonight if you insist on coming with.'

Glad of the excuse to end the conversation, I drag myself to my feet. When I lie down on the sofa to rest, guilt and shame paint the inside of my eyelids with the picture of Verity and Reenie beaming in front of the long view of fields and rolling hills outside West Wycombe, the tower with the golden ball rising above the distant treeline. The memory of Verity putting her head on my shoulder as we sat below the tower makes my stomach roll over afresh.

I cannot ruin this. But I also cannot tell Verity the truth about Claire Jeynes. She cannot know I am thinking about breaking the Rules.

I replay our conversation in my head but remember no lies, and yet something prickles at me.

Claire Jeynes . . . Her estranged father, the GP . . . The pills I stole from his house . . . The pills she took after she drove into my child . . . She drove into Hope then carried on home, where her father treated her hysteria so she could sleep safe and warm in her bed while my daughter lay dying alone in a freezing ditch . . .

Suddenly the pieces come together and I understand what I've been missing. And why I won't have to break the Rules after all.

Verity

The target of our current pro bono case lives just over an hour's drive away. We arrive a little after eight, parking on a quiet road along a stretch of woodland then setting off through the trees. The moon is full and the sky clear, so we have no trouble making out the well-trodden paths as dusk darkens into night. There's no slope and yet Pru is out of breath after the first hundred metres. We have to keep stopping.

'Let's go back to the car,' I say the third time it happens. 'We can try a different plan another day.'

Pru shakes her head.

'I can do it by myself. You stay here, and I'll be back in half an hour.'

'No solo jobs until your . . . training is . . . complete,' Pru grits out.

'You let me go and steal our first target's trash solo!'

'Stealing rubbish . . . is not . . . murder.' She takes a gulp of air as if coming up from underwater. 'It's not even . . . a crime.'

She gives me her most quelling Look, but I just stare back at her. 'Our target is going to be in the garage while we're creeping about the house. You can't cough or—' I gesture at her wheezing.

'He won't . . . hear us over . . . the racket he will . . . be making.' She trudges on.

What should have taken fifteen minutes drags into an agonizing thirty before we finally arrive at the fence along the back of the target's property. I lever myself up and scan the house and garden.

'No new cameras. No one in the garden. Can't see anyone moving around the house, and obviously the whole neighbourhood can hear what he's up to.'

'A lot of people will have far better lives after tonight's work.'

We both duck instinctively as our target's drumming reaches a new peak of cacophony. Exchanging grimaces, we scale the fence and drop down into the garden. Only Pru doesn't land neat and nimble but crumples forward on to her hands and knees.

She tries to push back to her feet, but her arms tremble. A moment later, she's pressing her arm across her face as a cough erupts. I grab the back of her jacket and drag her behind a shrub, heart thumping. In the garage next to the house, the drumming continues unabated.

'I can do this. Just stay here, OK?' I hiss into Pru's ear.

'I'll . . . be fine. Go get . . . the door open.'

I shake my head but scuttle off across the grass to the corner of the house. Placing one foot up on a heavy planter, I raise my arms above my head then push off, grasping the roof of the garage. Lifting my other foot up to the ledge of the kitchen window, I shimmy on to the garage roof. Rolling on to my knees, I reach into my pocket and draw out the stick and plastic bag we picked up in the woods on the walk over. I throw the bag at the boiler vent, then use the stick to shove it far enough into one of the openings for it to look like it blew up here and got caught.

Tucking the stick away, I crawl to where the garage meets the house, then reach across the brickwork to the drainpipe bracket next to the bathroom window. Leaning out, I brace my elbow on the windowsill. I don't have to fight the catch – the target has helpfully left the window open. Wriggling out further, I lower my elbow below the sill then release my grip on the bracket and bring my other arm over, too. Shoving off with my feet, I shimmy through the window, walking my hands across the floor until I can drop my feet to the ground, staying crouched on the bathmat as I catch my breath.

The target is still bashing away at his drums as I creep to the door, then slip into the hall, making sure I put my feet down flat and resist the urge to tiptoe. When I reach the stairs, I keep to the wall-side of the steps to minimize the creaking of the floorboards. In the downstairs hall, there's no carpet so I slide my feet along till I can glide around the door into the kitchen.

Pulling on disposable gloves, I carefully ease the garden door open. Pru is waiting outside.

While she makes a beeline for the boiler, gloves on and tools already in hand, I hurry to the carbon monoxide alarm. Popping open the battery compartment, I pull out the batteries and replace them with duds from a bag in my pocket. I am just snapping the compartment closed when the drumming stops.

My eyes dart to Pru. She is still focused on the boiler, but her head is tilted as if she's listening.

I strain my ears for the sound of the door into the house opening, but everything stays quiet.

Pru keeps working, her breath short and fast. I creep closer, hovering at her shoulder.

Finally, she eases the cover closed, letting out a little sigh of relief.

I see the panic on her face as the cough overtakes her. She slaps her hand across her mouth, but we can both hear someone moving across the garage.

I grab Pru's elbow, wrench open the garden door and shove her outside. Snicking the door to, I hook a hand under Pru's shoulder and drag her across the garden and behind the thickest shrub.

'Stay here!' I whisper.

Then I throw myself over the fence. Rolling on to my knees, I lift my arms and pound on the back of the fence, giving a hoot of laughter.

'Shut up, you drumming wanker!' I yell.

Forcing myself back to my feet, I kick the fence, then run on and throw my shoulder into it further along. 'Thinks he's Keith Moon!' I shriek.

'Sod off, you little hooligans!' comes the answering bawl from the house. 'You damage that fence, I'll have the police on you!'

'Oooo, he's gonna call the police!'

I give a low cheer, then a high-pitched whoop of laughter as I swerve away into the woods. I can't imagine he'll come over the fence to chase me, but still I run until my lungs seize.

When I'm sure I'm clear, I collapse to the ground and lie on my back in the leaves until my pulse steadies.

Eventually, I force myself to my feet and make my way slowly back to the target's house.

I search for a knothole in the fence and peek through to be sure he's not standing guard in the garden, though it seems unlikely. The garden looks empty. The lighted windows at the back of the house show there's no one watching.

I tap at the fence. A moment later there's a faint rustling, then a soft tap back, but Pru doesn't appear over the top.

'I need you to boost me,' comes her cracked whisper.

I'm over the fence with a speed and agility that even Pru would approve of – if she weren't crouched in the dirt, one hand clutching her chest as she heaves for breath.

Pru

Somehow, Verity gets me on to the top of the fence and down the other side without killing us both.

Somehow, she gets me through the wood. My head whirls, and the world whirls, and every part of me hurts, but even this is secondary to the weariness. It drags at me with every step. I want to care that we are both already on thin ice with the Sisterhood. I want to care that Verity's breath keeps hitching as if she wants to sob but will not let herself. I want to care that I am being a burden. That I am failing. But I am too tired for fear or shame.

Behind us, a man is (hopefully) dying. I can almost believe karma has tied my fate to his and, as he slowly dies, so am I. There is a terrible feeling in my chest, as if everything in me is just . . . stopping.

'Please, Pru. Just a little further.'

My feet drag. Brambles catch at my jeans. A line of thorns rakes across my ankle.

Verity. I am with Verity. On a job with Verity. I have to keep going.

Streetlights ahead, roving as if the world is spinning around me.

We stagger on. Someone is panting. Is it me? Verity? My chest burns for air.

A line of cars sways from side to side ahead of us.

Here is my car. I lean against the cool metal and sigh with relief.

A beep. The door beside me is drawn open. I am pushed down on to the seat. Someone swivels my legs inside. The door closes. I tip sideways and lean against the window.

The world is drifting. The woods, the night sky, the streetlights, the road.

My eyes are closed. There is just a reddish darkness, and then . . .

I jolt awake as the driver's door slams. A low moan escapes my lips.

I feel as if I have just hiked ten miles in the mountains. I did a job in Switzerland once. Shoved someone off a cliff. Quick. Effective. Good view.

Someone taps on the window next to my head. My eyes slowly focus on Verity's face through the glass. I fumble for the door handle, but she gets there first, hand out to brace me in case I topple on to my face in the gravel.

I twist and lower my feet to the ground, but when I try to push myself up my arms refuse to work. Verity reaches out and lifts me, then holds on as my head spins and everything giddies around me.

When I finally have my balance back, we shuffle up the path for what feels like hours, as if the distance has warped into miles. Then we are inside.

I stagger to a chair, lower myself into it, then fold my arms on the table and drop my head on to them.

'We should get you to bed. At least the sofa.'

'Tapentadol. Then caffeine. Makes it work faster.'

Time stop-starts. An age bent over the table. Then Verity with a pill in the palm of her hand. Pressing a glass of cold, delicious water to my lips.

I gulp at it, then cough and cough. Sagging forward again, I fight for breath.

I blink, and Verity drapes a warm wheatgerm bag around my neck, making me moan with relief.

Another blink, and my hand is wrapped around the handle of a steaming mug. I press it to my breastbone and sigh as the ache of my wheezing eases.

Gradually the world fades back in.

Verity is sitting opposite me. She scrolls on her phone, then taps at the laptop, then goes back to the phone.

'What . . .' I croak, then sip at my tea. 'What are you—'

'I knew you were up to something, so I took photos of your satnav history earlier. I've been sitting here figuring out exactly how much you've been lying to me. For instance, you didn't go to the hospital for a scan this week. You went to a residential road in a town forty miles away. Google can't help me with why – no public events, no deaths reported so far, no obvious connection to Claire Jeynes or Gavin Pieper or Hope.'

She zooms in on something. 'The week before, you went to a café instead of getting blood tests. Then there are the various supposed GP visits before that. The last of which apparently happened at the graveyard. Bit of a morbid location, but I guess "care in the community" has a pretty wide reach after all.'

She puts her phone down. 'I'd think you were just afraid to find out what's wrong, but the previous GP appointment you kept – it lines up with the date on the tapentadol.

That isn't something they'd give you without a serious diagnosis. Then, of course, there's the hydrocodone. You had that prescription before the cough – or at least before I knew about the cough. Maybe it was an old prescription. Or maybe you've been sick for months and months.'

She finally meets my eyes.

'Did you pick me because you were trying to wrap up loose ends while you could and you wanted to be sure that, even if you and I couldn't figure out what happened to Reenie in time, the Sisterhood would keep looking?'

'You already knew that was part of my reason.'

'Stop teasing it out of me!' Verity's voice breaks with the force of her shout. 'Just tell me the truth. Did you pick me because you knew you wouldn't have to live with the choice very long?'

I sip at my tea, letting it soothe my throat. 'I picked you because I was out of time to find another way to help you. I couldn't help your sister, but you were another matter.'

Verity tilts her head up and away, but I still see her chin wobble. 'You think you've helped me by bringing me into this literal life-and-death world that I'm not cut out for, then leaving me?'

'I haven't left you,' I snap, then have to pause, rubbing a fist over my breastbone. 'I keep telling you it is not a question of magically having what it takes. It's a decision—'

'And yours was to lie to me,' she hisses. A tear glints on her cheek. 'I've been trying so hard to do right by you – was worried sick I'd drag you down with me. But it never mattered, did it, because you'll be gone before—' Her eyes widen. 'The Sisterhood knows. That's why they've given me so many second chances. They know you made a mistake with me, but they think it's because you're ill.'

'I did not make a mistake, Verity. Look at tonight.' I reach out, but she pulls away, twisting to the side. 'You *will* be ready in time. You're nearly there now. We just need—'

'You need to go to bed.' Verity is suddenly on her feet, gathering her things. 'I need to be anywhere but here.'

A moment later I'm alone in the kitchen. I finish my lukewarm tea, though it curdles my stomach. I consider curling up on the sofa in the hope of hearing Verity come in so we can talk it out, but that is sentimental nonsense. We shall both be more rational in the morning.

I think about putting a chocolate on Verity's pillow, but it would be a pitiful peace offering.

Right now, she is too upset to see clearly. But despite all the complications and misadventures along the way, I have taught her more than she knows. She will understand one day. I have hope it will be in time for her to forgive me while I am still here. But it is enough to know it will come in time.

I drop my clothes on to the floor then crawl into bed without washing. I expect to plunge into sleep. Instead, I lie in the silent, empty house, starting at every sound. But it isn't Verity.

Not Verity.

Still not Verity.

I wake to my phone beeping and vibrating in my pocket. With a groan, I roll over and tug it out, squinting at the screen.

Then I tap frantically at the 'accept' button. 'Hello?' I quaver.

'Pru Lawson?'

'Speaking.'

'This is DI Strickland. You left your card with a police officer recently in connection with Verity Bannerman. We were hoping to reach her today, but her phone keeps going to voicemail.'

I lever myself up against the headboard. 'Why don't you stop by? Verity is staying with me – it's a long story, but I am rather ill so she has been good enough to help out. She should be downstairs, unless she has popped out for something at the shops. Do you have a pen?' I give my address. 'I shall get the kettle on and see if there are some biscuits about the place,' I promise, as we say our goodbyes.

The moment the call ends, I fling back the covers – at least I try to. It takes several clumsy attempts before I get to my feet. I immediately drop back down to sit on the edge of the bed, as the room dances around me. I force myself to breathe slowly and steadily, then stand again, waiting until the dizziness settles before I stride towards the wardrobe. I get one step before my chest pinches.

Again, I wait, breathing steadily – if angrily. Then I shuffle forward until I can reach the wardrobe. I pull out the sort of outfit that will hopefully put DI Strickland in mind of his mother or favourite aunt. It takes far too long to wrestle myself into the skirt and top, but finally I am dressed.

Grateful that my hair is short, I finger-comb it into an approximation of neatness, then shuffle into the bathroom to wipe the stray smears of mud off my hands, arms, legs and face. It's for the best that I look as tired and ill as possible, so I leave the make-up and start the slow journey across the room and into the hall.

Verity's bedroom door is open, the bed unmade. I turn to the stairs, having to take the steps one by one. I try not to think about whether this is a temporary state, brought on by over-exertion, or whether this is how things will be from now on.

I stop, wavering, halfway down. I do not want this. Or any of the things to come. I do not want to end my life like this.

Thank God I already have a plan that means I won't have to.

I hear a car crunch into the driveway and do my best to hurry, wanting to mutter curses but knowing I need to stay calm for the conversation ahead – assuming the car is Verity returning. If the police are here first, I shall have to adapt.

I step from the hall into the kitchen at the same time that Verity walks through the garden door. She is still in her outfit from last night and I can well believe she hasn't slept.

'The police are on their way,' I tell her. 'I take it you went to see Gavin.'

She closes the door then skirts around the table to put on the kettle. 'There aren't going to be any consequences for you with the Sisterhood since you're on borrowed time anyway, so I'm not interested in a lecture. As for the threat to take your one free kill, I'm sure your friends will see it through if there are ever any answers. That was just a way to keep me in line, but I get it now: it doesn't matter what I do – you're not going to lose anything, let alone be in any danger—'

'But *you* will, you stupid child!' The failed attempt to shout has me grasping at my chest.

Verity moves forward instinctively, then stops, her face hardening. 'It's my life, and you're not going to be around to see the mess I make of it, so why do you care?'

I sigh, shoulders slumping as I let my face show what I'm feeling. 'If you don't know the answer to that, then you really have learnt nothing.'

A new crunching of gravel heralds another car pulling into the drive.

'Say as little as possible. You have moved in because we have just heard about my diagnosis. Tell no lies, but do not tell any troublesome truths, either,' I snap.

'I'll say what I want,' Verity snaps back. 'You don't have to handle this for me, Pru.'

'Verity.' The word comes out as a weary breath. I close my eyes and force myself to stay calm. 'I have asked you for very little. Just this once, I need you to do what I say, not because you have to, but because I am asking.'

I head back down the hall before she can answer.

The doorbell rings.

'Coming!' I croak. I shuffle forward then draw the door cautiously open. 'DI Strickland?' I ask the suited man on the doorstep, as if he might be someone else.

He nods.

'Come in. Verity is just back. We were making tea, though I'm afraid I have not found the biscuits yet.' I beckon him after me as I shuffle down the hall, taking my time. 'Sorry for the pace.' I pause to cough into my elbow, flashing him an apologetic smile.

We step into the kitchen as Verity sets down the teapot. She has put out mugs, rather than the china, but there is sugar and milk on the table at least.

'Verity was just about to tell me what she has done now.' I limp over to the counter and reach up to the cabinet, then lower my hand and press it to my chest. 'Verity, would you see if we have any shortbread?'

Her gaze moves between me and DI Strickland, then she turns to the cabinet and fetches out the box.

'Put it on a plate, dear. No reason we have to live like savages.'

DI Strickland holds up a hand. 'Please don't bother on my behalf.'

I smile at him as I ease myself into my chair. 'The good thing about being ill is having an excuse to enjoy the things you have been saving for later.'

I reach out and check the pot, swilling the tea around, then pouring. 'So, Verity went to Gavin Pieper's house last night. I know you told her she was on her last warning – and I do understand how difficult she has made things. We had agreed' – I give Verity a hard look – 'that she would write a letter to Gavin and I would deliver it. See if he might let me ask a few questions about something Verity remembered recently that she thinks may have some bearing.'

I proffer the milk, pouring carefully when DI Strickland nods.

'The thing is, Detective Inspector, we had some bad news yesterday. Rather, I had some bad news a little while ago, and yesterday Verity figured it out before I could tell her. There was a row and, in her upset, she stormed off to confront Gavin herself.'

I raise my hands, turning a weary but fond look on my mentee. 'We have been working on her impulse control so that she can stop doing things that are destructive to herself and others every time she gets upset or has a fresh idea about her sister's case. But, you see, it was such very bad news and she is angry that I didn't tell her sooner.' I sigh. 'Perhaps it was a mistake, but I hoped she would be in a better place before she had to know.' I turn back to DI Strickland. 'Well, we all know what they say about good intentions.'

Verity leans back against the counter, arms crossed, her pose defensive but her eyes full of anger and hurt.

DI Strickland looks over at Verity. 'So, you admit you went to see Gavin Pieper last night. Was this at his home address?'

Verity nods.

'About what time?'

Verity shrugs. 'It was late. Eleven thirty, I guess?'

'And did you find him at home?'

Verity is frowning now. 'Yes. The living-room window was open, so I just leant in. He was on the sofa and . . . we talked a bit.'

'I expect Verity means she screamed a bunch of semi-coherent questions at him,' I say ruefully.

Verity flushes conveniently, biting her lip. 'I told him about the stars and . . .' She shuffles from one foot to the other. 'About a week or so before Reenie disappeared, we were in the garden one night, looking up at the sky, and she started going on about how Virgos, like her and Gavin, are meant to hold themselves and others to high standards. And I said she'd been a right dick to TJ lately, so that was hardly Virgo behaviour. And she started yelling about how men are only nice to get what they want and you can't ever trust them . . .' She tightens her arms across her chest.

'I know Mum said Reenie was fine before she disappeared, but she wasn't. I read the—'

I clear my throat and Verity cuts herself off.

'I mean, Pru's been giving me things to . . . to study. To understand why we reacted to Reenie's disappearance the way we did. I tried to tell you the truth, but Mum kept going on about how you'd get the wrong idea and it might mean you looked in the wrong places instead of finding Reenie.'

She glances at DI Strickland then down at her feet. 'I thought TJ must be the problem, but then I started remembering other stuff about the way she dumped Gavin out of the blue and the fact she wouldn't talk about him afterwards – like, at all. And she threw out all her star stuff after that night in the garden. Everything: jewellery, clothes, books, ornaments. She even scratched off the star decal TJ got for her car when she passed her driving test.'

'The memory about the star decal was what prompted Verity's little visit to TJ's house a month or so back, when I left your colleague my card,' I cut in. 'She thought maybe it was a sign that TJ had hurt her sister, but then she started focusing on what Reenie had – and hadn't – said about Gavin.'

I pat the table next to me and, after a moment, Verity sinks down in the chair beside mine. 'We have been discussing how best to tackle the possibilities this raised, only everything came crashing down yesterday. I had a bad episode and Verity put two and two together, and it seemed like a betrayal instead of my best attempt to keep helping her until I can't any more.'

Verity makes a soft sound and hunches into herself.

‘Returning to your visit to Gavin Pieper . . . After your loud exchange of words through his living-room window, what happened?’ DI Strickland asks.

‘I told him that Pru and I had got in touch with his ex-sister-in-law on Facebook. We saw from her page that she and Gavin’s brother had divorced, so we sent a message and she said she hadn’t felt able to say anything before, because she really didn’t know one way or another, but it was possible Gavin *had* gone out the night Reenie disappeared.’

‘And after you told Gavin Pieper this?’

‘He came to the window and shoved me back a step, then slammed the window in my face and pulled the curtains.’ She grimaces. ‘I bashed at the glass, shouting that I was going to call you and see what you had to say about his alibi, but one of the neighbours poked his head out, so I left.’

‘Then you came back here?’ DI Strickland looks at me.

‘I drove to the park,’ Verity replies before I can speak. ‘You know – the one we were at the day Reenie . . . Anyway, I wandered around for a bit, but there were some teenage boys drinking by the swings and they started shouting stuff at me, so I left.’ She reaches for a biscuit, rolling it back and forth on the table. ‘After that, I drove to the university, then walked all the way to our old house, then came back a different route.’ She gives an angry huff of laughter. ‘As if I was suddenly going to find a clue sitting there waiting for me – in the pitch dark, no less.’

‘And after that?’ DI Strickland prompts.

‘I went back to the car and just sat there until I nodded off. Woke up to a traffic warden knocking on the window because it's permits only after 8 a.m. Then I came back here, right before you arrived.'

'Apart from the traffic warden, can anyone confirm this?'

'No?' Verity stops rolling the biscuit about, tipping her head to the side as she studies his expression.

'My car was boxing hers in, so she took mine last night,' I chip in. 'The satnav should show where she went and when.'

DI Strickland smiles. 'Would one of you mind showing that to me quickly? No objections if I take a few photos on my phone?'

'Be my guest. Verity, could you take him to look?'

The moment they are out the garden door, I drag the laptop over and run a search for local breaking news.

Dog walker finds body on Heathtop Hill. Police cordon in place around summit.

No access to popular viewing point as police investigate discovery of a man's body.

Coughing wracks me and I double over my knees. A sudden flurry of noise and movement around me, then there is a hand on my shoulder.

'Pill,' Verity says, pushing one into my hand.

I shove it into my mouth, then fumble for my tea. Verity presses a glass of water into my hand instead. I force the pill down only for some of the water to come back up, spilling over my lips and into my lap. Verity crouches beside me, dabbing at my chin, then my skirt, with a napkin.

'Tea,' I croak.

She hands me the mug, then slips a hand under the

bottom as my arm trembles. I let Verity take the mug back once I have drunk, sagging in my chair.

Verity pushes to her feet and turns to DI Strickland. 'Do you have to caution me for going over there? Is it really harassment when I had something new to say, though I know I should have told you, instead of just . . .'

I glance up in time to see her eyes fall on the laptop. She freezes.

I gesture at it, turning to DI Strickland. 'Body . . . found . . . Is it . . .' I get out, then have to stop.

DI Strickland nods. 'A body we believe to be Gavin Pieper's was found early this morning in the woods behind the viewing point at Heathtop Hill.'

'And you think that I . . .' Verity grasps the back of her chair in a white-knuckled grip. 'I didn't! I wasn't there!'

'That is what the satnav indicates, since it shows you following the route you described, on the timeline indicated,' DI Strickland says calmly. 'However, we will be checking with the traffic warden you mentioned. If she confirms she saw you with the car at 8 a.m. by the university, then it follows that you didn't have time to walk to and from Heathtop Hill between when Gavin Pieper's neighbour says he left home and when the body we believe to be his was found.'

Verity's throat bobs as she swallows. 'I can tell you where I parked by the university. It was just down to the right from the main entrance, on the corner of the first or second street.'

DI Strickland holds up his phone. 'I've got the satnav details.'

'Oh. Yes. Of course. I don't know if anyone else saw me. Maybe there's dashcam footage?'

'We may not need to be quite that thorough, but, if so, I will contact you for more exact details of the route you took when you were on foot.'

Verity nods, wrapping her arms around herself. 'I guess you can't say how . . . what . . .'

DI Strickland casts a glance at me. 'A note was found at the scene, along with an empty bottle of vodka and several packets of medication. We will be authenticating the handwriting and forensically examining the note, so I can't say much for now. I can tell you that it mentions your visit yesterday and the accusations you made, particularly about the alibi. According to the note, Gavin *did* leave his home the night of Reenie's disappearance, in order to loiter near your house in the hope of catching her as she came home.'

Verity's eyes are wide. She reaches out a hand, as if searching for something to hold on to. I slip mine into it, squeezing back when her grip tightens almost painfully.

DI Strickland rubs at his chin, eyes on the table rather than on Verity. 'What you remembered about Reenie's upset fits with the picture the note paints regarding the reasons behind Gavin and Reenie's break-up.'

He lets the words sit for a moment, and I recognize the technique: when giving terrible news, it is important to be clear and straightforward, but also to lead the recipient to the knowledge before you confirm it so they are better able to process the information, despite their shock and distress.

He clears his throat again. 'The note states that he took things too far with Reenie – too far in a sexual sense,' he adds, voice tight.

Verity's breath trembles as first one then a second tear traces down her cheeks, but she doesn't look surprised. The lines that crease her face are ones of resignation and pain.

'After the . . . incident between them, she accused him of assaulting her and ended their relationship,' DI Strickland continues. 'He claims – rather the note claims – that he was there the night of her disappearance to apologize, but she never showed up, so eventually he went home.'

He glances at me, then looks back at Verity. 'The note ends by saying he couldn't live with the fact that Reenie must have taken some desperate action because of what he did to her.'

Again, he pauses.

'It seems Gavin believed Reenie killed herself because of him. He thinks she hid herself away somewhere so you and your mother wouldn't have to know what she'd done, and that's why she's never been found.'

Verity stares at him. Her hand is fever-hot in mine, oily with sweat.

'You think he's telling the truth in the note. That she . . .' She shoves her chair back from the table, hand pulling from mine. 'She wouldn't do that.'

DI Strickland's face goes impossibly gentle. 'Verity—'

'No! She wouldn't do that. She wouldn't have left me with our mother!'

Her eyes widen as if she can't believe she said that out loud.

DI Strickland sighs. 'Until we find some proof – of this or anything else – we won't *know* what happened. But I think it's as good a theory as we've ever had.' He holds up a hand, though Verity has made no further move to interrupt. 'From everything you've told me, your sister wouldn't have *chosen* to leave you. But a lot of people who take their lives aren't in a rational state. They're so distraught they can't think beyond the next moment. I can recall a dozen cases where family members have said exactly what you have – and I'm sure they're quite correct: in their right minds, their loved ones would never have made the choice they did.'

'Think what you like,' Verity snaps, her eyes on the garden as if she can't bear to look at him. 'But just because Gavin killed himself and said some stuff in a note doesn't mean it's true.'

'Correct,' says DI Strickland. 'We have come to no conclusions and we *will* look at all possibilities, just as we have always done. If I can find you answers, I will. I hope you can believe that.'

For a while we are silent, then I push my chair back and stand so I am shoulder to shoulder with Verity.

'You do not believe Verity is involved – except, perhaps, as a precipitator of the guilty conscience that was already eating away at Gavin.'

DI Strickland nods. 'For now, I'm satisfied that Verity was elsewhere during the relevant time period, though we will be seeking further confirmation of her story.'

I hold out a hand. 'Thank you for your time – and your patience. If there is any more you can tell us down the line, we would be most grateful. I am sure Verity would like to read what was written in the note. At least as regards her sister.'

DI Strickland nods, shaking my hand. 'I'll come back to you on that.'

'You should rest, Pru,' Verity says, squeezing past me. 'I'll see DI Strickland to the door.'

He tips his head at me, then follows her out of the kitchen.

'This needs to be the end of it now,' I hear him say as the front door opens. 'I know it's not a definite answer, but it's probably the best there will ever be. You've done everything you can for your sister. She'd want you to start living your life now – and stay out of trouble.'

A moment later the door closes, then footsteps come back along the hall. Verity stops in the doorway.

'You understand that this was your one free kill, don't you? Oh, I know you didn't kill Gavin,' I add, when Verity's face floods first with confusion then consternation. 'I'm quite certain everything happened just as you told DI Strickland.'

'Maybe I kept you in the dark, just like you did with me,' Verity says, tone biting.

'It would be fun to see you try.' I close my eyes. 'No, don't take that as a suggestion. It is the *last* thing either of us needs right now. The point is that, yes, you've learnt a lot – you are becoming quite accomplished in some areas of our work, and the rest is improving – but you aren't at the level needed to create and carry out the type of meticulous plan required to kill Gavin and lay down a trail of evidence to support the story you just gave DI Strickland. In any case, you'd have needed weeks to scout locations, pin down timings, identify potential CCTV traps, and I know for a fact you've been far too busy. The trouble is that the Sisterhood will never believe you aren't responsible.'

I let Verity take this in. Watch her straighten in fear.

'So now you have a choice – they can believe you misused your training, in which case they will come for you. Or they can believe that, in my worsening state, I mistakenly forgot to include the paperwork to authorize Gavin as the target of your one free kill, as per Rule 1, in my latest batch of forms and reports.' I have to pause to suppress the urge to cough, letting Verity sit with the realization of the danger she is in. 'Your one free kill is only meant to happen *after* I have signed off on your training, but, under the circumstances, they will understand the urgency.'

She continues staring at me, blinking slowly, face blank and eyes distant.

'Do you understand, Verity? From now on the truth is that we found out it was Gavin, and *I* dispatched him for you in fulfilment of your one free kill. The whole reason you went to his house last night – then did all the rest – was to create an alibi, as per our painstakingly detailed plan, that would prove to the police that you had nothing to do with it.'

'So, we just accept Gavin's story in the note and give up on finding Reenie?' Verity's voice wavers with mingled misery and fury.

'We can keep looking for the body. That would not be out of order.'

'But if we find it – or something else that points to a different culprit – we don't go after him. Even though I *haven't* taken my one free kill.'

'Yes, Verity, you have,' I say. 'You took it last night.'

She shakes her head, expression bleak.

'I am proof that a life in the Sisterhood is worth it, free kill or no. Of course, one day you may come across a pattern of crimes such as a series of girls who have been drugged and assaulted at parties and clubs within a certain geographic area. If there is enough to merit an investigation, and if that investigation is fruitful, the Sisterhood will take on the target as a pro bono case. It would come to the same thing. Only, this way, you will be alive to see it.'

Verity's chin wobbles, tears flecking her lashes.

'Last night was one mistake too many, Verity, and now there is a terrible price to pay. But it is worth it to keep yourself safe. It is worth it to save your place in the Sisterhood and the life you have in front of you.'

I meet Verity's gaze, waiting until the turmoil in her eyes fades into acceptance.

'Every aspect of your one free kill is done now, including drawing police attention and harassing suspects, since you have your answers and the culprit is already dead. The Sisterhood will be so glad to know your troublemaking is behind you and that you can now complete the final stages of your training in good standing. Because it is over now. *Isn't it?*'

Tears wash down Verity's cheeks, but she swallows then nods.

I turn away and start making a fresh pot of tea. 'I will make the relevant calls later today and backdate the appropriate paperwork while you work on your CCTV skills.'

'Thank you.'

I turn to find Verity staring at me with an unexpected look on her face: something like recognition, or perhaps realization.

'Thank you for bending the Rules for me. I know what lying to the Sisterhood will cost you,' she whispers. 'And thank you for your gift, Pru – thank you for giving me a place in the Sisterhood. I'm sorry I've been so slow to understand what it means. But I'm ready to choose it now. I think I finally understand what that means.'

We step forward at the same moment. A long time passes as we hug silently in the sunny kitchen.

Verity

Days pass and no one comes to kill me. I go out to the shops, take long walks, giving the Sisterhood plenty of opportunity, but nothing happens. When a fortnight passes with training and kills proceeding as normal, I start to believe I'm safe. Despite everything, Pru has succeeded in bending the Rules for me.

Our jobs now are small, close to home. Pru leaves me to do more and more of the planning, preparation and execution (literal and figurative). She is able to do less and less, but it's always enough: we're determined to see my training over the finish line.

I surprise us both with my competence. More than once, I catch Pru smiling proudly at me as I talk her through a plan.

Finishing my training and graduating to full membership of the Sisterhood is the only gift I can give Pru in return for all I finally understand she's been giving me, so I study and I practise and I learn. It turns out that Pru was right all along, and it really is that simple. I wish it hadn't taken me so long to realize that strength isn't something you store inside, nor is it something you can measure – 'I'm strong enough for X, but not for Y.' It's nothing more than deciding that you *will* meet the trials in front of you.

So, I'm strong now because I refuse not to be. Even when Pru starts throwing up every other day. Stops being able to eat what she wants. Starts losing weight. Stops being able to walk more than a few metres without losing her breath. Starts taking the painkillers regularly, then moves on to liquid morphine.

We're still looking for cases that might match Reenie's, though mostly so Pru can demonstrate what to look for, where to look, how to put the pieces together and make the leap from a bunch of nothings to a potential pattern.

Maybe it was Gavin. Or maybe his note was the truth and his actions pushed Reenie to do something desperate while drunk. Or maybe I need to look again at my final suspect – Charles Temple. With so much money, not to mention powerful friends and family, there could be a good reason why there's no dirt on him. Or maybe there was someone else from that night I've never even considered, like Nathan.

If there's something to find, Pru's training will ensure I do. And if not . . .

I think I can live with that. Now that I have the Sisterhood – a career and a purpose – I've got enough to start putting together a life. Part of that is going to be living up to Pru's gift and her legacy. I might have started as the worst mentee in Sisterhood history, but I'm determined to be a top-notch member for all twenty-five years of my service.

Everything plods along steadily for a while. Then, out of the blue, about a month later, Pru drags me away from CCTV training (despite the fact I'm still shit) and tells me we're going out for dinner. We change, then I help her into the car, and she guides us out of town and on to the motorway.

'Either we're going somewhere fancy, or I'm about to get a surprise. Is this a punishment surprise, a training surprise, or a reward surprise?' I glance away from the road long enough to see Pru smiling enigmatically. I groan and turn my attention back to driving.

We sail off into the sunset and, after about an hour, Pru directs me to pull up on the verge beside a line of posh houses set behind manicured front gardens. She climbs slowly and unsteadily out of the car.

'Will you get the stuff from the back seat?' she asks tiredly, leaning on the bonnet.

'Maybe a walking stick would help?' I dare suggest as I fetch out chocolates and a bottle of champagne.

Pru glares, then sighs. 'Maybe we can look online together tomorrow.'

I beam and offer my elbow. 'Madam, may I escort you?'

'Oh, for heaven's sake, Verity,' snaps Pru as she puts her arm through mine. 'If I've told you once, I've told you a hundred times, funny is not your colour.'

'Yeah, yeah, you're laughing on the inside,' I tell her.

We stop several times on the garden path, pretending to admire the plants. When I reach out to press the front doorbell, Pru tugs my arm.

'Good friends go straight to the kitchen,' she says, leading me around the side of the house.

A group of women are already laughing and chattering and pouring drinks and cooking as we let ourselves into a brightly lit kitchen.

There are cries of delight as Pru steps inside, and everyone descends to exchange hugs and kisses . . . with both of us.

'I've heard so much about you, Verity,' says a woman I'd guess is somewhere in her fifties, though her glowing skin and shiny curtain of black hair make it hard to tell. 'Come and tell me all about yourself.' She tugs me to a bench in the corner and passes me a flute of champagne. 'I know you're driving, so just a small one. You'll have about five hours and seven courses of food to get it out of your system.'

I glance over at Pru and see her being helped into a high-backed chair lined with cushions. Three women drag chairs around her and cluster close to clink their glasses.

'How do you know Pru?' I ask the dark-haired woman.

She grins, sipping at her champagne. 'We're all part of the Sisterhood, darling.' She crosses her long legs elegantly to the side. 'Pru and I have worked with each other on so many jobs over the years. All those impossible cover-story clients.' She quirks an eyebrow. 'All those beautiful places, and the food . . . There's nothing like finding yourself in far-flung parts for weeks on end, not speaking the language, to help people bond. Then there's the killing, of course.'

'I'm dreading when they send me off alone internationally,' I confess.

'Don't be! Some of the time you could end up with one of us – there are quite a lot of two-woman jobs, you know. And, of course, there're lots of others who are just as – well, almost as – delightful as we are.' She holds out a hand. 'I'm Nora. Well, Honora, if you want the whole thing, which I never do, so please don't call me that unless you're angry with me.'

Something about the way she moves plucks at a memory, but it slips away before I can pin it down. 'Have we met?'

Nora laughs. 'No, but we have crossed paths.' At my frown, she leans in with a grin. 'The job in Winchester – I stood look-out to make sure no one saw you come in or out of the garage.'

'You're the woman with all the shopping!'

Nora toasts me with her champagne, then takes a long swig. 'I should tell you upfront that I wasn't just there to help but also to write up your first observation report – every mentee gets at least two. Yours was glowing that day.'

'Oh.' I feel myself flush with pleasure. 'Thank you.'

'But don't hold it against Constance, when you meet her, that she had to be a little more . . . ambivalent. She was there in Prague for the, um . . . energetic defenestration.'

'Oh God.' I bury my face in my hands. 'No wonder Pru was so pissed.'

'Not your finest hour, but we've all been there. Well' – Nora bites her lip – 'maybe not exactly, but we've all had our . . . mishaps. Except Pru, perhaps,' she adds thoughtfully, looking across at her. 'She's quite the legend, you know. Highest number of kills in a term of service – though don't ask how many. All anyone will say is that it's a record. Graziella's half proud, half fuming about it.' She giggles, then sobers. 'But Graziella gets to have a second act.'

I frown, opening my mouth to ask what she means, but Nora waves a dismissive hand.

'Ignore me. I'm being indiscreet. I'm a bit drunk,'

she confides, leaning in close again. 'I want to be happy tonight – spending time with Pru, finally meeting you, but I'm too sad. So I'm going to be drunk instead, because it makes me silly, and that's close to happy, right?' She gives me a pleading look. 'You'll help make sure Pru doesn't notice the difference, won't you?'

I grimace. 'I can try, but I've never got anything past her before.'

We both look over at her. Just as I feel tears threatening, Nora jostles her shoulder into mine.

'We'll look after you, you know. When she's gone. Rule 2.'

I swirl the inch of champagne around the bottom of my glass. 'Did she ask you to—'

'Oh sweetie, no. Of course not! As if she'd have to *ask*.'

Pru seems to feel our attention and raises her glass in our direction. We solemnly raise ours in return.

'We'd do it for her, of course, but we won't have to, once we get to know you. I always get a sense about people I'm going to be fast friends with, so you'd better get used to having me as one of your Sisterhood besties.' She snorts. 'But don't tell Pru in those words. She'll pull the face where it looks like she just ate a slug.'

As I laugh, Nora slips out her phone and taps in her PIN. 'Pop your number in and I'll text you back so you've got mine, too.'

When my phone pings with her message, I add her as a contact.

'Now you can send me photos from tonight,' she says. 'I'm already too drunk to remember to take any, but you will, won't you?'

'Sure.' I look over at Pru. 'Shall I start now?'

'Perfection,' she cries, bounding to her feet so fast champagne slops out of her flute and on to the floor. She drags me over to the others. 'Verity's going to memorialize us! Lean in, Sisters!'

I nearly stumble over my own feet.

'Come on, Verity. I can't hold this smile all day,' Pru snaps, but there's only happiness on her face.

I lift my phone, then have to take a steadying breath when my hands tremble. 'Sisterhood on three . . . two . . . one . . .'

Verity

Pru hasn't mentioned Hope's case for weeks. Does she know I've been reading the file late at night, doing my own (useless) investigating every chance I get between training and jobs? Of course, it's laughable I'd find something Pru couldn't after all these years, but I have to keep trying. Only I find nothing, nothing, nothing . . .

There must be *something*. Some gap where there should be information. Some piece that doesn't fit.

The thought echoes in my head. There *is* something that doesn't fit – Pru lying to me about having friends over when she was really going to that community centre.

It's late afternoon, and Pru's resting in the garden, so I'm free to draw over her laptop and search for news on that date involving the community centre.

Claire Jeynes was speaking there that day.

The next time Pru lied about what she was doing, she went to the open garden at Claire Jeynes's parents' house.

Pru has put in days of work on this woman, even though she knew her time was short.

I type 'Claire Jeynes' into Google, Facebook, Instagram. Then I try the parents. A few things come up on the mother's career as a magistrate, though there's more about her community work. The same is true with the GP father.

A recent copy of the local newsletter has a piece on the open-garden event, and there he is, quoted first and foremost: 'I'm so proud of my little girl. She's had so many challenges and yet she's tried so hard to help others. If letting people into my garden can raise a little money for her charity, it's the least I can do. Though I didn't love it when an interloper had to get chased out of the house. Silly, really, when there's far more to enjoy outside!'

There's a picture of a charming orchard with moss-dappled stone walls, then another foregrounding a topiary animal in front of a lawn sloping down to a small lake, complete with mini island.

'We put in the water feature ourselves, but the island was a happy accident. One day our daughter swerved around a rabbit and drove straight into the lake. The car was clearly a write-off so we decided to upcycle it into an island to support diversification of habitat for local plants and wildlife.'

My heart thuds as if I've been running. Pru has spent twenty-six years looking for the car that hit Hope, following every possible lead, visiting garages and scrapyards, tracking down those convicted locally of driving under the influence, chasing up dozens of other possibilities, and yet she never traced the car. She figured it was probably owned by someone rich enough to hide it until suspicions wouldn't be raised when it was finally scrapped or taken to a garage, but what if it never got repaired *or* sent to a scrapyard? What if the person who killed Hope drove it purposefully into a lake to hide the damage, then let it rot away underwater? It's the perfect way to make a car 'disappear' in plain sight.

Am I making something out of nothing? My brain is now programmed to see how a crime can be made to look like nothing more than an innocuous accident. But why else would Pru be so fixated on this woman and her family?

I click out of the tab and draw up another, putting in the postcode for the open-garden event. Then I reach for Hope's file and find Pru's old address.

Pru's old house lies in a warren of narrow, winding roads between the site of the open-garden event and the nearest town.

I flick frantically through Hope's file until I find a map showing the place where she was killed. Someone walking from Pru's house into town would have met someone driving from town to the Jeynes's house along the exact stretch of road where the accident happened.

It's her. Claire Jeynes killed Hope.

Her family is clearly rich enough to have multiple cars, so it wouldn't have been hard to make up an excuse for not wanting to drive so she could hide the damage for a while. Then, when she finally did take her car out again, it would have surprised no one that she had an accident: a newly qualified driver who hadn't been behind the wheel for a while was exactly the sort of person who might crash on their very own driveway.

But what sort of person kills a girl just a little older than themselves, then carries on with their life, free and easy? Though if the drugs did come afterwards, and weren't the reason she hit Hope, maybe it wasn't that simple.

I change my search parameters to the year of the accident. Claire Jeynes was head girl at a fancy private school. I find a few photos of her beaming and bright on the 'First

Day of Upper Sixth', 'Autumn Term Open Day', 'Harvest Festival charity drive', 'Halloween party for low-income kids', according to the captions. She was part of various pre-Christmas theatrical and musical performances, as well as the tennis and netball teams.

I roll the search into the next year. Nothing. I find an 'End of Sixth-Form Prom' photo and zoom in. She's not there. I search for the netball and tennis teams again, then musical performance photos after that Christmas. Claire Jeynes isn't in a single one after the time of Hope's death. It can't be a coincidence. Not on top of everything else.

I stand up, stride across the kitchen, then run into the garden.

Pru is lying in a sun-lounger, reading. She blinks in confusion as I drop on to the grass beside her and pull the book out of her hands.

'When you went to the open garden, did you know about the car in the lake?'

Pru stares at me for a moment. Then she smiles. 'That is very good work indeed, Verity.'

Confusion wars with hurt. 'Why didn't you tell me? How long have you known?'

'About?' she asks, tilting her head.

'About the fact that Claire Jeynes killed Hope.' My pulse thrums in my throat. 'Was it a test? Did you give me just enough clues and opportunities to see if I could work it out?' Then I realize. 'It's my final job as a trainee, isn't it?'

Pru draws her chin in. 'Verity,' she says at the same time I realize I'm being stupid.

'No, it can't be, because I'm your mentee – and I live here now – so it would be too much of a risk, even though no one else knows about the connection between you and Claire Jeynes. So, *was* it just a test of my investigative skills?'

Something about it doesn't ring true. Could Pru really bring herself to use Hope's case for training purposes?

Pru settles back in her lounger. 'Why does the Sisterhood kill?'

'To stop dangerous people committing further crimes,' I say automatically, then, 'Oh. She didn't commit any other crimes. You've not just been investigating, you've been watching her, digging into her life . . .'

'She doesn't even drive,' Pru says softly. 'She never drove again after that day. She talked about it in an interview a few years ago.'

I search her face. 'How long have you known?'

'I guessed a while back, but I didn't *know* until I found the car-island. I still don't have anything that could be viewed as proof. In searching for it, I have had time to learn a great deal about her.'

Pru's eyes drift away to the rambling rose draping the trellis up the side of the house. 'The girl who killed my daughter grew into a woman who did her best to make amends, though there was nothing she could do to make things right. I do not forgive her, and I wish ill upon her. I am glad she didn't get to live the life she was expecting to have. I take pleasure in the fact that it has been hard and often miserable. It's the very least she deserves. But she is not the type of person the Sisterhood was created to target.'

'But you've earned the right to use your one free kill how you choose. Twenty-five years, Pru . . .'

She reaches out to take my hand in hers. 'I have a better use for my one free kill. I'm leaving it to you.'

My mouth opens, but I have no words. White noise fills my head.

'It has never been done before, but I have always wanted to be a trailblazer, and I expect the Sisterhood will honour my wishes. Officially or unofficially,' she adds with a grin. She squeezes my hand. 'Maybe you will find Reenie's killer. If you do, I am sure it will be via other victims – maybe not girls who have disappeared or died, but others who have suffered harm. You cannot claim a second free kill of your own, but you can put forward a target in my name and the names of his other victims. You could do it anyway, but this is a guarantee. You have twenty-five years of service ahead. And now you have the promise of the reward that comes with it.'

I swallow hard, chin trembling.

'Silly girl, what on earth are you crying for?' Pru asks, brushing a tear off my cheek. She struggles to sit up, then eases herself off the lounger on to the grass to hold me tight as I weep for her and for all the things I've failed to do.

'I wanted to help you find peace,' I get out between ugly, heaving sobs.

'All you need do is live a good life, full of purpose and service and all the happiness you can manage,' Pru whispers. 'That is all the peace I need from you – to choose as well for yourself as I have in choosing you to be my mentee.'

Pru

When I wake, the light is still fresh. The air is sweet with the scent of jasmine as I prop open the kitchen door.

Crouching by the cupboard beside the oven, I fumble around in the saucepan at the back, extracting the box of pills I stole at the open-garden event. I listen carefully until I am certain Verity is still upstairs, then I take the packet into the dining room and wedge it into the underside of the table.

Verity has been diligent with her CCTV drills, and I doubt it will be long before she comes across it. If it doesn't vanish within a week, I'll have to find some other sure-to-be-discovered place to hide it where she can believe she's stumbled across it by accident.

Pills re-hidden, I set out breakfast then start cooking for later.

When Verity lumbers downstairs in her usual tousled morning state, I feed her, then send her to the shops with a long list of very precise instructions.

'Stocking up for a siege?' she asks.

'We are expecting company. Now, off you go. That will take a while, then we have places to be if we are to time things right for today's dispatch.'

For once, things go smoothly: I cook until Verity returns

with the shopping, then we put it away and set out to kill a serial rapist. All very organized and domestic.

The traffic is light and, when we arrive at the viewpoint above a rock-strewn riverbed, the drizzle means we are quite alone.

We wander around under umbrellas, then, at the appropriate moment, Verity attaches a transparent string to her hat and tosses it over the railing to catch on a curl of bramble.

A few minutes later, a pair of Dalmatians comes skittering up the path and starts urinating on everything in sight. Their owner arrives shortly after. He pauses to examine Verity's bottom – she is wearing a particularly tight pair of jeans – then goes over to help with the hat. She smiles and moves aside so he can stand at the closest point (with the sheerest drop) to reach for it himself.

I bend to fuss with the buckle on my sandal while Verity positions herself.

It is a moment's work to knock out the man's knee and topple him forward, while Verity gives a sharp shove against his centre of gravity, and over he goes.

As I turn back to the car, I think about the faces of the three victims the Sisterhood is sure he assaulted. He likes blonde girls in their teens and early twenties. Well, he did.

Glancing back, I see Verity pluck at the fine thread attached to her hat; it comes sailing back to land at her feet, but she just stands there staring at it, her face clouded with discontent.

When I was five years into my term of service, I remember crashing through Paloma's back door unannounced one evening, brandishing a bottle of sambuca (her favourite) and frothing with frustration.

‘Did you even consider that I might have a visitor?’ she demanded, as she took out glasses and gestured me towards the fireplace. ‘Light that,’ she ordered.

I snatched the matches out of the mother-of-pearl box on the mantelpiece and set the pre-prepared curl of newspaper alight, feeding in kindling until, with a pop, one of the logs burst into flame.

When I turned, Paloma was sipping her drink. Her gaze was as sharp and knowing as ever.

‘There will always be more targets,’ she told me gently. ‘The point of the Sisterhood was never to wipe them out. It was to reduce their numbers as much as we can.’

‘It’s not enough,’ I whispered, suddenly too exhausted to even pull myself off the carpet.

‘What would be “enough”?’ She shrugged. ‘There is always something more we want. Fewer predators. More time.’

Something in her voice made my fury vanish, replacing it with fear. ‘Are you . . .’

‘The doctor says less than a year.’

I push the memory away, blinking the glaze of tears from my eyes. Paloma’s death was terrible, but I had Graziella, my other friends in the Sisterhood. I was ready, even if I didn’t want to be. Verity isn’t. She’s come so far, but she still needs me, and soon I will be gone.

I take out my phone, tap in the PIN and start sending messages. My plans for today are important, but they aren’t enough. It is time I put my faith in Rule 2.

When I look up again, the wind is blowing hard, raking lines of white foam on to the river and singing around me like a chorus of distant voices, warning us not to linger.

'Time to go,' I call to Verity.

She pauses to tie the Dalmatians' leads to a bench – the weather will turn shortly and one of the other dog-walkers who frequent the spot will be sure to find them within the hour – then we hurry back down the path to the car.

'Why didn't you tell me we had visitors coming when we were planning for today?' she asks as she guides us on to the road.

'That is not how surprises work. Anyway, we all know what trouble you get in when you are busy and distracted. I would hate to know what you would be up to if I let you get bored and complacent.'

'I thought there was a Rule against torture.'

I cross my arms and look out of the window. 'I am not long for this world, so even if I were – for the first time in my life – to break the Rules on my own account, I am bound to escape punishment, aren't I?' I shrug. 'Maybe I should experiment. Give it a go while I still can.'

I reach across the console. A moment later there's a hand in mine.

'Do watch the road, Verity. You are right on the edge of your lane, and I will not have you straying off the straight and narrow now,' I tell her.

Verity

When we get home, Graziella, Nora and a young woman I don't recognize are sitting around the patio table.

'You should be prepared for further socializing over the next few weeks,' Pru warns me as we click off our seat-belts. 'I have many people to catch up with – and introduce you to.'

As Graziella and Nora hug Pru, the third woman holds out her hand. 'I'm Constance,' she says.

I promptly feel myself turn scarlet. This is the woman who saw my 'energetic defenestration' in Prague. She must think I'm both a moron and a liability.

It must show on my face because she laughs, leaning in conspiratorially. 'Don't tell anyone, but it was hilarious. I couldn't give you a glowing write-up, but I did my best.'

I don't get a chance to thank her because Pru starts ordering everyone about. A folding table and a bunch of chairs are brought out of the garage and set up under the apple tree, along with a quartet of sun-loungers. When Pru starts coughing, Graziella pushes her into one, saying something that makes Pru subside meekly – for all of two minutes before she starts giving orders again. Still, she does it from the chair and, after a while, sinks back to watch us quietly.

Soon another two women arrive, then another four, and before I quite realize it, I'm at a party. I slip away to put on something a little more festive than the hiking clothes I chose for this morning's kill. By the time I rejoin the others, two more people have arrived with flowers and wine.

I hover by the 'poison patch', as Pru calls the flowerbed with the hemlock and monkshood. Nora is deep in conversation with the two newcomers and Pru is busy chatting with Constance. I don't know anyone else yet except Graziella . . . who is heading in my direction with two glasses of wine.

I gesture around. 'Is this . . . are they all . . . you know?'

'I suppose it's good you're not assuming,' she says dourly. 'And yes.'

I duck my head and wish I'd put on better shoes, but I'd gone for comfort over style. Graziella's sandals are gorgeous cerulean heels, with a pleated detail at the open toe. They look spectacularly uncomfortable. If they are, she gives no indication.

'Pru needs to stop now,' Graziella says, eyes on my mentor as she laughs then coughs as Constance rubs her back tenderly.

I nod, toeing at a loose bit of earth. 'Will I get to finish training with someone else? It would mean a lot to Pru. And of course I want—'

'She's going to need someone to look after her. Someone who can stay at the house and . . .' She purses her lips. 'If we arranged for you not to have jobs until after . . .' She stops, takes a deep breath.

'You mean, you'd – the Sisterhood – would let me have, like—'

Graziella glares at me.

'God, you're just like her,' I say. 'Fine. Are you saying that the Sisterhood would give me a leave of absence so I can be with Pru for the end?'

For the first time, Graziella's chiselled features soften. 'No one would expect you to turn nurse. If she needs that, we'll make arrangements, but she won't want a stranger around more than can be helped.'

'No, she certainly won't.' I take a sip of wine, my gaze going to Pru again. 'If she's happy for me to stay, I wouldn't want to be anywhere else.'

Graziella presses my hand. 'Come on then,' she says, beckoning me after her. 'Time for Pru to answer your other question.'

I frown, but it's not worth pushing my luck with Graziella, so I meekly follow her across the grass. Pru looks up as we approach, then struggles to her feet, Constance steadying her until another woman can pass her stick over.

Nora whistles loudly and everyone looks around, going quiet.

'Dearly beloved,' Pru announces, 'we are gathered here today . . .'

As she speaks, the rest of the party moves into a loose circle. Nora squeezes in on my right, jostling her shoulder into mine with a grin.

'Sh!' says Graziella.

Nora makes a 'zipping lips' gesture.

'We are gathered here today,' Pru repeats, looking around the circle, 'in the sight of . . . a nice round dozen of our Sisterhood to welcome our newest member.' She turns to me and raises her glass. 'Congratulations on successfully completing your training and embracing our purpose. Here's to twenty-five years of careful planning, preparation and successful dispatching – and then, to top it all off, having to find some absolute amateur, who has never killed anyone in her life, and showing her the ropes.'

Everyone laughs.

'It has been my great . . .' She stops, shaking her head. 'I am grateful to end my service with making the right choice of mentee – a woman worthy to join our ranks. Welcome to the Sisterhood, Verity.'

The others all raise their glasses, and this is it. My moment. My graduation party, with these strangers I'm now bound to.

Nora squeals in my ear as she hugs me. 'Happy Graduation Day, darling!'

She throws herself on Pru next, as Graziella turns to me. 'Do her proud,' she says.

I nod, and shake Graziella's offered hand.

Then the others surround me and it's hugs and kisses and exchanging numbers, and I finally understand that it's not just a graduation party. It's a way for Pru to introduce me to even more of the women she served with – the women who have comprised her second family – so that, when she's gone, I don't just have purpose and a career, but colleagues who will soon become friends and, eventually, more.

Today, Pru is giving me a whole life.

When I've been congratulated by all the guests, I turn to find Pru watching me from her sun-lounger. She pats the seat beside her and I sink down by her feet.

'Graziella says I don't have to start taking jobs yet,' I tell her. 'I can stay here with you. Just as well really. I know you wouldn't sign off until you thought I was ready, but we're both aware my CCTV skills are still a bit rubbish.'

'Adequate, Verity. They're adequate, or we would not be celebrating today,' snaps Pru. 'Honestly, what do you take me for?' Her eyes drift to where Constance and Nora are laughing as they examine the poison patch. 'You don't have to stay with me, you know. You could—'

I reach for her hand. 'Already trying to shove me out of the nest, and my graduation party not even over yet?'

Pru sighs. 'There's something I should tell you. I would rather not, but I think we have both had enough of the troubles that come from my holding back, even when it has been for your own good.' She looks over at Graziella, who nods, raising a glass. 'I don't want to suffer at the end. When it starts to get nasty – when I've had enough – I am going to finish things on my own terms.'

I sniff, swallowing hard. 'OK. I'll—'

'There is nothing for you to do, Verity, apart from be well and happy and stick to the Rules.'

I gasp out a laugh. 'You and the bloody Rules.' But they're not bloody to Pru. To her, they're beloved. In twenty-five years, she's never broken them, only bent them once, to keep me safe.

Now she has delivered on her one remaining duty: providing a trained replacement to serve the Sisterhood in her place.

'They have steered me well all these years' is all she says. 'And they will do the same for you, if you let them.'

'You'll tell me, won't you?' I get out. 'When it's time. You won't just let me find you . . .'

'I shall tell you when it is time,' Pru promises. 'It will be what I want. The way I want it. I deserve what peace I can get, and that is what I am planning, Verity. I'm planning peace.' Pru reaches into her pocket then thrusts a tissue into my hand.

I give a watery laugh, blowing my nose. 'Just give me notice when I need to start flat-hunting, OK? I know I won't have to leave immediately – there'll be the will and probate and settling the estate—'

'Oh, for goodness' sake, Verity,' snaps Pru.

I nearly poke myself in the eye as I jump in the midst of drying my tears.

'Who else would I leave my home to but you, you silly girl? You would think it was a big surprise, even after I have inducted her into the Sisterhood,' she tells the rosebush beside the lounger.

'I love you, too,' I whisper.

Her eyes are very bright as she pats my hand.

Pru

There is still too much to teach Verity and too little time, but we do our best. More important is building her bonds with those I trust the most. They can continue teaching and supporting her when I am gone.

I cook dinner for Graziella and Nora and Constance. Rather, I start to cook then order Verity through the rest. Her knife skills are diabolical, but she is learning to fold cream and whipped egg whites with a light hand, so that is something.

I try to teach her about the garden, but I am weary. I sleep more hours of the day than I spend awake. It becomes harder and harder to get downstairs. Harder to wash myself. Dress myself. Harder just to breathe.

I hate the morphine and the pills. The way they muddle me. But it is worse without them. The pain licks at my bones with a tongue like acid. Nausea swallows whole hours down into misery. I can eat fewer and fewer things without paying for it. Sleep drags me into darkness then spits me out, my heart hitting an off-beat to its normal rhythm, leaving me even more exhausted than the night before.

Verity drives when we go out. I expect I still could, but I

have no wish to end my life causing the type of harm that ripped Hope from this world, stealing her life, my life.

As the end approaches, I try not to dwell on who I would be if she were still here. How this would go if it were Hope, instead of Verity, with me at the last. But when my mind wanders there, the misery I expect to find waiting is tempered. Nothing about my grief has ever been tempered before, yet here I am. Of course, I wish time would run backwards and Hope could be in the world again, but she can't. And I am who I am now because of it. And so with Verity.

Day by day, I see that she is going to be better than OK. Her life will be strange and different, just as mine has been, but it will be good. She will be happy more often than not, and isn't that all anyone can hope for?

She is better because of the life I have had and the person I am. There is a strange restfulness in that, even as everything else grows sharp and thorny with pain, weariness and the end steadily drawing nearer and nearer.

I cling on and relish. I relish the food I love. My home. My garden and all the plants I have nurtured in it. I relish my friends and the meals we share. The evenings lying on picnic blankets gobbling down wine and cupcakes for dinner. The days we drive to the flaming autumn beech woods and Graziella meets us in the car park. Though I can't walk more than a few metres, it is enough for us to sit on a fallen tree and be there in silence together.

I want more. So much more. I want years of watching Verity grow and learn and thrive.

But slowly the relishing is getting harder. More and

more time is stolen by pain, by my body failing. Soon I will have had all the good there is in this life and, though I am frightened and angry, I am also so very tired.

One day soon I will have the last thing I want that this world can give me. Then there will be peace.

And triumph.

Verity

When I was younger, I didn't understand what people meant when they said that the fact flowers, youth, life itself, are ephemeral is what makes them beautiful. It's rubbish, because there are loads of beautiful things that don't age or die. I suppose even paintings, palaces and mountains decay or erode over time, but compared with a human life, there's so *much* time.

Summer has slipped into autumn, and Pru is fading with the season. I don't think she will reach winter. I am trying to make myself ready, trying to store up every memory, every moment, but of course that's not how it works. No hoard of memories will be enough once she's gone, and yet I lie awake every night, torturing myself with trying to remember every detail of the day. I'm keeping a journal, but that's not enough, either. I have filled up my phone with photos and videos, and it's still not enough.

Yesterday morning, when we were sitting in the garden, quiet apart from Pru's wheezing, she took my hand and smiled and said, 'Soon.'

I knew what she was telling me, and it was all I could do to cry quietly at her side and not run from it.

This morning Graziella visited again, staying through lunch then heading off to pick up her mentee ahead of a short-term cover-story job. Pru promptly dropped off in the lounger under the apple tree while I retreated inside to avoid disturbing her.

I peer through the kitchen window: she hasn't moved yet.

My heart clenches with pain. I need there to be more. Because nothing I have is enough if she's gone.

There's no new information on Reenie's case. All the time Pru's spent searching, and she'll never know the answer. Maybe I won't, either.

I thought that if I could just solve Hope's case, it would feel like I've given Pru something in return for all she's given me – and maybe even help me believe that eventually I'll solve Reenie's case, too. But of course Pru had already figured it out. I know I shouldn't be surprised that she's chosen to keep to the spirit of the Rules, not just the letter of them, though it needles like a splinter every time I think about it. But it's Pru's tragedy, not mine, so I have to respect her wishes.

Still, even if she doesn't want Claire Jeynes to die, what about prison? We could go to the police, if Pru doesn't want to turn to the Sisterhood, but what if they refused to drag the car out of the lake to examine it? What if they did drag it out and the evidence has washed or rotted away over the years? With no proof, would the police go after two rich, powerful locals on the say-so of a dying woman and her troublesome mentee?

There's something about the whole thing that doesn't feel right. I'm missing a piece of the puzzle, but I have no idea what it could be.

Growling under my breath, I stomp down the hall and

into the dining room, setting up a new CCTV challenge. Pru made me promise to do at least one drill a day till 'You believe you meet my standards,' as she put it. This is likely to be half past never, but it gives me a distraction when the reality of how little time we have left together overwhelms me.

Sighing, I pop the window latch, climb out into the flowerbed, then start wriggling back on to the sill. I don't want to disturb Pru, so I'll have to check the footage later to see if I succeeded, but it's time I learnt to do this alone.

Teetering badly, I have to cling to the window frame to stop myself toppling head first on to the floor. I close my eyes, take a deep breath and try to focus.

Instead, my brain goes straight to Pru saying she didn't take her one free kill because Claire Jeynes is spending her life showing she's sorry and trying to help others. Since she doesn't drive any more, no one else needs protecting from her. That all makes sense.

I extend an arm until my hand touches down on the seat of the chair in the corner. Then I reach out my other arm.

The problem isn't that Claire Jeynes never came forward – by the time she woke up from her drugged slumber, Hope was already dead – but rather that, whenever she gave interviews about how she got into charity work, she made it sound like she'd been sexually assaulted: like *she* was the victim. That doesn't smack of remorse or determination to make reparations for her crime. I just don't buy Pru being OK with that.

I transfer my weight on to my hands, then bring one knee down on to the chair, too. I get the other knee down, then crouch there.

Claire Jeynes claimed the sedatives were the reason she didn't go to the police because, by the time she woke up, it was too late to gather the evidence that would have made them believe her. That was a lie, too, so why bother mentioning it in the first place? It doesn't make any sense when not only did it become a hit-and-run the moment she drove away, if she'd called an ambulance from the scene, Hope might well have lived.

'Focus, Verity,' I snap, in my best impression of Pru, but it's impossible now I'm wondering why no one ever linked the timing of Claire's 'trauma' with her sudden aversion to driving. Were her family and friends just so worried they never considered other explanations?

Maybe they *were* oblivious, but it doesn't explain why she lied about wanting to make a police report. She said it in every interview. Was it a lie she told herself so she could blame her father rather than herself, and the estrangement was so that he couldn't puncture her pretence?

Carefully, I swivel, then arch my back as I crawl down and forward, under the dining-room table. I eye the door, trying to imagine the angles, but it doesn't compute.

Groaning, I bow forward and press my forehead to the carpet. I need more training. Why did Pru sign off on my graduation? She has to know I'm not ready to do this alone. Maybe I should go outside and ask her to come and help me.

I sit up so quickly I bash my head against the underside of the table.

As I clutch at the back of my skull, something drops down beside me. Squinting one eye open, then the other, I pick up a small box.

It's some sort of medication packet. My stomach swoops. What if this is the thing Pru has been hiding so that, when the time comes, she can go out on her own terms?

The combination of the blow to the head and the thought of Pru overdosing herself makes my teeth fizz with sourness. I don't want to look at what the medication is.

I move to stuff it back into place, then my eyes lock on the name printed on the label.

Owen Jeynes.

There's a ringing in my ears, though whether it's from bashing my head or the rush of realization I have no idea.

The only reason for Claire Jeynes to talk about wanting to make a police report in every interview is that it's true, but that doesn't fit with her leaving the scene of the hit-and-run *unless she left to get help*.

Maybe her phone was dead or she couldn't get reception. Her home was two miles away – her home with her doctor father. Maybe she simply went for the closest medical help available, but arrived so hysterical no one could understand her, so her father gave her the pills . . .

I am holding a packet of pills prescribed to Owen Jeynes.

I scramble out from under the table and dart down the hall, through the kitchen and into the garden. Pru has woken up and is now looking at an old photo album.

I march over and thrust the packet of pills under her nose.

'Why did Claire Jeynes go home instead of calling an ambulance from the scene of the accident?' I demand.

Pru gives me a look of such fondness I drop down on to the grass as if she's knocked the legs out from under me.

'I don't know, as I haven't asked her, but phone reception is bad around that area. Lots of dead-zones. What do you really want to know, Verity?' she asks, as if we're talking about the weather or what's for dinner.

'If she went home to get help, then why did no one call an ambulance? Even if she was completely hysterical, she was with it enough to drive, so she could've dragged her dad out to the car and shown him the damage, then he'd have understood. And she can't have driven straight into the lake that day because, if it happened at the same time as a fatal accident less than two miles away, someone would have put two and two together. Which means she must have hidden the car before going to find her dad . . . but how could she have thought that through *while* she was totally hysterical?'

My head whirls and I press a hand to the place where I bashed it. A lump is rising, but when I lower my hand there's no blood.

Suddenly the complications fall away and I see how simple the answer was all along.

'She tried to call for help at the scene but couldn't, so she drove home – maybe to find a working phone or maybe to fetch her father to provide first aid. Only he gave her the drugs so she would pass out instead. Then *he* hid the car.'

Pru nods. 'I expect he staged the car-in-lake accident, too – and came up with the idea of the island to permanently hide the evidence.'

'*That* was why Claire Jeynes cut all contact with her father during her recovery. She wasn't angry at him for giving her the pills that started her addiction. She was devastated that he'd betrayed her by drugging her in order to cover up what she'd done. He took away her only chance to save Hope before it was too late: he made her a murderer.'

Pru sets the album aside, sitting up and swinging her legs over the side of the chair so we're face to face. 'If she had gone to the police then, she would've faced charges for manslaughter. Her father would have been charged, too. So she kept her mouth shut and dived head first into the sedatives, then other drugs, so she didn't have to face up to what they had done.'

I stare from Pru to the box of pills in my hand. 'Why didn't you call in your one free kill after you went to the open-garden event and found out about the car-island? Why break into the house to steal this?' I wave the pill box. 'The community newsletter mentioned someone sneaking around the house – that *was* you taking this, right?'

'Yes,' Pru says.

'Were you investigating? You said there wasn't enough evidence, so was it about finding more, then you just grabbed this out of . . . what? Instinct? What are the pills for, Pru?'

Pru smiles. 'I expect you already know the answer to that question.'

'You knew all this before you gave me your one free kill. Why did you dodge my question about using it yourself?'

Pru sighs, the brightness in her eyes dimming. 'Because the Sisterhood might have said no to authorizing Owen Jeynes as a target, given both the lack of evidence and of further crimes. I couldn't bear the possibility. In any case, by the time I was sure about what had happened, I knew the chances of the kill happening while I was still alive to see it were low.' She shrugs. 'Mostly, though, I gave you my one free kill because I wanted to carry this one out myself, since I shan't have to face any consequences.'

'You stole these to break the Rules,' I breathe. 'You knew from him having the sedatives on hand to use on Claire the day of the hit-and-run that he would probably have a bunch of medications stashed at the house at all times. And you always told me that if you want to "accidentally" overdose someone, the best bet is medication prescribed to them or someone close to them. Were you going to kill Claire and pin it on her father so they both paid, or were you going to go after him?'

She shrugs again. 'I stole the pills to give myself options. But the truth is I don't want Claire Jeynes to be killed, or even her father, since there's no evidence he committed any other crimes, either. It is just as well because, after twenty-five years, it turns out I can't bring myself to break the Rules. If there were iron-clad evidence that I could take to the police, that would be one thing, but it doesn't exist any more, and it would be near impossible to fabricate a convincing fake after all these years, so that is that.' She smiles gently, reaching out to pat my hand. 'I knew what I was doing when I gave you my one free kill. It was my choice, and I expect you to respect it.'

She swivels her legs back on to the lounger and lies down again, reaching for her album. 'Be a dear and throw the pills away, then tear that box up. I'm not going to be using it.' She muffles a yawn. 'While you're in the kitchen, perhaps you could make me a nice cup of lemon-ginger tea and find some biscuits? After that, you can set up the CCTV array so it captures the front of the house, the driveway and the nearest edge of the patio – not the patio table, though: be absolutely sure of that. Then you can work on routes into your bedroom.' Her eyes are already back on the pictures.

I sit for a while, watching her, then push to my feet and storm inside, tearing open the pill box and opening the bin. I tip the box, watching the sleeves start to slide out, then snatch my hand back before the pills can fall.

I believe Pru doesn't want Claire Jeynes dead, but between killing Owen Jeynes and letting him get away with leaving Hope to die in a ditch . . . I just don't believe Pru would choose to let it go.

I stare down at the pills. Pru didn't steal them to 'give herself options'. The moment she went into that house, she broke the Rules. The question is why she didn't follow through.

It isn't because she feared the Sisterhood coming for her – whether she had one month left or seven, they were bound to let nature take its course. But she wouldn't have acted before I graduated, in case they discontinued my training. Now I'm a full member, they can't punish me for anyone's sins but my own, so since then she's been free to—

The world tips over.

Pru didn't kill the man responsible for Hope's death because I kept causing trouble. One thing after another. So many messes to clear up. So many things to teach me, then teach me again when I learnt too slowly, delaying my graduation. So she waited, then waited some more, needing to be sure I was safe and secure.

She waited until she was too ill to follow through.

I could call the Sisterhood on her behalf, but what if her worst fears are right and they say no? What if they say yes, but there's too little time? It could work if I hand the pills over, but it would mean shaming her by revealing she'd intended to break the Rules. The whole reason she didn't is that she was busy protecting me. I can't disrespect that sacrifice.

But I refuse to do nothing. Which means there's only one choice.

I close the bin and tuck the lid of the pill box in securely before slipping the box itself into the side pocket of my handbag.

I thought my gift to Pru would be keeping to the Rules from now on, like she's taught me. And I will. But first I'll break them one last time, for the best reason of all.

Whatever the consequences – and they'll be mine and mine alone – there's a certain satisfaction in finally finding a purpose for my Rule-breaking, troublemaking tendencies. For the first time, I won't just be flailing around in desperation. I'll be making a choice.

After all, if I look at all my past misbehaviour as training, maybe I've not just been learning how to follow the Rules, but how to break them and get away with it.

Pru

It is morning and I am already tired from having an accident on the way to the toilet, then having to wash and change my clothes.

It takes me a full twenty minutes to get downstairs, wriggling on my bottom. Then I have to call Verity to help me to the kitchen. Everything I try to eat curdles my stomach.

There is another accident. Verity says nothing, just helps me with gentleness, kindness, love. Cleans me. Puts on the laundry. Then again.

But I hate it. By the time we're done, there is a dagger of pain between my breasts that will not ease. My lungs feel as if someone is not just squeezing them, but digging their nails in, too.

When Verity goes out into the garden to hang up the laundry, I check that the pill packet is tucked into her handbag, then pick up my mobile and make the call that comes at the end of things.

My heart beats triple time as I wait to learn if I am right, or if I shall have to go to my grave without knowing beyond any doubt who killed Hope.

I have my answer when everything is arranged within two minutes.

I sit back as adrenalin and relief and fear and grief and fury rush through me. Then a strange sort of stillness comes upon me. I hoped it would, and here it is. I reach beneath my collar and press Hope's ladybird pendant against my skin, feeling it warm to my touch. If I were a superstitious idiot, I would believe she is here with me and my sudden ease is her doing. Instead, it is nothing more or less than the solace that comes from certainty. This is what I want. For her, for me.

'I think sometime before today is over,' I tell Verity ten minutes later, as she lifts my feet on to the sofa so I can recline.

She freezes as she processes what I mean, then crouches to hug me. 'OK,' she whispers. 'There's something I need to do, though, before . . . before. It should only take me two hours or so. Will you be OK here for a little while? I could call—'

'A little peace would be lovely,' I tell her, stroking the hair back from her face. 'I phoned someone I need to see, so I shall have company while you're out.'

She is crying, lips pressed tight together so she doesn't sob. She nods then staggers to her feet and dashes off to get ready.

When she checks in on me before leaving, I catch her hand and squeeze her fingers. 'Thank you, Verity. I have everything I need now for the peace I deserve.'

She shakes her head, clinging with both hands around mine. 'I should have been better.'

'We have got here, so you have been good enough. You can be better tomorrow, can't you?'

'Not tomorrow.'

'No, maybe not. But the day after. You have everything

you need, even if it's not everything you want. Make the most of it.'

She nods, hugging me tight again. 'Thank you,' she whispers. Then she's gone.

The door closes, the gate squeaks, tyres crunch on the gravel.

I swivel my feet to the floor and start the slow trek to the kitchen. I take the stolen pills out of the saucepan at the back of the cupboard, then prepare a tea tray, using only the mugs I do not care about. I set out packets instead of a sugar bowl and a biscuit plate. The milk stays in the carton. I check my watch, take some morphine, then a little more. I go to the toilet.

It all takes a ridiculous amount of time, and yet it is just enough that, when I set the tea tray down on the patio table and ease myself into a chair, I only have to wait ten minutes before I see a man walking up the lane. He will have parked his car a good way off, of course.

I take out my phone and tap Verity's number. A moment later she picks up.

'Are you OK? Do you need me? I can—'

'I hope you are on hands free,' I tell her tartly. 'Can you pull over anyway?'

There is a moment of dead air, then I hear the change in the sound of the engine as she slows, slows, stops.

'When we finish talking, I need you to call the police. Tell them you checked the home CCTV system and saw something worrying.'

'Pru—'

'Once you have done that, you can turn back if you like. The police should get here long before you do.'

The man is looking at the house numbers, getting closer now.

'I am telling you that it's time, Verity. I promised I would, so I am.'

'You have to wait for me!' she wails. 'I have something—'

'You have a lot of trouble is what you have. Honestly, after all this time, is your parting gift to me to break the Rules? No, it is not. Instead, it is *your* time to promise *me* something. We are neither of us breaking the Rules today, but I am still going to get everything I want. Remember that – there is always a way to do it properly. Just think it through.'

Owen Jeynes is checking out the cottages on the other side of the street. Of course, I gave him the house name instead of the number to ensure I had enough time to see him coming.

'How did you know where I was going? What I was going to do?' she whispers.

'Oh, Verity. I could not love you if I didn't know you, so of course I'm aware that you have spent the last hour heading towards a certain big house about two miles from where I used to live. That is the whole point, my dear. You are safely miles and miles away, just as I planned when I left that box of pills for you to find. Do make sure you throw it away before you return, won't you?'

'He's there, isn't he? You sent me off to find him while you brought him to the house—'

'Shh,' I say. 'Be careful what you say on this phone call. You wouldn't want to ruin everything for me at the last moment, would you?'

She takes a breath like a sob.

'Everything is exactly as I arranged it. You are in the car, not breaking the Rules after all, and I am here, not breaking the Rules either and still getting the end that I deserve after twenty-five years of service – an end that represents a last moment of purpose. It's what I want, Verity. And I know you love me, too, so you will be glad of it, won't you?'

Owen Jeynes has found the house, but, as expected, he walks on to the end of the road. He will double-back soon and find his way into the drive instead of coming to the front.

'Pru—'

'I have to go now. So why don't you call the police, then Graziella? She can be waiting here when you get back to handle the official side of things – and make sure you behave.'

'I will. Just—'

'I am going now, Verity. Look after yourself, won't you? It is the only gift I want from you.'

I tap the 'end call' button as Owen Jeynes crunches across the drive.

He squeaks open the gate and comes striding up the garden path.

I wave to him, and he stops, blinking in surprise. I see the moment he recognizes me, though of course he thinks I was at his open garden to nose around for clues to old crimes, not to set up new ones.

The moment he told the tour group about the car in the lake, I knew there was no chance of finding sufficient evidence to get anyone sent to prison for killing Hope. Then, when I realized who the true culprit was, I recognized I'd have to get him sent to prison for a different crime – one where I could guarantee that all the evidence tied neatly back to him: means, motive and opportunity.

As Owen Jeynes approaches, I watch him pat his left pocket. Has he brought something to finish me off? If so, he will still want to talk first, hoping to persuade or bargain before he resorts to the drugs – the only method that could give him a sense of control and ensure he doesn't have to get his hands dirty. It's possible he will get cold feet. Or, of course, that there is nothing in his pocket but his phone.

It doesn't matter. Whatever happens in the next ten minutes, he is going to end the day in a police cell and spend the rest of his life in prison, because in the flowerbed behind me is the pill bottle I stole during the Open Garden. Since the prescription label is in his name, chances are that it bears his fingerprints: I've been careful not to add my own. The contents are in my tea.

I swill the last of the liquid in my mug as he walks towards me, making sure the pills are fully dissolved.

The new CCTV array I had Verity set up doesn't catch the table where I'm sitting, or the flowerbed behind, as per my instructions. But it will show him walking across the drive, up the path and on to the patio, then leaving. The metadata will show he was present during the window of time in which I was poisoned. My phone call to Verity will further pin down the timeline to ensure everyone knows he is guilty.

I drink the last of my tea as he steps off the garden path and comes towards me.

He may not have been the one to hit Hope with the car, but he drugged Claire so she wouldn't call an ambulance. Then he went about covering up her crime while my Hope lay dying in a freezing ditch. He wanted to maximize the chances that she wouldn't be found in time, and he got his wish. Now, he is going to pay for that – and pay in a way that gives me triumph and costs me nothing. A perfect close to a life I have lived as well as was possible after Hope was killed.

Dr Jeynes hasn't had a lot of time to think or plan since I called and told him I knew what his daughter had done. That I knew about the car and the lake. That I had managed to get a confession from Claire and did he want to come and discuss it with me before I called the police? I knew if he called her, she wouldn't pick up – and he knew it, too – so I was sure he would come straight over. And here he is, hoping against hope that there is some way out.

But I've already won – and without breaking a single Rule. I couldn't prove he killed Hope, but I've made sure there will be no doubts that he killed me. If he has plans of his own in that regard, they will only cement my case. Either way, he is done. He just doesn't know it yet.

I smile as I sit back in my chair and enjoy my garden, my home, my victory.

This is the ending I want, and here it is, just in time.

Verity

Graziella takes charge of everything, though in the end it's simple enough.

Since it's clear from the CCTV footage that the retired doctor who just killed my mentor never came into the house, all the forensic investigations are focused on the drive, garden and patio. I have free rein of my home and will be able to sleep in my own bed tonight.

Graziella must have called Nora because she turns up in the evening with takeaway and hugs, then tells me she's sleeping in the guest room tonight, though she has to leave for a job in the morning. It means the house isn't empty, this first night without Pru.

In the morning, Graziella is already working at the kitchen table when I come downstairs.

'Just as well I retired the day before yesterday, isn't it?' she says when I ask how long she can stay.

We are kept busy with the police, and the paperwork, and the will, probate, notifications to the bank, the utility company, insurance . . . Pru left clear instructions, of course. Including that there is to be no funeral. Instead, people come and go with food and condolences and company. I figure a garden party for close friends from the Sisterhood will be a good idea for the spring. A memorial instead of a funeral. I can think about it once the burial is over.

Nora stays over the night before, so I've got company in the morning, and in the car on the way to the graveyard. Pru's orders said there was, under no circumstances, to be any fuss with a funeral cortège, so it's just me, Nora and Graziella waiting in the car park when the undertakers arrive, though behind them comes another car with Constance and two more of Pru's friends.

'She never said we couldn't carry her to Hope ourselves,' says Graziella.

So, with the undertaker instructing us, we slide out the coffin and lift it between us by the handles along the sides. It's both far too heavy and far too light, and I can't stand that she's in there and not in there at the same time, so I focus on the fact that we're carrying her home.

When we arrive at the reopened grave, the undertakers show us how to lower her down so her coffin rests on Hope's. It'll be months before we can have her name added to the headstone, but Graziella's already arranged it. Pru left instructions for that as well, so I know that the message will read 'Mother, Sister, Mentor.'

I am too busy crying to hear the words the others speak at the grave, then suddenly someone is handing me a white rose and I'm dropping it on to the coffin, then Graziella is doing the same, but when I turn it's no longer just the six pallbearers.

At least four dozen other women circle us, each with a white rose in her hand.

Graziella stands at my shoulder, with Nora on my other side, her arm around me. Another rose falls into the coffin, then the woman it belongs to comes over to me. I'm not ready to do a receiving line. There's snot down my lips and I'm trembling, and if I open my mouth I'm going to sob in someone's face.

But the woman just smiles sadly and holds something out. It looks like a business card.

'Rule 2,' whispers Nora.

'In case of need,' says the woman. 'Though I'm sure we'll be setting the world to rights together before long.'

She nods and moves on for the next woman to take her place.

Soon Pru's coffin is strewn with roses and I have a stack of cards and as many promises of mutual purpose. The final woman to step up looks to be a little younger than me – maybe mid-twenties. She smiles shyly.

'I'm Faith.' She flashes Graziella a look. 'I've just finished training, too.'

Graziella sniffs. 'My mentee,' she says. 'I wasn't sure you'd work out, so I waited to see before introducing you.'

Faith holds out a business card with a mobile number scrawled across the top. 'We'll be working together on the job in Italy.'

'The Sisterhood likes to pair new members starting their term of service around the same time as a sort of support system. You won't always be working together, but you'll see a fair amount of each other, so you'd better keep your more troublesome habits to yourself,' Graziella tells me so tartly I hear Pru in her words. But then Pru must have been her partner, just as her mentee is mine.

'Can't we go to that café round the corner and do all

this over cake?' Nora asks. 'I'm starving and miserable, but at least the first can be fixed.'

Seven months ago, Pru suggested the same thing, and I said no. Now, I nod and tuck my arm through Nora's and the four of us make our way out of the graveyard together.

I look towards Mum's headstone, but I can't see it. I expect to hear her voice floating after me, mournfully scolding me that I could at least visit her and Reenie before leaving, but it's Pru's voice that whispers in my ear – *I see you're finally taking my advice. Better late than never.*

If I were alone, I'd say, *I promised I would, so now I will.*

Instead, I look over at Faith. 'Did your mentor ever mention you'd get a partner in crime? Mine didn't say a word, even though it would have been a real comfort to know I wouldn't be working solo for the next twenty-five years.'

'She just kept telling me to work stuff out for myself,' Faith replies.

'I hate that. Do you think that's just Pru and Graziella, or do all of them do it?' I ask.

Graziella heaves a put-upon sigh, while Nora laughs. The pale December sun casts patterns of light and shadow through the branches of the yew trees as we make our way to the gate, discussing our plans for putting the world to rights.

Seven months ago, when I first met Pru in this graveyard, I was alone, about to lose my job, my home, even Boudicca.

Seven months ago, I couldn't imagine a life worth living where I didn't know what had happened to my sister.

Now, I have learnt to move forward with my ghosts walking beside me, not standing in my way. I will never finish grieving the life I never got to live – the life Reenie never got to have – but where before it seemed impossible that I could ever be happy more often than not, now I know I will be. Just as Pru wanted.

Author's Note

A lot of my fiction explores the gulf between the ideal of justice and the reality of the criminal justice system.

Recent figures suggest that only one in six victims of rape and attempted rape make a report to the police. There is a charge or summons in under 5 per cent of cases: the conviction rate is similar. This is one of the reasons that reporting figures are so low: even after finding the courage to go to the police, victims know that is as far as most cases go. For many, it's simply not worth the additional trauma of a report, a physical examination, a years-long wait and potentially an adversarial cross-examination if the case goes to court.

Women and girls are the majority of victims of rape by a very large margin, just as they are the majority of victims in cases of domestic violence, coercive control and other sexual offences. Few female victims of male violence ever see a positive criminal justice outcome; even when they do, the process is usually long, almost invariably painful and often (re-)traumatizing.

According to the latest UK government figures, over 12 per cent of adult offenders (the vast majority of them men) were proven to have sexually reoffended within the last year alone. The lifetime recidivism rate is hard to pin down, but many studies suggest the rate of reconviction stands around 20 per cent. Given how many offences are never reported, let alone pursued, let alone lead to a conviction, the real rate is likely to be substantially higher.

As for the ideal justice . . . Humans the world over, since the start of civilization, have struggled with the question of how to put this value into practice. What does it mean to 'give someone justice'? Is it ever possible with crimes like murder and sexual offences? If not, what can be achieved, and how? What do we prioritize in our approach? What does it do to victims, offenders and society as a whole if we know the vast majority of rapists and other sexual offenders are not likely to face any punishment for their crimes? What does it do to victims to live with the fact that the person who chose to hurt them will probably suffer no consequences whatsoever?

I don't have any answers. Instead, I write with the hope that my books will leave readers asking questions. This book begs two key questions:

- What type of injustice is worse – murdering repeat violent and sexual offenders to stop them from creating further victims, or letting additional people suffer harm at the hands of repeat offenders, and
- How should we define 'worse' when we ask this question?

Actualizing an ideal like justice isn't simple in theory, let alone in practice. But in pursuing justice we tend to neglect to ask the obvious questions – if all that's on the table is a range of injustices, which ones are we choosing, and what are we saying with our choices?

Ultimately, I doubt there *are* good answers to these questions. The solution, then, is to change society so that these questions no longer need to be asked in the first place.

Acknowledgements

I owe a thousand thanks to my family for being so wonderful and supportive. Biggest love and hugs to my dad, who made a lovely corpse at every murderous birthday party of my entirely normal childhood. Thanks and love to my mum, who read various (rubbish) early drafts and cheered me on when I was stuck, not to mention lending me her criminological expertise to ensure that, implausible hook aside, everything that flows from the premise is grounded in how and why women commit violence – it made all the difference to have your help and input when I was floundering and the voices just wouldn't come.

Tons of love to the Anglo-Italian-American hordes: Giudi, Julian and George, Lori and Julian, Erin, Alice and Ella, Kieran and Aidan (with love for Auntie Liana and Uncle Benito), Uncle Bym (with love for Auntie Mira), Rich and Josie, Sophie and James, with a shout-out to Auntie Ann and all in Wales. Love to my Ros – you would have liked this one best of all, I think, but then I always think that about a new book.

Thank you to my beloved Aunty Pat, who edited all my early work many, many times and taught me so much of what I know as a writer.

Huge thanks to my amazing Godmother Dany, who gave me a home to adventure from and who is always there with support and clever advice.

Love and hugs to my brilliant godbrother, Malcolm.

And to Collett – thank you so much for putting up with my hopelessness while I struggled through writing and editing this one!

I owe so much to my fabulous friends. All my love to my author friends who help me navigate the brilliantly mad world of publishing, especially Karen (hugs for Naomi and Will!), Christi and Jack, Holly (hugs for Connie and Will!), Anna (hugs for Ally!), Kate and Liz, Louisa, Gina, Fauzia and Stuart, and all the other fantastic writers who make my life (and everyone else's) so much better. Hugest hugs and love to all the lovely friends who help me keep track of the world outside the publishing bubble, particularly Dr Emma Milne, Riki and Fran, Katja and Alexia, Lizzie (with hugs for Micah and Phil), Tony (with love for Aoife), Ian and Kitty (hugs for Rosalba), Mike P (hugs for Sarah and the boys!), Andy (hugs for Ruth), James and Myrren (hugs for Toby and Amber), Chris (with love for Carmel), Katie (with love for Peter), Katie (hugs for Isabella Lily), Jens, Annie C and family (thank you for reading and staying in touch – whenever I see your name pop up, I know Ros would be so happy), and everyone I'm too blotto from editing to remember if I forget to come back to this! Special thanks to Simon, Sue and Katharine for all the lovely times sharing our passion for stories – I do so appreciate your appreciation for the murderous tendencies that run in the family. Big thanks to my blogger friends, especially Luna.

Shout-out to friends and family in Italy, particularly everyone in Sarnano – Maura, Luca and Roberta, Gabriella and Fabio, Roberto and Lilli, and everyone else!

There wouldn't be an acknowledgements section in the first place if not for agent extraordinaire Dr Kristina Pérez. Thank you for believing in my writing and for being a brilliant editor. My books are so much better for your clever, insightful input and advice. I couldn't ask for a better partner and advocate. It is a joy to know and work with you.

I am so grateful to my wonderful editor, Harriet Bourton. Thank you for helping make this book everything I hoped it would be. Many thanks for additional edits to Laura Gerrard, and to Rosey (Roseanna Battle) for being the glue keeping it all together! Thank you to fantastic copy-editor Sarah Day for her eagle-eye and light, clever touch! Huge thanks to Amelia Evans in rights for being so kind and supportive, and to lovely Monique Corless. Big thanks to Natalie Wall in editorial; Annie Underwood in production; Sam Fanaken, Ruth Johnston, Caitlin Knight and Autumn Evans in sales; and Jessica Adams in international sales. Huge thanks to Alisha Kruse for my stunning cover. Biggest thanks to Nadine Jendrusch and everyone at dtv in Germany! And to all the other editors, translators, designers, publicists, marketing folks and more helping my books reach new audiences across the world. Many, many thanks to PLE's Jack Mozley for all the financial wizardry and to Isabel Lineberry for all the support and social media graphics!

Thank you to my friends and colleagues at BSU. And to my students – it is such an honour and pleasure working with you all and being part of your journeys, as you've been a part of mine. Special thanks to Janette, Dashe, Sam and Alex for listening to many, *many* whinges about how this book would just not go right. Hugest gratitude and admiration, too, for brilliant author and fabulous co-founder of Literature across Borders, Meghaa Gupta – and to all our international partners, colleagues, students and volunteers. This project is one of my great joys and I can't wait to see what comes next.

Thank you to Paul and Catriona, Russ Holland and Patrick Mayer for helping me figure out all the financial stuff, and to Viv, Cindy, Andrew and all who helped keep the house from falling/burning down mid-edit.

I am so inspired by all my colleagues and clients in human rights, but particular thanks and admiration must go to those I've worked with on issues of male violence against women and girls. I hope I have done justice to everything I've learnt from working with you.

And finally, thank you to those who've bought, read and reviewed this book. I wouldn't have the career I love without you and your support.

Book Group Questions

1. If someone offered to mentor you into the Sisterhood, what would you do, and why?
2. Do you feel satisfied or frustrated by the fact that Pru and Verity don't solve the mystery of Reenie's disappearance?
3. Are you more invested in one of the two protagonists than the other? If so, which and why?
4. What surprised you most in the book?
5. Do you agree or disagree with the idea that the best a society can hope to achieve when creating Rules (i.e. laws) to deal with people who mistreat others is the least overall injustice? Can a criminal justice system ever deliver on the ideal of justice?
6. If there was a TV / film adaptation, who would you cast in the key roles?
7. What was your favourite scene or line?
8. If you could ask the author one question, what would it be?
9. What questions do you still have about the Sisterhood and how it works?
10. If you could add one Rule, what would it be?

If you enjoyed *The Sisterhood of Invisible Murderers*, read more from Alexia Casale in

THE BEST WAY TO BURY YOUR HUSBAND

Four new friends. Four dead bodies. One big problem . . .

Sally never meant to cave her husband's head in with a skillet. Or at least she didn't until suddenly, she did.

But Sally isn't the only woman in town being pushed to breaking point. When coincidence brings four strangers together, a surprising solidarity is formed.

So can they find the best way to bury their husbands – and get away with it?

Darkly funny and with a big beating heart, *The Best Way to Bury Your Husband* combines four very different women, one unexpected friendship and several spades in this irresistible page-turner.

'A darkly comedic story . . . I loved it'

Jesse Sutanto

'Poignant and funny, dark and searing'

Andrea Mara

'Perfect for those who like feminism with their dead bodies'

Julie Cohen

'Tense, funny, moving and strangely cosy'

Holly Bourne

On a station platform, with nothing to read,
and a four-hour train journey stretching ahead of him...

That's where the story began for Penguin founder Allen Lane. With only 'shabby reprints of shoddy novels' on offer, he resolved to make better books for readers everywhere.

By the time his train pulled into London, the idea was formed. He would bring the best writing, in stylish and affordable formats, to everyone. His books would be sold in bookstores, stationers and tobacconists, for no more than the price of a ten-pack of cigarettes.

And on every book would be a Penguin, a bird with a certain 'dignified flippancy', and a friendly invitation to anyone who wished to spend their time reading.

In 1935, the first ten Penguin paperbacks were published. Just a year later, three million Penguins had made their way onto our shelves.

Reading was changed forever.

—

A lot has changed since 1935, including Penguin, but in the most important ways we're still the same. We still believe that books and reading are for everyone. And we still believe that whether you're seeking an afternoon's escape, a vigorous debate or a soothing bedtime story, all possibilities open with a book.

Whoever you are, whatever you're looking for,
you can find it with Penguin.